GET A FREE JAK]

Sign up for the no-spam r
of the Sawyer prequel n

C000226053

Check the details at the end of this book.

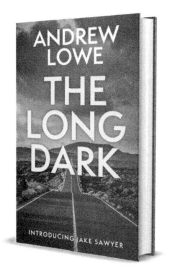

Email: andrew@andrewlowewriter.com
Web: andrewlowewriter.com
Twitter: @andylowe99

First published in 2023 by Redpoint Books
This edition April 2024
Cover photographs © Shutterstock
Cover by Book Cover Shop

For Tom and Josh

I dreamt the past was never past redeeming.

— *RICHARD WILBUR, 'THE PARDON'*

PROLOGUE

The man shook his head like a wet dog, splashing the floor with sweat and blood. He slumped forward, his matted hair hanging between his legs, shoulders propped on his knees.

A hand gripped his chin, raised his face.

'Y'still with us, son?'

The man tried to jerk his head away, but the hand held him firm. The light from the overhead bulb was tepid, but his swollen eyes squinted, craving the dark.

The hand released him, and he slumped forward again.

They'd worked in shifts; two at a time. Knuckle dusters. Cudgels. A cricket bat for the stomach.

As a four, they'd had him up against the wall; arms held by one pair while the other two worked his kidneys. He'd kicked and scuffed his feet at the start, but the pickaxe handles put a stop to that.

The heavy door scraped open and the four men parted to make way for a fifth. He pulled up a chair and sat in the centre, facing his captive. He took a puff from a Sweet Afton cigarette and tapped ash onto the floor. Smoke spiralled up, coiling around the bulb.

'Well, now.'

Handlebar moustache, deep-set eyes in shadow beneath heavy brows.

The man piped the smoke out through his nostrils and smoothed back his thick dark hair.

He leaned forward. 'You've had better days, Connor. Am I right?'

Connor slowly raised his head and peered at the new man, then slumped forward again. 'Who the fuck are you?'

'I'm gonna let you call me Patrick.' He leaned back. His silver medallion glinted in the light. 'I'm hoping you'll acknowledge the courtesy, Connor. You shouldn't bother wasting your time being tough and obnoxious. Nobody here will care or be impressed by that. And we'll make sure your family knows you cried like a newborn, however this goes.'

Patrick took another puff and stamped out the cigarette beneath a heavy work boot. He shuffled his chair closer.

'I know you're terrified, Connor. I know your bowels are loosening.'

Connor raised his head. 'Where are we?'

Patrick glanced up at one of his men. 'Omeath. Little village about halfway between Dublin and Belfast. Normally, I wouldn't be seen dead here. You don't have a choice, though.'

One of the men gave a grim laugh.

'Have you worked this out yet, Connor? It's sort of a debrief. We're both soldiers, am I right?'

'If you're Nutting Squad, you've got shite intel.'

'I thought we were being courteous.' Patrick grabbed a fistful of Connor's hair and tugged back his head to face him. 'I'm engaged in a righteous struggle against an occupying oppressor. Your role is a bit more complex, yes? I can assure you, our intel on you is far from shite. We're internal security. They call us the Nutting Squad because of the bullets we put into informers' brains. But that moment is a long way down the line for you, Connor.' He pointed. 'You've had the good bit. There's a lot of bad to come. The kind of bad is up to you.'

Connor raised himself upright and leaned back in his chair. He spat to the side. Mostly blood. 'Whatever you do to me here, you're not my judge.'

Patrick nodded. 'You're a good Catholic boy, then. Used to be my way, too. I heard the pastoral call. And then the loyalists killed my father, and I got distracted.'

'I was just trying to save lives.'

Patrick waved him away. 'I don't want to know your story. I've got the basics. I want to know how you were recruited. Security service contacts. Names, network, handlers. I know a lot of it already, but I'm looking for a few connections to confirm. To help me take others like you out of the game.'

Connor's head lolled and he drew in a shallow breath, mouth opening.

Patrick leaned forward.

Connor spat onto the floor between them. 'Not an inch.'

Patrick sighed. 'You're going to feel a lot of pain now, Connor. It'll go on for a long time. Days. And then you're going to die.' His fingers went to the medallion. 'Now, we're clearly not going to get a confession, and I'm sorry to say that we're all out of holy oil. So when we're done with the work, we'll have to skip to the prayer, then send you on your way.' He leaned forward, finding the eyes, the faltering defiance. 'I'm just a seminarian, Connor. A deacon. I might get back to my studies when all this is over, but right now, I don't have the authority to absolve you.' He studied his captive. 'Most people, they live out their lives, some part of them goes wrong, and they check out. After a short illness. Suddenly. Peacefully in their sleep. Your end will not be like that.' He scraped the chair over and shuffled in next to Connor, leaning close to his ear. 'You will not be visited, comforted, soothed by the love of your family. Nobody's going to hold your hand while you travel towards the light, Connor. It's all dark for you now.' Patrick reached out and prodded Connor's forehead with a finger. 'Until that bullet goes into your brain.' He sat back. 'By the time that cold barrel pushes into your skin, it'll feel like a blessing. Like an answered prayer.'

One of the standing men pushed a black hood over Connor's head and handed Patrick a length of rope. The man held Connor firm while Patrick secured the hood with the rope.

He waited for Connor to settle, with his hooded head drooped forward, then leaned in close again.

'I know you're afraid of divine judgement. But it's nothing compared to mine.'

PART ONE

FALLEN

1

Liam Barber crested a hump in the single-track road, catching a half-second of airtime. He hung his arm out the window of his silver Range Rover Sport, slapping his palm against the door to the rhythm of the music inside: 'Own It' by Stormzy.

The young woman in the passenger seat took off her sunglasses and pivoted to face him. 'Slow down a bit, babe.'

Barber glanced over and grinned.

'Sarah. You're like an old woman. Enjoy the ride. Do you know the stats for Rovers? Adult occupant protection up in the early nineties. You couldn't be safer in a tank.'

Barber angled his head and took a gulp of morning air, as he gazed across the rippled pastures on the edge of Sterndale Moor. A scattering of cows grazed in the shade, tails swishing.

He nudged Sarah's shoulder. 'Hey. Bet you didn't know this. Cows have four stomachs.'

Sarah slipped the sunglasses back on and turned to face forward. 'I did know that, actually.'

'Yeah? But do you know why?'

She shrugged. 'Break down their food?'

Barber gaped at her. 'Very good. They chew the food enough to swallow it. Then the unchewed food goes to the first two stomachs, where it gets stored. The cow feels full up and rests. Later, she coughs up bits of it—'

'Cud,' said Sarah.

'What?'

'*Cud.*'

'Oh. Yeah. Cud. So, that gets chewed again and goes to the third and fourth stomachs, where it's digested. Some of that nourishes the cow. But the rest goes into the bloodstream, travels to the udder, and gives you something to stick on your Corn Flakes.'

Barber rounded a corner, too fast. The road straightened out and narrowed, bordered by tall dry-stone walls with only a few inches of verge. He crunched through a pothole and Sarah winced.

She sipped from a flask of water. 'So, you going into the family business?'

He laughed. 'Not until the old man pops his clogs. Won't let anyone near his herd. Calls them his girls. Bit weird. Milks the buggers twice a day still. He'll stop when he drops.' Barber flipped down his sun visor and squinted at a car up ahead, travelling much slower. 'Fuck's sake.'

'Does your mum still work?'

'She rears the calves. Does all the paperwork. Dad wanted me to be an agronomist. Manage the arable crops and grassland. I reckon that's more for my sisters, though. I want to focus on my garage. No money in farming. It's all shovelling shit and early mornings.'

Barber squeezed the brake as they closed in on the car in front: an orange-and-black Mini Convertible.

Sarah took another sip. 'Not a lot of future in selling petrol cars, either. It'll be all electric soon.'

He scoffed. 'You just have to diversify. Build a new electric business, shift the petrol and diesel into used.'

She turned the music down. 'Nobody will want used petrol and diesel if they're illegal on the road.'

'Like I said, we're diversifying. Mum wants to start a pop-up ice-cream business in the summer. Jersey cows. Creamy milk. Fucking rude not to, really. I want to do up the old barn, start a boxing gym. Dad gave me the old "we'll see".'

Sarah pointed at him. 'Which means no.'

'Yeah. Mum wants to turn it into an Airbnb.' He gestured with the hand outside his window. 'What is this clown doing?'

Sarah patted Barber's knee. 'Speed limit, babe.'

'It's sixty on a single-track. He can't be doing more than forty. Fucking tourists. They moan about tractors blocking the roads, but they're just as bad.'

Barber eased the Range Rover a few feet from the Mini's back bumper. He flashed the lights and waved his arm in a scooping, hurrying motion.

He called out of the window. 'Hey, Captain Slow! While we're young!'

The Mini maintained its speed for a moment, then accelerated away.

'Thank fuck for—'

The Mini's brake lights flared as the driver slowed again, easing the car into a near-crawl, causing Barber to brake hard.

Sarah yelped in surprise and reached for Barber's arm.

He grinned at her. 'Oh. Here we go. He wants to play silly buggers.'

'Liam. Can we not? I don't want to start the day with—'

Barber gave a prolonged blast of the horn. 'We've got another two miles of this.' He waved from the window again and shouted. 'Get a fucking shift on!'

Another hoot of the horn.

The Mini crawled on for a few hundred yards, then slowed further and came to a stop, forcing Barber to do the same. As he pulled up behind, he lightly clunked the front bumper into the Mini's back.

Sarah patted his knee again. 'Bloody hell. Seriously, babe. Let's not do this.'

Barber reversed the Rover a few yards and stared out at the stationary car ahead. The driver had parked at a slight angle, allowing just enough space for the Rover to pass, if it dropped its left wheels into the shallow roadside ditch.

'Just ignore him. Go past.'

The Mini's driver side door opened and a tall man with unkempt neck-length black hair stepped out. He was slim but broad in the shoulders, and snugly fitted into a black suit, with white shirt and dark tie.

He closed the door and studied the Mini back

bumper for a moment, then walked towards the Rover. There was a sway to his gait, just short of a swagger.

'Oh, Jesus. *Liam.* Please. Not again. Just go round him. He looks like a bloody gangster.'

Barber laughed. 'He's a streak of piss.' He opened his door but didn't get out straight away.

The suited man stopped walking and sat down on a flat section of stone wall, studying his phone.

'Stay here.' Barber climbed out of the car and closed the door behind him. He rose to his full height and walked along the verge towards the man. Barber was beefy up top, but light-footed, in shorts and sport trainers. An elaborate tattoo covered the back of his right calf: a tall galleon with sunset backdrop.

He stopped a few feet from the suited man and folded his arms.

The man looked up from his phone and slid it into his back pocket. He raised his head, fixing Barber with glinting green eyes.

'A great philosopher once wrote... Be kind. Everyone you meet is fighting a hard battle.'

Barber scowled. 'Right. Who was that, then?'

The man shrugged. 'Some say Plato. Others think it was Philo of Alexandria.'

Barber took a step forward. 'Yeah? Do you know my philosophy? Shift your little toy car before I knock your fucking head off.'

The suited man smiled, holding Barber's gaze. 'You sure that isn't Socrates?'

Barber glanced back at the Rover, where Sarah

watched with a clenched expression. He turned back to the man. 'Listen. I'm in a hurry.'

'Evidently. Hearts? Lungs?'

'What?'

The suited man hitched down off the wall. 'I assume you're carrying transplant organs or something.' He nodded to the car. 'Or your girlfriend's waters have broken.'

'Wow,' said Barber. 'So, we're really doing this?'

The man moved forward through the short grass and stopped in a patch of sunlight. He tilted back his head and basked for a few seconds.

'You're used to being in charge, aren't you, Liam?'

Barber took a sharp breath. 'What?'

The man trained those green eyes on Barber again and smiled, activating a deep dimple in his right cheek. 'People move to your tune, yes?'

Barber stepped closer. 'How the fuck do you know my name?'

The man considered this. 'You look like a Liam. I'd say you're the eldest of brothers.' He pointed. 'Or you might be the only boy, with a sister or sisters. What I'm saying is, you get your way, don't you? If people stand between you and what you want, they have to step aside to accommodate your needs. Just like me and my little toy car.'

Barber leaned forward, in arm's reach. 'Right fucking smartarse, aren't you? Well, did you know that driving too slow is statistically more dangerous than driving too fast?'

The man nodded. 'Old Isaac Newton might have

something to say about that.' He stifled a yawn. 'Slow driving is only a factor in accidents because of associated behaviour from other drivers. Particularly risky overtaking. And tailgating.' He pointed again and grinned. 'That's your thing.'

Barber frowned. 'Ah. You overheard my girlfriend say my name.'

'Are you a fool, Liam?'

'What?'

'*Only a fool breaks the two-second rule.*'

Barber lurched forward. He grasped the man by the throat, pushing him back. The man spread his arms behind him, steadying himself on the low wall.

Sarah got out of the Rover and called over. 'Liam!'

The suited man gave a triumphant smile.

Barber leaned in close to his face. 'Move this fucking car now, or you're walking away with less teeth than you started the day with.' He released his grip and stumbled back into the road, turning to the Rover.

Sarah stomped around the front of the car and threw open the driver side door. 'Liam. Please, babe. This is stupid. Let's *go*.'

'Shut up, Sarah. Fuck's sake.' Barber eyeballed the suited man as he moved away from the wall, rubbing his neck. 'Nice suit, dickhead.' He sneered and walked back towards his car.

'We need to swap details,' said the man. 'You ran into me.'

'Bollocks,' said Barber, not turning round. 'Barely touched you.'

'You're legally required to give me your details if I have reasonable grounds to ask for them.'

Barber stopped, turned.

'There's a mark on the bumper. That's reasonable.' The man took a notepad from his inside pocket and wrote something. 'Here's my registration. Name and address. Phone number.'

Barber swiped the paper from the man's hand and read it. *'Jake Sawyer.'* He looked up and frowned. 'Rhymes with *lawyer*. You look the part, but I don't know many lawyers who drive Minis.'

Sawyer grinned. 'Good thinking, Liam. But I'm not dressed for work.'

Barber tilted his head from side to side, cracking his neck muscles. Eyes fixed on Sawyer, he took a card from his wallet and flicked it through the air towards him. It fluttered into a patch of long grass.

Sawyer picked it up and read both sides. *'Liam Barber... Sterndale Motors.* Is this your own business?'

'None of your business.'

Sawyer raised an eyebrow. He reached down to the grass, pocketed the card and turned to Sarah. 'This isn't the first time, is it?'

'Hey,' said Barber. 'Don't fucking talk to her.'

Sarah walked round to the passenger door but didn't get in. She laid a trembling hand on the door frame, watching the men.

Sawyer nodded. 'You've had to sit through this scene before, haven't you, Sarah? Those tremors are a panic response. These scenes are like micro traumas for your body. It stores them away. It keeps the score. I bet you get them every time, don't you? Somebody gets in Liam's way, or he doesn't get what he wants. He threatens them. Maybe even grabs their neck. Has he ever grabbed your neck, Sarah?'

Barber lunged for Sawyer, swinging a punch in a wide arc. Sawyer stepped across it, turned and faced Barber, grinning. Barber rebalanced himself and sprang forward, drawing back his fist. Sawyer parried it with his forearm—*bong sao*—leaving Barber's body wide open.

Barber was quick to react; he jinked himself back, out of Sawyer's range, and raised both fists up in front of his head, ducking down, keeping low. He stepped forward and faked a left punch, then threw another right.

Sawyer read the feint and blocked the punch with his forearm again, then parried Barber's follow-up left with a scooping, palm-up thrust—*tan sao*—but paused before delivering the typical headbutt *coup de grâce*.

Barber stood there for a second, pinned in position, both arms trapped by Sawyer's subtle adjustments of pressure. He grunted, trying to disentangle himself for another strike, but Sawyer hooked his left foot under Barber's right and swept it aside, sending him tumbling to the ground.

Sawyer planted his feet wide and side-on, in classic Jeet Kune Do fighting stance. He slid back along the road, gaining distance on Barber.

A royal blue Audi pulled up a few yards behind the Rover.

'You've done a bit of boxing, haven't you, Liam?' said Sawyer.

Barber scrambled to his feet, slipping on the loose earth.

Something predatory flashed in Sawyer's eyes. 'I didn't want to humiliate you in front of your girlfriend. See, that was me being kind. But you insisted.'

Barber came again, more cautious this time, moving over to the verge, as if the long grass might camouflage him. He'd grazed his elbow in the fall, and as he raised his guard, a few beads of blood dropped onto the grass.

'Hey!'

A shout from the Audi. The driver—a middle-aged woman—had lowered her window.

A small dog in the back seat barked in alarm.

Sawyer took a sharp breath and put a hand to the back of his neck.

His breathing quickened.

'Grow up, the pair of you!'

Barber's blood, trickling down the grass.

He edged closer to Sawyer, keeping low, bobbing and weaving with the sun at his back.

He dipped his head; Sawyer raised a hand to shield his eyes from the sun flare.

'Excuse me!' The Audi woman's voice, shrill and insistent. *'Some of us have to get to work.'* She stepped out of the car, staying behind the open door.

The dog yapped, rapid and urgent.

Sawyer squatted down, breathing hard now. Panting.

He put a hand to the grass, dropped to his knees.

Soil through his fingers.

As he hauled himself upright again, Barber threw another punch. Sawyer jerked his head to the side, but too late. The blow hit him on the side of his mouth and he collapsed into the long grass.

Barber shuffled forward, standing over him, fists raised. 'There you go. There you go, you fucking smartarse.'

He aimed a kick at Sawyer's midriff; Sawyer rolled away in time to take the sting out of it. He steadied himself on the stone wall, with his back to Barber.

'Liam! Stop this!'

Sarah, pulling him away.

Barber stepped to the side, against the wall, trying to see Sawyer's face.

He barked out a laugh. 'Oh my fucking god. He's crying over here.'

Sawyer kept his head down, shoulders shaking.

Barber turned to Sarah, delighted. 'Mr big man. Crying like a little girl.'

The dog poked its head out of the Audi window, barking and barking and barking.

'Bobby! Quiet!' The driver got back into her car and slammed the door.

Sarah took a few cautious steps forward, stopping in front of Barber. She squinted through the sunlight, studying Sawyer.

'He's *laughing*, babe.'

'What?'

Sawyer turned and hitched up onto the stone wall. His face was flushed, but his breathing had slowed and he wore a broad, toothy smile.

The laughter ramped up: short bursts between

rasping breaths, then longer, louder, with an edge of delirium. He kept his eyes down as he laughed.

Sarah stumbled back, gripping Barber by the arm. 'Let's go. Now. Seriously.'

Barber gazed at Sawyer, resisting, but then followed Sarah back to the Rover, shaking his head. He opened the driver door, began to climb in.

'*Fewer.*'

Barber popped his head over the door. 'What?'

Sawyer pointed at him, stifling more laughter. 'You said *less* teeth. If you're going to rely on verbal threats, at least learn to speak the fucking language properly.'

Barber looked in at Sarah, then back to Sawyer.

He climbed in and closed the door.

Sawyer backed further into the wall and squatted down, steadying his breathing, shaken by spasms of laughter.

Barber started the Rover and veered away from the Mini, left wheels skimming the edge of the roadside ditch. He screeched past, clipping and closing the left wing mirror, and sped away.

Sawyer hauled himself upright and waded through the long grass, back onto the road. He stood by the Mini, leaning on the bonnet, gaze fixed on the Rover as it disappeared into the distance. The laughter had faded now, but his grin stayed broad and fixed.

The Audi woman leaned out of her window. 'Hello! Are you alright?'

Sawyer turned to her, waved a hand. 'Never better.'

2

Curtis Mavers rocked forward on the sofa, using the momentum to haul himself to his feet. He grimaced and clutched his arm, then pivoted towards the door.

Another knock. Five taps. Polite, measured, half a second apart.

He shuffled over and lifted his dark glasses to peer through the peephole. His face was puffy, with faint purple bruising around his eyes. He took a slow, shaky breath, then slid aside the deadbolts and trudged back to the sofa.

A key turned in the lock, and the door opened wide, but nobody entered.

Mavers flopped down and took a sip from a glass on the coffee table. 'Coast is clear. Just the two of us.'

Dale Strickland stepped into the apartment and closed the door behind him. He burned a glare into Mavers's broad back and stepped around to face him.

'No visitors?'

Mavers scratched at his greying beard. 'I thought I'd

defer the dinner parties to my next destination. And I don't think I'm the right colour for the Didsbury swingers.'

Strickland wrinkled his nose at something and walked over to the closed blinds. 'You can let some air in, Curtis. We're five floors up.' He slid a hand through the slats and pushed open a window.

'You think I'm worried about a drone strike? Or fuckin' Spider-Man popping in?' Mavers tried to laugh, but collapsed into a coughing fit. He gripped the centre of his chest.

Strickland took a seat in an armchair opposite Mavers. He loosened his tailored blue shirt and ran a palm over his close-cropped white hair. 'I hope you're not getting through my Glenfiddich too quickly.'

Mavers scoffed. 'Medicinal purposes.' He raised his eyes to Strickland for the first time. 'Looking a bit ragged, Dale lad. Don't suppose you're getting much sleep. Join the club.' He paused. 'I need something stronger for the pain. The shit you gave me isn't touching the sides. Tap up your old drug contacts. Mix me a potion.'

'I'm not a magician,' said Strickland. 'But I'll help.' He slipped on a pair of thick-rimmed glasses and fixed his chilly blue eyes on Mavers. 'It's time to move things forward, Curtis. I appreciate you've suffered—'

'Someone watching your boy?'

Strickland sat back. 'You mean my son?'

Mavers nodded. 'Young Luka.'

'He's in the car outside, with my driver.'

'Missing his mum, is he?'

Strickland toyed with the face of his gold watch.

Mavers whistled. 'What was that piece again? Not Rolex, is it?'

'Audemars Piguet.'

'Classy, but conspicuous. That's very you, isn't it?'

Strickland sighed. 'You can project wealth and power without being vulgar.'

Mavers kissed his teeth. 'You should see Stokes's place. Fucker's got gold taps.' He took his time pouring himself a fresh glass of whisky. 'Status symbols don't really do it for me, Dale. I heard knowledge was power.' He slurped his drink, grimaced as it went down.

Strickland leaned forward, propping his elbows on his knees. 'As I say, I appreciate you've suffered, but it cost me a lot of money to get you away from Leon Stokes and it is time to—'

'Deliver the goods?'

'Yes. My wife is being held by a murderer who believes I wronged him in the past. The man who took my son for the same reason several years ago. If you want me to provide genuine safe passage, I need to know what you know.'

Mavers drained his glass and clinked it down on the coffee table. He rolled up the sleeve of his right arm, revealing a vast smear of disfigured skin: raised welts, blistered and fibrous; a tattoo image, with only the edges visible behind the scorched and peeling epidermis.

'Stokes had a doctor there, you know. Cleaning up after his pet psycho had done his work, prepping me for the next session. He topped me up with blood after one beating. Then that cunt took off my tattoo with a blowtorch. A good friend of mine did that tattoo. Sound

21

fella called Murray. Known him since we were kids. He was a brilliant artist. Used to draw amazing stuff on my skin in felt pen. Me mam went mental. But he died a couple of years ago. Even if I get grafts, I can never recreate his work. So you're seriously spot on about the suffering, Dale.' He carefully rolled down his sleeve. 'I don't want your bird to pay the price for your misdeeds, but the last time you arranged "safe passage", it didn't work out for me.'

Strickland took off his glasses, cleaned the lenses with his shirt cuff. 'You should never interrupt the enemy when he's in retreat, Curtis. You see, I'm winding down. New job. New outlook. New life. I want to move on from my enemies, not make new ones.' He replaced his glasses. 'You can't win 'em all, and you have to know when to cut your losses. Our venture didn't work out, and I apologise for my paranoid reaction. But this time, it's in my interest to make sure you put plenty of distance between yourself and this fair isle. If we keep this beef going, we can only do each other harm. Do you know what a pyrrhic victory is?'

'One where you win and lose at the same time.'

Strickland smiled. 'Sort of, yes. You win, but suffer such damage that the triumph seems hollow. Curtis, if you hold out on me now, and my wife dies, you get revenge, but no chance to put things right for yourself. So, we can either both lose, or both win. And I assume you've set up some insurance in case I fuck you over again?'

Mavers nodded. 'Let's just say if I get yanked by the bizzies, or Stokes's crew turns up before I leave British soil, you'll be the first to know.' He poured himself another glass and downed it in one. 'When I was watching your place in Bakewell, I saw a car. Dark green. Looked like a Focus. This is late afternoon. Fuck-off big fella got out, strolled on up the path. Couldn't see exactly, but someone answered, and he went inside.'

Strickland took out a ballpoint and slid a card from his wallet. 'And you got the registration?'

'Oh, yeah. Soon after, this fella came back out to the car with your missus. She didn't look too happy, but not hurt as far as I could see. He drove her away in the Focus.'

Strickland clicked the end of the pen. 'Curtis. Registration.'

'RG17 5NJ.' Mavers took a drink. 'Hope you find her. And him.'

Strickland wrote the number and got to his feet. 'I need to check this.'

Mavers nodded. 'It's legit.' He peered over the top of the dark glasses. 'That's me done, Dale. Now. Work your magic. Make me disappear.'

———

Strickland walked out of the apartment block and into a small courtyard car park. As he strolled to a white Mercedes S-Class parked in the corner, a stocky man in a well-fitted suit stepped out of the driver seat and walked around to open the passenger door.

The back window rolled down and an adolescent boy hung his head out. He swished his floppy blond hair off his face and called to Strickland.

'Can we *go*?'

'Two minutes, Luka.' He waved a hand at the man, who eased back into the driver seat and closed the door.

Strickland walked to the car park entrance gate and tapped a number on his phone. The recipient didn't answer immediately, and he stepped behind a tree, out of sight of the car. The morning sun was dampened by a streak of cloud, but he lifted his face to the sky, anyway.

The call connected.

Strickland kept his voice low. 'My witness came through. I have a reg, and I assume you can bring your expertise to bear. I need to know it's a valid number, quickly. Then I need to know where the car is, and how it got there.' He turned and hurried back towards the Mercedes. 'I'm talking to Derbyshire tomorrow. But I'm also making independent enquiries.'

3

'I know you think you skipped the depressing part. But have you seen the sandwiches?'

A heavy hand landed on Sawyer's shoulder, and he turned. Frazer Drummond narrowed his eyes.

'You're supposed to start fights at weddings, Sawyer. Not funerals.'

'My old JKD instructor said you should aim to end fights before they start.'

Drummond scoffed. 'How very zen.' He leaned in closer. 'You've done a decent job with... concealer?'

Sawyer nodded.

'But you did it while the initial bruising was still forming. The redness is peeking through.' He stood up, regarded Sawyer. 'So, not at the funeral. Did you piss off the postman?'

'Someone scuffed my bumper. Things got punchy in the insurance exchange.'

Drummond slipped out of his black suit jacket and draped it over his arm. 'And how's the other guy?'

'I left him alive as a warning to other tailgaters.'

Drummond smiled and glanced around the crowded function room. The mourners kept the conversation muted, with a few cautious laughs.

'What's this place called again?'

'Bull's Head.'

Drummond waved a hand. 'Ross never drank here. You'd think his family would pick something with more meaning than a white-bread country hotel.'

'I don't think he cares now.'

They walked over to a narrow trestle table beneath the windows of the function room. Layered plates of bought-in finger food; jugs of juice and soda, ungenerously iced; nasty florid tablecloth. Sawyer transferred a few sandwiches to a paper plate and took a seat below the mic stand at the edge of a shallow stage.

Drummond hovered as Sawyer opened the sandwiches, inspecting the fillings.

'Dig in, Sawyer, for fuck's sake. You look like you last ate a week ago.'

Sawyer winced and pushed the plate away. Drummond filled a cup with juice and handed it to him. He watched, stern, as Sawyer sipped, staring ahead.

'She'll be back.'

Sawyer drained the cup. 'No guarantee.'

'Aren't you Little Mr Sunshine today? The brain is a fucking wonder, okay? It repairs itself. But she needs the downtime to give the process a chance.' He leaned down. 'Just make sure you're in shape to greet her when she rejoins the cruel world.'

The crowd by the main doors shuffled aside, as

several new mourners entered and lined up at the food table. Principal SOCO Sally O'Callaghan; DI Ed Shepherd; DS Matt Walker. DSI Ivan Keating—in full uniform—arrived last and embraced a young woman in a family group by the bar. Keating kept his head bowed as they spoke, catching Sawyer's eye as he looked over her shoulder.

Shepherd broke away and took a seat opposite Sawyer. Drummond nodded and moved off.

'Sir. Good to see you. Didn't fancy the service?'

'I don't do prayers.'

'It wasn't that religious. The readings were nice.' Shepherd studied him. 'How are you?'

Sawyer toyed with the empty cup. 'Let's go for *functioning*.'

'I wish I could say you haven't missed much, sir.'

'I hear you don't have to call me that anymore. Technically.'

Shepherd smiled. 'It's a respect thing.'

Sawyer looked up. 'Congratulations on your promotion. But I'd find someone else as a role model, if I were you.'

'DI Shepherd.' Keating pulled back another chair at Sawyer's table. 'Sorry to interrupt, but I'd like to speak to DI Sawyer in private for a moment.'

Shepherd held Sawyer's eye for a second, then sprang to his feet. 'Of course, sir.' He glanced at Sawyer and headed back to join the others.

Keating placed his cap on the table and ran a palm across his cropped white hair.

'I know you weren't best friends with Detective

Moran, Sawyer. But you could have at least paid your respects.'

'I had a car moment. A prang from behind.'

'Did you caution the driver?'

'Kept it domestic, but ran a PNC check. The guy was an arsehole but disappointingly clean.'

Keating sat. 'Any update on Maggie?'

'Stable, but no sign of revival. It's been a week now.'

'And how's your health?'

Sawyer angled his head. 'Fluid. Got out of the hospital day before yesterday.'

Keating eyed him. He laid both hands on his cap, drummed out a pattern with his thumbs.

'But enough about me,' said Sawyer. 'What's happening with the enquiry?'

Keating gave a grim laugh. 'It's more than an enquiry. It's national bloody news. Government level. Political condemnation. We've been locked down as a crime scene. ISC interest. There was even an MI5 meeting about potential change to the National Threat Level. Home Office has set up a task force based in Derby. The bloody Home Secretary is the SIO, Sawyer. Hands-off, but conducting an illustrious orchestra of Met brass. It's basically a pop-up force. They're considering it an attack on the regional police, and they've been sweeping the place for the last week. They've also been raking over ongoing cases, interviewing our MIT. Even the support staff.'

Sawyer lowered his eyes. 'Any breakthroughs?'

'No. Quite a few lines, though. There's a lot of interest in Austin Fletcher.'

'His actions slowed down the attack.'

'Yes. And he probably helped Maggie. But they want to know why he was insisting on only talking to you, and they're elbow deep in the discovery of Scott Walton and the other bodies. They think Fletcher might have been Walton's accomplice, and they fell out.'

Sawyer glanced at him. 'They think wrong.'

'If only we could find him and find out.' Keating shuffled his chair around the table, closer to Sawyer. He lowered his voice. 'I lose no sleep over Scott Walton. But three people died in what looks like fallout from Fletcher's involvement in his death, including one of my detectives. Unless you have your own take on why a group of armed, masked men attacked the police station where he was the sole prisoner?'

Sawyer gazed across at the mourners, chomping on their cheese and pickle and toasting Detective Constable Ross Moran with tepid plonk, then confronted Keating's steady glare.

'Fletcher called in connections to get him out,' said Sawyer. 'But he went rogue as soon as he got his hands on a gun.'

Keating nodded, unconvinced. 'But why not just let the men spring him? And why did they shoot a custody sergeant, a solicitor, an anonymous officer managing the cells?' He leaned forward. 'And why is Fletcher shooting them when they've arrived to get him out of prison?'

Sawyer shrugged. 'He's not exactly a team player.'

Keating took a drink and fixed Sawyer with a pained smile. 'If you're well enough, the task force wants to interview you tomorrow. Be warned, though. There's a lot of unresolved questions swirling around about your involvement in Walton's death. Stoked up by your detractors, admittedly. But you'll need to be convincing, and your seat is going to feel pretty uncomfortable in that interview room.'

'No support, I assume?'

'I asked. They declined. Conf room. NCA officers on video. I'll be present as senior rank. Independent, though.'

'You could always hold my hand under the table.'

Keating didn't smile. 'We also have the small matter of a missing person, also connected to you.'

'Eva Gregory. Why connected to me?'

Keating raised an eyebrow.

A middle-aged man and woman approached him, and he stood, head bowed, as they said their sad goodbyes and headed towards the function room's external door.

Keating sat back down. 'Jesus Christ. Moran's brother and sister. That's what guns do, Sawyer. It's not just about the bodies the bullets hit. Those people are bloody well broken.' He took a breath, recomposed. 'So, yes. Eva Gregory. There's been no contact since Dennis Crawley, apparently, called Strickland eight days ago. Demands, I can work with. Threats, bluster, ransom requests. But I'm not a fan of the silent treatment. Sally got work boot imprints from outside their drive. Also tyre tracks. Too generic, though. No witnesses. Nothing useful in the passive data.'

'I assume the father of Eva's son has been a feature?'

'Strickland's had his beak in, yes. He's moved into the family home to look after the young lad.'

'Dad of the year.'

'Whatever you think of Strickland, he's in line for Greater Manchester mayor, and he's been the only contact with Crawley so far.'

Keating broke eye contact, fiddled with his shirt cuff.

Sawyer smiled. 'He wants me to help. He's asked after me.'

'Of course he has. You put Crawley away when he came calling last time. Saved Strickland's son. If I were him, I'd want you involved, too. If only as someone who's been up close with Crawley before.' He picked up his cap, turned it around on the tip of his fingers. 'So, are you well?'

Sawyer watched Moran's brother and sister. The sister had to hold the brother's arm around her shoulders to keep him upright.

'No. But I'm well enough.'

4

Sawyer parked the Mini at the end of the gravel drive and gazed across the moor to Ramshaw Rocks, an ugly-beautiful clump of gritstone at the edge of the Staffordshire Roaches. As ever, his father's voice came through.

'A crag with teeth.'

And more.

'There is nothing in darkness that will not be disclosed.'

For the first time, the religious meaning fell away, and Sawyer caught the tone of a task laid down for him; something his father was trying to communicate.

The sinking afternoon sun lit up fresh blottings of heather, busy colonising the moor in shades of pink and purple; an underlay for autumn.

As Sawyer approached the house, Justin opened the door, nodded, and turned back inside. Rufus and Cain clambered over each other and bounded over, panting in the heat. He fussed them, catching their sour breath, the soapy sweetness of their fur.

The dogs escorted Sawyer down the hall and scurried out to the back garden as he diverted into the sitting room.

'Do you want a drink?'

Justin closed the door behind them and took a bottle of water out of a mini fridge beside Maggie's work desk.

Sawyer took it. 'Thanks.'

Justin sat, perched on the edge of the chocolate brown futon. Loose-fitting white T-shirt, Adidas shorts. A few days' beard growth; blond with flecks of ginger. His rigid features had wilted, and he kept his sunken eyes on the vast bay window overlooking the moor.

Sawyer unscrewed the bottle. 'Been for a run?'

Justin scoffed. 'After a fashion.'

'You stopped smoking.'

'I've stopped everything.'

Sawyer took a sip. 'How are Mia and Freddy coping?'

'Freddy is shut away with his console. He has a summer activity camp thing, but I can't convince him to go. Mia is just...'

'Angry?'

Justin glanced over. 'Yes. I think she has a boyfriend. Some lad called Joshua. So, how are you?'

'Stiff. Mild traumatic brain injury, apparently. Glorified concussion. Sounds worse than it is.'

'Are they interviewing you?'

'I'm up on Monday.'

Justin nodded. 'Significant witness.' He drank from a

plastic tumbler, clunking it against the vase of drooping lilies on the coffee table. He yanked a tissue from a box and mopped at the spillage, staring at his reflection as he wiped.

Sawyer took a seat. 'Justin. We'll work this out.'

'She opened her eyes.'

'When?'

He turned and held Sawyer's eye. 'This morning. But it doesn't necessarily mean… They define consciousness in two parts. Wakefulness and awareness. The neurons and connections that support wakefulness exist in one region of the brain, while those that provide awareness are in another. First, they establish wakefulness. Then, awareness. After that, there's a process for coaxing the patient back to consciousness.'

'So, the eyes just signify wakefulness? Not awareness.'

Justin nodded and turned back to the window. 'I suppose it's progress. But it's all so damned abstract. One thing doesn't lead to another. No promises. No definites. Sometimes it all feels like bloody voodoo or something.'

'You're used to the law. Rigorous. Defined. Cause, effect, consequence.'

Justin raised his glass, peered into the water as it caught the sun. 'Go on, then. What's the legal prognosis? What are they going to ask you that they don't already know?'

'It's usually more about trying to gauge a response to the things you know already. That gives you a strategy to get to the stuff you don't know.'

'Fucking hell, Sawyer. You're worse than the doctors. What's their angle?'

Sawyer forced a smile. 'Fletcher. He was the only

prisoner at the time the building was attacked. And he wanted to speak to me.'

'Why?'

'That's what they'll want to know.'

Justin sighed. 'And do you know?'

'No. But they won't believe me.' Sawyer looked around the room. 'Why did Curtis Mavers come here, Justin?'

'What does that have to do with anything?'

'Maybe a lot.'

Justin got up and walked to Maggie's work desk. He opened a drawer, tidied it. 'That piece of filth wanted to... Mia.'

'Mavers?'

'The other one. Wilmot.'

'He's dead.'

Justin nodded. 'Finally, some good news.' He looked out to the moor. 'I'm seeing Holsgrove tomorrow.'

'On a Sunday?'

'There's a private ward there. As usual, money buys flexibility. Come along if you like.'

'They sent me photographs of you after the beating.'

Justin closed the drawer and walked over to Sawyer. 'This is when you were hiding?'

'They were trying to flush me out. The message was clear. You first, Maggie next. They knew I couldn't stomach that.'

Justin leaned in to him. 'And who the fuck is *they*, Sawyer?'

Sawyer's phone buzzed in his pocket.

'I have ideas. But, as you said. No definites. Yet.

Maggie wasn't a target in the station attack. But I'd like to ask her what she saw and heard before I got there. And I'm sure Mavers can help with our enquiries. If we can find out who hired him to target you, then we might get to more things we don't know.'

'You think he was involved in the station attack?'

'Yes.' Sawyer took out his phone. A call from Shepherd. 'Maybe not directly. But I got a home visit just before, from someone who was looking for him. My uninvited guest was definitely involved in the attack. So Mavers could be the missing link.'

He connected the call. 'You've found Eva Gregory.'

'Your radar's off, sir,' said Shepherd. 'It's not about Eva. And remember. Nobody takes the good news first.'

'Is there good news?'

'No.'

5

Sawyer edged the Mini into a shallow passing place at the side of the single-track Kinder Road, and walked down to the Scientific Services unit van, parked in a dead zone between two strips of red-and-white cordon tape. He showed his warrant card, and a uniformed officer logged him, then lifted the tape, letting him duck under.

The man pointed. 'Straight across, sir.'

Sawyer followed his finger. 'Kinder Bank wood?'

'Yes. Just off the reservoir path. Outer search is complete. All clear from Sally.'

He hopped over a dried-up stream and crossed the open field, shielding his eyes from the luminous low sun. Shepherd stood at the other side, beneath an overhanging tree, talking to two FSIs in white Tyvek suits.

'Is this new policy?' said Sawyer.

'Sir?'

'Funeral wear to scenes.'

Shepherd shrugged. 'Haven't had a chance to change.'

The Tyveks nodded at Sawyer and walked past him, heading back to the van. Shepherd moved off, deeper into the patchy woodland along the lower valley slope.

'New birches around here,' said Shepherd, nodding at a fresh plantation along the field edge.

'Uhuh. Where did you put the Rover?'

'I didn't.'

'Detective Sawyer.'

Sally O'Callaghan stood at the edge of the inner cordon in her turquoise Tyvek suit, beckoning Sawyer with both arms. He stepped under the tape, followed by Shepherd. O'Callaghan's crop of peroxide hair flashed in the gloom as she flipped back her suit hood.

She studied him for a moment. 'You look like a man who needs a hug but doesn't want one.'

'I wouldn't get too close. That doesn't go well for most people.'

'Fucking hell, Jake. Not self-pity. I can't go down to that cellar. It's only the hide of impenetrable cynicism that keeps me moving.'

She pivoted and led them through the trees.

'How are you?' she turned, caught his eye.

'It's good to get out of the house.'

She barked a bitter laugh. 'Indulge in something life-affirming. I hear Maggie is through the worst.'

'Hard to predict.'

'God, yes. But the brain is a remarkable lump of gunk. Resilient little bugger.'

'That's what Drummond said.'

O'Callaghan gave a mock gasp. 'Sympathy from Frazer? Get that bottled.'

'It only took a near-death experience to get it.'

'Hell of a business, though. Do they know what the bastards were up to yet?'

'Working on it,' said Shepherd.

She guided Sawyer under the inner cordon tape, giving his shoulder a squeeze.

Sawyer and Shepherd put on plastic shoe protectors and latex gloves, and approached a charred oak tree stump with exposed roots. The air was dense, caustic. Scorched flesh. Baked soil.

Sawyer crouched, gazing at the man's body: blackened and burned. His hands and feet were secured with metal cuffs, the hand restraints locked behind the thick end of a root. Despite the short length of the chain links, he had curled into a foetal position with his hands clenched into fists, raised in front of his face.

'Pugilist stance,' said Sawyer. 'Standard for burners.'

O'Callaghan nodded. 'Flexed elbows and knees. Shrinkage of tissues and muscle because of dehydration caused by the heat.'

'Hard to tell,' said Sawyer. 'But it looks like he's been beaten, too.' He sniffed, looked up at O'Callaghan.

She nodded. 'Petrol. Or some kind of accelerant.'

Sawyer edged his face closer to the corpse. 'He seems relatively young.' He stood up. 'We'll need Drummond to examine his lungs.'

'Why's that?' said Shepherd.

'Smoke-damaged tissue indicates inhalation,' said O'Callaghan. 'Clear tissue means he died before the fire was on him.'

'If he was burned alive,' said Sawyer, 'he would have

been in agony, with terrible damage to his feet, legs and hands. But death would ultimately be from smoke inhalation.'

'Keating has called a briefing first thing,' said Shepherd.

'That'll be popular,' said O'Callaghan. 'Sunday morning.'

Sawyer walked to the clearing edge, parting branches. 'As usual, the number one priority is victimology. We need to know who he was, so we can learn about the time leading up to his death.' He glanced at O'Callaghan. 'Before the evidence. Before the act. We go back to the past. That's where the answers will be. How the killer and victim related to each other. How and why they converged.' He looked down through the trees at the reservoir surface, glowing in the sunset. 'Beautiful spot for an immolation.'

O'Callaghan gave Shepherd a look.

'Good to have you back, sir,' said Shepherd. 'I couldn't do this without you.'

Sawyer turned, raised an eyebrow.

Shepherd scrubbed at his beard. 'Rover's conked out. Need you to do the driving.'

6

Catherine Brennan shut down the computer and closed the wooden blinds at the open window of her home office.

Her nose twitched.

Barbecue embers. Citrus from the outdoor candles.

Ralph's voice drifted up from the kitchen: stentorian, mock exasperated. Marshalling their two girls inside while he cleared away. She had promised them the first half of *Toy Story 4*. If she left now, she could be back by Buzz's carnival escape. Sweep up the children while Ralph called his ailing father.

Brennan crouched in the corner and tapped a code into the wall-mounted keypad, unlocking the custom-made Banham safe. She opened a drawer inside the safe and took out a black leather folder. She slipped the folder into her Kate Spade shoulder bag, then locked up and headed out and down the stairs.

The girls chattered to Ralph at the back of the house. She called through.

'Going out. Back in half an hour.'

Brennan had the door open, but Ralph came barrelling through from the kitchen.

Heavy hands snaked around her hips. Ralph smelt of garlic and Tom Ford.

'It's dark, Cat.'

She sighed and turned to him. 'I'm a big girl. Accounts were a bastard. I could do with a little drive. Clear my head.' She rested her forehead on his chest and tucked her deep red hair over one ear. 'We can get the terrors to sleep as soon as I'm back.' She lowered her voice, angled her head to catch his eye. 'We're due an early one.'

He grinned and released her. 'How long will you be? I'm making hot chocolate.'

She hurried out. 'It'll still be warm chocolate by the time I'm back.'

————

Brennan waited in an isolated bay at the corner of the Lamb Inn car park, watching two young men in chef uniforms chatting and smoking at the back door, under a pale overhead light. She took the leather folder from the glovebox and rested it on her knees, trying to steady her ragged breathing. Sparks flew up as the men ground out their cigarettes on the stone wall before stepping back inside.

She got out, crossed Hayfield Road, and walked down a sloping path that ran parallel to the road before veering away to an old packhorse bridge and a narrow track into trees at the edge of farm outbuildings.

She switched on her phone light, keeping it low to the ground; enough to navigate a few feet ahead in the dark, but not high enough to make her visible from a distance. Nightfall had chilled the muggy air, and she hitched up her jacket collar as she stopped at the corner of a dilapidated dry-stone wall.

She pressed a thumb over the phone light and looked up at the black sky, holding her gaze as the stars came into focus. Shimmering constellations. Spangled nebula. A celestial light show unmuted by electrical pollution.

Brennan touched the slender crucifix at the end of her pendant necklace, and navigated to the what3words app, where every three-metre square in the world was mapped by three words unique to the location. She opened her Favourites list and tapped on the entry for *purchaser.flukes.blinder*.

Three minutes' walk to a spot at the far side of the outbuildings.

She pressed on, taking it slow, holding steady in the centre of her constricted puddle of phone light. After a couple of minutes, the swish of traffic on the main road fell away, and she found herself alone with her mulchy footfalls.

She stopped at the destination: a long forgotten patch of rubble from another collapsed dry-stone wall.

Brennan's neck prickled, and she looked back the way she'd come, swinging the phone light around the open field. She paused, then turned and stepped over a mound of rocks, crouching behind what remained of the wall.

She took out the folder and aimed the phone light at the rubble, looking for a suitable spot.

Movement from the trees a few metres away.

A man's voice.

'Well, now.'

Brennan sprang upright. 'Jesus! Scared the life out of me.'

'Really, Catherine? Taking His name in vain.'

'Not without good reason.'

The man stepped out, but stayed in shadow. 'You should be shifting. Get back to your fella.'

'I tried to get here earlier. Couldn't get away.'

The man lit a cigarette, shielding the match flame from the breeze. His face glowed as he took a deep drag. He turned his head to the side and blew out a thin jet of smoke. It billowed and drifted across his wide shoulders.

'I've been here for half an hour. Thought you'd bottled.'

He took another pull on the cigarette. The glow caught a glint of something around his neck.

'Couldn't be helped,' said Brennan. She held up the folder. 'Might as well just give it to you now.'

'Just leave it there. Get yourself back. Don't want your ol' man getting nosey.'

He walked to a tree and sat at the base.

Brennan hovered for a few seconds, then turned to go.

The man took another drag, spoke through the

smoke. 'Next one will be a different spot. Watch the app. And let's tighten up. Sort out your timekeeping.'

She paused. 'It's kids. I couldn't—'

'Plan better. Leave earlier. Get cover. Whatever it takes.'

She nodded.

He tilted his head. 'Still good with this, girl? We staying the course?'

'Yes.'

He waved the cigarette. 'I know it's hard for youse.'

Brennan turned back to face him, square. 'The Lord does not hand us something we can't carry.'

7

A battalion of insectoid spacecraft whirled across the TV screen, shedding a blizzard of missiles that raked across the playfield. Sawyer jinked his ship in and out of the narrow safe channels as the missiles burst into swirls of deadly shrapnel. His thumb spasmed, and the ship ran into an overhanging rock, where it disintegrated in a spiral of flames.

'Fuck it.'

He sat upright on the sofa. Squinting, dizzy on hyper-focus.

He dropped the joypad to the floor and jabbed the power button on the TV remote, extinguishing the only light in the room.

Sawyer sat there for a while, waiting for his heart to steady, basking in the synthetic electrical hum from his phone's YouTube app. *Blade Runner Apartment Ambience.* Two hours into a twelve-hour audio loop.

The register of the drone effect rose and fell. Rhythmic, repetitive. Supposedly soothing.

His mind got busy filling the vacuum. Babbling voices, visions, leering faces, earworms, lyrics.

Hello darkness, my old friend.

He let it run. Listening. Watching the faces form in the blackness, then melt away, merging with others.

What was it his meditation app had told him? *Pay them no mind. Apply no judgement. Don't try to get rid of them.*

As his eyes adjusted, he reached forward and picked up his glass of beer. Tepid, almost full.

Sawyer sipped at the foamless surface. Swallowed. Winced at the sourness.

He set the glass back down and reached his foot across to the floor switch, clicking on the dim corner lamp.

The room was unchanged, wedged in reality. Cluttered coffee table; TV and PS4; empty microwave meal tubs stacked beside the full recycling bin.

A mound of Blu-Rays and DVDs sat by the TV. Difficult world cinema. Bergman, Haneke, Ozu, Tarkovsky.

The drone of the YouTube audio rose and fell, rose and fell.

Sawyer pulled a paper bag from the coffee table shelf and took out two rectangular packets. He popped two pills out of the first pack and swallowed them with a swig from a bottle of Diet Coke, then chased with a single pill from the second pack.

The drone dropped away, replaced by his ringtone.

He ignored it, and groped further along the coffee

table shelf, pulling out a small hardback notebook with a dark orange cover and a handwritten white label.

Jessica Mary Sawyer
My life and thoughts

Sawyer set the book aside and glanced at the phone. The Caller ID read *MIKE*.

He sighed and connected the call.

'Hey.'

Sawyer winced. His brother's voice came over too loud, too clear. He lowered the volume. 'Hey yourself. What's going on?'

'Working on some contractor code. It's crawling with bugs. This is my Saturday night now.'

Sawyer browsed the notebook. 'I can beat that. I'm playing video games. Alone.'

'Where's your cat?'

'It's night-time. Bruce is at work.'

A tinging metal sound at Michael's end. 'I'm making you a cup of virtual tea.'

'Well, you certainly don't drink real tea.'

'Herbal tea is still tea. Are you playing *Bullet Symphony*?'

'You know I am.'

Michael made a slurping sound. 'That game makes my head hurt just thinking about it.'

'I'm back at work.'

Michael paused. 'Hargreave said to rest.'

Sawyer closed the journal. 'Holsgrove. I can't sit around, Mike.'

'You have to heal, Jake. You can't rush it.'

'There's no other damage. Bit of wear and tear. I've got some painkillers. I bought a couple of things online. Non-addictive.'

'For the pain?'

'It's just... to help me sleep. You know. It's hard to shut down.'

'I do know. What brands?'

Sawyer closed his eyes. Faces again. Animated, contorted. Maggie shouting. His mother, open-mouthed, trying to push away her attacker.

'Tramadol. Methylphenidate.'

A pause. Clicking keyboard at Michael's end.

'Okay,' said Michael, 'so you're taking an opioid painkiller and a medication for ADHD.'

'I don't take the painkiller often. And the methylphenidate... It tones it down.'

'Tones what down?'

'All of it. The chatter. The compulsions. Without it, I feel like... my mind is on a ship in a storm. With it, I'm still out to sea. But the waters are calm.'

More clicking.

'It says you shouldn't drive. Headaches, low appetite. I've had Tramadol. It gave me bad dreams.'

Sawyer picked up the phone and walked over to the kitchen. 'I don't think I've ever had good ones.' He opened a few cupboards, checked the fridge. Packet noodles, ageing yoghurt, curling pizza slices, unopened salad long past its best.

'Are they investigating what happened at the station?' said Michael.

Sawyer tipped a few Shreddies into a bowl. 'Yeah. Talking to me on Monday.'

'Going through it all again?'

The milk was on its way out, but still drinkable. 'Not really, but it's a hoop I have to jump through.'

Michael puffed out a sigh. 'And how's Maggie doing?'

Flash of the explosion.

'Stable. There's some progress.' He slid the bowl onto the coffee table, spilling the milk. 'Their main job is to keep her blood pressure steady. The coma drugs suppress it. So, they give her more medication to keep her heart regular.' He crunched through a mouthful of cereal. 'But you know all this, Mike.'

'What do you mean?'

'You came through okay.'

'Did I?' A long pause. 'It's strange, you know. Whatever they gave me when I was in that coma... It's like it flushed a few things away. Some of the dark stuff. Just gaps there now.'

'What do you mean, gaps? In your memories?'

Michael took a few breaths, gathering himself. 'Yes. Before, there were images, sounds. They followed me around. Fucking haunted me. I couldn't escape them. Now, they're more like distant memories. Faded. But Maggie's trauma was a lot worse than mine. Be prepared, Jake.'

'For what?'

'For her to be changed. At least to start with. She might need a lot of care.'

Sawyer nodded. 'I live to give.'

8

Sawyer pushed through the double doors and hurried past the evenly placed offices with yellow frosted windows. He kept his head down as he waited for the lift, but couldn't resist a look as he stepped in.

The junction at the end of the corridor had been barred with a yellow flexibarrier. Two men in Hi-Vis vests and white helmets leaned over the custody suite, studying a document. A broad-shouldered man stood before the barrier, a lanyard with the word *SECURITY* printed on the ribbon hanging over his fitted suit.

Sawyer raised his eyebrows at the man, who returned the faintest nod. The lift doors closed, and the car rose away from the sound of drilling in the cell area beyond.

On the open-plan MIT floor, the main desks were empty, with the major players packed into the central glass-walled conference room. Keating stood by the head chair of the twenty-seater table, scowling down at the master touchscreen linked to the large wall monitor behind.

Sawyer glanced across to the closed door of his office, and entered the conference room in silence, taking a seat next to Shepherd.

'Sir.'

Sawyer logged in to his individual touchscreen. 'How's the Rover?'

'It's going to be a week or two. Had to cab it. Theo thinks it might mean a late start to the school year.'

Sawyer forced a smile. 'Tell him Jake's Taxis will make sure he doesn't miss a second of geography.'

Keating sat down. 'Let's dive in. I apologise for interrupting your Sunday.' He swiped at his screen. 'But blame the bastard responsible for this.'

The central monitor displayed a scene photo of the blackened corpse, curled with raised fists, shackled to the tree root. Sawyer scrolled through several autopsy images on his own screen and skimmed the prelim pathology findings.

Keating switched the main image to a shot of a heavily bearded man standing before a white background. He stared down the camera lens, head tilted back.

Sally O'Callaghan spoke up. 'He was in the system. Jermaine Cunliffe. Aged thirty-three. Released from prison only ten days ago.'

'Fucking hell.' A detective sitting opposite Sawyer smoothed out his slicked-back hair. 'He didn't waste any time pissing somebody off.'

'And he was out of practice, DC Myers,' said Shepherd. 'Model prisoner at Wakefield. Served fourteen years for his part in a murder. Sir...'

Keating tapped his screen, handing control of the main monitor to Shepherd. He stole a glance at Sawyer.

Shepherd swiped his screen and a new image appeared on the wall monitor: a smiling middle-aged man in a saggy suit and tie. He stood outside a grand public building, in the centre of a group of relaxed-looking teenagers in school uniform, resting a hand on two of the pupils' shoulders.

Sawyer raised his eyes to the main monitor as Shepherd spoke.

'Thomas Brennan. Forty-five. Headmaster of St. Anselm's private school in Bakewell from 1990 to 2007. In 2007, he confronted some rowdy teenagers outside his house in Duffield. Got beaten badly for his trouble. Died on the way to hospital.'

'I remember the press conference with his wife,' said Keating. 'She publicly forgave the killers. The kids.'

Shepherd nodded. 'Tanya Brennan. Devout Catholic family. Well off. Thomas was born in Kilkenny, where he married Tanya in 1988. They came to the UK two years later when he got the St. Anselm's job. Four teenagers were convicted of the murder.' He looked down at his screen. 'Damon Morris, Jared White, Rory Burrows and our friend, Jermaine Cunliffe. All got life with minimum terms, which was seen as lenient at the time.'

'How old was Cunliffe then?' said DC Matt Walker, seated next to O'Callaghan.

'Nineteen,' said Shepherd. 'The eldest. Burrows and White were both eighteen. Morris was seventeen. Even though he was the youngest, they all threw him under the bus at trial, claiming he was the ringleader. A neighbour testified they heard Morris urging the others to "bust his fucking skull".'

'And Cunliffe was the last to get out?' said Myers.

'Yes,' said Shepherd. 'Morris got out three years ago, Burrows and White last summer.'

'All of this might be irrelevant,' said Keating.

'Maybe the first three got together,' said Walker, 'and waited for Cunliffe to get out.'

Myers scowled. 'Why, though?'

'Maybe his was the loudest voice trying to make Morris the fall guy,' said Shepherd. 'And Morris worked them both onto his side.'

'You need to mind your ankles,' said Sawyer, keeping his eyes on his screen.

Shepherd narrowed his eyes. 'Our ankles?'

Sawyer looked up. 'It's easy to fall down a rabbit hole. We're working a murder case, not devising a crime drama. We need to focus on Cunliffe's story. His ten days on the outside. What took him from the prison gates to being chained to a tree?'

'Induction, not conjecture,' said Walker.

Sawyer gave a small smile. 'Exactly. The murder is a tempting link, but it shouldn't be a distraction. How did Cunliffe die? Then look at the whys. And the possible whos. We start with the science.'

'Allow me,' said O'Callaghan, beaming. She nodded at Keating and pointed to her screen. He transferred control, and she swiped through several images as she spoke. 'We have reasonable 3D visuals on tyre tracks, but there are lots of different samples from the surrounding roads. My techs can narrow down to type and brand, but we'll need a cross-ref to be certain. Boot prints are only latent, but the freshest ones connect to the dirt road on the edge of Kinder Bank. I'm seeing multiples here, too, but only one type pointing towards the tree and also pointing the other way. Impressions are stronger coming than going.'

'Carrying the body,' said Sawyer.

Shepherd caught his eye. 'The killer might have been carrying the live Cunliffe.'

'Or unconscious,' said Walker.

O'Callaghan looked from man to man, mouth open in mock respect. 'You boys are good.'

'Drummond is calling COD as smoke inhalation,' said Sawyer, staring at his screen. 'Still early, though.'

'Plenty of accelerant,' said O'Callaghan. 'Concentrated in the earth and grass around the tree. Quite a lot of blood in there, too.'

Sawyer looked up.

'All Cunliffe's.'

'Any blood near the boot prints? Away from the tree?'

'Not that we can find, DI Sawyer. And we've looked *really* hard.'

Sawyer closed his eyes. 'He was subdued, cuffed. Then driven to the dirt road, carried to the spot, secured. He was beaten, covered in accelerant, set on fire. The killer watched for a while...' He opened his eyes. 'Then he walked back to his car and drove away.'

'He might have been dead before the killer lit him up,' said Myers.

Sawyer shook his head. 'We need Drummond to

know for sure. But it's a lot of effort to just beat a man to death.' He scrolled through the scene photos in silence.

Keating stepped in. 'As Sawyer says, focus your teams on victimology. The Brennan murder sticks out, but it might be unrelated. Assume nothing. Look into it, but also dig into Cunliffe's connections. Relatives, friends. Any records or potential history. Did he make enemies inside? Fourteen years in a high-security prison is plenty of time to grow a few grudges. DI Shepherd is SIO on this.'

'I thought we could drop in on Cunliffe's aunt in Brassington,' said Shepherd. 'She's been putting him up. Parents not around anymore. Get a sense of what he's been up to since he got out.'

Keating nodded, sat back. 'Work with DI Sawyer. But be aware that the NCA enquiry into the station attack is ongoing, and Sawyer will need to be available, as he was present on the day.'

'How is Maggie?' said Walker.

Eyes turned to Sawyer; he kept focus on his screen. Swiping, scrolling.

'She's stable,' said Keating. 'The signs are positive. I'll let you all know when there's any more news. Now. On top of all this, we have a crime in action. As you all know, Eva Gregory, the wife of the Manchester Deputy Mayor, Dale Strickland, hasn't been seen for over a week. I spoke to Strickland at the weekend, and he's certain the person who called him on the day of her disappearance was Dennis Crawley, the man we caught and convicted of three murders back in 2018, when Crawley also abducted Strickland's son, Luka. The case was handed to East

Midlands Special Ops Unit because of the situation here following the attack, and because Crawley absconded from a medium secure unit in Nottingham. But now we're up and running again, Strickland is insisting we take the reins.'

'How does that work, sir?' asked Myers.

'Passive data shows that Gregory's last known position was her home in Bakewell. East Mids have made little progress, and there's been no more contact. Strickland has requested a meeting with myself and DI Sawyer tomorrow.' He drummed on the desk. 'So, there's a lot going on.' He bowed his head. 'And, of course, we're a man down on the MIT now.'

'Sir,' said DC Myers, 'this is a mid-sized team. There's no resource to run two concurrent investigations.'

Sawyer raised his head. 'I got here as fast as I could, DC Myers.'

'You'll work it out,' said Keating. 'You have plenty of support staff. Use them to the full. Keep it all bagged and tagged in HOLMES. Share and share alike. Don't trip over each other. There's a lot of heat still on the attack enquiry, and I'll cover media with Stephen Bloom. We might have to do pressers, depending on what arises in the cases. Strickland has already done a public appeal about his wife, but got nothing.' He sprang to his feet. 'That lazy Sunday pub lunch is officially cancelled. We'll update later or tomorrow, when we have something to update on.'

He strode out of the conference room towards his office.

The others followed, but Walker hung back.

'Sir. It's good to see you again. How are you feeling?'

Sawyer logged out of his touchscreen. 'Brain's foggy.' He offered a weak smile. 'But it'll take more than a maniac with a shotgun and grenade to put me down.'

9

'Rise and shine, ladies!'

Leon Stokes snapped open the window blind and shielded his eyes from the flare of morning sun.

'Can we not?'

The two men sitting opposite each other at the dining table turned away from their card game. Wesley Peyton tugged on his sky-blue Manchester City baseball cap and pulled the brim down over his bloodshot eyes. Jakub Malecki squinted into the light and tracked Stokes as he padded across, barefoot, to the purple sofa.

Stokes grinned. 'Sorry, Wes. I wouldn't want to compromise your vampire looks.' He set a tall foamy drink down on the glass coffee table and lowered himself onto the sofa, grimacing. 'Fuck me. Think I might be overdoing the pull-ups. It's good pain, though. I've been watching that *Westworld* show up in the gym. One character says, "When you're suffering, that's when you're most real." I like that.' He took a slurp from the drink.

'That looks fucked up,' said Peyton.

Stokes raised the glass. 'Healthy shake. Protein powder, almond butter, berries, oat milk.' He patted his belly. 'You get out what you put in.'

Malecki and Peyton shared a look.

Stokes nodded to Malecki. 'How's your pain? How long for the break to heal?'

Malecki rubbed at the strapping around his elbow. 'Hairline fracture. Few days.'

Stokes nodded, holding the moment before calling out, way too loud. *'Boyd!'*

Malecki and Peyton startled; both covered their ears.

Stokes laughed. 'Fuck the Pope. Have you two been up all night?'

'Got here a couple of hours ago,' said Peyton. 'Party in town. Had to get this fucker a dose of fanny, now the love of his life's out of action.'

Malecki stared up at the ceiling and raised his middle finger to Peyton, who swatted it away, laughing.

'You mean his hand, right?' said Stokes. 'That's a sophisticated joke for you, Wes.'

'Decent girls,' said Peyton. 'Had to pay, mind. He's used to that, though, aren't ya?'

Boyd Cannon entered and sat next to Stokes in the other corner of the sofa.

'Women that old should pay us,' said Malecki.

Peyton took a sip from a takeaway coffee cup. 'No such thing as a free fuck, my friend. Us men always have to pay somewhere down the line.'

Cannon sighed. 'We have a meeting.' He put on a

pair of thick-rimmed glasses and began setting up his laptop on the coffee table.

'Why so fucking early?' said Peyton. 'On a Sunday.'

'He's in Japan,' said Cannon. 'Tokyo.'

Stokes pointed at Malecki and Peyton. 'You two. Quiet for this. Doyle doesn't know we had Mavers, remember?'

'And what's the strategy?' said Peyton. 'I'm still vague about why that Scouse cunt is still breathing.'

Stokes tilted his head. 'Big picture. Ending him didn't serve our needs. Sometimes you have to see past your own pride. It's the leaders who take everything personally who don't last.'

'We had our fun,' said Malecki. 'He knows he met me. He knows it when he looks at his arm where his tattoo used to be.'

Peyton gave Malecki a shove. 'Like you know you met Sawyer, eh?'

'He was a naughty boy,' said Stokes. 'We taught him a lesson. He won't do it again. And he's turned out to be a valuable bargaining chip with Strickland. He'll take care of Mavers. Good to have the future boss of Manchester police on side.'

'Yeah,' said Peyton, 'but we didn't exactly keep our part of the bargain, did we?'

Stokes sat back in the sofa. 'No. You didn't. You made a mess of it.'

'There was someone else at the station,' said Malecki. 'In the cells. He had a gun.'

'Yeah. A handgun. You had a fucking shotgun!'

Stokes slammed his hand down on the table; the protein shake wobbled but didn't topple.

Cannon snatched up his laptop, laid it back down. 'Strickland isn't the issue. He's distracted, anyway. His wife has gone AWOL.'

'His missus is missing,' said Peyton.

Cannon continued. 'Strickland is probably pleased about the chaos we brought to Sawyer's station. We can revisit once he secures the mayor job. The Mavers thing... It's passing into history. Doyle is the acute problem. Mavers killed one of his men. He wanted us to deliver him. We need to square that before it gets out of control.'

Peyton stood up and leaned over the dining table. 'Yeah. And I'm asking again. What's the strategy?'

'Delay,' said Stokes. 'Management. Strickland has control over Mavers for now. So we let that play out. The resolution will make Doyle happy. He just doesn't know it yet.' Stokes finished his drink. 'The guy in the cell was one of Strickland's old hands. Fletcher. Think they've fallen out, though. And he's disappeared, anyway.'

'Let's remember to ask Strickland where he is, then,' said Peyton.

Cannon looked at his watch. 'Two minutes. Before we start, we have another acute problem.' He turned the laptop screen to face Stokes. 'Accounts are in the toilet. We also lost Ant Finney and Billy Rice in that Buxton mess. They were strong earners.'

Stokes shook his head. 'We'll be fine. New people coming in. Lots of fresh product. The raids have stopped. And once we get round to Strickland, we'll be untouchable.' He squinted at the spreadsheet on Cannon's screen. 'What the fuck is *this*?'

Cannon checked. 'Care home.' He glanced at Stokes. 'Your mum.'

'Jesus wept. Do they feed the old dears *foie gras* in that place?' He waved the laptop away and stared into his glass, sloshing round the residue. 'I still don't get how Sawyer got the best of both you players.'

'I told you,' said Peyton. 'He's fucking Houdini. Got out of Jakub's cable ties and fought him off, then sucker-punched me at the station.'

Stokes nodded slowly. 'And then he got distracted by the red-haired woman.'

'Maggie Spark,' said Malecki.

'And you lobbed over a grenade and legged it?'

'I told you,' said Peyton. 'We were masked up. Guns are untraceable. Explosion would have covered any other tracks. Dibble we took down shot Ant, and this Fletcher cunt did Billy. I didn't see what happened after I chucked in the grenade. I was well out of there.'

Cannon finished setting up the Zoom call. 'We know Sawyer survived.' He looked up. 'Any news on the woman's health?'

'Fuck the woman's health,' said Peyton. 'I lost two good mates.'

'She's alive.' Malecki snatched a sip of Peyton's coffee. 'But in a coma. Centre for Clinical Neurosciences in Salford.'

'And you're absolutely one hundred per cent certain that Sawyer didn't recognise you from your visit to his house?'

Malecki's eyes swivelled to meet Peyton's. 'I already told you. I wore the same balaclava. But he doesn't know who I am. He has no name to connect it to.'

Peyton drew in a sharp breath. 'Oh. Fucking *fuck*.'

Cannon sat up. 'What?'

'I just remembered. I used Jakub's name.'

'When?' said Stokes.

Peyton closed his eyes. 'Fletcher killed Billy. He shot at me, but I took cover in a side room. Jakub took a shot at Fletcher, and when he dived into the room with the woman, Jakub ran out of the door, through the reception and out of the station. I shouted after him.'

Stokes got to his feet and walked over to the dining table. 'And you shouted what?'

Peyton opened his eyes. 'I used his name, I'm sure. I called him a cunt or a shit-out or something. For leaving me there.'

Malecki dropped his head.

'CCTV there has no audio,' said Cannon.

Stokes pulled out a chair and sat by Peyton. 'Who might have heard you say that? *Think*.'

Peyton caught Stokes's eye, then stared down at the floor.

'Sawyer wasn't there then,' said Malecki.

Stokes drew the chair closer. 'Yes. So, who was in earshot? Who might have heard you?'

Peyton snapped his eyes up. 'Fletcher. And the woman. All the others were dead.'

'Doyle's bailed,' said Cannon. 'Zoom message. *Leon. Sorry, lad. Something's come up. We'll meet when I'm back in England. Need to sort the M situation. Some disturbing rumours. Stay in touch.'*

'What does he mean by "disturbing rumours"?' said Peyton.

Cannon closed the laptop. 'Maybe he's heard that we had Mavers and let him go. Not great. And all this "we'll meet" and, "stay in touch". Not, "let's meet" or "I'll be in touch".'

Stokes shrugged. 'Power trip.'

'He's losing his patience,' said Cannon.

'I know the feeling.' Stokes walked over to the giant Auerbach painting on the back wall. He stared into the yellow-and-red abstract for an uncomfortably long time, leaning in close, studying the lines. 'Boyd. Talk to Strickland about the Mavers clean-up. Laurel and Hardy. I'm giving you two a special project.' He turned to look at Malecki and Peyton. 'Maggie Spark. I'd like an extensive health update. We cannot have her coming round and recalling a distinctive Polish surname.' His eyes shifted to Malecki. 'Because that will lead to you. Which will lead to me. Which will not happen, no matter how many more coppers I have to put in the ground.'

10

Shepherd opened the Mini glovebox, showering the footwell with empty sweet wrappers. He gathered them up and rummaged through the packets.

'Are you importing this stuff now?'

Sawyer glanced over. 'I shift around. Chocolate limes, barley sugars, Murray mints.'

'Old man sweets.'

'Nothing wrong with that. The Jolly Ranchers are modernist in comparison, yeah. I get them from the Georgian House Sweet Shop in Bakewell.'

'Some of them are *blue*,' said Shepherd. He pulled out an empty packet and tidied the wrappers into it. 'I'm sugar free for three months now. First few weeks were hell. But now, just the idea of it makes me shudder.'

Sawyer rounded a corner, shifting to the left to make way for an oncoming car. The driver shot him a look.

'You're a touch central,' said Shepherd.

Sawyer glared at him.

'Sir.'

'I told you. No need to call me that now, DI Shepherd.'

Shepherd fiddled with his phone's Maps app. 'I'm in transition. It'll take a while to get used to it.'

'You're on course. Don't take any bribes and you'll be Keating inside ten years.'

Shepherd laughed. 'Still a long time. And you think you need to stay clean to make brass?'

'Same with anything. Either stay clean or get good at hiding the dirt.'

Shepherd looked across the low dry-stone walls flanking their route out of the Southern Peaks, down to Brassington. The farm fields ran flat to Matlock in the east, but sloped up westward. The road was barely double track, but Sawyer kept the Mini in the middle.

Sawyer glanced over at Shepherd's hands, tapping the side of his phone. 'Good visibility either side. Comfortable vanishing point. Just holding the road. No need for nerves.'

Shepherd touched his window down a couple of inches and inhaled the earthy morning air. 'Roadside grass showing its age.'

Sawyer nodded. 'It's all time with you, isn't it? Three months off sugar. Ten years is long. Seasonal change. Do you not agree with Carlo Rovelli?'

'And who's he?'

'Theoretical physicist. He says our perception of time doesn't correspond to reality. It's an illusion. We string together these sequences of events in the past, present and future, and call that reality. But that's just a human construct. The universe actually runs on quantum mechanics and thermodynamics.' Sawyer turned and grinned, a manic flash in his eye.

'Spent a lot of time down online rabbit holes while you recovered, then?' said Shepherd.

'Reading books. Some people still do that.'

'None of it is remotely provable.'

'Good excuse if you're late for something, though.'

Shepherd leaned over and pointed out of Sawyer's window. 'We're just over the ridge to Minninglow. Neolithic burial chamber, 3000 BC. Not sure what that comes to in quantum time. You'd have to ask yer man, Ravioli.'

Sawyer sighed. 'You had any more incidents?'

'Panic attacks? No. Apart from the mini meltdown when I saw the bill for the Rover.' Sawyer side-eyed him. 'My counsellor is sound. Once a week. It gives my brain a rinse out.'

'Life's good for you, then. Got your head straight. Promotion. Setting up the new team in Sheffield.'

Shepherd turned to the window again. 'Had a wobble at Moran's funeral. Just... the emotion of it. The...'

'Finality?' Sawyer slowed for a tailback behind a dumper truck. 'He was a hero, you know.'

'Thought you were best of enemies.'

'You can be a hero and an arsehole at the same time.'

Shepherd studied him. 'Didn't deserve to die, though.'

'Didn't say he did.' Sawyer lurched into the road, driving down the wrong side past four cars, then cut back in front of the truck as it turned into Hoe Grange Quarry.

Shepherd put a hand to the dashboard. 'What's the rush? I thought you didn't believe in time.'

'Moran kept her safe.'

'Maggie?'

Sawyer nodded. 'He must have authorised the evidence room unlock. He knew Fletcher's gun was in there. Fletcher got out of his cell somehow and helped, but it was Moran's decision to unlock the evidence room that saved Maggie.'

'Oh, I'm getting this now.'

'What?'

'It's guilt.' Shepherd ducked down, peering up the hill to the Minninglow tree circle. 'You think Moran did more than you. He kept her alive. You almost got her killed.'

'But what's the point?' Sawyer raised the volume; close to shouting.

Shepherd turned, keeping his eyes forward. 'She got caught up in something. Moran happened to be there, too. He got her to safety, but you kept her alive.' No response. 'What do you mean, "what's the point?"'

Sawyer whipped his head around to face Shepherd. 'What's the fucking point in her being alive if she doesn't get to live?'

A car rounded the oncoming curve, too fast. The driver gave a lengthy blast on his horn, forcing Sawyer to swerve to the left.

Shepherd gripped the dashboard with both hands. 'For God's sake!'

'Sorry.' Sawyer's shoulders rose and fell as he took slow, measured breaths.

They drove in silence for a while. As Sawyer stopped at a bottleneck ahead of a narrow bridge, Shepherd pulled a packet of wine gums out of the glovebox. He opened it, held it out to Sawyer, jiggled it around.

Sawyer shook his head.

'Can I ask a question about the station attack?' said Shepherd.

The traffic thinned out; Sawyer looked over as he pulled away. 'You want to know what I was doing there in the first place.'

'Yeah. How come you turned up when you did?'

'That's one for the NCA interview tomorrow.'

Shepherd snapped the glovebox shut. 'You can tell me, sir. I'm a DI now.'

'Long story,' said Sawyer. 'Still working on it.'

11

Anne-Marie Parker sat in a corner armchair, kneading and tugging at a handkerchief in her lap. She rocked back and forth, in long, slow movements, shifting her eyes between Sawyer and Shepherd.

'Did either of you two see our Jermaine?'

'We both did,' said Sawyer. 'I'm so sorry this happened, Mrs Parker.'

She scoffed, pitching so far forward she almost toppled out of her chair. 'How long was he here? Two bloody weeks. He was so decent. So different. He wanted to give something back to the world. He'd studied, you see. Distance learning. NVQ in catering. Restaurant management.' She checked Sawyer's expression, then Shepherd's. 'I know he did wrong. But it was so long ago. He was just a kid. It broke Joanna's heart.'

'Your sister,' said Shepherd.

She nodded and hustled her long hair up into a messy ponytail. 'His father, Darrell, had long gone by then. He had diabetes, you see. Got himself a personal trainer to get some of his weight off.' She waved a hand. 'Turned out he was upgrading. Joanna was just the little woman after that.'

Sawyer glanced at Shepherd. 'They separated?' She nodded. 'How old was Jermaine?'

'Thirteen, fourteen. Darrell didn't want to know after that. Typical. My Joanna always had a way with men. She was too bloody good for them all. And they knew it. Took advantage while it lasted. Moved on when they got bored.'

Parker dropped the handkerchief. As she leaned over to pick it up, a shaft of sunlight flared through the window behind the sofa, exposing her puffy eyes and tear-stained cheeks.

'Were you planning for Jermaine to stay with you indefinitely?' said Sawyer.

'As long as it took. He knew he'd been given a second chance. He had every intention of making the most of it.'

Shepherd took out a notepad. 'Can you tell us about Jermaine's routine since he got out of prison? Did he go out much? Did you see him with anyone?'

'Couple of times he didn't come home. But I wasn't keeping tabs on him. His licence said he had to stay in contact with his probation officer, stick to his approved address. Here. He wasn't allowed to leave the UK. We'd put a bit of money away for him and we were using it to build him a small annexe out back. Nothing much. Bed, little office. He never brought anyone round here, but I don't know where he was going in the evenings. Listen. I've asked. But nobody is telling me anything.' She dropped her voice to a near-whisper. 'What exactly happened to him?'

DC Patricia Highfield leaned forward and reached out a hand to Parker; she swatted it away. 'We're still trying to establish the details, Anne-Marie. Remember, it's best not to dwell—'

'I'm not a child,' said Parker. 'I want to know.'

'There was a fire,' said Sawyer. 'We think he died of smoke inhalation. We'd rather not say more until the full pathology report.'

Shepherd eyed him. 'Did Jermaine have any links to Kinder Bank? The woodland near Kinder Reservoir.'

Parker dabbed her eyes with the handkerchief and fixed her gaze on the carpet. 'Not that I know of. We last saw him the day before yesterday in the afternoon. I'm a maths tutor. I was leaving to go to a pupil's house and Jermaine was in his room. I could hear the telly was on. I looked in on him, said I'll see you later. That was that. Nothing seemed off. He said he was going out for a drink. Didn't say who with.'

'What happened to Jermaine's mother?' said Sawyer. 'Joanna.'

Parker looked over at Highfield. She closed her eyes. 'Pickled her liver. She was always a drinker, but she really went to town after Jermaine was sent to prison. Didn't stop until she was dead. Took her five years, mind.'

'And his father?'

'Darrell lives somewhere in Greece. That's where his trainer comes from. He'll be freeloading with her family. He's been there for years. I tried to call him when I got the news, but couldn't get hold of him. Always the way.'

Highfield nodded at Sawyer. 'We're covering that.'

'Do you know if either had any connections you weren't sure about?' said Shepherd.

She frowned. 'Connections?'

'Unusual. Criminal. Any debts. Any disagreements.'

'Nothing like that, no.'

Highfield got up and opened the curtains at the back window, revealing the rose gold wallpaper, florid upholstery, mock zebra skin rug. Moneyed bad taste.

Sawyer edged along the sofa, into the shade. 'The other boys who went to prison. Do you know if Jermaine stayed in touch with them?'

Parker scowled. 'Yes, I do. And the answer is no. He wanted nothing to do with them. When I went to visit, he often talked about how that was the worst day of his life and he wished he could go back in time and make it all better. Keep that poor man alive. We can all relate to that, can't we? Regrets. Things we wish we could do differently. My husband is a councillor in Matlock. He was going to help Jermaine get a job at the town hall café. Work his way up. We had a talk on the day he got out. He said he'd had therapy inside, and they'd agreed that you can't change the past, so it's silly to keep harking back. He was looking to the future. Those lads were part of his past and he was done with all that.'

'We might be done with the past,' said Sawyer, 'but the past is never done with us.'

Highfield and Shepherd exchanged a glance.

'How did Jermaine react to the death of his mother?' said Shepherd.

Parker heaved herself upright and hobbled over to the

fireplace, blocked with ornamental white brickwork. She took a photo from the mantelpiece: a toddler and a young woman on a beach. The boy leaned forward, laughing in delight as a wave approached; the woman looked on, face flushed with joy.

'I think Joanna blamed herself for what Jermaine did. She had to work when he was little. She could never give him the attention he needed, and Darrell wasn't much of a father.' She sat on a footstool, staring at the picture. 'I couldn't have my own kids. I wanted to be the one to give Jermaine that new start. But I could never replace his mother, of course.' She aimed a fractured smile at the detectives. 'Fathers protect their daughters, and they bond with their sons. Mothers pass on that female energy and wisdom to their daughters. But mothers and sons? That's special. The most special job of them all. That's women helping to shape the men of the future. Giving them the love and the space to grow into themselves. Discover who they are. Give them the tools to love and to pass on that love. Joanna tried to do that, but the booze got inside her. Poisoned her.'

Sawyer sprang to his feet and fumbled his phone out of his pocket. He held it to his ear and hurried out of the front door.

'Please excuse me. Urgent call.'

———

Shepherd crunched up the curved garden path.

Sawyer sat on the Mini's bonnet, with his back to the

house, gazing across the sunlit dales on the southern fringe of the National Park.

'Sir?'

He stood a few yards back, watching the rise and fall of Sawyer's shoulders.

'Sounds like Jermaine distanced himself from the others involved in the Brennan murder,' said Shepherd. 'Like Keating said. Assume nothing.'

Sawyer didn't turn.

Shepherd kept talking. 'Nice work, giving her something about cause of death. But not too much.'

At last, Sawyer cleared his throat. 'You don't study for a vocational qualification, plan to make a clean break and reinvent yourself as a restaurant manager. And then, ten days after release, get involved in something new that goes wrong so quickly, someone makes the effort to drive you to an isolated rural area, chain you to a tree and burn you alive.' He held Shepherd's eye. 'Why that place? Why burning? Death is the end product, but what's the killer getting out of the specifics? What's the agenda?'

'There's a lot of risk,' said Shepherd. 'A lot of trouble.'

Sawyer nodded, stood up and walked to the driver's door. 'It's overkill. He set it up so Jermaine would suffer. But there's also a detachment. It's hands-off.'

'He might have just got private kicks from watching the suffering. The burning.'

Sawyer unlocked the car. 'I'll zoom in on the forensics. Get Walker to check Cunliffe's movements since getting out. Who he's been drinking with. You look into the Brennan family, and set up meetings with the other three boys. Men. I'll drop you at Buxton.' He caught himself, held up a hand. 'Sorry. Forgot. You're the SIO.'

Shepherd smiled. 'It's fine.' He held Sawyer's gaze across the top of the car. 'Not sure you are, though.'

'You know me. Going down to the cellar. That always sorts me out.'

12

The lift car ground and clunked into the shaft wall as it descended. Sawyer looked up at the ceiling light; the filament just about held its feeble glow, barely bothering to flicker. He stepped into the corner by the illuminated button panel and bowed his head.

'How many times have you read it?'

He turned. A figure stood in shadow in the opposite corner; green eyes on him, piercing the gloom.

Sawyer turned back to the buttons. 'Into double figures, I'd say.'

'If I'd known my private journal was going to be studied by someone else, I'd have taken more care.'

'It's all I've got, Mum.' He closed his eyes, listened for her breathing, movement.

Just the rattling car; the whining motor.

'What are you looking for, my darling?'

He took a long breath, rested his forehead against the cold lift wall. 'Peace.'

'You won't find that in my old troubles.'

'The last thing Dad said to me.' He looked back at the figure, the eyes downcast now. 'The Bible verse. *There is nothing in darkness that will not be disclosed. Nothing concealed that will not be brought to light.*'

'*All shall be well,*' said Jessica.

'No.'

The lift hissed to a halt. Sawyer grappled with the inner security door, dragged it open.

The basement corridor strip lighting flushed away the shadows.

'Dad wasn't reassuring me it would be okay in the end. Saying it would all come good. He was telling me there's something concealed. Something to bring into the light.'

He looked back; the lift was empty.

———

'In here!'

Sawyer headed down the corridor, past the deserted pathology lobby, and paused at the pale green door.

Scented coffee. Salty bacon tang.

He walked into the converted storage room. Frazer Drummond leaned back in a cheap chair at the low beechwood table, squirting a sachet of ketchup into the centre of a sandwich. Two white plastic cups sat on the table, either side of a black A4 folder.

'No PA today,' said Sawyer.

'Day of rest.'

'No rest for the wicked.'

Drummond smiled and bit into the sandwich. 'Speak

for yourself.' He chewed, gesturing for Sawyer to sit. 'I got you a milky coffee. How nice am I?'

Sawyer took a seat and looked into the cups: one black, one frothy white.

'No strychnine. Promise.'

'Thanks.' Sawyer sipped, winced. 'No sugar, either.'

'Fuck me, Sawyer. They were all out of cinnamon sprinkles, too.'

'No resupply. That's the trouble with Sundays. I was expecting you to be a touch more surly about being here today.'

Drummond swiped a napkin across his mouth. 'I'm okay with working today. One of Sophia's old school friends has named her godmother, and she's attending the christening.' He took another bite. 'I'm not a fan of christenings.'

'Interesting symmetry for the week, though. One in, one out.'

Drummond gave him a look. 'I prefer to wet the baby's head with a glass of Montoya. Little fuckers don't care either way, do they? Synaptic density is pretty sparse until nine months. Early babies aren't much more than food tubes.'

'Don't you have teenagers at home now?'

'Fuck, yes. Speaking of food tubes.' He picked up the folder. 'There's a do later. I might drop in. Pull a few faces at the poor little bastard. Give him his first nightmare.' Drummond paged through his reports. 'So. How's you?'

'You mean, apart from the insomnia, guilt, trauma, hallucinations?'

Drummond frowned. 'Hallucinations? Visual or auditory?'

'Both.'

'I'd get that seen to. Probably PTS from the explosion. You're back at work indecently soon, Sawyer. Whatever you might think, there are others who can do your job just as well.' He leaned forward and stared into Sawyer's eyes. 'A fucking blind man could see you need a rest. You're way more lean than mean, Detective.'

'You told me that. At the wake.'

'It's got to be stress. All that cortisol can seriously mess with your metabolism. Don't just take my word for it. Ask the internet. Google "HPA axis". You know when people say they can't take it anymore? They mean it literally. They're drowning in cortisol. It scrambles your hormones, changes behaviour and impulses, brain chemistry. Add that to the cognitive impairment you're still recovering from after the station attack... Seriously. What the fuck happened there?'

Sawyer sniffed his coffee; scorched and waterlogged. 'I'll explain that to the enquiry tomorrow.'

Drummond laid out a few sheets from the folder on the table. 'I read about your London exploits. Pretty fucked up, even by your standards.'

'Enough about me.'

Drummond nodded. 'Jermaine Cunliffe. Interesting history. Good luck finding who he might have fucked off enough to want to burn him alive.'

'He was alive?'

'Not for long. He was marinated in accelerant. Nothing exotic. I'd go standard paraffin. Lung tissue is completely toasted. There would have been lots of smoke, and he couldn't get away from it. Happens quickly. Once you inhale smoke at that density, you can't get enough oxygen through your system to carry on living. Too much carbon monoxide in the lungs, no carbon dioxide release. He was out in the open, but with the restricted movement... Unconscious in two to five minutes. Brain death in ten.' He shuffled through the papers. 'His grey matter was exceedingly abnormal. Astrocyte activation, neuronal and myelinated axon damage, haemorrhage. All consistent with my findings. Did you know, Sawyer, they used to burn traitors alive? And heretics. If the executioner didn't like the victim, he'd wet the wood to make it burn slower, prolonging the agony.'

'Any other injury?'

Drummond tried to take a sip of coffee, spluttered. 'That not enough for you? Yes. A lot. Broken ribs, dislocated jaw. Our friend even smashed in Cunliffe's kneecaps first. TOD probably early hours Saturday.'

'Anything in his system?'

'Bit of alcohol. Someone went to a lot of trouble to get him to this location. Difficult to reach. Specific.'

Sawyer skim-read one of the papers. 'Specific is always interesting. He must have prepared the tree earlier. Made sure it was isolated enough to not cause any extra fires.'

'I'll give him that.' Drummond took another chomp of his sandwich. 'More environmentally aware than the bloody tourists with their portable barbecues. And it's a glorious spot. Almost as if he wanted him to die with a decent view.'

Sawyer stood up, stretched. 'He doesn't care about that. There's no personal connection. There's just... too much of everything.'

'Beating *and* burning?'

'Yes. So why beat him?'

'Anger. The desire to see him suffer as much as possible.'

Sawyer glanced up to the ceiling; a veneer of ancient nicotine stains. 'Or the opposite. He wanted it to *look* personal. The burning took a lot of planning. He could just control, secure, gag. No need for the beating.'

'Sawyer. If you were so lacking in empathy that you're happy to burn a man alive, then I don't see why you'd be averse to giving him a kicking first. Just for fun.'

Sawyer shook his head. 'This isn't about fun.'

13

Robert Holsgrove clasped his hands together and placed
them on the edge of the desk, keeping his elbows at his
side. His custard yellow tie was immaculately knotted,
and his glass-top desk looked new and unused; empty
apart from a flat black keyboard and mouse, and a
matching monitor pivoted to the side.

He offered a brief, on-then-off smile that barely
dislodged his dense grey moustache.

'You should be encouraged, Mr Perkins.'

Justin glanced at Sawyer as they took their seats.

'Any more signs of wakefulness?' said Justin.

'Not that we've seen. The opened eyes are, as I say,
encouraging. But there's a process. We need to see a
consistency before I can risk moving things along.'

'Risk?' said Sawyer.

Holsgrove held up a hand. 'Forgive me. That's
inelegant. I meant more *justify* than risk. We've fitted
Maggie with a more permanent breathing tube. A
tracheostomy. Inserted through the front of the neck,

directly into the trachea. I'm reluctant to continue intubation in patients of this nature for longer than necessary, due to risk of ventilator-associated pneumonia. She's comfortable and well-nourished with liquid food delivered directly to her large bowel via nasogastric tube. I have no concerns about irreversible muscular atrophy at this stage, but I'm afraid I can't offer you any plausible neurological prognosis, although the wakefulness is good news. And I'm happy with kidney and liver function. There's quite a high dosage of blood pressure drugs, sedatives and opiates. Maggie is metabolising it well.'

'What do you mean by needing to see a consistency?' said Justin. 'What might happen next?'

Holsgrove paused and took a sip from a bottle of Evian, which he settled back on a circular coaster at the far corner of his desk.

'I'm keen to see Maggie open her eyes regularly, and for longer periods. Then I'd look for purposeful response. Awareness. Movement such as pushing away at a painful stimulus. Purposeful response contrasts with the automatic reflex movements we see in coma. I would then hope to see a response from simple commands, such as "look at me", or even "hold up three fingers" or "try to mouth words". Those are all commands that require some thinking ability. At this stage, she may respond to certain voices, phrases. Sometimes music. Famously, of course, we think of the eyes as windows to the soul. In reality, open eyes don't necessarily indicate consciousness. The window may be open, but the soul remains inscrutable.'

Sawyer took a sharp breath.

A flash of his mother. Face pulped. Eyes staring. Hand reaching out.

'After that, we would remove the tracheostomy, taper off the sedatives but keep the opiates. Then we monitor, move to physiotherapy. As I said, that's when we learn about any complications or compromises.' He held up his hands. 'For now, we're in a holding pattern.'

————

They sat in the corner of the Costa concession. Sawyer slurped on a bucket-sized milky tea; Justin nursed a small decaf.

'Busy for late Sunday,' said Justin.

'Not sure they do regular time in hospitals.'

Justin eyed the patrons. 'Reminds me of the casinos in Las Vegas.'

Sawyer narrowed his eyes. 'Feels like a stretch.'

'I mean the timelessness. The sense of purgatory.'

Sawyer snapped a shortbread biscuit in half, showering the table with crumbs. 'This whole place is the private ward, yes?'

'Yes. The NHS unit is part of the main hospital.'

'I suppose your analogy works, then. If people want to give you their money, you make it easy for them to do it. Throw off the restrictions.'

They shared a moment of silence, as Sawyer dunked the biscuit and took a bite, awkwardly synchronised with Justin sipping his coffee.

'So,' said Sawyer. 'Why did Mavers and Wilmot come to your house?'

Justin sighed. 'This again?'

'Yes. This again. Justin, we both want Maggie to get well, but we have no control over that. I do have control over tracking the people who put her in here. Who nearly killed her.'

'And you.'

'Curtis Mavers is the link. The goon who visited me at home was desperate to find him. When he didn't get what he wanted from me, he turned those people loose on the station.'

'How do you know?'

Sawyer took a slug of tea. 'I tracked his car.'

'Ah. So the enquiry will want to know why Fletcher was asking for you alone, *and* what the hell you were doing, arriving at the station in the nick of time.'

'I can handle that. But there's something you're not telling me.'

'Oh. The mind probe. Maggie mentioned this.' Justin took a long, strategic plunge into his coffee. 'Why do I get the feeling you're about to arrest me?'

Sawyer rubbed at his eyes. 'What would the charge be? I'm just trying to get a sense of where Mavers fits into all this. Why a man was sent to torture his location out of me, and why, when he or his employer weren't happy with the answer, they murdered three people and tried to murder two more.'

Justin paused until a young barista finished clearing the adjoining table. 'Glenroy Valance. Yardie enforcer from a Manchester crew. He was running a county lines operation in Macclesfield. I got him off a crack supply charge around a year ago. Given his record, he was looking at double figures.' Justin propped his elbows on the table and held his face in his hands. 'On the day he left court, he took me aside and told me he owed me and if I ever needed anything... I know, I know. Stupid.'

'Suicidal.'

'I was angry, Sawyer. Humiliated. I called him and—'

'He sent a couple of his boys to take issue with Mavers and Wilmot. And you thought it would all settle up there. Evens.' Sawyer sat back, stared down at the table. 'Actually. Stupid *and* suicidal. How did you know—'

'I recognised Wilmot from another case. He didn't remember me. He was... peripheral.'

Sawyer's phone buzzed with a call. 'So, I assume it didn't go well?'

'I assume not. I haven't heard from Glenroy, though. Mavers mentioned it at the house.'

Sawyer checked his phone. Shepherd.

He screened it.

'Mavers has got a brain. He probably bested Glenroy's boys, and they took a kicking for it later.'

'So, we're even in his eyes now?'

'Naturally. So, how did they track Wilmot and Mavers down?'

Justin shrugged. 'Underworld grapevine?'

Sawyer leaned forward. 'Can you ask him? Nicely.'

———

Sawyer drove home through the dusk, into an unremitting storm that shrouded the motorway in spray and steam. He used voice control to skip through music: albums, playlists, individual tracks. But nothing stuck. Not even the organic fuzz of his favourite album, *Loveless*; usually such a reliable meditative balm.

He pulled into the last service station before the Snake Pass, bought Coke, an egg sandwich and a box of custard tarts, and parked by the garage wheelie bins, watching the patrons dashing in and out through the rain.

His phone rang again; he connected through CarPlay.

'Walker's been busy,' said Shepherd. 'Are you frying bacon?'

'Rain on the roof. I'm in the car.'

Sawyer's eye was drawn to an elderly woman struggling to replace the pump nozzle after fuelling an orange Minivan.

'Did you see Maggie?'

'Spoke to her neurosurgeon. More encouraging signs, but nothing definite.'

The woman finally slotted the nozzle home and ducked her head as she emerged from the shelter of the awning, braving the downpour.

Shepherd paused for a moment. 'All the Jermaine Cunliffe stuff checks out. The catering qualification, the plan to get his life restarted with restaurant management. Anne-Marie's husband, Rowan, had visited him several times over the past few months. As she said, he's a Matlock councillor. Looks like he helped steer Jermaine through the parole process. Therapist reports seen by the board stack up.'

At the kiosk door, the woman turned and seemed to look directly at Sawyer. Her cheeks were droopy and jowly, and her eyes hung low in the sockets.

Shepherd's voice grew muddy and distant.

'This boy really worked on himself, sir. He did a terrible thing and seemed determined to build a fresh life.'

Sawyer's stomach flipped as he sensed the woman's anger at the perceived intrusion. It was violent, disproportionate.

'He'd even been meeting one of his Listeners from inside. An older fella. That's who he was drinking with on his last night.'

But she was surely too far away. And how could she notice him through the rain?

'Alibi checks out.'

Shepherd's voice sank deeper behind the crackle of the rain.

Sawyer blinked, as the woman pushed through the door, and her facial flesh trailed behind like a retinal afterimage. The glaring eyes hovered by the door as she joined the queue inside, then faded, followed by the undulating flesh.

He blinked again, holding his eyes closed.

'Sir?'

Sawyer opened his eyes, fumbled with the sandwich pack.

Look down. Away from the movement outside.

He opened the sandwich. The contents were dry and coagulated, but unmistakably egg.

'He's cleaner than the two of us put together, sir.'

Sawyer opened the bottle of Coke, sipped. The fizz

felt electrical on his tongue. 'The Thomas Brennan murder is his only outlier,' he said eventually. 'There has to be a connection. His widow?'

'Tanya. Died last year. Breast cancer. Fifty-six.'

The woman walked out of the kiosk. Sawyer braced for her to turn and look at him, but she dashed through the rain and got straight into her car.

'Close relatives?'

'Two adult daughters. Catherine and Laura.' He paused. 'Thirty-three and thirty-one.'

Sawyer took a bite of the sandwich. He chewed, but had no impulse to swallow. He forced the mouthful down with a sip of Coke, bit off another.

'We should talk to them both tomorrow.' He gagged on the food, just about managed to swallow.

'Busy day for you,' said Shepherd. 'Station attack enquiry. And you and Keating are due with Strickland, right?'

Sawyer unwrapped the custard tarts. 'Right.'

'I can cover the Brennan daughters with Walker if it's easier.'

He sniffed the box, recoiled. Nutmeg, sugar. 'It's fine.' He threw the box onto the passenger seat.

'I could attend the enquiry interview with you?'

The rain ramped up, pummelling the car windows, rendering them opaque.

'Significant witness only. No support.'

'They're not sweating you?'

Sawyer took two pills from his pocket, swallowed them with more Coke. 'No. Just a lot of moving parts.

High-level. Thanks, but I'll be fine. Brief me if anything new comes out of the main briefing.'

Sawyer hung up and drove off the forecourt, through the wind and the rain. He could have taken a more direct route around Kinder, down through Hayfield. But he craved the height of the pass; the dip and swoop overlooking the Hurst Reservoir, as the road climbed through the invincible moorland.

Near the summit, he pulled away and parked in a lay-by, hazards flashing.

The storm surrounded him, and he took out his wallet and slipped the razor blade out of its protective sleeve.

He lifted his shirt and touched the edge of the blade into his flexed pectoral, gasping as the muscle dented, but the skin didn't tear.

He held it, trying to steady his trembling hand, visualising the swipe. The heat of the blood. The pain externalised.

Sawyer pulled the blade away, slid it back into its sleeve.

His whole body was in tremor now, and he bowed his head.

Sobbing. Roaring.

14

Luka Strickland knelt before the giant TV screen and pulled out a box from under the coffee table. He browsed the video games, selected *Elden Ring* and inserted the disc into the PS4.

'Eggs?'

Luka flicked his blond hair out of his eyes and looked up towards the kitchen. Dale Strickland stood in the doorway, in a white dress shirt with the sleeves rolled to the elbows.

He held up a spatula.

Luka shook his head and fished his controller from the clutter of glasses, plates, empty Doritos packets.

Strickland walked over and knelt down by the side of the TV. 'What's the plan today?'

Luka shrugged. 'Seeing some mates when they're back from school.'

'Are you thinking of going back yourself soon?'

'I've thought about it, but decided against it.'

Strickland shuffled into Luka's eyeline. 'I heard you calling out last night again. Bad dreams?'

'Yeah.' Luka tapped through the game menu and started the loading sequence. 'Pretty mental.' He stared at the screen: a caped warrior hunched beneath a skyline of interconnected flaming rings.

'How long does this take?' said Strickland.

'Couple of minutes.'

'Would it be quicker on the new version?'

Luka took a drink from a mug. 'PS5?'

'Yeah. I could get you one of those. Belated birthday gift.'

Another shrug. 'That would be cool.' He tossed back his hair, keeping focus on the progress bar.

'Bit gloomy in here,' said Strickland. 'Can I open the blinds?'

'Dad. I've told you. I can't see the screen with the blinds open.'

A shadow passed over the window from outside; the letterbox flapped.

'I have to work today, Luka. I'm driving myself in the new car. Jonah and Vincent will be out front. Do you have everything you need?'

'Yeah.'

The game began, and Luka entered his character's attributes screen and hopped from box to box, selecting and deselecting.

'You have my number. Cameron is working out back, from the office. Jonah is in charge. I'll brief him before I leave. Please let him know when you go out. And let me know where you are.'

Luka nodded. 'I don't think he'll let her go.'

'What? Who?'

'Dennis. He hates you, and he tried to hurt me. But Jake rescued me and put him in prison. I bet he hates him even more.'

Strickland reached out to Luka, resting his hands on his shoulders. Luka paused the game, then turned and fell forward, submitting to an awkward hug, burying his face in Strickland's chest.

'Hey,' said Strickland, squeezing. 'Luka. We talked about this. Don't worry. We'll find Mum.'

Luka pulled away, hiding his face. 'Have you checked the caves? Where he took me?'

'Of course.'

He got back to the game. 'You think Dennis is stupid. But he's not. He knew you'd go there. So you wasted your time looking. You wasted Mum's time.' On-screen, Luka engaged an armoured guard in one-to-one combat, ducking and leaping to keep away from his sword strikes. 'So he's got her somewhere you won't find her, and he won't let her go like he did me.'

'You're *wrong*.' Strickland raised his voice, softened it as he continued. 'I've found something out, about the day Mum disappeared.'

Luka paused the game and turned to him. 'What?'

'Just... something. I'm going to look into it today. I'm sure it will help us.' He got to his feet.

'You won't find Mum without Jake,' said Luka.

Strickland sighed. 'He'll have a part to play, Luka. It's his job. I'm getting all the top people to help.' He headed out into the hall.

Luka listened, as Strickland collected the post, paused, and left the house by the front door. He peered round the edge of the blind, watching, as his father climbed into the back of the Mercedes, but left the door open. The car rocked as he gesticulated to the men in the front.

Luka leapt up and hurried out to the hall. He slowed, as he passed the office, and the sound of Cameron talking inside, then dashed through the adjoining door to the garage and slipped the black key card out of his pocket. The red-and-black Tesla Model S gave two muted beeps to indicate the proximity unlock.

Luka opened the back door and took out a small black disc—a Bluetooth tracker—fixed to a double-sided sticker pad. He peeled away the outer edge of the sticker and reached under the front passenger seat, pushing the sticky side up into the plastic.

He closed the door quietly and slipped back past the office.

The Tesla sounded a single beep to lock as it detected the key card's position.

Back in the hall, the front door closed as Strickland came back inside.

Luka diverted into the kitchen.

Box of eggs on the table. Bread. His father's mug, with fresh coffee.

'Hello?'

Luka opened the fridge and tossed the black key card onto the floor, where it slid across the polished wood and came to rest by the table leg.

Strickland entered as Luka took a carton of milk from the fridge.

'Change of plan. I'm not leaving you alone today.'

'Why?'

Strickland looked down, spotted the key card.

He raised his eyes back to Luka.

'Must have dropped it,' said Luka, pouring milk into the smoothie jug.

Strickland retrieved the card. 'Police are coming here soon, Luka. To talk to me. Don't worry—'

'You've gone red.'

Strickland took a drink from his mug.

'Dad. What's happened?'

He stared ahead, breathing fast. 'Crawley.'

15

'DI Sawyer. You are to be commended for such a full and frank report, considering the situation. I would have liked to conduct the interview in person, but I know your MIT is running two major enquiries at the moment.'

'We appreciate your understanding,' said Keating, seated beside Sawyer in the Buxton conference room.

The main video screen was horizontally split between two stern middle-aged men in good suits. The man above was older and leaner than his colleague below, who mostly kept his eyes down. Both wore wireless earpieces.

'I should also confirm that this interview is being remotely monitored by the NCA investigators. I apologise for their non-attendance, but we're also spinning multiple plates. Normally, we would take a statement here, but your report will suffice. I'm DI Edwyn Lynch. This is DS Bryan Weaver.'

Weaver looked up and smiled. 'We've been keen to

talk to you, DI Sawyer. The narrative is pretty clear now, but we're hoping you can eliminate a few fuzzy spots.'

'Oh,' said Lynch. 'And this is absolutely not a formal interview. Just an addendum to your report and statement. You're not under caution.'

'How are you, Detective?' said Weaver.

'Recovered,' said Sawyer. 'Physically, at least.'

Lynch's expression morphed from stern to sympathetic. 'It must have been a distressing event. Compounded by the injury to your colleague. I hear she's doing well.'

Flash of Maggie. Foetal in the station corridor. Screaming.

Sawyer nodded.

'The main point of confusion,' said Lynch, 'is the motive for the attack. Since we're no further towards identifying the offenders, we're dealing in one-sided speculation. But, as someone who was present, do you have any insight? Why did somebody go to the trouble of ordering a coordinated armed attack on a police station housing a Major Investigation Team?'

Sawyer glanced at Keating. 'An OCG connected to the station's only prisoner. Austin Fletcher.'

'They were springing him?' said Weaver. 'So why go in with guns blazing? They would know nobody would be armed.'

'Maybe they were enemies of Fletcher. Or friends of his enemies. Judging by their actions, I'd say their intent was to kill him rather than free him.'

Lynch leaned forward. 'But he got hold of a gun himself, didn't he?'

'It was the gun he was brought in with,' said Keating. 'I assume that DC Ross Moran released it from the evidence room when he realised the danger.'

Weaver looked down, consulting something. 'And his arrest was because of his presence at a location where three bodies were discovered, relating to a previous case.'

'That's correct,' said Keating. 'We were acting on information that Fletcher could have been involved in those deaths. We were trying to find out more when the attack happened.'

Lynch nodded, pondering. 'We spoke to DCI Robin Farrell of Greater Manchester Police, who claims to have received information about Fletcher's alleged involvement in those murders from your DC, who was sadly killed in the attack.'

'He was present for Fletcher's interrogation,' said Keating.

'Ah!' said Weaver. 'And, Detective Sawyer, do you have any idea why, during that interrogation, Fletcher would only say one word? Your surname.'

'I... I've become something of a celebrity recently,' said Sawyer. 'I am what the tabloids might call *troubled*. My mother was murdered when I was a young child. I was present, and also attacked. In recent years, my father took his own life when my investigation led me to my mother's killer. I've been the subject of several media profiles.'

Weaver nodded. 'You're saying that Fletcher had heard of you?'

'It's plausible.'

Lynch took a sip from a glass of water. 'Yes. It is. And what brought you to the station on that day, at that time? Were you fulfilling Fletcher's request?'

'We don't offer suspects a choice of interviewer,' said Keating.

'Of course not,' said Weaver. 'So, DI Sawyer, can you explain how you entered the station at that time? During the attack?'

'I'd arranged to pick up Maggie Spark. She was attending the Fletcher interview to assess his psychological condition. But I had an ulterior motive.'

Weaver looked up sharply. 'Which was?'

'DCI Keating had expressly ordered me not to get involved in Fletcher's interview. He explained that specialist interrogators were being brought in once Ross Moran and Maggie Spark's efforts had been exhausted. In my experience, characters like Fletcher are quick to judge the agenda of specialists, and to either steer them away or give them a false version of what they're looking for. I felt that if I could find an excuse to speak to Fletcher in his cell, I could loosen him up.'

'So, you went to the station intending to speak to Fletcher, against DCI Keating's orders?' said Lynch.

'Yes. But I wanted to make it seem incidental. I felt DCI Keating's assessment was misguided and wanted to help the enquiry without seeming to be directly disobeying his order. I was certain that, once Fletcher had opened up, the underhand tactics would be forgiven.'

Sawyer glanced at Keating; he kept his eyes firmly forward, on the monitor.

Lynch smiled. 'A means to an end.'

'The greater good,' said Sawyer.

'I've thought long and hard about this, Detective Sawyer,' said Weaver. 'The only reason I could think of for your presence was a distress call from Maggie Spark, once it was clear the station was being attacked.'

'Yes,' said Sawyer. 'But you surely know that didn't happen, having studied her phone records.'

Lynch gave an askew smile and peered at Sawyer from the screen. 'The CCTV footage is rather unhelpful. One camera was damaged in the blast, so we have a limited perspective.'

'The coverage only takes in the main door,' said Weaver. 'DC Moran emerges with a handgun. He shoots, then falls to the floor, having been shot himself. Soon after, there's brief imagery of Austin Fletcher holding what looks like the same gun, firing back at the attackers. But he's then pushed back into the evidence room with Maggie Spark. That's when you come in.'

Sawyer nodded. 'I saw one attacker, armed with a single-barrel shotgun, advancing on the evidence room. Knowing that the gun would only fire one shot before the attacker would need to reload, I distracted him, and then, once he'd fired, I disarmed and subdued him.'

'It might have been helpful if you had actually arrested him,' said Lynch. 'Instead of leaving him to head down the corridor, where we have no coverage. Why did you do that?'

'To check on Maggie. Given the commotion, the shots, the bodies, I'd say my concern was justified.'

'I agree,' said Weaver. He winced. 'I just wish you'd

have detained the attacker, given that the others had left and seemed to present no threat at that point.'

Keating gave him the side-eye; Sawyer ignored him.

'I didn't know what I was going to find in the evidence room. I didn't know if Maggie was in danger in there. Possibly from Fletcher. I judged that her safety had to take precedence over the arrest.'

Weaver consulted something off-screen again. 'The attacker then attempted to kill both you and Maggie with a hand grenade. The footage shows him sliding it along the corridor. How did you survive the blast?'

'I couldn't assume there was enough time to throw the grenade back to the attacker. A cell door had been torn off one of its hinges in a struggle. I pulled it away and used it as a shield.'

'I assume this was Fletcher's cell door?' said Lynch. 'It's still unclear how he got out. Did you see him leave the station by the courtyard door?'

Sawyer took a breath. 'Yes. He backed out through the door, holding the gun on myself and Maggie. I had no choice but to let him go.'

'And any idea where he might be now?'

'None.'

Lynch looked down, typing something. Two in-line images appeared on the monitor: zoomed-in CCTV stills of the station corridor.

Two men. One in a light-coloured balaclava, holding a shotgun at his side; the other in a darker, two-tone balaclava, aiming a handgun.

Both images were grainy, focused on the men's eyes.

'This is the best we could do with enhancement,' said Lynch. 'Detective Sawyer, do you recognise these men?'

Sawyer squinted up at the screen. 'No, I don't.'

A phone rang. Lynch looked down, frowned.

'My apologies. We're almost done. I just have to take this call.'

He disappeared off-screen.

'Oh. I wanted to ask...' Weaver pointed at the screen. 'The custody sergeant on the day. Gerry Sherman. You called him, didn't you? Not long before he was shot.'

Sawyer nodded. 'I did. As I say, I was due to pick up Maggie. I wanted to check the status of the Fletcher interview.'

'Why not call her direct?'

'DS Weaver,' said Keating. 'I don't care much for the tone of your enquiry. Is my DI under suspicion in any way?'

Weaver sat back. 'Apologies, DCI Keating. I've been curious about this detail and I hoped that DI Sawyer might—'

'I didn't want to interrupt her,' said Sawyer. 'Evaluating a difficult subject can be delicate and complex.'

Weaver's lips set into a thin line. 'Indeed.'

Lynch reappeared in his half of the monitor. 'DCI Keating. DI Sawyer. Thank you for your time today. That's been extremely helpful. I assume you didn't bring your phones into the conference room?'

Keating looked at Sawyer. 'No. Why?'

'I... made it clear that we weren't to be disturbed. But the caller overruled me.'

'Dale,' said Sawyer.

Lynch gave a sage nod.

'Yes,' said Keating. 'He's coming in. But we're not due to meet him for another—'

'He said it couldn't wait.' Lynch cut across him. 'He wants you both to go to his house immediately.'

16

'When did it arrive?' said Keating.

Sawyer and Keating stood before the boxy desk in Strickland's home office. At the other side, Strickland dropped his head and leaned forward, gripping the edge of the desk with both hands.

'About an hour ago.'

The door opened and a short but powerfully built man in jeans and black T-shirt hovered in the doorway. 'Mr Strickland. Sorry to interrupt.'

Strickland took off his glasses and raised his eyes. 'This is my assistant, Cameron. Detective Inspector Jake Sawyer. Detective Superintendent Ivan Keating.'

Cameron nodded. 'Just the usual postman on the doorbell cam, Mr Strickland.'

Strickland nodded. Cameron moved to leave, but Strickland waved him in. He closed the door behind him and stood to the side.

Sawyer snapped on a pair of latex gloves and stepped forward. He took the Polaroid photograph out of the brown envelope and held it up to the light from the open window that overlooked the back garden.

Eva Gregory sat slumped on a high-backed chair in front of a plain light blue background, scowling into the camera. Her normally glossy black hair looked ragged and unwashed, and the lenses of her brown-rimmed Tom Fords were revealed as murky by the camera flash. She wore no make-up, and looked unharmed.

'Eva had a Polaroid camera in her room,' said Strickland.

'Bedroom?' said Keating.

'Just a private study room out back, off the kitchen. I just checked. The camera is missing. It's the first time I've noticed.'

Sawyer studied the photo. 'Did forensics sweep that room?'

'They did the whole place,' said Strickland. 'Even Luka's room.'

Sawyer picked up the envelope. 'Is Luka at school?'

'He won't go. Says he can't.'

Sawyer caught Strickland's eye. 'Is he here?'

'Upstairs. I declined your offer of protection for him, as I wanted to use personal associates. I'm sure your men are competent, DSI Keating. But Crawley took Luka from under police guard at the hospital, so you'll forgive my lack of faith.'

'The address is handwritten,' said Sawyer. 'We need to confirm it's Crawley. Prison and hospital forms. It was delivered locally, but there's no sign of when the photo was taken. The camera flash might have caught something in Eva's glasses.' He held it close to his face, scrutinising. 'We should fast-track forensics on the photo and envelope. Get Rhodes on image enhancement.'

Strickland sat at the desk and smoothed down his cropped white hair. 'Why not do the usual thing of having her hold the day's newspaper? To show when it was taken.'

'He doesn't care,' said Sawyer.

Keating sighed.

'About what?' said Strickland. 'Eva?'

Sawyer shook his head. 'He doesn't care about showing us proof of life. He didn't send this for reassurance, or to back up a demand. He's turning the screw. He wants it to hurt. He wants to remind you that you have no power.'

Keating stepped forward. 'Mr Strickland, I apologise for DI Sawyer's frankness in this matter.'

Strickland waved a hand. 'I'm a big boy.' He laid both hands on the desk, clasped them together. 'But this is the only development in the investigation since it began, and it was provided by the kidnapper. Not the police. Not the team in Nottinghamshire. Not your team, DSI Keating. I agree with DI Sawyer. This delusional psychopath has all the power. He's running the show. Now, I've been using private operatives to protect my home and my son. If I see no progress from official agencies, then I'll do likewise for the active investigation. As I'm sure you appreciate, I have many high-level contacts who could help.'

'I can assure you,' said Keating, 'that all lines of—'

Strickland stood up. 'I've arranged a meeting with the lead detective on the Nottinghamshire team. The ones looking into Crawley's escape. When I take the job of full-time Greater Manchester mayor, I will look into options for merging forces in the North and Midlands. There's too much bureaucracy and pointless protocol. We need more directness. Particularly in cases like this, where someone's life is at stake.'

'I appreciate your frustration,' said Keating. 'But there are unique resource pressures at the moment. After the attack.'

'Of course. I'll set you up with some GMP staff. You could use them for this investigation or assign them to other cases.' Strickland paused, stood upright. 'DSI Keating, surely we're not horse trading over a woman's life here.'

Sawyer slipped the photo back into the envelope and looked up to the open window, catching movement. A shadow.

Dale's tone softened. 'I'm aware of the unusual events at your team base, DSI Keating. Of course, that will have slowed things down. But we need to pick up the pace.'

'The station is almost fully operational again,' said Keating. 'I'll fast-track forensics on the envelope and reassign the detectives. I'll also send someone down to meet with your Nottinghamshire contact. I can offer you regular updates—'

'I'd appreciate it if you could call on a detective who has encountered Crawley before. The abscondment is his last known activity before he took Eva. I would like DI Sawyer to liaise with Nottinghamshire and look over the details. His insight would be invaluable.'

Sawyer nodded at Keating as he opened the door. 'It's fine. It's a good idea.'

He stepped out into the hall and walked through to the kitchen. Cameron stood near the fridge, looking at his phone. Steam from the kettle rose around him.

The cord on the back door blind swung slightly.

Cameron turned. 'Everything okay?'

'Did you just go outside?'

He frowned. 'No. Why?'

Sawyer turned back and hurried down the hall, past the office where Keating and Strickland were still talking.

He paused at the bottom of the stairs.

Lingering body spray. Male. Something cheap and sickly. Synthetic musk.

'Luka?'

He climbed the stairs, catching Luka Strickland heading into a bathroom.

Luka turned.

'Hello, Jake.'

Soil on the stair carpet. A fresh smear on the wooden floor of the landing.

Luka hesitated at the open doorway. 'Are you helping find her?'

Sawyer nodded. 'Were you listening in?'

'No!'

Sawyer walked forward and squatted down, close to Luka. He softened his voice. 'Luka. I know this is difficult. But she is strong, and we're doing everything in our power—'

'Do you think he's killed my mum?'

Sawyer caught his breath. 'Of course not. You've a

right to be anxious, but… don't assume the worst. When you were taken, I promised your mum I'd find you. And I did, didn't I?'

Luka nodded, head down. 'I need a wee.' He squirmed.

'I know you want to help. But if you get involved, it could put you in danger again. And it could also make things even harder for your mum.'

'So, go on. Do you promise you'll get her back safe?'

Sawyer stood up. 'I promise to try.'

17

Robert Holsgrove tidied his papers into the corner of the table and sat back as the waiters laid out his regular Monday lunch.

The younger man set down the dishes as his older colleague commented.

'Good afternoon, sir. We have the houmous, baba ganoush, tabbouleh, falafel, natural labné, cheese samboussek. And on the side, haloumi, flatbread and pickles.' He arranged the food for ease of access and added a final dish himself. 'And the lentil soup with pita crisps.'

'Many thanks, Farez.'

The waiters retreated. Holsgrove took a sip of lemon water and gazed through the awning entrance, out at the thrusting young lunch crowd scurrying across Spinningfields Square. Most wore shades and short sleeves. It was hardly balmy, but sustained sunshine in central Manchester was not to be wasted.

Holsgrove loaded a plate with an assortment of delights and pulled out a journal from his papers: *Practical Neurology*. He would get his nose into the piece on localisation in focal epilepsy, then work through a few research notes.

He stirred a spoon through the soup and tried a sip.

He turned to the article and wedged the journal open under the rim of his plate, then put on his readers.

Two men sat down opposite each other at the adjacent table, and Holsgrove glanced up. His nose twitched at the smell of something fruity. Gum? Vape?

Farez brought menus for the men, then retreated.

Holsgrove forked in a mouthful of tabbouleh.

'Have you been here before?'

'Couple of times, yeah. The lamb wraps are good.'

'Don't fancy that. Excuse me, pal.'

Holsgrove looked up.

One of the men pointed at Holsgrove's food. He smiled and took off a sky-blue Manchester City baseball cap. He was callow and drawn, with predatory eyes. The smile was cartoonish, ill-fitting.

'Sorry to interrupt your reading, my friend. What's that you've ordered? If you don't mind me asking.'

'Of course not. It's a mezze platter for one. I heartily recommend it. You can get them for two.'

The man spluttered a laugh, too loud. 'I'm not paying for his fucking lunch. He can have my scraps.'

The other man didn't react. He kept his eyes down on his menu, straight black hair hanging down. The first man was puffy, carrying too much weight. The second

113

was bulky, too, but broader shouldered, proportional. He wore a surgical strap around one elbow.

The first man got up and took the seat beside Holsgrove.

'Do you mind if we join you?'

Holsgrove whipped off his glasses. 'Actually—'

The first man slapped him on the shoulder. 'I know, I know. You're catching up with a bit of work, yeah? This is a business lunch for us, too.'

The second man slipped over onto the seat opposite.

The first stuck out his hand. 'I'm Georgi. This is Sergio.'

Holsgrove reluctantly shook. Warm, damp. Georgi squeezed and tried the smile again.

'Look,' said Holsgrove, 'I don't mean to be rude—'

'Don't be, then.' Georgi looked up at the sign above the awning. '*Comptoir Libanais*. What's that mean?'

'It's French. Lebanese counter.'

Georgi took a falafel from Holsgrove's plate and pushed it into his mouth, whole. He chewed, wide eyed.

At last, Sergio looked up. He pushed his hair out of his eyes. 'How is Oscar?'

Holsgrove looked at Georgi, still chewing. He tidied his yellow tie and placed his hands on the edge of the table.

'I'm sorry. I don't recognise either of you. I'm not sure—'

'He goes to Seashell Royal School, right?' said Sergio. 'Down in Cheadle Hulme.'

Georgi wiped his mouth with a napkin. 'For mongs.'

Holsgrove picked up his notes and tried to stand.

Georgi clamped a hand on his shoulder and eased him back into his seat.

'Oh. Sorry. Can't say that any more, can you? Complex special needs, isn't it?'

Holsgrove jerked away from Georgi's grip. 'What do you want? This really isn't very bright of you. I could call the manager at any moment. Have him contact the police.'

Georgi shook his head. 'That wouldn't be good.' He mopped up some houmous with a flatbread. 'For Oscar.'

'This can work out for everyone,' said Sergio. 'All we're asking for is one phone call.' He took out a pen and wrote a number on the back of a restaurant card.

Holsgrove looked at the card, then at Georgi and Sergio. 'What is this? Who *are* you?'

'Concerned parties,' said Sergio.

'Concerned about what?'

'About the welfare of one of your patients. Maggie Spark.'

Holsgrove scoffed. 'I can't share confidential details—'

Georgi slapped a hand on his shoulder again. 'Yeah. You can. No fucking problem.' He lowered his voice. 'We won't tell if you don't.'

'We're not asking a lot,' said Sergio. 'If Ms Spark shows any signs of being able to communicate, you just call this number. You speak to me before *anyone*. Including her family.'

'And especially police,' said Georgi. 'We need fair warning, Mr Holsgrove. Because if anyone speaks to Maggie Spark before we do, and if we hear the police know about our meeting today, then someone will drop in on your lad at the Seashell Royal.'

Sergio leaned in close and stared into Holsgrove's eyes. 'And I promise you. His special needs will get a lot more complex.'

18

Laura Brennan set down a tray of drinks: two glasses of white wine, a pint glass of water, and a Diet Coke.

Shepherd took the water, raised it in thanks.

Laura smoothed down her skirt and tucked herself under the pub table. She took a sip of wine. 'Catherine is running late. I'm so sorry. She'll be here any minute.'

Laura adjusted the pin holding her bleached blonde hair in place. She was short and tidy, with wide, worried eyes.

Sawyer drank from the glass of Coke. 'Thank you for agreeing to speak to us. We couldn't host you at the station. It's still being...' He glanced at Shepherd. 'Refurbished.'

Laura smiled. 'Oh, it's no problem. This is our local, so...'

The beer garden of Ye Olde Bowling Green Inn sat on high ground, overlooking an expanse of farm fields that rippled down to the Hope Valley, blanketed in gauzy evening light.

'It's gorgeous out here,' said Laura. 'Such a divine view. I love this time of year. The end of summer blending into autumn. I remember how Dad adored the valley. He was a big walker. He used to tease my mum when she asked him if he loved the Peaks more than her. He said it was a close one.'

'Did you walk with him?' said Shepherd.

She smiled, bittersweet. 'He tried to get us to go, but... Teenage girls. Of course, now, I'd give anything to go back and walk with him. But you can't live in the past. You can only go forward.'

'According to Stephen Hawking,' said Sawyer.

'Yes, well. He's not a popular figure at Bible Group.'

Sawyer nodded, sipping his drink. 'He didn't see it as a zero-sum thing. The origins of all this.'

'Of course. But that's the whole basis of our faith. It's the path we've taken. I believe the way the universe began was chosen by God for reasons we can't understand. I take it you believe it was determined by a law of science?'

'I do.' He looked over to the double doors in the pub conservatory, as a red-haired woman pushed her way through and hurried towards their table. 'Hawking thought the concept of the divine could be personal, though. A higher force we can feel and describe which seems magical. He said you could call the laws of science *God*.'

Laura smiled. 'Or nature.'

'Yeah. He just didn't believe in a creator being. Someone you could meet and put questions to.'

'This sounds bloody heavy,' said Catherine Brennan, as she embraced her sister and took a seat beside her.

Laura smiled. 'Just a little debate about theology.'

Catherine nodded to Shepherd and Sawyer. 'Ah. So, I take it we're in the presence of atheists?'

She tucked her red hair behind her ear.

Flash of Maggie, screaming.

'This is Detective Inspector Ed Shepherd,' said Laura. 'And Detective Inspector Jake Sawyer.'

Catherine took a slug of wine. 'So, what do we call youse? *Officer* or *detective* or what?'

'Atheist One and Atheist Two,' said Sawyer.

Catherine smiled. 'Don't worry, Mr Sawyer. We're humble Bible bashers. We won't be preaching or doing conversions. Not on a weekday, anyway.'

'We're hardened detectives, Ms Brennan,' said Shepherd. 'We don't convert easily.'

'Ah,' said Catherine. 'This is your little debate, yes? Evidence. The law of science versus faith.' She held Sawyer's eye for a moment. 'Laura said you wanted to talk about Jermaine Cunliffe.'

Laura frowned and lowered her head. She toyed with a silver crucifix hanging around her neck.

'We do,' said Sawyer. 'I'm afraid he was found dead on Saturday evening, up in Kinder Bank wood.'

'I saw it in the *Times* this morning,' said Catherine. 'Such a shame.'

Sawyer glanced at Shepherd. 'Some might say that's a surprising response.'

'I mean to spoil that area. It's beautiful woodland round there.'

'Have either of you had any contact with Mr Cunliffe since he was released from prison?' said Sawyer.

'None,' said Laura, looking up. 'We've spent the last fifteen years trying to forget him.'

Catherine stared into her drink. 'How did he die?'

Shepherd cleared his throat. 'We're still working on—'

'He was burned,' said Sawyer. 'Someone beat him, then poured petrol over him and set him alight.'

Laura groaned and turned her head to the view across the fields.

'We didn't do it.' Catherine took a deep drink of wine, keeping her eyes on Sawyer over the top of the glass.

He smiled. 'I know.'

'We wanted to ask you about your father, Thomas,' said Shepherd. 'Connections, interests. Jermaine Cunliffe was one of the men, boys, convicted of his murder. The link is too strong to ignore. You can appreciate that. I hope this isn't too difficult for you.'

'No,' said Laura. 'I enjoy talking about Dad. It brings him back a little, you know?' She set down her wine and twirled the crucifix in her fingers. 'He met Mum back in Ireland. They got married and moved here when he got the job at St. Anselm's. Mum was pregnant with me when they married. Cat was born in Ireland. I was born here.' She paused for a moment, settled herself. 'When I think of Dad, I just feel his love. It was like... a glow he had. It made you feel warm.'

'Your mother died recently,' said Shepherd. 'Is that right?'

Catherine nodded. 'About a year ago. Breast cancer.

Mastectomy didn't catch it all. She had a decent four years, although the last few months were hard.'

Sawyer winced at a volley of braying laughter from a group at a nearby table.

Catherine took another swig of wine.

'Cunliffe's death might be unrelated to what happened to your father,' said Sawyer. 'But we need to ask if you can think of anyone connected to him, or your family, who might have seen Cunliffe and the others as fair game.'

'You mean revenge?' said Laura. 'All this time later?'

Shepherd sighed. 'It's possible.'

'I would have done it myself, back then,' said Catherine. 'I wanted them all... just...' She closed her eyes. 'My wonderful dad. He was such a beautiful soul.'

'Done what?' said Sawyer.

She finished the glass. 'Oh, I don't know. I was eighteen. Laura was sixteen. Full of hormones. It's a cliché, but the night it happened still feels so recent.' She looked out at the fields. 'That old rubbish about time being a healer. It just never seems any further away. Does that make sense?'

'It does,' said Sawyer. 'You want to erase it from your mind, but you feel guilty for thinking that.'

Catherine stared at him.

'You try to focus on the good parts, but the horror is too powerful. It won't let you.'

'That's right. You feel guilty because—'

'You don't want to forget,' said Sawyer. 'It seems wrong. As if you could ever forget someone who was, and still is, so deeply a part of you.'

Catherine studied him. 'I had to pull his tongue out of his throat.'

Laura groaned again. She got up and walked to a vacant table.

'On the night?' said Shepherd.

Catherine nodded. 'They'd beaten him so badly. It was unbelievable. Kicked him in the head. His tongue was blocking his breathing. And he was choking. They'd run away by then. I tried to tilt his head back. But I had to put my hand in his mouth and clear his throat. There was so much blood. Mum ran to us, screaming and screaming. Laura was shouting after the boys. His face was so swollen. His eyes closed. He was trying to say my name. Laura's. Mum's. But he was spluttering, coughing. He tried to stand, but couldn't. We were holding him, covered in his blood. Crying, screaming. The ambulance was there quick enough. And that was it. At the start of that day, this lovely man was our dad. At the end of it, he was with the Lord.'

They held their silence for a few moments. Laura stood out of earshot, gazing out at the view, twirling her crucifix.

'Your mother, Tanya,' said Shepherd, quietly. 'She gave that incredible press conference.'

Catherine gave a deep sigh. 'She had to forgive them. It was her way. It was the only way.'

'Thomas was a headmaster,' said Sawyer. 'St. Anselm's. Was he popular?'

'Oh, yes. Hugely. Everyone loved him.' She leaned forward. 'He was a good man, Detective Sawyer. And evil came for him.'

Catherine's hands slid across the table. She caught herself and picked up Laura's glass, took a sip.

'You believe in absolutes?' said Sawyer. 'Good, evil.'

She scoffed. 'I'm a Catholic. Take a guess. I believe we want to be good, but we're all capable of bad. Of evil.'

'Original sin.'

'We're all flawed, and vulnerable to temptation, sin. You serve the law. That's a construct of humans. But humans are flawed, and so is the law. God is not flawed. His love is absolute.'

Sawyer stared her down. 'Have you forgiven them?'

'Matthew's good on that. 6:14. *If we don't forgive men their trespasses, neither will our Father forgive ours.*'

'Did your mother really forgive them?'

'Oh, she did. Most of the family followed her lead. Except my father's brother. Uncle Dylan. He came over for the funeral and stayed with us.'

Laura started to walk back.

'He didn't forgive them?' said Shepherd.

She shook her head. 'I remember him standing round the coffin. Everyone was distraught, but he just looked angry. At the wake, he tried to clear the tables, shoving the sandwiches back behind the bar. Saying how it was all disrespectful and we shouldn't be using it as an excuse for a piss-up.'

Laura sat down. 'Uncle Dylan was good to us, though. He was just distraught.'

'Older or younger brother of your dad?' said Sawyer.

'Bit older, I think.'

'Where is he now?'

Laura shrugged. 'Back in Ireland, as far as I know.'

She rescued her wine from Catherine and took a drink.

'He was here for Mum's funeral,' said Catherine.

More loud laughter from the nearby table. One woman shrieked; close to a cackle. A scream.

Face down in the grass. Head raging from the hammer blow.

His mother, howling. Screaming in agony and outrage.

Sawyer turned to the table. 'Will you *shut the fuck up?*'

Two men, two women. Twenties. All turning, shocked.

A beat of silence. Other tables looked over.

Sawyer turned back. He sipped his Coke, steadied his breathing. 'Sorry.'

'*Hey!*' A male shout from the table behind. '*Fuckin' 'ell. Keep your hair on, mate.*'

Female voices, hushed.

'*Who's he think he is?*'

'*Is he staff or something?*'

A second male voice.

'*Wanker.*'

Sawyer closed his eyes. The images swirled.

Leering faces, morphing and warping.

'You okay?' said Shepherd.

He opened his eyes. 'What about pupils at St. Anselm's? Did your father have any specific connections there? Anyone we could investigate? Violent history, criminal record.'

Catherine and Laura recomposed themselves, glancing at each other.

'Nobody comes to mind,' said Laura. 'I remember he was close to one teacher. Kieran something. Geography, I think.'

Catherine nodded. 'Kieran Leith. They did a lot of walking together. Particularly when Mum was unwell. He was the head of some hiking organisation or something.

'Sorry to have to raise this,' said Shepherd. 'But you received a lot of hate mail from one boy's family, didn't you?' He looked at his notepad. 'There's a complaint from you on record.'

Catherine grimaced. 'Not his family. It was *him*. Damon Morris.'

Laura looked away. 'I can't stand to hear his name.'

'Or someone could have sent it on his behalf,' said Sawyer. 'What kind of things?'

'It was after he'd been released,' said Catherine. 'Not long after Mum's mastectomy. He'd obviously got wind of it. He sent the foulest things. Defaced photographs of Dad. Sexual threats. Nasty little notes sent in envelopes covered in filth, so the postman would see it. Someone wrote *CANCER BITCH* on the front door. We had phone calls. I answered one. A man said, "Die soon, cunt", then hung up.'

'Morris got the lightest sentence, right?' said Sawyer.

'Yeah, he was the youngest. And the worst. He started the attack on Dad, and he was always angry at being caught. As if it wasn't something that deserved a jail sentence. He blamed us for his loss of freedom.'

Laura gasped. 'What kind of sick mind actually believes that?'

Sawyer drained his glass, stood up. 'Thank you both for your time. That's been really helpful.'

Laura looked up. 'Let us know if you need anything else.'

He leaned over the table. 'Sorry for the... moment.'

Catherine reached over and patted Sawyer's hand. 'Don't be silly. We all have our soft spots. With me, it's people blowing their nose.' She shuddered. 'We're all flawed, remember?'

Sawyer looked down at Catherine's hand. Diamond engagement ring, matching wedding band.

'We're all flawed,' said Sawyer. 'But God isn't.'

She withdrew her hand, took a sip of Laura's wine. 'You're getting it, Detective Sawyer. Yes.'

'So, are you not afraid of this all-powerful force?'

'I prefer to think of it as reverence. Respect.'

'I like James 4:14,' said Laura. '*You do not even know what will happen tomorrow. What is your life? You are a mist that appears for a little while and then vanishes.*'

'We know He can destroy us in an instant,' said Catherine. 'But God is a good Father. He's filled with love for us. It's the cornerstone of our faith. We trust His promises, and we believe that if we have faith, if we follow Him and obey His demands, then He will bless us, not destroy us.'

———

Sawyer flopped back in the Mini driver seat.

'Something's off.'

'About what?' said Shepherd.

'Maybe they're lying about not having contact with their father's murderers since they were released.'

Shepherd puffed out a sigh. 'Are you sure? I didn't get that.'

Sawyer started the engine, pulled out of the pub car park. 'If not that, then there's something they both know they're holding back.'

'You've looked into their God-bothering souls, right?'

'Just their eyes. If they're not lying, they're at least avoiding something.'

'The uncle?'

Sawyer squinted through the dusk. 'Could be.'

Shepherd pointed. 'Lights?'

He switched on the headlights and joined the road heading back to Shepherd's house.

'How long for the Rover repair?'

Shepherd scrolled through something on his phone. 'You sick of me already?'

'I was thinking of heading back into work. Assuming you're done for the day.'

Shepherd gave a slow nod. 'I am. Yes. Done for the day. You should be, too. You not sleeping?'

'Why do you say that?'

'You're going full Hulk on a bunch of kids having a good time. Remember. Self-care.'

Sawyer nodded at Shepherd's phone. 'Walker?'

'Detail on Cunliffe's last movements. He was with Ray Carlisle, the manager of the Matlock café his aunt mentioned. Walker checked him out. They'd been meeting at the same pub regularly. Couple of times a week. His uncle connected them. The fella said Jermaine was impressive and wanted to make a go of it.'

'Did he travel the same way every time?'

'Carlisle told Walker Jermaine always walked it, yeah. Fifteen minutes. Walker also says Carlisle checks out.'

'Go see the whites of his eyes, anyway. But this doesn't feel like a new enemy Cunliffe has made since getting out.'

Shepherd tapped his phone on the dash. 'No. Could still be a coincidence, though. Might be nothing to do with the Brennan murder. We shouldn't try to fit everything around it.'

'Catherine's rings weren't cheap.'

Shepherd looked at him. 'Yes. Touchy, too.'

Sawyer scoffed. 'I think it was more of an empathy thing.'

'They're minted, though. Plenty of money in Thomas's family back in Ireland. Tanya ran the family business. Local insurance. Very successful. They both did a lot of work for a Catholic Church near the family home here. All Saints in Hassop.'

'Let's look at Uncle Dylan. He'll be knocking on a bit now, though. And we should talk to Thomas's walking buddy.'

'Kieran Leith.'

'Yeah.'

They drove in silence for a while.

'You seeing anybody?' said Shepherd.

Sawyer scowled at him.

'I mean therapy, not women.'

Sawyer faced the front. 'No.'

19

Rory Burrows jolted awake. He twisted away from the shower of freezing water, scraping his bound legs over the stone floor.

He blinked his eyes clear and turned, into almost total darkness. His breaths were rasping, rattled, and each inhale sent a flex of pain across his chest.

Burrows tried to sit upright, but his hands were bound, too. Behind his back. He dug his heels into the wet floor and slid along, through the puddled water, until his head clunked into a stone wall. He shuffled around, pushing himself upright against the wall.

Agony, as he rolled. From one of his arms, both legs. He tried to cry out, but a gag blocked his mouth, pulled tight and taped to his cheeks.

He slumped, staring out at the room, watching the shadows form as his vision adjusted.

Low ceiling. Uneven stone floor. A table at the side. Cases stacked against the facing wall. A staircase against the far wall; cold light peering through an ajar door at the top.

A cellar.

His nostrils flared.

Piss and iron. Soil and rot.

His forehead throbbed. Blood trickled down into his eye.

'*Well, now.*'

Burrows startled at the voice.

A tall shadow moved out of the corner by the staircase.

A flash of flame as the figure turned into the wall to light a cigarette.

'I'm guessing you've had better days, Rory.'

The man puffed out grey smoke. It swirled like a phantom in the blackness.

Burrows cowered as the man approached, still in shadow.

He reached down and tore away one strip of tape, then yanked away the gag, taking the second strip with it.

The man stepped back, ran his fingers through his hair. The light from the door cast him in faint outline as he tilted his head.

Burrows spluttered. '*Fuck.*' He spat. 'What do you want? I've done nothing, man. Please. Let me go. I promise...' He howled. 'My fucking leg!'

The man held up a hand.

'Seriously, Rory. I thought we were private down here, but you make a lot of noise.'

Burrows spat again. Blood. 'Listen, listen. You don't want to do this. Whatever it is. I can help.

Whatever you need. Just tell me. *Why?* Look. I've got kids, man.'

'That's not true, Rory. You've been in prison.'

'Yeah. Fourteen fucking years!' He moaned and writhed. 'Ah, fuck. It *hurts*.'

Silence from the man. More smoke.

'It's a long time, Rory.'

'What? Yeah. Yeah, it is.'

'Long enough?'

Burrows stared up at the figure. 'Fucking hell. I can't help that. I couldn't—'

'You made your choice.' He upped the volume slightly. 'You know what you did.'

'Yeah. I was stupid. I was eighteen. Tanked up. I've regretted it every day since. It was... It was stupid and wrong. But I've done my time.'

'Did you atone?'

'What? I just told you. I regretted—'

'How did you atone?' The man stepped forward. 'Is this what you'll do when you stand before your maker? Whine about how you've *done your time*?' He forced the gag back over Burrows's mouth and taped it back in place, then turned and walked to the table.

Burrows sobbed and writhed.

Sparks puffed up from the man's feet as he stomped out his cigarette.

He dragged something heavy from the table and stood with his back to Burrows.

'No matter how much you regret, or suffer for your sins, you can never pay the full price of making good the injury. Because you are much less worthy than God.' He turned. 'So, Christ died to make up the difference. Because his life was worth so much more to the Father.' He walked towards Burrows. 'And in that way, man's debt to God was satisfied.'

Burrows caught sight of the object he was carrying: a long-handled felling axe with a broad, curved blade. The man let the blade drop to the floor, dragging it across the stone floor as he walked.

Burrows cried out behind the gag, kicking and shuffling himself into the corner.

'So, no. Rory. You did not atone. There was no self-sacrifice. Only self-pity. And man's justice has proven unworthy. So now, I deliver God's justice. *Saint Michael. The Archangel. Defend us in battle. Be our protection against the wickedness and snares of the devil. May God rebuke him, we humbly pray. And do thou, O Prince of the Heavenly Host, by the power of God, thrust into hell Satan and all evil spirits who wander through the world for the ruin of souls.*'

He placed the axe on the floor, crouched, and swung a heavy right hook into Burrows's head.

And again.

And again.

Burrows slumped, unconscious.

'Amen.'

20

Sawyer gazed up at the vast slow-shutter photograph, gold-framed and mounted on the off-white wall. The waterfall at Lumsworth, suspended in time; the water draped over the rock; the stream below like white paste, foamed and frozen.

Alex Goldman sat opposite in her mauve armchair. She kept her head slightly bowed and her hands clasped, resting on her knees. She was as unchanged as the picture: blow-dried grey hair, beige rollneck. Still, but unyielding. The silence amplified a slight whistle in her exhales.

Sawyer shifted at the edge of the black *chaise longue*. He glanced across at the wall clock: 8:50am.

'What's the record?'

Alex jumped a little. 'For wordless sessions? You're not even close yet. Twenty minutes is mild. I had one chap go through two hour-long appointments without saying a word. He didn't show for the third booking. I never saw him again.'

Sawyer turned back to the photo.

'I know you don't like that image, Jake,' said Alex. 'As an aesthetic. But you're still drawn to it.'

'Your chair is new. It's the same model as the old one, but new.'

She smiled. 'It was sagging a little. My condition isn't getting better.' She rubbed at her thigh. 'And, as I spend a lot of time in my consulting chair—'

'Spend your money where you spend your time.'

'Precisely.' She gestured to the tray sat on the curvy-legged side table. Teapot, cups, plate of biscuits. 'Will you have tea now?'

He sighed. 'I'm not stopping.'

Alex leaned forward and took a sip of her own tea. 'How do you mean?'

'It's not you. It's me.'

She said nothing.

'In London,' continued Sawyer, 'I saw this moving shadow on walls, in room corners. Like an insect or spider. Now it's bigger, amorphous.'

'A hallucination.'

'I assume so.'

'We talked about your... visions of Jessica.'

He rubbed at his forehead. 'They're back.'

'Since the incident at the station? The explosion.'

'Yes. I know it isn't real. But plenty of people find comfort in things that aren't real. Ideas. Myths.'

'Faith?'

Sawyer nodded. 'Whatever works, I suppose. Whatever helps.' He looked up at the picture again. 'Have you heard of Carlos Rovelli?'

'Vaguely.'

'He thinks reality is just something we've constructed, and everything actually runs on quantum physics. Reality is what we call this network, onto which we project all these little sequences of events. Past, present and future. He sees the flow of time as subjective rather than objective. A feature of the way we experience the universe, rather than an objective part of its fabric.'

Alex set down her cup. 'It's a bit early for this, Jake. What does it have to do with hallucinations?'

He shrugged. 'It's too easy to dismiss them as delusional. Could they be glimpses into alternative sequences of time? Perhaps there's a way in which traumatised people can access those alternative sequences?'

Alex leaned forward, frowning. 'Tell me about Maggie, Jake.'

He closed his eyes. 'She's alive. I'll take that for now.'

'Have you heard of CS Lewis?'

'Of course. He wrote *The Lion, The Witch and the Wardrobe.*'

'He also wrote a wonderful meditation on the grief he suffered after his wife's early death. He was driven by Christian faith. But this tragedy tested it to the limit. He worked it out by writing *A Grief Observed*. In the end, he saw the time he'd been given with his wife as a gift from God. He said the pain he felt after her death was the price he had to pay for his happiness when she was alive.'

Sawyer kept his eyes closed. 'If someone told you that grief is the end point of all love, it wouldn't stop you from loving.'

'No. But it is a process. Like healing. And perhaps you're trying to reject these processes. Shut them down. By deconstructing them with this... I don't know, quantum theory. This muddling of time is a major part of trauma. You feel the pain of the past over and over, in the present.'

'It makes the past feel like the present.' He opened his eyes, went back to the picture.

Alex sat back. 'I have a question. About Maggie.'

'Survivor guilt. We've done this.'

'No. We know you've spent your life regretting how you couldn't help your mother. Couldn't save her. And then your father.'

He looked at her. 'You're wondering if I feel that DC Moran did more to help Maggie than I did. I had the same question from a colleague.' He hesitated. 'Of course I do. He ended up losing his own life. I kept Maggie alive, but only technically. Biologically.'

'But that's progress. You were present at the death of your mother and father, but they're no longer with us. Maggie, though—'

'She's no longer with anyone. She's in limbo. You could say that's worse.'

Alex angled her head. 'And would *you* say that?'

Sawyer stared up at the picture again, staying silent.

After a few minutes, he gave a deep, shuddering sigh, breaking the reverie.

'My father had this thing. From the Bible. *There is nothing in darkness that will not be brought into light.* He said it to me just before he died.' He held Alex's eye. 'I'm thinking it's not just his way of imparting wisdom. I'm thinking his fixation on that idea is hinting at something deeper. And I'm seeing things in Mum's diary...'

Alex took another drink. 'You should be careful of only seeing what you want to see. Confirmation bias.'

'I think that Mum's death was just the subjective part of a wider reality. The part that hurt me the most.' He shifted forward in his seat. 'And it's so huge that it sits there in the centre, obscuring everything else.'

'But how can you ever know the truth of this, Jake? Won't it always be just an idea you torture yourself with?'

Sawyer squeezed the three middle fingers of his left hand with his right, cracking the bones. 'You mentioned healing. I think there's something profound going on, in my perception. It's as if the pain is forcing it to the surface.'

'Jake...'

'And healing will suppress it. It almost feels like I'm evolving.'

She sipped her tea.

Sawyer smiled. 'You think I sound crazy.'

'I think you sound like you're in pain. Surely you don't believe you're growing some kind of third eye.'

'If you like.'

'Jake. All these ideas. Just conjecture. And, I hesitate to say this, but it sounds like fantasy. Possibly even paranoia. Looking for patterns, perceived secrets... You need to embrace healing as a process. Something deep and difficult, but reachable. A journey of change.' She pushed her hands together, as if in prayer. 'The methods you've tried so far might not have worked. So, embrace new methods. I was reading earlier, about EMDR—'

'It's just talk therapy with a gimmick.'

She sighed. 'You are suffering, Jake. You're in the grip of Post-Traumatic Stress. And not PTSD. I don't believe it's a disorder. It's trauma, based on tangible events. I suggest you discard the abstract, intangible ideas and focus on the physical realities. You don't have to be forever stuck in the past. You *can* change. You might not believe it now, but you can heal.'

He stood up. 'Thank you. Alex. For everything. For trying. For seeing me again. But all the self-examination is just sending me round in circles. This is no good for me. I'm no good for you. I'm going to do my healing in my own way.'

21

DCI Jonas Whatley led Sawyer into his glass-walled office and slid the door closed, sealing them in with the aroma of furniture polish and citrus cologne.

He opened the window halfway and stood beside a floor-mounted beechwood table in the centre of the room, gesturing for Sawyer to sit.

'Nice to put a face to a name, Detective Sawyer. I feel like I know you already.'

Whatley was bulky for his height, but nimble enough, and salon-groomed. His hair was closely cropped, with an immaculate fade and evenly trimmed beard.

Sawyer sat, ran his fingertips across the smooth tabletop. 'You've read the articles.'

'I haven't, actually.' He walked over to the standing desk in the corner and transferred a small box onto the table. 'Your name has come up several times in the Crawley files.' He popped the top button on his waistcoat and took a seat.

'Any progress at all?' said Sawyer.

Whatley grimaced, shook his head. 'It's your gaffer's gig. We've been mainly investigating the abscondment. But now, of course, there's a complication that falls under your jurisdiction.'

'A complication,' said Sawyer. 'You mean kidnap?'

'So it would seem. Dale Strickland's wife. Mr Strickland detained me for quite a lengthy phone call the other day. Insisted I speak to you. Is he Greater Manchester Mayor now?'

'Not yet.'

Whatley placed his weighty hands on the table. 'Any movement on the kidnap?'

'A couple of lines. He sent us a photo of Eva Gregory, the victim, yesterday.'

'Forensics?'

'Clean.'

Whatley nodded, pondering. 'Any demands?'

'It's not that kind of kidnap.'

'What kind is it?'

Sawyer looked over his shoulder, through the window to the open-plan office with partitioned desks. 'Crawley has a beef with Strickland. He blames him for his mother's death. A few years ago, he murdered three people he thought were connected. Kidnapped Strickland's son. I made the arrest.'

'He wasn't harmed himself?'

Sawyer turned back. 'No. How is DI McBride doing?'

'Sonia? You know her?'

'We worked together on the David Bowman case.'

'Of course.' Whatley just about managed a smile. 'She's a capable detective. That was a tough case for her, emotionally. And for you, too, I imagine.'

Sawyer looked past Whatley, through the window. 'You imagine right.'

'An unfortunate outcome.'

Sawyer held his eye. 'For Bowman, yes.'

'Perhaps unfortunate is the wrong word. Regrettable.'

'In what sense?'

Whatley clasped his hands together. 'Any case that ends with the suspect's death is hardly a great advert for justice. And there's not a lot we can learn to prevent similar offences in the future.'

'Bowman hasn't murdered anyone since.'

A warmer smile this time. Whatley held up his hands. 'No judgement, Detective Sawyer. I'm aware of the extraordinary circumstances.'

'Have you had any sightings of Crawley? Near the hospital he escaped from? Rural areas?'

'None. Hard to imagine him choosing to hide out in Nottinghamshire, though.'

'Why?'

Whatley shrugged. 'Would you?'

'Are you not disposed to your jurisdiction?'

Whatley opened the box. 'I live in Loughborough. And anyway, Crawley is a Derbyshire man, right? Any sightings at his old haunts? Criminals on the run often gravitate to the familiar.'

'He has an uncle. James. We're watching his place and a few others.'

'You say Crawley blames Strickland for his mother's death?'

'He says Strickland assaulted and raped her in his presence. Crawley was thirteen. She was in a wheelchair. Paralysed from the waist down. She died two years later. Naturally, Crawley links the two events.'

'Jesus Christ.' Whatley looked up. 'Have you gone back a few years? Places he used to go with his mother, maybe. Anything there?'

'Yes, and no.'

Whatley sighed. He patted the box. 'This is everything since Crawley's time at Manchester. Take it away if you like. Files. Reports. Letters from crazies. A few personal effects from his original admission.'

Sawyer stood up. His phone buzzed with a call. He screened it and shoved the handset into his back pocket, then grappled with the box.

'Do you need any help with that?' said Whatley. He got up and opened the door for Sawyer.

'I'm fine.'

Sawyer backed out, turned.

Whatley rested his hand on the door handle, clearly itching to shut Sawyer out. 'Good luck with the case, Detective. I get the feeling you'll need it. Caught between Dennis Crawley and Dale Strickland.'

'I appreciate your time.'

Whatley pushed out his smile again. 'Short and sweet.'

'One out of two isn't bad.'

———

In the entrance corridor, Sawyer's back pocket buzzed. He set the box down on a side table and took the call.

'The plot thickens,' said Shepherd.

'Uncle Dylan?'

Shepherd spoke to someone in the background. His voice crackled for a moment, then smoothed out.

'Sorry, sir. Bad service here. What was that?'

'You've found something interesting on Uncle Dylan.'

A group of junior officers walked in from outside. Sawyer ducked into an alcove.

'No,' said Shepherd. 'But I think we can safely double down on a connection to the Brennan case.'

'Why's that?'

'Someone cut off Rory Burrows's head.'

22

Dale Strickland raised his thermos cup. 'You look like a man in need of caffeine.'

'I had my fill of it last night.' DCI Robin Farrell kept his eyes on the scenery outside the tinted window. 'Not the most thrilling stake-out I've endured.'

'But we have something, yes?'

'Absolutely.' Farrell tapped a breath mint from a canister and flicked it into his mouth. He reclined into the padded back seat and surveyed the car interior. 'This your new toy, then? What happened to the Merc?'

'I still have that. It's with my associates back home. This is more for me. It's a Tesla Model S with a performance upgrade.'

Farrell shrugged. 'Befits your status. Not my thing.'

Strickland slurped his coffee through the spout. 'Too obvious?'

'Showy.'

'I'm a high-profile figure, Robin. I can't lurk in the shadows anymore.'

Farrell turned back to the window. 'That's my job.'

'Well, yes. Own it. Do you.'

Farrell winced. 'I took a long look at the place. It tallies with ANPR data on the reg you gave me. I mean, assuming the source of the reg was reliable, and we're not being led around by our nostrils as payback for someone you've pissed off.'

Strickland glared at him. 'It's reliable. Not cheap, either.' He browsed a folder of photographs: various angles of a one-storey cottage set back from a winding lane, backing onto lush woodland. The shots were grainy and artificially brightened, but serviceable. Strickland held one up to the window light, squinting. 'I don't think Rankin will have any worries, Robin.'

'Who?'

'Never mind. Tell me more about the car.'

'Olive green Ford Focus,' said Farrell. 'Stolen, of course, from a rural car park only a few miles from the ophthalmologist Crawley escaped from. I couldn't get CCTV without them knowing I was sniffing, but there's nothing in that area.'

'You're off the naughty step now, yes? They trust you with ANPR.'

Farrell sighed. 'It's a separate system. And, yes. The investigation has been dropped.'

'You're no longer suspended.'

'It wasn't a suspension.'

Strickland gave a knowing smile. 'But your GMP boss called you in, yes? And confirmed you're free to assume your DCI role officially.'

Farrell turned, eyeing him. 'He did.'

'You must have an angel watching over you, Robin.'

Farrell crunched on the breath mint. 'ANPR puts the car at your place in Bakewell on the day of Eva's abduction. He took a rustic route to get there, and then to this place.' He pointed at the photos. 'But not rustic enough.'

'Two minutes, boss.'

Strickland waved a hand. 'Thank you. Farouk Abadi, my new driver,' he said to Farrell.

The driver caught Farrell's eye in the rear-view mirror. He was suited, with a bushy moustache and black leather driving gloves.

Strickland slapped a palm onto the photos. 'So, whose house is this?'

'Victoria Kendal. Divorcee. Landscape gardener.'

'What's her connection to Crawley?'

Farrell shook his head. 'Late forties. Family friend? There might be no connection and it's a place he's staked out in the past.'

'And how is Ms Kendal's health?'

'Haven't got that far. You said you wanted to see the house first.' He cleared his throat. 'Don't take this the wrong way, Dale...'

Strickland raised an eyebrow. He took off his heavy-framed glasses, polished the lenses with his shirt cuff. 'Go on.'

'It looks like a multiple murderer has kidnapped your missus. You don't seem too eager to get her back.'

Strickland smiled. 'I agree with our mutual friend.'

'Who?'

'Mr Sawyer. He said that Crawley wants to torture

me. Not kill Eva. But you're right to be anxious. I would like to end this quickly now.'

'Coming up on the right, boss.'

Farrell pointed. 'Just over there. Get a look from here. If you turn right, you'll have to pass by close. This car will get noticed.'

'Just stop for a few seconds in the lay-by, Farouk,' said Strickland.

Abadi slowed and parked the Tesla at the side of the road. Strickland leaned forward and looked out of the right-hand windows at a house in the middle distance across the fields; clearly the one in the photos.

Abadi passed Strickland a small pair of binoculars; he replaced his glasses and studied the house.

'No cars. Blinds all down.'

Farrell sighed, nodding. 'I established this yesterday.'

'And you saw nobody coming or going?'

'No, Dale. I would have mentioned that by now.'

Strickland handed the binoculars back to Abadi. 'How does the ANPR data connect to this house?'

'Nothing else round here. And the route checks out. Next steps are to make a connection between Victoria Kendal and Crawley.'

'And to find out where that car has gone. Why it isn't here now.'

'It hasn't shown on ANPR for over a week.'

'He might have dumped it somewhere,' said Abadi. 'Or found a barn to hide it in. I wouldn't want to leave it parked outside in full view.'

Strickland grinned at Farrell. 'Drive on, Farouk. Let's head up to Manchester.'

He pulled out and drove away.

'Crawley has sent you a picture of Eva?' said Farrell.

'Using her Polaroid camera.'

'What does he have against you again?'

'He's delusional. A psychopath who thinks I had something to do with an assault on his mother when I was a teenager. He took my son a few years ago, and I suppose now I'm higher status, he's decided to have another go.'

'That was when Sawyer tracked him down, right?'

Strickland took a long drink of coffee. 'Right.'

Farrell ruffled his waxy black hair, smoothed it out again. 'Dale. Whatever you think, whatever Sawyer says, we need to go official on this. If Crawley is based here and he's taken Eva somewhere else, and he's sending you items to prove he has her... It shows he's thought this through. There's a plan in motion. Time is crucial. These things rarely have happy endings if you just let them play out. What are Keating's team doing? Is Sawyer involved?'

'He is. They're examining the picture of Eva. Sawyer is talking to Nottinghamshire detectives investigating Crawley's abscondment.'

Farrell kept his eyes on Strickland. 'We can't just storm into that place back there, Dale. We need resource on it. Covert surveillance. In case he comes back with the car. We need to build an idea of what we might find. If we go official, we can use professional negotiators. Technology. Thermal imaging—'

'Robin. Are you not a high-ranking detective?'

'Yes.'

'Well, then. We *are* "official". I'm using the resources

148

available to me. You're a part of that. And I'll make sure your cooperation doesn't go unrewarded. When I take the mayor role officially, I'll be looking for someone to oversee a northern police hub. Incorporating Nottinghamshire, Yorkshire. Derbyshire.'

Farrell glanced at the driver, catching another unfriendly glare in the rear-view mirror. 'So, let me run it all. I can share the car info with GMP colleagues. We can back-channel it. Resolve it without Keating, if you're looking for a political score.'

'That doesn't work. You and I have too much crossover. I'd rather we kept it private and personal. I'll make sure you get your share of the glory. And in case you're in any doubt, the reboot of your professional reputation didn't happen out of the goodness of your DSI's heart. I'll have my men investigate the house more closely later.'

Farrell turned back to the window.

Strickland slid the folder over to Farrell. 'I know what you're thinking, Robin. Law. Order. I'm sure you know your Aristotle. Good law is good order. All that.'

'Yes. But you can't be selective about which laws you follow. That's the path to chaos.'

Strickland slapped him on the shoulder. 'In the midst of chaos, there's opportunity.'

23

Sawyer ducked inside the forensic tent.

He nodded to Sally O'Callaghan, propped on a trestle table near the entrance, and took out a mini pocket torch.

He crouched by the man's severed head and aimed the beam around the cheeks and jaw, then lifted the hair away and studied the section of neck, then the scalp. Finally, he trained the light on the eyes: half-open, eyelids webbed with blood.

'Clean.' Sawyer stood up, turned to Shepherd. 'No hacking. No missed blows.'

Shepherd nodded. 'Efficient. Can't assume historical skill, though.'

'There's no sign of abrasions in the neck flesh. One slice and off. Surely an axe or heavy sword. But we need Drummond to confirm.'

'It's Rory Burrows,' said O'Callaghan. 'His body's in the bushes nearby.'

Rain rattled against the canvas.

They stood there for a moment, gazing down at the head, resting in a small recess of earth.

O'Callaghan twirled a pen in her fingers. 'Well, this is cosy.'

'The killer hid the body but not the head,' said Sawyer.

'We're lucky the walker saw it before his dog,' said Shepherd. 'It was out in the open. No attempt to cover it.'

O'Callaghan started to pack her kit bag. 'We pulled a few fibres from one ear. Might give us something. The rain has fucked us on tracks, though. And Bamford Edge is well trodden.'

'Fast-track PM,' said Shepherd. 'Keating wants a gathering later.'

Sawyer kept his eyes on the head. 'He hides one thing, displays another. That should tell us something. Maybe there's shame about the body, about the overall kill, but triumph about the head. The face.'

'Not much to display with Cunliffe,' said O'Callaghan. 'Charred remains.'

'Is he communicating something?' said Shepherd.

Sawyer turned, walked to the tent opening. 'If I were Damon Morris or Jared White, that's how I'd take it.'

'Do you want to see the body?' said O'Callaghan. 'It's intact.'

'I'll pick it up with Drummond.'

He ducked outside, followed by Shepherd.

They walked to the ridge footpath and sheltered from the rain under a pop-up awning at the back of the Scientific Services unit van. The signature view down to

Ladybower Reservoir, with the submerged arches of the Ashopton Viaduct, was greyed out by the rain, but still postcard perfect.

'I used to bring my niece up here,' said Shepherd.

'I have a vague memory of coming with my mum and dad. I wanted to stand on the rock but they wouldn't let me.'

Shepherd did a double take. 'You mean the Instagram cliché? On the overhang?'

Sawyer nodded. 'So, why display the head but not the body? Why here?'

'Not exactly easy to get up to this spot.'

Bleating from behind. They turned in unison.

Two black-and-white-faced sheep trotted along the far side of the footpath.

'Derbyshire Gritstone,' said Shepherd. 'Markings on their faces like Rorschach tests.'

They turned back.

'Here's a question,' said Sawyer. 'At what point does a decapitated animal stop being alive and start being dead?'

'Jesus. Sir. Can we do this over coffee?'

'Is it the moment the heart stops beating?'

'That's usually terminal, yeah.'

Sawyer shook his head. 'Hearts can be restarted. CPR. Lazarus syndrome.'

'Is that a sci-fi film?'

'It's real. So, how about brain death?'

'Well. The heart feeds the brain with oxygen, so I suppose there's still oxygen in the brain when the heart stops. Not for long, though.'

'So. Brain stem death?'

Shepherd squeezed his eyes closed, opened them again. 'Is this a test?'

'I was reading about it after speaking to Maggie's doctor. When someone is on life support, they can show signs of being alive, even when the brain stem is technically dead. They have clinical tests to declare brain stem death, which gives the legal green-light to withdraw life support. But the tests are pretty rough. Stroking the eye with a tissue. Pinching the nose. Feeding ice-cold water into the ears. But you can also keep a body alive, even though the brain stem is dead. Even if the head is severed.'

Shepherd scoffed. 'Yeah. In the *Saw* films or something.'

Sawyer's eyes flashed. 'No. It's technically possible. Ethically questionable.'

'Just a bit.'

'In the nineties, two American scientists beheaded a sheep that was about to give birth to a lamb. Then they connected the headless body to a breathing machine with a tube plugged in to its severed neck. Soon after, they performed a caesarean section and the headless body gave birth to a baby lamb. Now motherless.'

Shepherd gulped in a deep breath. 'And how is this going to help me sleep?'

'The point is, the scientists argued that a headless body isn't necessarily dead. Or, to put it another way, we have ways of keeping a headless body alive, so decapitation doesn't have to mean body death.'

Shepherd turned to him slowly. 'You've been

spending too much time with Drummond.' He checked his phone. 'Keating wants a midday briefing.'

'Double down on the Brennan family. Either this is directly related to Thomas Brennan's murder, or his killers have fallen out with each other or someone else during their time inside. One out of four could be unrelated. Two out of four is a trend. Get protection on Morris and White. And I want to talk to them both. I have a hospital appointment. You go see White straight after this. But we should both talk to Morris before the briefing.'

'Why?'

'The trolling of the Brennan family. The threats. The way the sisters were repulsed by the mere mention of him.'

The rain had eased. Sawyer walked out of the awning, closer to the drop at the edge of the ridge. Shepherd followed, but stayed further back.

'So, what about the locations?' said Shepherd. 'Touristy spots.'

'We can speculate. But let's dig deeper into the Brennan angle first. And see if Drummond and Sally come up with anything on Burrows.'

Sawyer turned back to the view. 'Burning. Beheading.'

'I know. What next? Boiling oil? It's all so medieval.'

'Or biblical.'

24

Laura Brennan settled herself in the confessional booth. The priest shifted in his seat opposite, obscured in partial shadow behind the latticed partition.

She closed her eyes, took a few breaths.

'In the name of the Father, and of the Son, and of the Holy Spirit. Amen.' She opened her eyes. The priest's outline was still, and he sat with his head bowed. 'Bless me, Father, for I have sinned. It is many days since my last confession. I've done a terrible wrong, Father. It is a terrible wrong in the name of the Lord. I believed it to be directed by His hand, but now... I have doubt. I have great shame, Father. So great that I have struggled to come to confession.'

The priest sniffed. 'Please. Take your time. As our Holy Father once said, confession is difficult and delicate. It is also exhausting and demanding, but one of the most beautiful and consoling ministries of the priest.'

Laura knitted her fingers together, flexing and unflexing.

'Father, it is difficult for me because I believe I have acted on the will of the Lord. In my heart, I know it is wrong. But if the will of God compels me... Am I not a mere vessel?'

The priest flattened his voice, keeping it soft but firm. 'This is a common source of struggle. How we can reconcile our human frailties and temptations with our service to the Lord. It is often difficult to connect our service to the spiritual realm with the reality we experience in our daily lives. Have you sought counsel from others?'

'No!' She hissed it out, gathered herself. 'No, I have not. This is a private struggle, Father.'

The priest paused. 'You have done the right thing in coming here today. The sacrament is an instrument of grace and forgiveness. I'm sure you're not alone in your struggle. But you will receive God's love, mercy and grace.'

'Father... Can the Lord speak through the actions of his believers? Does he really communicate directly with us?'

'I have no doubt. And we communicate directly with him through prayer.' His seat creaked as he shifted again. Something glinted through the partition, reflecting the booth light. 'Can you tell me more about your "terrible wrong"?'

'It's my mother... A conflict over honouring her wishes. She was a dedicated servant. I would say that she devoted her life to God. And now she has joined my father in eternal rest.'

The priest shuffled closer to the partition. 'We all wish to honour our Earthly parents. The sacrament is a process. You are here today because you are experiencing the first part of that. Contrition. And in being here, you are enacting the second part. Confession.' He raised his head. 'Your presence is testament to God's love. He has sent you to me. And, as I'm sure you know, you sit here, not confessing to a priest, but to God himself. Only God has the power to take you to the next step. Absolution. This is where you will be restored and renewed by his gift of sanctifying grace. You entered this booth a sinner. You will leave it absolved of your sins, and given the grace to repent. To heal the wound caused by the sin.'

'But how will I achieve true contrition?'

He paused again. 'Do you fear punishment?'

'Yes.'

'The sacrament exists to ease that fear. Once you have completed the process, you will realise that true contrition means to recognise that you have displeased the one who loves you. That is the moment you receive forgiveness.'

Laura looked down at her hands, patterned by shadow from the partition.

Flex, unflex.

The priest continued. 'And if you feel unsure about whether you can achieve God's forgiveness, then consider your mother. If your "wrong" is to honour her, and she was, as you say, a devoted servant, then surely God is repaying her service by directing your actions. And you should stand firm with your faith. With *her* faith.

Because, although you may worry that your actions are questionable in the Earthly realm...' He leaned forward, peering through the partition. 'God is with you.'

25

Kevin Tsong pivoted his monitor, displaying the image to Sawyer: his brain, as rendered by MRI. Mint blue on black, with a highlighted section glowing slightly brighter than the rest.

'The schwannoma is stable,' said Tsong, putting on his silver-rimmed glasses. 'I'm confident we can move to bi-yearly checks, if you continue to be asymptomatic.' He wheeled his chair to a side desk and pulled a pen from a drawer. 'Any advance on the dry skin?'

'Comes and goes. Usually in the same areas. Little patches.'

Tsong looked up. 'Well. I'm sorry to have to break it to you, Mr Sawyer, but you're not as rare as we suspected. We've had fewer than three hundred cases of Urbach-Wiethe disease, and I don't think we can add you to the roster. It sounds like you have a touch of common or garden eczema. Or maybe plaque psoriasis. Both have connections to stress. The skin is the largest organ, and internal pressures often manifest outwardly.' He laid out a document, clicked his pen. 'Bear with me a moment.'

Sawyer looked over Tsong's showroom-tidy desk. Wood polished to a shine. Grey phone. Black keyboard. Blue-and-white *Mr. Grumpy* mug. A stack of books: *The Secret Barrister*, *And Finally* and a biography of Alan Turing.

Tsong smiled as he wrote. 'I sense I'm being assessed, Mr Sawyer. Or can you turn your detective side off?'

'Oh, no. It's a shadow. Always with me.'

'And what do you see? Be frank. I'm fascinated by your work. I'm a big fan of crime drama. Particularly the Scandinavian shows.'

Sawyer nodded to a black doctor's bag on the floor beneath the window. 'The side pocket of your bag is unzipped, with papers sticking out.'

Tsong smiled and turned back to Sawyer. 'Go on.'

'But I would happily eat dinner off your desk. Either you don't use this office often enough to make it messy, or the bag is against type. I know you practice in several places, so I'd go for the former. You probably share with others. Rotate schedules. That's backed up by the lack of personal touches. The muted colours may be part of that, but as you're the senior clinician here, you would have the strongest say in the decor, and the fact that you've chosen to avoid strong primaries suggests you were raised in an atmosphere of utilitarian simplicity. Perhaps there's a cultural connection there, given your surname. The Turing book makes me wonder if you might be gay, but the *Mr. Men* mug suggests children. Or at least a healthy relationship with a gay partner.'

Tsong beamed at him. 'I'm going to give you three out of five. You're spot on with the office details, but I'm not gay. I just have an interest in computer science. And the mug was a Secret Santa from the hospital I used to work at.'

'I'll do better. Although I do have an excuse at the moment. I'm recovering from a traumatic brain injury.'

'I was going to ask about that. I can see from your record that you were treated at the Salford neuroscience centre recently. What happened?'

'Armed men attacked the station I work at. We're still trying to establish the reason. I was caught in an explosion.'

'Good grief.'

'Could have been much worse.'

Tsong looked through a few papers. 'Are you on pain medication?'

'Not officially.'

Tsong raised an eyebrow. 'Are you suffering after-effects?'

'Nothing I'm not used to.'

Tsong set down his pen. 'In what sense?'

'Flashbacks. Sleeplessness. Impulse control. Anger.'

'In our previous consultation, you mentioned this sense of detachment. Also, hallucinations.'

Sawyer's eyes drifted. 'All of that. Much worse.'

'As I've said before, I'm not a psychologist. Have you consulted any therapists?'

'Yes. Some insight. No real progress.'

Tsong frowned. 'Mr Sawyer. I fear we have reached the limit of how much I can assess you physically. You clearly have a keen analytical mind, but unless you resolve this deeper trauma, your inner life will remain complex and corrosive. Try to see yourself as one of your cases. A puzzle in your own right.'

'The unexamined life is not worth living.'

'Indeed. Our friend Socrates was fascinated by the human condition. Employ his methods on yourself. In a constructive way.' He paused. 'If you're self-prescribing painkillers, then you're entering a rather dark realm. You may compound your troubles rather than easing them.' He caught himself, turned back to the document. 'Please forgive the lecture. But I've seen many patients in similar positions who have tried to wrestle with this business alone.' He folded the paper and handed it to Sawyer. 'Stronger hallucinations. That's concerning.'

'It's mostly my mother. We talk. I know I'm really talking to myself. But it's so vivid. And it's a comfort. She feels as real and present as you do now.'

Tsong held the moment. 'Do you have auditory hallucinations? Negative voices, saying you're unworthy or pointless? Urging you to harm yourself?'

'I have those thoughts. But I don't have schizophrenia.'

Tsong took a sharp breath. 'I hope you can find some comfort, Mr Sawyer. Please follow my advice. There are many wonderful trauma counsellors.' He reached out and shook hands with Sawyer, placing his other hand on top. 'You don't have to fight your own way through this. You don't have to live in fear.'

Sawyer fixed his gaze on Tsong. 'I don't feel fear. I don't feel much of anything.'

26

Curtis Mavers squinted through the door peephole.

A short, slender man in dark glasses stood a few feet back with his head bowed. Decent suit. No tie, but sharp shirt. Early forties. Thinning on top.

'Not today, thanks.'

The man raised his head. 'I come bearing gifts, Mr Mavers.' He smiled up at the peephole.

Mavers cocked the silenced Glock, held it at his hip, and opened the door.

He stepped around, away from the frame.

'Step in, lad.'

The man walked through into the flat, and Mavers closed the door behind him.

He set down a small brown briefcase and took off his glasses.

Stern eyes; just the right side of hostile.

Conciliatory smile.

'Do you mind if we do this face to face? Without recourse for insurance.'

Posh, but not high born. Faint northern twang.

'Let's see how it goes.' Mavers prodded the gun towards the sofa. 'Park your arse. Turn and face me. Case by your side.'

The man complied.

'I'm Lawrence Crutchley. A mutual friend sent me.'

'Acquaintance.'

Crutchley smiled. 'Of course. I've been given specific instructions, and I can assure you, there's no ruse.'

Mavers pushed a pizza box off a chair and sat facing Crutchley, keeping the gun low.

'I'm getting the feeling I've gone up a few pay grades, Lawrence.'

Crutchley nodded. 'Our acquaintance couldn't be here today, and for that he sends his regret. I've known him for a good few years. We met in prison.'

Mavers spluttered a laugh and grimaced, clutching his arm. 'You from the parole board?'

'I forged a will. Well, I forged many things successfully before that. But I was caught forging a will.' He opened the case. 'Five years.'

He took out a padded brown package, cleared a space between the mugs and glasses on the coffee table, and emptied out the contents, item by item.

'Fake passport. Exemplary quality. UV proof. Optical variation. Intaglio ink. Securely printed. Watermarked. To call it a forgery would be a gross insult. It's better than the real thing.' He tapped a second document. 'Work visa. Again, highly legitimate. You're an engineering contractor, Curtis. In Jamaica for six months, overseeing specialist maintenance work.' Crutchley pointed to a plastic card. 'Debit. PIN details inside. To memorise, naturally. Bank of America. You'll be met at Montego Bay airport by a local chap called Mr. Spence. He'll take you along the coast to a small town called Fairy Hill.' He winced. 'Sorry about that. Beautiful place, though. There's a cabin there for you. A local contact will look after you for a couple of weeks while you settle yourself. I'm told you can leave the house and have your toes in white sand within two minutes. After that, there's a place for you down south. In Heartease, near Mandeville.'

'That's where my dad was born.'

Crutchley smiled. 'Spiritual homeland.'

Mavers shuffled the chair closer to the coffee table. He raised the Glock and slowly lifted the barrel to Crutchley's forehead. 'When?'

Crutchley kept his cool, with the slightest hint of irritation. 'Tomorrow. Plane ticket is in the package. Civilised afternoon flight from Heathrow. Business class. Eight and a half hours later, you'll never see another Betfred or Poundland again.'

Mavers nudged the Glock barrel into Crutchley's forehead.

The man sighed. 'As I said, Curtis, this is no ruse. Check your account later. There are details for online login. You have enough money in there to lie on the beach until next Christmas. Cabin rental is covered for as long as you need it. After that, our acquaintance has contacts to keep you honest.'

Mavers reached out with his free hand and flicked through the passport and visa. He held Crutchley's eye. 'You're a liar, Lawrence.'

For the first time, Crutchley showed a flicker of concern. 'No. I can assure you—'

'A professional liar. You just told me.'

Crutchley shook his head carefully. 'Just documents. Forgery. This arrangement is legitimate. Our acquaintance is planning to restart his life. He accepts that he's made his mistakes. As have you. This is a chance to turn a toxic past into a healthy future.' He leaned forward, pressing his skull into the gun barrel. 'Nothing personal. But he wants you far away. A clean exit. He's grateful for your work, and your help in the search for Ms Gregory.' He glanced down at Mavers's bandaged arm. 'You've suffered, Curtis. Physical disfigurement. Emotional torment. This is where you replace the pain with pleasure.' He paused, averted his gaze. 'Jayne never got a second chance. She would want this for you.'

Mavers lowered the gun, let his head drop.

Crutchley kept silent for a few moments, then closed the case and got to his feet. 'Pack your toothbrush. You're going home.'

27

Damon Morris opened the front door and stepped out onto the porch, then backed into the doorway, sheltering from the rain. He was tall and scrawny; all elbows and knees in baggy T-shirt and boxers. Sawyer and Shepherd could have comfortably sidestepped past him on either side.

'Oh, here we go.' He sniffed the air. 'I can smell pork.'

They showed their warrant cards; Morris kept his frozen sneer on their faces. He was over-tanned and shaven headed, with a scruffy black goatee flecked with grey. He passed a large smartphone from one hand to the other, twirling it with each pass.

'Damon, this is Detective Inspector Jake Sawyer. I'm Detective Inspector Ed Shepherd.'

Morris hissed a laugh. 'Fuck me. A bin-dipper. Shouldn't you be lifting the local hubcaps? Listen. I've already had you lot mithering me. I don't want your protection, yeah? I learned one thing inside. Look after number one, yeah?' He jabbed a finger into his own chest. 'You fuckers put me away for fifteen years. Why should I trust you to look after me now?'

'You murdered a man, Damon,' said Sawyer. 'I assume you're aware that's illegal.'

Morris stared Sawyer down. 'Didn't mean to kill him.' He shrugged. 'He started on us. Posh twat. We were just messing about.'

Shepherd brushed the rain off the top of his head. 'Damon, we have a couple of questions about your co-defendants. Do you mind if we come in? It would make this a lot easier.'

'For you. I'm alright under here. Nice and dry, yeah? Look. I've had fuck-all to do with the other three since I went away. Now I find out someone's topped one of 'em.'

'Two,' said Sawyer. 'How does that make you feel?'

'Can't say I'm arsed. Like I say, I didn't even know they were still alive. So... No loss.' Morris grinned, baring a mouthful of stained teeth. 'State of you pair. Didn't you bring umbrellas?'

'We assumed you'd be a half-decent human being and let us come in.' Sawyer smiled back. 'We assumed wrong.'

Morris hissed a laugh through his teeth. 'Hey.' He patted Shepherd on the lapel. 'Why don't you give it the old, "we can do this the easy way or the hard way?" line? I love that.'

'Jermaine Cunliffe was burned alive,' said Sawyer.

'Was he bollocks!'

'Rory Burrows was beheaded.'

Morris pondered, nodding.

'Did you kill them, Damon?' said Shepherd.

The laugh again. ''Kin 'ell. You're not interrogating me on my own doorstep, are you? I might have to put in a complaint, yeah?'

Sawyer hitched a thumb over his shoulder. 'Would you rather we arrest you?'

'You seriously think I murdered them two?'

'No,' said Sawyer. 'But I washed my hair this morning.'

'Listen. I've been banged up half my life with some seriously nasty bastards. You're not going to shit me up with a few threats.'

Sawyer puffed the rainwater from his nose. 'You're a fan of threats, aren't you?'

'Eh?'

'You've sent them to the Brennan family.'

Morris laughed. He took out a cigarette and lit it. 'Nah. I didn't send threats. I'm not that stupid.' He took a puff. 'Just a bit of abuse. That interfering twat put me in prison. It was only fair his family got some shit in return.'

'Wasn't the murder enough for you?' said Shepherd. 'Depriving them of a husband. A father.'

Morris rolled his head round his neck. ''Kin 'ell. I've done all this with the counsellors and parole board. I thought you was coppers, not social workers.'

'*Cancer bitch*,' said Sawyer.

Morris smiled, sheepish. 'Good one.'

'Did that make you feel better? Mocking the widow of a man you've kicked to death?'

Morris leaned forward and puffed a mouthful of smoke in Sawyer's face. He widened his eyes. 'Yeah.'

Sawyer grabbed Morris by the throat and pushed him into the door frame, holding his mouth close to his ear.

'He was choking on his own *fucking* blood.' He sprayed rainwater as he spoke. 'The blood you'd beaten out of him. One of his daughters had to shove her fingers into his mouth to help him breathe.'

Shepherd put a hand on Sawyer's shoulder, but he shrugged it off. Morris writhed, but Sawyer tightened his grip on his throat, making him gag and flail his arms.

'*Imagine it.* Watching your own father die. And you can't do anything to stop it.' Sawyer released Morris, shoving him back into the hallway. 'You're not worth protecting.'

Morris stumbled, holding his throat. He crouched with his back to the door, coughing and retching. When he'd finally got his breath back, he turned to face Sawyer, smiling, showing the teeth again.

'Wow. My friend. You are in the wrong fuckin' job if this is how this shit gets you.'

———

They spent the first ten minutes of the drive back to the station in silence. As Sawyer stopped at a T-junction outside Saltersford, Shepherd ducked down to look across at the isolated building on the corner: an ancient-looking farmhouse with an adjoining tower.

'I was reading about this place. Jenkin Chapel. Looks like a cottage or something, but it's actually a church.

Built by locals in the 1700s. Mad to think that George the bloody second was on the throne when they started worshipping here.'

Sawyer moved off, turning onto the Buxton road. 'You think I returned to work too early.'

Shepherd sat back. 'It had crossed my mind.'

Sawyer glanced at him. 'Are you going to report it?'

'I'm obliged to, but we've got enough to worry about. Horrible little bastard.'

'Still common assault, though.' He winced. 'I can still smell his breath.'

'Can you describe it in a word?'

Sawyer thought for a moment. 'Feculent.'

'Delightful. If Morris complains, I'll have to witness. But I'll back you.'

'What about Jared White? Was he any less odious?'

'He was quiet. Seemed a bit damaged, really. Happy to accept temporary surveillance, but we'll need to go further up the chain for long term.'

The rain ramped up; Sawyer flicked on the wipers.

'All eyes on victimology. We have to call it as some kind of delayed revenge for the Brennan murder. I'd almost say he's the first victim of this case, with Cunliffe and Burrows two and three. We need to urgently speak to the uncle, Dylan, and Leith, Brennan's teacher friend.'

Shepherd nodded. 'I also want to know more about Brennan himself. Maybe he wasn't such a squeaky clean, God-fearing pillar of the community. That's what they thought about BTK, you know.'

'Is this your staple reading diet? Country churches and serial killers?'

171

'More local history than churches in particular.'

'Lots of that in this case.'

'What?'

'Time. Ancient history. Plenty of years between the Brennan killing and now. But memories can be long.'

Shepherd rubbed his eyes. 'And someone is in no mood to forget.'

'Or forgive.'

28

Keating burst into the conference room.

'Two victims relating to the Thomas Brennan murder in 2007. Even though that case is closed, it has to be our focus now. What do we make of Cunliffe and Burrows murdered so close together?'

'It might be over,' said Sawyer. 'Just those two. The killer had to wait for Cunliffe to get out before he did them both. Maybe he was worried about the Burrows killing getting back to him inside.'

Keating crashed down in his seat. 'Mights and maybes, Detective Sawyer. I'll add one of my own. Maybe it isn't over, and the other two Brennan killers are next. Which suggests someone connected to Brennan. Have we rooted round deeply enough in family connections? Friends? Links back to his roots... where was it?'

'Kilkenny,' said Walker. 'I've checked out both vics. Cunliffe's aunt tells a story of him wanting to start again in restaurant management. He'd made a contact through his uncle, and that seemed to be happening. Burrows was a junkie when he was convicted. Cleaned up inside. Model prisoner. Completed two OU courses. He wanted to work with addicts in prison. He'd been volunteering at a Sheffield rehab centre.'

'Doesn't exactly sound like they were on the road to recidivism,' said DC Myers. 'What were Burrows's OU degrees?'

Walker checked his notes. 'People, Work and Society. And...' He looked up. 'Criminology and Psychology.'

'Last movements?' said Sawyer.

'Burrows lived alone. Flat on the High Peak estate. Part-time job at the local Tesco Extra. Manager there said he was his best employee, and he could see him going a long way. I suppose he was still young. Thirty-two.'

Sawyer pulled up the crime scene photos on his touch screen. Cunliffe's scorched and curled-up corpse. Burrows's head, resting on the grass, as if his body were buried beneath.

Keating nodded to Sally O'Callaghan.

'Not much,' she said. 'Not a scrap of trace evidence. Tyre tracks at the Cunliffe scene are retreads, which you usually find on trucks. But the wheel base, turning radius and track width indicates something smaller. Probably a van. You often find cheap retreads on transits. No way to narrow it down further, though. There's similar up at the Edge, but the weather made it impossible to compare, and there are hundreds of other tracks mashed up.'

'That's a fuck-ton of ANPR cross-ref,' said Myers.

O'Callaghan smiled. 'Appreciate the insight. We also have fibres from Burrows's head. Carpet. From the killer's shoes or boots, I'd say. According to Drummond's prelim, one of his cheekbones was broken. Also his jaw, nose, left arm and both legs. Blunt trauma for the limb breaks. No similar fibres there, though. Drummond is going with some kind of club or maybe an axe handle.'

'Did he use an axe to cut off the head?' said Shepherd.

'Looks that way. Or a heavy cleaver. Only one strike, and a clean slice. Drummond suggests the facial damage was the killer knocking Burrows unconscious before the beheading. Easier to hit a stationary target, I suppose. Nothing unusual in the carpet fibres. I could match, but we'd need a sample. Oh, and the chromatography shows the accelerant used to burn Cunliffe was kerosene. Safer and less volatile than petrol. Non-flammable vapours and no feasible way to track its source. You can get it at garages.'

'House to house,' said Keating. 'Estates near to both scenes. Also near both vics' homes and last movements. Restrict ANPR to twenty-four hours before TOD. Filter out the vans and pick-ups. Might help us connect a suspect. Once we have one.'

'Which way was he facing?' said Sawyer.

Shepherd looked over. 'Who?'

'Burrows. The head. Which way was it facing?'

'Hold on,' said O'Callaghan. 'I have some photos before we set up the tent.' She swiped through her touchscreen. 'Roughly northwest. Why?'

'So, in the direction of the aqueduct?'

O'Callaghan looked again. 'Yes.'

Sawyer nodded, looked up from his screen. 'Two carefully planned killings in two days. If he's working through the Brennan killers, maybe the van or truck is rented. Cross-check local rental details of relevant vehicles. Filter against records, Irish background, Irish family connection. The Brennan daughters said they have an uncle, Dylan, who was notably angry at his brother's funeral.'

'Chasing,' said Walker. 'No joy. He moved to Cork a few years ago. No answer from the number I got. I left a message, saying I was an old friend of his brother's.'

'I'll get on to the Garda in Cork,' said Keating. 'I know the Chief Super there. Byrne. He's a prick, but if we can get an arrest, we can check phone records. What about local connections here? The Brennans were big in the Catholic community around their home.'

'We could drop in on their preferred place of worship,' said Shepherd. 'Church of All Saints in Hassop. There's also one of Thomas's close teacher friends. Kieran Leith. The daughters said he might know about links to the Brennan family.'

Keating noted something in a pad. 'Low priority. Let's eliminate the uncle first, then try for lateral lines with the teacher friend. How about ex-pupils at Brennan's school? Any standouts? Maybe some old loyalties that have been biding their time?'

'Done lots of work on that, sir,' said Walker. 'Nothing jumping out in terms of cross-reffed records. Maybe Leith can help us with that. I'm also checking the killers' time inside. Prisoners they shared cells with, or who might have links to the Brennans.'

Keating massaged his forehead, screwed his eyes closed. 'Where are we with the two remaining Brennan killers? White and Morris.'

Shepherd glanced at Sawyer. 'Real and immediate danger. Delivered the Osman warnings and wrote them up in HOLMES. We had to tell them about the context of the threat, but didn't share unsanitised intelligence.'

'Personal alarms?'

'White took one, but Morris wasn't interested. White was okay to have an officer posted. Morris refused.'

Keating shook his head. 'Mark calls from his address as urgent. We can't do any more. I don't have the resource to put him on round-the-clock watch.'

'Gotta say,' said Walker, 'there's a big fat elephant in the room.'

'We're assuming the same killer,' said Sawyer. 'We're assuming the Brennan link.'

'Indeed. We're sketching out a path and looking for ways to pave it. The methods of both murders are wildly different.'

Sawyer turned to Walker. 'Maybe that's the idea. But the connection is too strong to ignore. We'll confirm the link by establishing motive. What is he getting out of the murders? And it will be a he. Both are linked by control and power.'

'And planning,' said Walker.

'Exactly. He killed Burrows off-site somewhere and transported him to the scene. He killed Cunliffe at Kinder Wood, after subduing and transporting him. This is well planned, precisely executed. It's someone confident, maybe even arrogant. He's probably done something similar before. We know he can wield an axe. He's strong enough to carry bodies. Let's get support staff doing work into similar crimes and get them busy with the van ANPR and rental checks. And we really need to talk to Uncle Dylan.'

Keating nodded. 'We also have movement in the Eva Gregory case. Someone, presumably Dennis Crawley, sent Dale Strickland a Polaroid photo of Eva. She looks well, but there's no way to tell when it was taken.'

'No demands?' said Myers.

'And no forensics.'

'I have a box of his stuff,' said Sawyer. 'Documents, correspondence. Mostly covering Crawley's time inside. Might be something there.'

'I've got a couple of new researchers,' said Walker. 'Could get them digging through it?'

Sawyer nodded. 'Have them focus on anyone who wrote to him and lives within reasonable distance of where he absconded. Even better if their home is remote. And we should run a conference.'

'Why?' said Keating.

'I don't think Crawley will kill Eva. This is more about seeing Strickland suffer. So, we should give him what he wants. Have Strickland make an emotional appeal for her safety. If he can. It might shake Crawley out.'

'But where does that end?' said Walker. 'Isn't that just pandering to him?'

Sawyer closed his eyes, paused for a moment, then

opened them again. 'Crawley has spent a lot of time planning this. His two goals are to enhance Strickland's pain, and to feel that his own pain is being acknowledged.' He glanced at Keating. 'A conference will cover both.'

29

Luka Gregory crouched low and clambered over the rubble of an old dry-stone wall. He lay prone on the rain-soaked earth behind a clump of trees, and studied the building. It looked more like a cabin than a house: one storey, with a grey slate roof and wooden door. A single white plastic chair sat on the small front porch beneath a pillared awning. A short path cut through a trimmed lawn out front, bordered with geometrically arranged beds of brightly coloured flowers. The windows were all obscured by dark blinds.

Luka took out his iPhone and checked the location of the tracker. The Tesla was on the M67, moving away from Manchester towards Derbyshire.

He crept closer to the side of the house, staying hidden in the undergrowth at the edge of the treeline. He slotted in his AirPods and grazed on a few podcasts and YouTube videos, killing time, eyes fixed on the house. After half an hour with no sign of anyone at home, he pushed himself upright, swished his hair from his eyes, and fitted a black balaclava over his head. He pulled on a pair of thin black football gloves and walked around to the back of the house, where he slipped a cheap wooden-handled folding knife from his back pocket, unfolding the blade.

Luka crouched by a raised door at the top of a small set of steps and tried the handle. It made a rusty crunching sound as he lowered it.

Locked.

He set down the knife and slid an oblong black box from a pocket inside his backpack. He took out a pair of kirby grips, bent one pin into a ninety-degree angle and slotted it into the keyhole, creating a makeshift handle. He slid the other pin in above the first and shifted it around, feeling for the tiny jaws that held the lock closed. After a few minutes, the lock clicked, and he tried the door handle again.

Luka eased the door open an inch and replaced the pins in his backpack.

He listened.

No noise or movement from inside.

He picked up the knife, slipped inside, and closed the door behind him, clicking the lock back into place.

The house was dark and smelt stale. Luka switched on his phone light and stepped through the short entrance hall into a compact kitchen with a white dining table in the centre. He swung the phone light around. The surfaces were clean, uncluttered.

He studied a wall-mounted corkboard by the fridge. Leaflets, business cards.

Futurescape: The UK's Leading Landscape Exhibition.

Gardens Illustrated Summer Show.

Hampton Court Palace Garden Festival.

He passed the phone light under the table, over the floor.

Two empty pet bowls on a large place mat; no sign of pets.

Luka walked through an open door into a low-ceilinged sitting room. Tall pot plants in the corners. Two-seater sofa. Armchair. Bookcases lined up across the back wall.

He paused, listening. Nothing but the ticking of a gold carriage clock at the side of the TV stand.

A glass vase of wilting flowers sat on a side table next to a TV remote and a neat pile of library books: PD James novel, biography of Capability Brown, a chunky illustrated encyclopaedia. He checked the dates; all were a couple of days overdue.

Luka paused again, holding his breath.

A metallic crunch from the back of the house.

He switched off the phone light and looked back through the sitting room door.

Someone was trying the back door handle.

He froze.

The door shook, rattling the frame.

Luka snatched up the TV remote and pressed the *STANDBY* button. The red light on the TV flashed green.

More noise from the back. The door shaking harder.

The screen lit up. Picture and volume: low but audible. Early evening game show. Unctuous host chatting to contestants.

Luka tossed the remote back on to the table and hurried through into the kitchen, across the hall. He turned to the front door.

A figure stood outside, distorted through the frosted glass.

The back door crashed open.

He ducked into the bedroom. Double bed. En suite. Back window, blinded. Possibly locked.

Bathroom. Small window set high in the wall, near an extractor fan.

A large patch of what looked like dried blood ran out from the bath, soaked into the bedroom carpet by the door.

Luka bit into his knuckles, muting the shock.

Heavy footsteps in the kitchen.

Chatter and laughter from the TV.

Luka looked under the bed; it was blocked with storage boxes and a bulky vacuum cleaner.

He dashed across to the far corner, behind the open door, out of view of the hall and sitting room.

He stood still, gripping the knife handle, his hand slick with sweat.

The footsteps moved through the kitchen and into the sitting room. They paused, then carried on into the hall and down towards the front door.

Now.

A bolt slid away at the front door.

Out through the back.

A male cough, from the back door, and a call. Foreign language.

The man at the front door replied, in a similar-sounding language, and clumped back down the hall into the kitchen.

Music from the TV. Adverts.

The men spoke, in the strange language, making no attempt to be quiet.

Luke dropped his head, trying to steady his thoughts, calm his breathing.

More dried blood, pooled around the foot of the bed.

The room lurched, and he rested a hand against the wall, grounding himself.

Footsteps as the men walked through into the sitting room.

Advert chatter from the TV.

Luka carefully poked his head around the edge of the door frame.

Both men stood at the sitting room side table, with their backs to the door. One barked a command at the other, and he picked up the remote and pointed it at the screen.

Using the sound from the TV as cover, Luka crept across the hall and into the sitting room. He sidestepped towards the adjoining door into the kitchen, a few feet from the men.

The room darkened as the TV switched off.

He made it through the adjoining door. The back door was a few feet away, and wide open.

One man turned, saw him, shouted.

The other switched on a torch.

Luka lunged for the back door, but clattered into the dining table and stumbled.

Strong hands gripped his shoulders and twisted him round.

His assailant was a hulking shadow in the torchlight. His shoulder-length hair whipped across as he wrestled to keep Luka still.

The other man stepped in and shone the torch in Luka's eyes. He grinned. 'There you are. What the fuck are you doing here?'

Luka wriggled against the man's grip, but he was too powerful. He lowered his head and butted him in the stomach. The man laughed. He grappled with Luka for a few seconds, then peeled him away with an impatient jerk, keeping a powerful grip on his forearm.

'We saw your light. Idiot.'

The second man crouched, gripped Luka under the chin. He had a thick black moustache. 'You got keys? You know who lives here?'

Luka shook his head.

'Then how the fuck did you get in?' said the first man.

The second man tightened his grip. He raised the torch above his head, aiming the beam down on Luka from above.

'Get the mask off,' said the first man.

Luka swiped the knife around, slashing him across his forearm. He yelped in pain and released Luka, who scurried to the back door, and sprinted out to the trees.

Shouts from behind, as both men pursued.

Luka made it to the adjacent road and leaned forward, ramping up the sprint.

He risked a look back, squinting through the dusk.

The men were slowing, giving up. They were too bulky to match his speed.

He ran for a few minutes, head down, until he reached the disused bus stop where he'd locked his bike.

Luka turned. If the men were still following, would he have time to unlock the bike and ride away?

But they had long gone, and he pulled off the mask and crouched by the bus stop, gasping.

He unlocked the bike, then switched on his phone light and held it to the knife blade. A faint smear of blood ran along the sharp edge.

Luka folded the knife and stashed it in his backpack. He pulled the moustached man's wallet from his back pocket and tossed it in after the knife. He zipped up the backpack and pedalled away.

30

Dale Strickland kept his head bowed for a moment. He sat at the wide beechwood table at the front of the old station conference room, flanked by Keating in full cap and uniform and Sawyer. A few of the journalists in the front seats stepped up and nudged their micro recorders and omni mics closer to him. A banner on the wall behind displayed the Derbyshire Constabulary insignia, along with a web address and phone number.

At the back, a line of branded TV cameras faced the action, while assorted old-schoolers lined the walls, notepads in hand. Stephen Bloom, the MIT media relations officer, stood off to the side, swiping at a mini tablet. He was tall, blond and leggy, in fitted business dress. He looked like a Nordic fashionista misdirected to a council coffee morning.

'Accustomed as I am to public speaking,' said Strickland, 'this is the toughest crowd I've yet faced.' He looked up, aiming his gaze above the heads of the observers. 'A few years ago, my son Luka was taken by the man I now believe has abducted my wife, Eva. Dennis Crawley. An old schoolfriend. As a result, Luka has suffered greatly, when he should be enjoying the unburdened pleasures of childhood. Luka is in terrible pain at the disappearance of his mother. Eva and I have had our difficulties over the years. But she is my wife, and she has stuck by me as I've rebuilt myself as a politician and campaigner. And now, I find myself in a state of terrible, constant panic at her absence. I appeal to the man who has control over Eva's fate...' He looked ahead, focusing on the largest TV camera. 'If your goal is to terrorise me, for whatever suffering you believe I inflicted on you in the past, then you have succeeded. But hurting Eva will not soothe you, or change what you believe has happened in the past. It will simply hurt a young boy who has only recently turned thirteen and has already suffered badly. So, I implore you...' He pushed his palms together, as if in prayer. 'For the sake of our son, please return Eva to us unharmed. Please do not let the past inflict further agony on an intelligent young boy with a bright future.' He averted his gaze and removed his glasses, settling himself. 'You have shown great fortitude, and strength, in taking Eva. I now ask you to show courage, in returning her to us, as we work on reconstructing ourselves as a family unit.' He patted a hand onto his heart. 'Meet with me. I will hear your complaint personally, so that we may find resolution. Maybe even redemption. If not, then you can easily just let her go, and live your own life. Make a friend, not an enemy, of your own future. *Please.*' His voice cracked. 'Eva is loving, giving. A beautiful person on the outside and inside...'

Strickland slumped forward, head down, shoulders shaking.

Cameras clicked.

Keating rested a hand on his shoulder. 'Thank you, Mr Strickland. I understand this must be incredibly difficult for you.' He turned to address the camera. 'To the man we believe is holding Eva, I say this. We have your personal effects taken from the institutions where you've been a guest in recent years. I would be willing to return everything, but that can obviously not happen while Eva continues to be away from her family. You can speak to me directly on the number on the banner behind. There is still time to turn back from this dark and dangerous road. It can all be done safely and anonymously. Equally, I would ask anyone with information on Eva's whereabouts to please call the Crimestoppers number. Again, all anonymous.'

Keating put his arm round Strickland's shoulders. More camera clicks.

'I'll take a couple of questions. But please be sensitive to Mr Strickland's presence.'

A hefty journalist in the front row raised a hand. Bloom nodded to him.

'Dean Logan. *Derbyshire Times*. Why now?'

'How do you mean?'

'Ms Gregory has been missing for over a week. Why have you only just got round to a public appeal?'

'We've been pursuing other lines. Now they're exhausted, we felt it right to—'

'Have you received contact from Crawley? Is that it? Is there now definite proof that he's the one behind this?'

'We believe he is, yes. But we obviously can't divulge specific intelligence at this stage.'

Logan nodded, doubtful. 'So why would he respond to this? You're not offering him anything.'

'Sorry, Dean. This isn't a negotiation. We're not entering some kind of trade here.'

'Has he made any demands?'

Keating side-eyed with Sawyer. 'We're not prepared to reveal that—'

'*At this stage*, yes,' said Logan. 'It's just... With every respect to you and to Mr Strickland, if I were Crawley, and I was watching this conference, I would take a lot of pleasure in Mr Strickland's pain. Then, everyone here is going to write it up, put out TV and radio packages... Crawley will see some of those. Again, enhancing his pleasure.'

'Is there a question, Dean?' said Keating.

'Yes. What's the point? Do you really believe that this is going to work? Appealing to the better nature of a man who's murdered three people, and now kidnapped two? He has something you want, but what do you have for him?'

Sawyer stood up. He reached into his pocket and laid something on the table, by the cluster of microphones.

A few photographers stepped forward and took shots of the object.

'This is an item taken from Mr Crawley during his original incarceration,' said Sawyer. 'It's his mother's tooth, set into a ring.' He looked down at Keating, who was glaring up at him, red faced. 'I've looked Dennis Crawley in the eye. I've spoken to him about the wrong he feels was done to his mother.' He leaned forward on the table, slapping down both his palms. 'I understand the agony of losing your mother to violence at an early age. How you would do anything to have her back. How you would treasure anything that could connect you to her. Particularly something that literally used to be part of her.'

Stephen Bloom hurried over, behind the line of chairs at the top table. He leaned in to Sawyer, whispering something, but Sawyer shrugged him away, and raised his eyes to the central camera.

'Dennis. You've achieved your goal. Dale and his son have suffered. But Eva is an innocent. She is not part of your complaint. Surely the last remaining evidence of your mother's existence is more important to you than a woman who just happens to be connected to a man who has done you wrong.'

He picked up the ring and held it above his head. Multiple flashes and camera clicks.

'Return Eva safely, and I promise I'll return your mother.'

———

Keating stomped into his office, waited for Sawyer to enter behind him, then slammed the door.

He walked across the room to his noticeboard, overloaded with pamphlets from crime victim funeral services. He paused, keeping his back to Sawyer.

'When will it be enough, Jake?'

'Sir?'

'Suspensions. Enquiries. Deaths. Injuries. Maimings.' He turned. 'All this fucking *drama*. Do you really need all this to keep you distracted?'

Sawyer took a couple of steps into the room. 'It might work. We don't have any other ideas. For all we know, Eva might already be dead.'

Keating slumped into his chair. 'It was a cheap stunt. We have to assume that Eva is still alive. And this might antagonise him further.'

'I know Crawley. He's a psychopath, and he's not interested in making Dale or Luka happy. He has no capacity to empathise.' Sawyer sat down. 'He's not interested in their pain, because he can't imagine it. He can't feel it. He feels nothing. Not for anyone else, at least. He believes Strickland brutalised his mother, punched her, knocked this tooth out.' He took out the ring, held it up again. 'That is the central event in his life. It's our key to getting him to do what we want. Sir. We can't appeal to his better nature, because he doesn't have one.'

Keating took off his cap, rolled it around the tips of his fingers. '*They fuck you up, your mum and dad*.'

Sawyer nodded. 'One of Larkin's greatest hits. The core of pretty much everyone we've ever put away.'

Keating waved a hand. 'They made their choices. You can't just be like a bloody local newspaper letter writer. Blaming the parents.'

'It's trauma. It infects. It poisons. It outlives individuals but passes down generations. It's hereditary.

And if we're going to help Eva, we need to understand Crawley's trauma.'

Keating sat back, sighed. 'I'm going to act on my trauma, after so many years of doing this job. I made plans last week.' He gave a pained smile. 'Early retirement.'

'Not that early. Sir.'

'Cheeky bastard. You'll miss me when I'm gone.'

'So, why now?'

'I'm not hanging around for Strickland's merger plans. You get to a certain vintage, and you just haven't got the energy for change.'

'Change is the only constant.'

Keating nodded. 'That's not Larkin. Sounds like Confucius or something.'

'Heraclitus.'

Keating pivoted his chair to face his computer. 'So, what now? We wait for Crawley to get in contact? Assuming he sees the conference.'

'Well, sir. The fucking drama. Sometimes it serves a purpose. The picture of his mother's tooth will be on the front page of every newspaper. Like I said, acknowledge his pain, his trauma. Make him realise he can't address it by holding on to Eva.'

Keating clicked through a few emails, turned his chair to Sawyer again. 'In other news, I spoke to Aidan Byrne, the Garda chief in Cork. Dylan Brennan has gone AWOL. Hasn't turned up for work in two weeks.'

31

Sawyer clicked the arms of his Wing Chun wooden man training dummy into place. He took a few steadying breaths and began the conditioning drill, driving his forearms into the roots of the stubby, limb-like poles. He cycled through the discipline's core blocking and parrying techniques, pivoting from horse stance to fighting stance, ramping up the force and intensity.

It was still dark outside, but by the time he'd finished his workout, the faint glow of dawn fringed his bedroom window blind.

He flopped onto the bed, face down, basted in sweat, gasping for air.

He closed his eyes, and immediately, the images danced and warped. Flashes of sinking underwater in his old Mini; of the lights on the train approaching as he walked towards it down the tracks; of David Bowman's neck, axed and fissured; of his mother, walking along the lane outside Wardlow village, haloed by the sunlight.

Sawyer opened his eyes, but still saw the images in the darkness at the foot of the window: morphing faces, pleading then sneering then raging; recurring scenes, shifting and switching. It was like channel-hopping through his past.

His arms and back screamed from the workout, but the discomfort was no match for the internal agony. He couldn't soothe this eternal existential mauling with temporary physical pain. Or maybe he hadn't been trying hard enough.

But there were ways to drive back the beast.

He reached into the drawer of the bedside table and took out two packets.

He walked through to the kitchen, fetched a glass of water, and downed two pills from each packet. He crouched by the fridge and bowed his head. His black-and-white cat, Bruce, entered through the back door cat flap, and Sawyer hauled himself to his feet, breathing deep and slow. His arms were bruised from the wooden slats, his nerve endings sleepless and raw.

'Early for you, big man.'

Bruce head-bumped his leg, miaowing. Sawyer slopped out a sachet of cat food and walked back into the bedroom.

He sat on the bed and reached into the bedside drawer again, taking out his mother's journal.

He'd marked the page with a piece of card.

Jessica's neatly inscribed words shimmered in the half-light.

June 1987
Ivan was here, with Harold. I was in the bathroom taking
off my make-up and I heard them talking. Ivan said they
can't just 'let the thing with Bill go away'.

He put the journal back in the drawer and took out
his father's *Memento Mori* medallion, flipping it through
his fingers, reading the words of Marcus Aurelius in the
inscription.

YOU COULD LEAVE LIFE RIGHT NOW

Sawyer reached into the drawer and found the small
plastic sleeve.

He slipped out the blade and rested the edge against
the top of his exposed pectoral, testing the pressure, then
shifted it to his bicep, pushing it into the flesh lightly.
Then harder.

The skin broke, and a trickle of blood ran down the
muscle, pooling in the crook of his arm.

The pain was bright and instant; a jagged rebuke,
spreading across his arm and shoulder.

Sawyer peeled the blade away, slowly, then tossed it
onto the bedside table. He pressed his fingers into the
wound, stifling it.

He tilted back his head and closed his eyes. He
pushed harder with his fingers, raising the pain, feeling
the heat of the blood as it oozed beneath his fingernails.

———

He drove down to Tideswell, through the morning mist, and parked outside the church. A few figures lingered in the graveyard, slumped and spectral. Sawyer took the Polaroid of his mother out of his wallet and looked at her, poised outside the garden gate in her orange bathrobe.

Always the panic. That the picture was fading too fast.

That there was less of it to see each time.

And, as ever, she held his gaze now, as she had done that Christmas morning. The eyes, heavy with devotion; the smile, frail and dutiful.

'What's in the darkness, Mum?' he said out loud. 'What's left to come to light?'

He closed his eyes.

'So, when will it be enough?' Jessica's voice from the back seat.

Sawyer kept his eyes closed.

'You're saying that because Keating said that.'

'If you like.'

'You said I feel too much. Like *The Go-Between*.'

A pause.

'I only knew you for six years, my darling.'

'So, you mean me back then? I felt too much.'

'That's who you were. Who you were becoming. Your heart was so open. It was as if you wanted to test yourself against the world. To prove you could take whatever it could throw at you. You saw so much because you were open to everything.'

'But then I lost that innocence.'

'Too soon.'

He screwed his eyes shut tighter. 'I tried to get tough. But only to cover the vulnerability inside.'

'You were tender. But not vulnerable.'

'I want to get back there. Guided by what I feel.' He opened the car door, stepped out without looking back. 'But I don't know the way.'

Sawyer walked to the gravesite, and gazed down at the rose-white headstone, the plain black lettering.

JESSICA MARY SAWYER
1954-1988

WHAT WILL SURVIVE OF US IS LOVE

He bowed his head, listening to the early birds, the wind jostling the trees, the sound of his breathing.

Footsteps on the path behind.

'That's a really lovely stone, if you don't mind my saying.'

Sawyer turned.

A man in his late middle-age wearing a jacket and tie stood on the path between the graves. He tried on a smile. 'Forgive the intrusion. I'm Perry. I teach English up at Salford University. I'm afraid I'm a bit of a poetry geek. Particularly Larkin. Plath and Sexton if I'm feeling brave.'

Sawyer shifted from Jessica's gravestone onto the path beside Perry.

He nodded. 'Jake.'

Perry frowned. 'Jessica was young. I'm so sorry. The

quote caught my eye, but also the age. My son's in a plot round the corner.' He nodded to the stone. 'Was Jessica your mother, Jake?'

'Yes.'

He held Sawyer's eye for a moment, as if struggling to select an appropriate comment. 'We had Ethan quite young. He died suddenly. Eighteen.'

'How?'

Perry gave a weighty sigh. 'Meningococcal septicaemia.' He smiled. 'Ethan was a wonder. A musician. Bursting with creative energy. So kind and full of curiosity about everything. We thought he had flu. And I brought him up some tea and toast one Sunday morning and he was just... cold. After the inquest, we brought his body home and laid him out in his bed, so his friends and family could see him, say goodbye. I know, I know. It sounds macabre. But I believe we shouldn't medicalise death. It's part of us all. We should see the dead, in their final repose. To give us something to compare with. They shouldn't just... disappear from our lives and memories, as if they've just gone to live in Australia or something.'

Sawyer lowered his gaze. 'How did you survive it?'

Perry shrugged. 'I didn't think we would, at first. I felt like there was a void where my heart used to be. Where all the nuances of emotion used to be. I felt guilty for experiencing pleasure or interest in anything else.' He caught himself. 'I'm sorry, Jake. I am intruding, I know.'

'It's okay. I'm sorry for what happened to Ethan.' He nodded to the stone. 'I assume you know the poem?'

'Of course. *An Arundel Tomb*. Inspired by the

sculpture of the deceased medieval couple rendered hand in hand, in Chichester Cathedral. That line before this. *Our almost-instinct almost true.* It seems to qualify the following line, which many read as Larkin offering comfort in the idea that love survives. He could be saying that perhaps love isn't a good thing, because it's a romantic ideal, and it's better to accept the reality. That death is part of life, and everything ultimately erodes. Even the figures in the poem. And they're made of stone.'

'I agree,' said Sawyer. 'But you could also read it as a call to savour the moment. The now. The present is all we have. Everything else is just empty sentiment.'

Perry smiled and swept an arm across the expanse of the graveyard. 'Well, that would certainly free you of the fear of this. The fear of the future we all share. It's why I envy those with faith. I used to have it. Before Ethan.'

'Why envy?' said Sawyer.

'If you have faith, it's baked in, isn't it? You're automatically freed from fear of the future. As long as you say your prayers.'

'I'm with Plath,' said Sawyer. '"The sky is empty." Nobody is watching over us. Life is random. Anything could happen at any moment. Faith. It's just stories. That's what we do. We add meaning and significance to comfort ourselves against the randomness. Big ideas. Reality. Time. God.' He shrugged. 'And when tragedy finds you, it makes it even harder to believe that you ever had agency. That you could have kept it away by following the ideas in a dusty old book.'

Perry nodded. 'And it's easier to imagine it could find you again and again, with no higher logic or divine mercy.' He stepped forward and gazed down at Jessica's grave. 'That's the thing about grief that nobody warns you about. The way it feels like fear.'

32

'Tell me more about Uncle Dylan.'

Sawyer sat facing Catherine Brennan across the smoked glass dining table: polished, with minimalist grey coasters and a central vase of flowers, expertly arranged.

Brennan dropped her head forward, letting her red hair cascade onto the table surface. She gathered it up into a high ponytail.

'He was a hothead. Lost his faith way before Dad died.' She sipped from a mug of coffee. 'Laura and I, we often heard talk of his connections back home.'

'In Ireland?'

'Yes. I remember I was doing a school project on the Troubles, and Dad said I should speak to Dylan. Said he would remember the time well. He married young, I think. Lived with her up in Antrim for a while. Came back South when it broke up. That would have been the mid-1980s.'

Sawyer glanced at the fridge: Smeg, mint green. 'How many children do you have, Catherine?'

'Two girls. Seven and nine.' She leaned forward and grinned, flashing a mouth of perfect white teeth. 'Oh. You're wondering why no fridge magnets. Ralph, my husband, is obsessive. I go with it. We're not very knick-knacky.'

Sawyer stirred his coffee. 'Your parents were wealthy, weren't they?'

'Insurance, yeah. Laura and I run the show now. Well, we Zoom with the managers weekly, catch up when we can. Dad's folks were in property. I've got a vague memory of visiting them in a big house near Dublin.' She clasped her hands together. Long manicured nails. Glossed, painted burgundy. 'Mum looked after the money. Dad never cared about it much.'

'Do you?'

'No. We live well, but I keep perspective. If you let money rule you, then you get obsessed with losing it. You start to make your decisions based on that.'

'Root of all evil.'

She raised her eyebrows. 'It's family that matters to me. And my faith.'

Sawyer took a drink. 'Dylan is missing. Two weeks.'

She sat back. 'Oh, no.'

'Have you heard from him?'

'Not since he stayed with us after Dad's funeral. Getting on for fifteen years.'

'And he has made no contact since?'

She shook her head. 'It took me a long time to get myself together after Dad died. I was focused on Mum and Laura. Then I met Ralph, the kids came along...

203

Mum might have stayed in touch with him, but not me, or Laura, as far as I know.'

'Laura said he was good to you.'

Brennan looked down at her hands. 'To her, yes.'

'But not you?'

She sighed. 'I was coming up to eighteen. He came to my room one night. Tried his luck.'

'Did you tell your mother?'

'Of course not. She had enough to deal with. He was tanked up, anyway. He said I was beautiful, wanted to touch my hair. He was insistent at first, but when I pushed him away, he left it. Went back to his room.'

Sawyer eyed Brennan's hands. No tremble.

She got up and took a scented candle from a drawer by the sink.

'You said he was angry after the funeral,' said Sawyer. 'About his brother's death being turned into a party.'

'Oh, my. Yes. He was furious. Trying to clear everything away. Snatching drinks out of people's hands.' She lit the candle, placed it on the table. 'I excused him because of the shock.'

'Excused him for coming on to you?'

She picked up her coffee mug, rinsed it at the sink, slotted it into the dishwasher.

Sawyer let the silence hover, as Brennan stood staring out the kitchen window at the back garden.

'The main thing is...' She turned and sat down again. 'He stopped. He took no for an answer.'

'This is your uncle, Catherine. Not some teenage date. Some would say he shouldn't have asked the question in the first place.'

She scoffed. 'You think I'm downplaying it.'

Sawyer shook his head. 'I think you want me to think that.'

Brennan bristled. 'Wind that back a bit. You're saying I'm hiding something?'

He smiled. 'Possibly. Or you're trying to divert me.'

An aroma of lemon and vanilla wafted over from the candle.

Brennan glared at Sawyer. 'Why do I feel like I'm in confession, Detective?'

'Because you have something to confess?'

Brennan lowered her gaze, sucked in a long breath. 'Shall we lose the dance?'

'Dance?'

'Yeah. If I'm going to be straight with people, I need them to be straight in return.' Brennan leaned forward again, held out her hands, palms up. 'What's on your mind, Mr Sawyer?' She locked her eyes onto his. 'What do you want from me?'

He took a drink, keeping his gaze on her over the top of the mug. 'I'm wondering if Dylan is killing the men who murdered your father and you know about it. Possibly Laura, too.'

She didn't flinch. Just shook her head. 'That's not true.'

'Did Dylan ever openly threaten to take revenge on the men?'

'I don't remember. Probably.'

'Tell me more about these connections he had back in Ireland.'

Brennan looked up at the ceiling and retied her

ponytail. 'He had Provo sympathies. I remember Dad saying they argued about it. We were Catholics. Firmly in the Republican corner. But Dad thought the violence was ugly and futile. He talked to me about his memories when I did the school project. He said it should have all ended at least ten years before the Good Friday Agreement, but the politicians kept it going. Dad wouldn't tell me anything specific about Dylan. He told me to ask him for the story direct. But I never got the chance.'

'If he gets in touch, will you let me know?'

She smiled. 'Do you think I will, Detective Sawyer?'

'I read people. Not minds.'

'I'm a good reader of people, too.' She pointed at Sawyer. 'You strike me as a man with a lot going on beneath the surface.'

He nodded. 'Isn't that how everyone sees themself? Classic cold-reading technique.'

She hitched her chair around, closer to him. 'But there are ways to tell if someone's lying or holding something back. Little tics and tells.'

'Yes. But I don't think of it as a science.'

'People cover their mouths, don't they? When they lie.'

'It's not usually that blatant.' Sawyer nodded to the candle. 'I wondered if you'd lit that to obscure something in the air. An uncomfortable truth you wanted to sanitise. Or at least good old Catholic guilt.'

Brennan laughed. 'Oh, wow.' She tapped Sawyer's knee. 'There *is* a lot going on behind those green eyes. But I'd say you're overthinking that one.'

She tilted her head to one side, letting her ponytail slip onto her shoulder.

Red hair.

Flash of Maggie screaming.

Sawyer blinked it away. 'Well. You don't always look for the obvious stuff. You tune in to the distance. The dissonance between behaviour and reality. Between what someone says and what they do. You can often tell more from what isn't said.'

Brennan looked dreamy and distant. 'Yeah. The subtext.' She sat up. 'Okay. Let's see if you can tell when I'm lying.'

'I don't really have—'

'I love my husband.' She grinned, waiting for his response.

'True.'

'Correct. Wait... I want my daughters to be gymnasts.'

'True. Something about the way you said "gymnasts".'

She flapped a hand in the air. 'Ah. Half-true. I only want one of them to be a gymnast. The one who's not very talented, and loves it. The other one is good, but isn't interested. Kids, eh? Okay. One more. When I was nineteen, I kissed a fifteen-year-old boy in an alley round the back of a cinema. He wanted to have sex with me, but I wouldn't let him.'

Sawyer pondered. 'Some of that happened, but not in that way.'

'Very good. I was fifteen. He was nineteen. I turned him down. He tried to do it anyway, but a guy came out for a smoke, and he legged it. I did like him, though.'

'So why did you turn him down? The age difference?'

'Fuck, no! What can you do? I was a good Catholic girl.'

'Was?'

Brennan smiled and raised her eyebrows, holding the tension. She stroked the silver crucifix on her pendant necklace.

'You and Laura both have the same necklace.'

She looked down. 'White gold, 18k. Mum gave them to us on the day she passed.'

'When did you last talk to Uncle Dylan, Catherine?'

She tapped her nails on the table. 'At my dad's funeral.'

Sawyer stood up. 'I believe you.'

33

Keating swiped at his touchscreen, and a mugshot of a scowling man appeared on the conference room central monitor. He had an oblong face topped with a crop of white hair, and an overgrown beard the colour of cigarette ash.

'Say hello to the number one suspect in the Cunliffe and Burrows murders. Dylan Brennan. Sixty-one. Brother of Thomas Brennan. Lives in Cork. Not seen for two weeks. Garda took this last March. He chinned someone at his village boozer. St Patrick's Day festivities.'

Myers whistled. 'North of sixty and still brawling.'

Sawyer looked up at the screen. 'I spoke to Catherine Brennan again. No contact with Dylan since her father's funeral. I don't think she knows where he is. She claimed Dylan came on to her around that time, but he backed off when she objected.'

'Big of him,' said O'Callaghan.

'She insists Dylan didn't directly threaten his brother's killers, but he's not short on testosterone, and she implied connections to political violence in Northern Ireland in the 1970s and 1980s.'

Keating scoffed. 'I'm not going down that rabbit hole. I assume we've checked Dylan's travel?'

'No evidence he's left Ireland since a flight to the UK a few years ago,' said Shepherd. 'He was on both planes.'

'What about Laura Brennan?' said Walker.

Sawyer zoomed in on Dylan's image on his touchscreen. 'Hoping to catch up with her later.' He looked up. 'It makes sense, but it feels wrong. There's money in the family. Plenty of means. But Dylan seems a bit of a mess to me. Like we said last time, this is an organised killer. I'll look at that Brennan family church and speak to Laura.'

'Church of All Saints,' said Walker. 'The Brennans' money practically kept it standing. It's more of a church to them than to God.'

'What about the other lines?' said Keating.

'Nothing from house to house,' said Shepherd. 'No sightings of any vans or vehicles that could match the tyre tracks. No hits on van rentals. We've checked the databases of all the key national online rentals and local indies. No hits on records or connections to the Brennan family. So far, the eligible vehicles picked up on CCTV or ANPR all check out. We've got a guy on the resource team who's hot on stolen vehicles. Nothing there, either.'

Keating sprang to his feet and paced. 'Last sight on Burrows?'

Shepherd checked his screen. 'Timings connect with the end of Burrows's shift at Tesco. His path home was through the park on the edge of his estate. No CCTV.'

Myers groaned. 'Sawyer's right. He's organised.'

'We're still checking prisoners the Brennan killers spent time with inside. Nothing yet.'

'I know it's lateral,' said Shepherd. 'But we're due to see Thomas Brennan's teacher friend Kieran Leith tomorrow. He's been in Scotland for a few weeks.'

Keating closed his eyes, pinched the bridge of his nose. 'And the other two? Morris and White.'

'Nothing to report,' said Sawyer. 'White has an officer posted and a personal alarm. Morris doesn't.'

O'Callaghan twirled her pen in the air. 'Is nobody going to ask me if we have any DNA from the scenes that could link to Dylan Brennan's DNA, which we have on record?'

All eyes turned to her.

She smiled. 'Because the answer would be no. Whoever is doing this must have experience in covering tracks. We have precisely fuck-all apart from the fibres, and contact trace from weapons.' O'Callaghan pulled up a gallery of mortuary shots and tethered her screen to the main monitor. 'Drummond says Burrows was beaten with something spiked.' She zoomed in on detail photographs of the torso, revealing scattered areas of puncture marks. 'But the injuries and broken bones indicate blunt trauma.'

Sawyer leaned forward, squinting at the image. 'Bruising around the puncture marks. Any impressions?'

O'Callaghan shook her head. 'Drummond thinks something thin, rather than, say, the head of a shovel. The bruising isn't wide enough.'

'Iron bar?' said Walker. 'Or baton?'

Sawyer flipped to Dylan's image on his screen. 'Trench club?'

'What's a trench club?' said Myers.

Keating winced, took his seat. 'First World War. Allied soldiers used them during night-time raids on enemy trenches, to make quiet surprise attacks. They were bats with hobnails hammered through.'

'That sounds a bit improvised,' said Walker.

'It was a serious tactic. Some units manufactured them in bulk, using professional carpenters and metal workers. They also used knives, bayonets, knuckledusters, hammers.'

Sawyer took a sharp breath. He braced for the images, but nothing came. 'The murders feel performative,' he said. 'The beatings feel personal. They're for him. If it was purely about revenge, why not just beat them to death? Make them suffer. But he goes to a lot of trouble. There's a big disconnect between presentation and signature. How he fulfils himself. Makes it worth his while. Beheading, burning. Two different methods. But the beatings are consistent.'

'And why dump the results out in the open?' said Shepherd. 'Why choose established outdoor spots over anonymous woodland? Is he making a point about tourism?'

Keating shook his head slowly. 'That's a reach. But there might be significance in the locations. Look into rangers. Connections between Kinder Wood and Bamford Edge.'

They pondered in silence for a moment. A group of detectives in the office outside walked past the conference room. Sunlight from the floor windows flashed across the table.

Sawyer ground his teeth at the swell of nausea.

Clear as yesterday, he saw his mother in silhouette, falling to the ground, into a patch of longer grass at the side of the verge.

Sunlight flared behind as she fell away, unblocking its path.

Sawyer raised a hand, shielding his eyes. But by now, the conference room was uniformly lit again.

The detectives winced as he jerked back his chair, grinding the legs against the floor.

Metal on bone.

He snatched up his plastic cup of water, guzzled it down.

His brother's scream. Shrill and thin. Strangled by panic.

His mother's face. Drowned in blood.

The word came. Unstoppable. Crashing from the past into the present.

'No!'

The detectives turned to him.

He came round. 'We're assuming too much. With the location connections.'

Keating's hard stare was on him. 'You feel strongly about this.'

Sweat tickled Sawyer's forehead; he swiped it away.

'Yes! I do. We should... focus more on the methods. And victimology. Instead of speculating about locations.'

O'Callaghan narrowed her eyes. 'To be fair, Detective

Sawyer, at the last briefing, you made a point about which way the head was facing at the Edge.'

Sawyer breathed in through his nose. Deep and slow.

Walker's cologne, or bath gel. Fruity.

O'Callaghan's coffee. Bitter, over-brewed.

He projected forward: a vision of his vomit splattering across the table, soaking the touchscreens.

He tipped back his head, draining the last drops of water.

'Both causes of death. They're found in the Bible.'

Side-eyes around the table.

'The Christian Bible?' said Keating.

'There are five burnings. Uh...'

Shepherd cut across him. 'Oh yeah. A couple of them were the fellas who dared to use unholy incense.'

'Yes,' said Sawyer. 'Aaron's sons. He was the brother of... of Moses. God burned his sons alive.'

Sawyer's phone buzzed in his pocket. He reached for it, but couldn't get it free. He stopped, and stared down at his trembling hands for a moment, then shifted them off the table and laid them out of sight, on his knees.

'And God himself is referred to as an "all-consuming fire".'

Sawyer lowered his gaze, focused on his hands. He listened as the sounds faded. The screams and barking. The hammer. The decoupling of past and present was almost complete. But he would need to speak again soon, here in the now.

O'Callaghan rescued the silence. 'John the Baptist. A Biblical beheading. And Herod took off his brother's head a few years later.'

'Didn't David behead Goliath?' said Walker.

Keating sighed. 'This is nothing. Follow the lines. I also want to look into the possibility that Morris and White might be working together.'

'We have no motive for that,' said Walker. 'Sir. And they were in different prisons. It's hard to see how they could have had much contact over the past fifteen-odd years.'

'Well, let's explore that, Detective Walker. Nicely volunteered. We also have some other business. Eva Gregory.' He gave a thin smile. 'Detective Sawyer's... moment at the press conference has certainly sparked a lot of publicity. How did we get on with Crawley's other belongings? Anything in his correspondence?'

Walker spoke up. 'I cross-reffed the crazies who wrote to him inside with proximity to his escape location and expanded it to the Cygnet Hospital in Nottingham. Two or three wrote to him regularly. One of those dropped off in the last year.' He checked his notes. 'One name jumps out, for the intensity and frequency of her letters. Victoria Kendal. Late forties. Landscape gardener. Lives in a fairly remote spot out by Miller's Dale. Her letters are a mixture of sympathy over what happened to Crawley's mother, and a weird teenage lust.' Walker looked up. 'She wrote to him every month in the last two years.'

Sawyer took out his phone, checked the message sender ID.

Luka.

34

Curtis Mavers slid his Bank of America card into the Westfield Shopping Centre ATM and checked the balance. As Crutchley had promised, the figure was generous, and he got busy indulging himself. He bought a Samsonite and wheeled it around his favourite outlets, stopping occasionally to pack in his purchases.

Breitling watch; iPad and AirPods; dark red blazer and trousers from BOSS; Cuban ankle boots from Geiger; gold metal Gucci Aviators; a stack of T-shirts, beach shirts and polos from Reiss; CK underwear and socks; sliders, shorts, and trainers from Vans; a basket of upscale toiletries from John Lewis.

He sank a beer at a sterile chain bar and took an Uber to the airport.

The driver, a fidgety young Londoner with an ungroomed chin beard, glanced in his rear-view mirror. 'Where you off to, mate?'

Mavers smiled. 'The promised land.'

The driver kept quiet for the rest of the journey.

At the airport, Mavers bought a fistful of Jamaican dollars, then found a toilet cubicle. He stripped, binned his stale old clothes and changed into new socks and underwear, crisp white polo, boots, blazer, trousers. He washed, combed his hair, and spritzed on a little Eau Sauvage.

He stared himself out in the mirror. A new man. His facial bruising wasn't fully settled, but the contrast with the rest of his look gave him an air of upscale toughness.

Mavers straightened his sleeves and winced at the shot of pain from his bandaged arm. Did that sleeve look thicker than the other? Slightly. But his build could carry it.

He bypassed the ragged Economy queue and strolled up to the over-staffed Business check-in desk. The clerk studied his forged passport, then his real ticket.

She smiled. 'Lovely to see you, sir. I'm afraid I have some bad news.'

His stomach lurched. 'What's that?'

'Unfortunately, the flight is oversold in Business. I believe there's a conference of some sort at the Montego Bay Convention Centre.' The clerk checked her screen. 'But... we have a couple of options for you. I could offer you a later flight on Sunday. Guaranteed seat in Business. This would include a compensation voucher for the inconvenience.' She looked him over. 'Or I'd be happy to offer you a complimentary upgrade to First on today's flight.'

Mavers turned his head, catching his reflection in the mirrored surface of a pillar. There he stood. Shop-fresh. New. Improved. From prison number to VIP.

At last, the world was lying down to him.

Status. Drinks on demand. Individual flat bed. Complimentary loungewear.

But it was all surface; as fake as his passport.

The persistent thrum of pain in his arm sharpened, then radiated. Undiminished.

He turned to the clerk.

'I'll take the Sunday flight instead, thanks. Still got a bit of business to sort out.'

35

Sawyer stepped up onto the wooden decking in front of the café. Luka sat at an outside corner table, head in his phone. He glanced up as Sawyer approached, but then swept his fringe to the side and refocused on the screen.

'Hello, Jake.'

'For me?' Sawyer pointed to the tall glass of hot chocolate in the centre of the table.

'Yeah.' Luka waved at a similar half-empty glass. 'Had one, too.'

Sawyer raised the glass. 'Cheers.' He sipped, then sat. 'What are you playing?'

'*Clash Royale*. Dead game, really. Normally I play *Clash of Clans,* but they've done a really good update. Still pay to win, though.'

Sawyer looked up at the sign. *Savoir Faire*. 'Fancy title for a park café.'

Luka shrugged and finished his drink in one. He clunked the glass down on the table and turned his phone screen down. 'I have to do that.'

Sawyer smiled. 'Addictive.'

'Yeah.'

Sawyer looked out across the sun-baked lawn, swamped with lunchtime picnickers. Joyful shrieks rose from the other side of the tree-lined path; from the plastics and primaries of the toddlers' play area.

'How are you doing, Luka? What's up?'

Luka gazed down at the table, rocking a little. 'I know where Mum is.'

'Really?'

'Well. I know where she was.'

Sawyer leaned over the table. 'Where?'

'There's this cottage. You take the road out of Cressbrook village. It's all by itself. It's got a weird garden. All neat. Like it's on show or something.'

'And how do you know your mum has been there?'

Luka lifted his eyes. 'I got in. Had a look round.' His voice wavered. 'There was some blood on the floor.'

'Is it abandoned?'

'No. Someone definitely lives there. Loads of recent stuff lying around. Food bowls for pets.'

Sawyer sat back. 'But the owner wasn't around?'

Luka shook his head, then went silent and looked across to the path and play area. 'I used to come here when I was little.'

'I don't understand, Luka. What makes you think this place is connected with your mum? How did you come across it?'

Luka rocked for a moment, then turned back to face Sawyer. 'I followed my dad.'

'Dale has been to the house?'

'I think so.'

Sawyer eyed him. 'Did you see him go in?'

Luka shifted his gaze again. 'No. But he went in his new car. It's a Tesla. Sometimes he drives it himself. Sometimes he has a driver. This time, his driver took him.'

'There's a lot you're not telling me here, Luka. If this is something to do with your mum, give me the full picture so I can help.'

Luka turned, held Sawyer's eye. 'What do you think I'm not telling you?'

'This isn't a game, Luka. How did you follow Dale? We're not the best of friends, but I wouldn't call him an idiot.'

He shrugged. 'On my bike. Kept my distance.'

'Is it a magic bike? Faster than a car?'

Luka lowered his eyes. 'There was loads of traffic.'

'What else did you see at the house?'

'Two guys were there. They caught me, but I got away. I was wearing a mask.' He pulled the balaclava out of his pocket and held it up.

Sawyer sighed. 'I warned you about getting involved yourself. This might have nothing to do with your mum, but if it does...'

Luka nodded, a skewed smile forming.

'What?'

He took out a plastic sandwich bag and laid it on the table.

Sawyer lifted it up to the light and examined the contents: a folding knife. The inside of the bag was smeared with a small amount of blood.

'I slashed one of them. That's how I got away.'

'Jesus Christ.'

Luka shifted his chair closer and laid a black wallet on the table. 'I lifted that from the same guy.'

Sawyer opened the wallet and took out a driving licence card. The moustached man glared out at him. He read from the card. '*Farouk Abadi*. Have you seen him before? Do you know the name?'

'I think I've seen him pick up my dad in the Tesla.'

Sawyer sat for a moment, processing. 'Could you direct me back there? To the house.'

'Easy.'

Sawyer raised his eyebrows. 'Really? After one visit.'

Luka snatched up his glass and tipped his head back, trying to draw out a few final drops of hot chocolate. 'I think so, yeah. It's a bit out of the way.' He laid the glass back down on the table and lowered his head, avoiding Sawyer's gaze. 'You promised.'

'Promised what?'

'To help find my mum.' He looked up, fixed Sawyer with misted eyes. 'I've done more than you, and I'm not even a proper detective.'

Sawyer picked up his phone and placed a call, then paused, waiting. 'Luka, what are you doing this afternoon?'

He shrugged. 'Still off school.'

'Let's go for a drive.'

36

Dale Strickland turned his back on the ceiling-high window and leaned against the ledge. The hustle of midtown traffic drifted up from street level, six storeys below. He took off his glasses and lowered his head, rubbing at the bridge of his nose. His white hair was growing out, exposing sparseness around the crown, and his skin looked dull and weathered.

'No sign of the car?'

His visitors shifted on the silvery grey couch.

'Tracks,' said the man with shoulder-length hair. 'But no vehicle. We checked every corner of the house. There's no evidence that your wife was ever there.'

Strickland looked up. 'The blood?' He cast his eyes to Farouk Abadi, at the far end of the couch.

'It's not hers, boss. I did a strip test. O-positive. Your wife is A-negative.'

'Could it be Crawley's?'

'Can't say without a sample. Can you get your guy to check NDNAD?'

Strickland stared ahead. 'Yes. I'll link you up.' He pushed off the window and lunged for his desk, swiping an arm across the surface. He let out a loud roar, as papers and folders flew onto the floor, and a mug shattered against the wall.

He leaned on his chair, with his back to the men, breathing hard.

They glanced at each other.

A sharply groomed young man tapped on the door and stuck his head round. 'Everything okay, sir?'

Strickland raised his hand, not turning. 'Fine, Oliver. Apologies.'

The man retreated and closed the door.

'He's too far ahead,' said Strickland.

'Crawley?' said the first man.

Strickland nodded. 'He was there, Reuben. It all connects. The car he used to abduct Eva was there. I've learned that the house owner, Victoria Kendal, used to write to Crawley in prison. My contact has seen the correspondence. He spent a lot of time flattering her, engaging her. "*You're not like other women. You make me want to be a better person. You're so beautiful.*"' He sneered. 'She's not. He also uses reverse psychology. "*You can do better than me.*"'

'He put the work in,' said Abadi.

'Exactly. It was a project. A long game. So, when he turned up unexpectedly, she would have been delighted, overwhelmed, unwary.' Strickland walked to a shelf and took down a bottle of Glenfiddich. He filled a shot glass, downed the whisky in one. 'He subdues her—'

'Maybe it's her blood,' said Reuben.

224

Strickland glanced at him. 'He brings Eva inside. Probably took the Polaroid...' He paused again, staring ahead.

'What do we know about Kendal?' said Abadi.

'Landscape gardener,' said Reuben. 'Forty-eight. Never married. Worked for herself. Private clients, contract work. She did something at Chatsworth last year.'

Strickland raised an eyebrow. '*Did something*?'

He shrugged. 'Planted some flowers?'

Strickland winced. 'If Crawley has held her at the house since arriving with Eva, maybe he's cancelled work for her, to avoid suspicion if she doesn't show.'

'We found some business cards in a desk drawer,' said Reuben.

'Check around. He might have forced Kendal to call herself and cancel.' Strickland's clear blue eyes flashed. 'I would. I'll get my contact working on phone data. He probably used her own phone, but I assume it's still with him. So, there could be a digital trail.' Strickland walked to his desk, unsteady. He slumped into the chair. 'You say there wasn't a lot of blood?'

'Pretty big patch in the bathroom,' said Reuben. 'Few days' old, I'd say. A bit more at the foot of the bed.'

Strickland rubbed his nose again. 'But the rest of the house was clean?'

'Yes, boss.'

'He's bothered to cover his tracks, but left the bloodstains.'

'He's taunting you,' said Abadi.

Strickland was silent and still for a while. 'Get onto

those client calls. Tracking Kendal might be the key to Crawley. I'll get my contact back on the car.'

'He might have taken a new one,' said Abadi. 'Dumped the old one. I would.'

Strickland sighed. He waved a hand to the door. 'Go.'

Abadi and Reuben got to their feet.

Strickland checked something on his screen. 'Reuben.' Both men stopped and turned around. 'Are you injured?'

Reuben glanced at Abadi. 'In what way?'

Strickland pointed to his screen. 'The main door entry scanner shows a white patch on your right arm. Too low down for a tennis elbow support.'

'There was a kid there,' said Abadi.

Strickland looked up. 'A kid?'

'Just snooping round.'

Strickland watched Reuben; he lowered his gaze. 'Was he already there when you arrived?'

'Yeah.'

'So, how did he get in? I assume Crawley didn't just leave the door unlocked.'

Abadi stepped forward slightly, doing the talking. 'We didn't see. Maybe there was a window left open.'

Strickland got up and walked past Abadi. He stood close to Reuben, drawing his eye. 'How old was this kid?'

Reuben shrugged. 'Teenage? Hard to tell with the mask.'

Strickland stared at Abadi. 'A *mask*?'

'Ski mask,' said Abadi. 'Balaclava.'

'And the injury?'

'He had a pocket knife,' said Reuben. 'Hit me with a surprise slash across the arm. That's how he got away.'

Strickland paced back to his desk, sat down. 'And you were about to leave without mentioning this?' He studied the two men. 'You're big boys. I can't imagine you being too scared to tell me. Which means you must be embarrassed about something.' He got up again, walked over. 'Is it that you let him get away?' He paused; no answer. 'Could he have found something you missed?'

Abadi shook his head.

They stood there in silence for a moment.

The traffic revved below.

'He got my wallet,' said Abadi.

37

Sawyer parked the Mini in a lay-by off the lane that wound past the Kendal house. The surrounding woodland glittered in low afternoon sun, and Sawyer flipped down his windscreen eye shield. They sat there for a while, windows open, listening.

Drowsy birdsong from the trees above. Distant bleating.

Sawyer took a pair of mini binoculars from the glovebox. He held out a packet of boiled sweets; Luka shook his head.

He leaned out of the window and surveyed the cottage, a light rain spritzing his face.

'You haven't even asked me if this is the right place,' said Luka.

'It is, though, isn't it?' He lowered the binoculars and sat back in his seat.

'Yeah. You got the address from someone on the phone. I'm not stupid.'

'I know.'

Luka leaned over, opened the glovebox. 'You've got loads of sweets in here. I can't believe you've got Jolly Ranchers. They're horrible. American sweets are rank. Their chocolate tastes like sick.'

'That's because they use a type of acid.'

'Yeah. Hershey's.' Luka prodded a finger into his open mouth. 'Smells like sweaty feet and tastes like sick.'

'You should suggest that as a new advertising tagline.'

Luka closed the glovebox. 'Who lives here, anyway?'

'A woman called Victoria Kendal. She used to write to Dennis Crawley when he was in prison. He might have used it to hide out.'

Luka scoffed. 'Well, he's not there now.'

'The men who were here. What were they doing?'

'Dunno. They came in after me. I don't think they saw me get in. One of them said he saw my phone light.'

'He spoke English?'

'To me, yeah. But not to each other. Sounded like Indian or Arabic or something.'

Sawyer closed the windows. 'I need to look around.'

Luka took his backpack from the back seat. 'I'm not staying in the car.'

'I know.'

———

Sawyer climbed over the crumbling wall, keeping his head below the undergrowth at the edge of the surrounding trees. Luka followed, and they crouched, watching the house.

'Has anything changed?' said Sawyer.

'Don't think so. The plastic chair is still there, and the blinds are down.'

Sawyer looked at him. 'I have a burning question I've been saving, Luka. How did you get in?'

Luka turned away. 'Window wasn't locked. I forced it.'

'Show me the window.'

Luka opened his backpack. 'Okay, okay.' He took out the box with hairpins. 'I picked the back door lock. You can't be angry about it. You taught me.'

Sawyer sighed. 'When we get your mum back, let's not tell her about this.' He moved off, keeping low. 'Stay close.'

They crept through the woodland, around to the back of the house. At the door, Sawyer waited, listening.

No signs or sounds of life from inside.

'You're up.' He turned. Luka was crouched, steadying himself against a porch pillar. 'You okay?'

Luka breathed, deep and slow. 'Just dizzy. It happens sometimes. Doesn't last long.' He lowered his head, focusing on his breathing. 'I've got a burning question, too.'

'What's that?'

'Why does Dennis hate my dad so much? I know he thinks he hurt his mum, but my dad says it's not true.'

Sawyer hesitated. 'It doesn't matter.'

'What doesn't?'

'If it's true or not. Crawley believes it.'

'So, if he really believes it and he hates my dad, why hasn't he just killed him or something?'

Sawyer closed his eyes. 'Because then it's over. His revenge. He's grown used to his anger. It's part of who he is. He told me he saw revenge as a stone you throw in a lake, and it sends out ripples, affecting more than just the subject of the anger. It impacts them, but also causes their loved ones to suffer. Their partners. Their children. Future generations. If the focus of your revenge dies, then...'

'The ripples don't go so far.'

'Yes. It can't be satisfied by a single death. You've carried your pain around all your life. It feels heavier than one person. Your revenge has to match that pain. But when you dedicate yourself to it, it's like a psychosis.'

'A what?'

'A madness. You become blind to everything else. Blind to reason. Blind to your own well-being. It becomes your life's mission. It takes over your life. It can destroy you. There's a saying. *If you seek revenge, dig two graves.*' He held Luka's gaze; his breathing had settled. 'Take your time.'

Luka rolled his eyes. 'I'm not scared.'

'I know.'

Sawyer tried the door handle. It was loose, and the door opened easily. He stooped to examine the lock. The deadbolt was buckled and the faceplate had partially detached from the frame.

'I didn't do that,' said Luka. 'I locked it from the inside when I got in.'

They stepped inside.

Sawyer switched on his phone light and walked

around the kitchen, studying the surfaces, the floor, the cork board leaflets. Luka followed him into the sitting room, where they were greeted by the ticking carriage clock.

Sawyer passed the light over the furniture and walls, the dead flowers, the table and books.

'You said the blood was in the bedroom?'

Luka nodded. 'And bathroom.' He led the way, across the hall.

Sawyer diverted and checked the front door. 'It's been forced, too. But the lock hasn't held so well.'

'One of them got in that way.'

In the bedroom, Sawyer aimed the light at the floor by the bathroom entrance. He crouched and examined the bloodstained carpet.

He stood up, cast the light across the light blue walls, then down at the bed. The headboard wasn't quite flush against the back wall.

He walked back into the sitting room, noted the high-backed chairs against the table with the books.

'Your mum was here,' said Sawyer. 'But I don't think that's her blood.' He swung the light up to the door.

Luka had retreated into the hall, eyes shining with tears. 'Where has she gone, Jake? Why has Dennis taken her somewhere else?'

Sawyer didn't answer; he walked back into the kitchen, cast the light down at the barren pet bowls. 'Did you look around the woods outside?'

Luka sucked in a deep breath, held it for a moment. 'No. I had to run when the men got here. I locked my bike up by an old bus stop.'

Sawyer eyed him. 'Why not just hide it in the woods before you came inside? Keep it closer.'

Luka hesitated. 'Didn't want it to get nicked. And it'd be harder to cycle away in the woods than on the road.'

Sawyer walked out to the back door and carried on across the edge of the plot, ducking into the trees. The woods at the back of the cottage were dense and wild, but thinned out as they trudged away from the road.

Sawyer turned to Luka and held up a car key. 'I know you don't want to. But I insist.' Luka rolled his eyes; Sawyer crouched down, held his shoulders. 'If we're both looking around here, we won't know if anyone else turns up to the house. I need a lookout. Call me if you see anything.'

Luka snatched the key. 'Call *me* if you find anything.' He stomped away.

Sawyer stayed crouched, studying the ground. He touched his fingers to the grass, knowing what would happen.

Flash of his mother's face; blood pooled in her eyes.

He sprang to his feet and inhaled the damp and loamy air, then ducked through the thick perimeter trees into the sparse surrounding vegetation. He walked on slowly, holding a straight line from the house, scanning the ground.

The trees soon opened out to a small clearing. Scatterings of soil lay around the fringes. In the centre, a patch of freshly disturbed earth had been patted down. A small cross, fashioned from two pieces of kindling, was driven into the mound.

Sawyer turned and barged back through the trees. He hurried into the kitchen and threw open the cupboards. In a tall storage closet near the door he found a shelf of neatly arranged gardening tools: gloves, secateurs, trowel. Several larger items hung against the back wall. He snatched up gloves and a shovel and ran out again, through the trees.

At the mound, he dug in slow, narrow scoops, sliding in the shovel head laterally. After a few minutes, the resistance slackened, and he dropped to his knees, emptying the damp earth in double-handed scoops.

Over the next half-hour, Sawyer emptied the hole, handful by handful, using the shovel to dig out the clumps of earth furthest away from the woman's body.

He slumped back, took off the gloves, and wiped the soil from his forehead. He let his eyes drift up the woman's fully clothed body.

Arms rigid at her side.

Mouth agape; eyes wide.

His phone rang in his pocket, and as he took it out, he caught movement behind.

Luka. Running out of the trees, into the clearing.

Wailing.

Sawyer dropped the phone and scrambled to his feet, blocking Luka's path to the hole. 'Hey! Luka. It's okay.'

Luka fought to get past him.

'*Luka!* It's not your mum.'

Sawyer guided him back, away from the hole. He crouched, held Luka's shoulders again. The phone carried on ringing.

Luka sniffed, wiped his eyes. 'You've been ages.'

'I know. I found… It's the woman who lived here.'

The tears came now. Luka's face crumpled in agony. 'Why did Dennis do that? What's he done with my mum?'

The phone. Still ringing.

Sawyer held him. 'Listen. This will help us. It means we can understand what he might want. What he'll do next. And he hasn't hurt your mum.'

Luka screamed at him. 'You don't know that!' He went limp, sobbing. Sawyer lowered him to his knees. He buried his head in his chest and gave a full-throated scream. 'Where is she? *Where is she?*'

He pulled back, staggered away, and slumped beside a tree at the edge of the clearing.

Sawyer watched and waited, letting the storm settle.

'I don't know, Luka. But she's not here. That's good, for now.'

He reached for the phone, took the call, expecting Walker or Shepherd.

It was Keating.

'Detective Sawyer. Whatever you're doing that takes you two minutes to answer your phone, stop it now and get over here.'

'Sir?'

'The protection officer at Jared White's place says he hasn't arrived home from work. He's an hour late.'

'What else?'

Keating paused, too long.

Sawyer steeled himself, turned away from Luka. 'Eva?'

His phone pinged with a message.

Keating cleared his throat. 'More contact. Crawley has sent another present. Just forwarded a picture.'

Sawyer opened his messages and zoomed in on the image: an extracted human tooth.

PART TWO

SINKING

38

The guy was humming. Standing over by a table, back turned, busying himself with something. His gruff voice stumbled tunelessly from note to note.

Jared White squeezed his eyes shut, opened them again. But the darkness in the room smothered him, yielding only faint outlines: the man; some kind of arched opening at the far end; the hint of a low ceiling; a dim, low-lying light obscured by the man's body.

White was seated, propped against a damp brick wall. His legs were tightly bound at the calves and his hands tied behind his back. He took short, cautious breaths through his nostrils, partially exposed above a strip of tape wrapped around his face. The tape secured a balled-up cloth gag that tasted bitter and leathery.

Humming.

Metallic clanks. Hammering?

White's nose twitched. Mildew. Rotting socks. Tobacco.

He felt for the floor. Cold, wet stone.

The man moved his head, triggering an aura of light from the lamp behind. Smoke drifted towards the far opening, and White picked out what looked like the base of a staircase leading up and out.

He shuffled in place, shifting his knees over. Pain spiked from a sore spot at the back of his head as he bumped it against the wall.

The man turned and took a step away from the table. The light from his lamp cast a jittery shadow.

He took another puff on his cigarette and balanced it on the edge of the table.

'Well, now.'

He walked towards White. Heavy boots on stone.

White squinted as the light from behind stung his eyes. He turned his head away, but the man reached down and held his chin firm.

A silver medallion spun at the end of the man's neck chain as he tore away the tape and pulled out the gag.

He turned and walked back to the table, retrieving his cigarette.

White spluttered and spat to the side. 'Look. Help us out, yeah? What do you want? My folks have got a bit of money, but I don't... Is it something my dad's done? I've hardly seen the fucker. I've been away.'

The man nodded. 'You mean prison.'

White shifted position, raising his head, trying to get a look at the man. But he'd turned his back again.

More sounds from the table. Thuds. Clangs.

'Yeah,' said White. 'Listen. I paid my debt.'

The man gave a dark laugh. 'Here we go. You did your time.'

White coughed and spat. 'Yeah.'

'And so you consider yourself absolved.'

'Only a priest can do that.'

The man froze, half-turned his head. 'Are you Catholic?'

'Yeah. I mean, no. I converted. I accepted Christ's love. I'm born again, yeah? Ah! My head is fucking ringing. Did you hit me with something?'

The man lifted a metal bucket off the table and walked towards White again. He placed it down on the floor.

White kicked his legs. He fell on his side, cheek against the stone floor. 'What's in the bucket? Please. Don't. Whatever—'

'You're trembling.'

White shuffled himself upright, against the wall. He looked up at the man, flinched at the light, bowed his head.

The man stepped closer, took a pull on his cigarette. 'Are you afraid, Jared?'

'Of course I'm fucking afraid.'

The man was silent for a moment. 'I used to be afraid. But then I heard the call.' He crouched. 'I heard the call when I was at my most afraid.' White looked up, found the man's eyes, flashing beneath heavy grey brows. 'You say you accepted Christ's love. But only because you were afraid, yes? You thought God might protect you. And he did, for a while. But now, he has brought you to me, to deliver his justice.'

He stood up.

White shook his head. 'No, no, no. I did wrong. But... what about forgiveness? The Lord is with us all in our suffering. *The Lord is near to the brokenhearted and saves the crushed in spirit.*'

'Psalm 34,' said the man. 'But also in that passage, Jared... *The Lord is against those who do evil, to blot out their name from the earth.*' He turned. 'Thomas Brennan wasn't afraid, was he? You didn't give him the chance.'

'I was—'

The man held up a hand. 'I know. You were young. You were stupid.' He dropped his cigarette end. Orange sparks scattered against the bucket surface. He turned to face White. '*Saint Michael. The Archangel. Defend us in battle. Be our protection against the wickedness and snares of the devil. May God rebuke him, we humbly pray.*'

White squirmed and groaned, tugging at his bonds. 'Wait! Fucking hell. *Wait.* I know that. It's the archangel prayer.'

'*And do thou, O Prince of the Heavenly Host...*'

'Michael is a protector, not an avenger.' Spittle hung off White's chin. 'You fucking psycho.'

The man paused for a second. '*...by the power of God, thrust into hell...*'

White's eyes widened as he jerked his neck forward. 'You have no *right*. You have no mandate. From the Lord.'

'*...thrust into hell Satan and all evil spirits who wander through the world for the ruin of souls.*'

White ramped up his rant. 'And what about you? What *are* you? What makes you so... good?'

The man turned away. 'I used to be nobody, Jared. Nobody who thought he was somebody. Doing wrong in the name of right.' He picked up the bucket. 'I'm not without sin. But I'm not afraid anymore.'

39

Dale Strickland walked to the open window of his home office and rested a hand on the sill. He kept his back to the room, shoulders rising and falling as he took in the sharp morning air.

'Can I get you something to drink, Mr Strickland?' said Cameron, standing by the boxy desk.

Strickland turned. He took off his glasses, cleaned the lenses with his shirt cuff; slower than usual, in grim fascination. Grey stubble shaded his chin and cheeks.

The silence lingered, became a presence, fouling the air.

Keating cleared his throat. 'We fast-tracked forensic odontology. The tooth matches up with Eva's records, but it's hard to be sure with just one sample. As the extraction was recent, we should be able to take some pulp and match against DNA, but—'

'I believe you've discovered the location where Eva was held,' said Strickland, his voice low and wavering.

Sawyer glanced at Keating, got the nod. 'I looked into the correspondence Crawley received in prison, and cross-referenced it with isolated locations near to where he escaped. We believe Crawley manipulated a woman named Victoria Kendal to let him hide out at her home near Miller's Dale. I was there yesterday and discovered Ms Kendal, deceased.'

Strickland's eyes jerked up. 'Where?'

'In the woods at the edge of the property. I saw a room where I believe Eva was held. The fittings match those in the Polaroid. There was also some blood inside the house, which we've matched to Ms Kendal.'

'He wanted us to find her,' said Strickland. 'And he knew we'd connect things up with the room.'

Keating nodded. 'I think so.'

Strickland made his way back to his desk, sat down hard. 'Was the woman buried?'

'Yes,' said Sawyer.

'Was she hard to find?' He rummaged through a drawer.

'Not really,' said Sawyer. 'As you say, Crawley clearly wanted us to find the body. He probably enjoyed the idea that you might have learned of the discovery and thought it could have been Eva.'

'Could the tooth belong to Ms Kendal?'

Keating shook his head.

Strickland frowned. 'Was this woman not missed? By her work?'

'Her phone was buried with her,' said Sawyer. 'She was a self-employed landscape gardener. I imagine

Crawley used the phone to buy time with her clients. Maybe forced her to feign illness. It's likely he—'

'Why so long?' Strickland closed the drawer and held Sawyer's eye.

'There was a lot of correspondence to work through,' said Keating. 'Four years' worth.'

'How sick do you have to be to write to convicted killers?' said Strickland.

Keating shrugged. 'It's common. Kendal proposed marriage to Crawley in one letter.'

Strickland laid a piece of paper on the table; lined and torn from a standard notepad. 'I received this, too. With the tooth.'

Sawyer took the facing seat and examined the paper. The note was handwritten in small, right-leaning script.

Dale,

They say time heals all wounds. This was not the case with the debasement and injury you inflicted on my mother. You've enjoyed your freedom from punishment for too long. I can't stand by and watch you achieve your cynical political ambitions.

I will return your wife if you publicly confess to the assault on my mother and make a full and unreserved apology. You will then receive her intact and alive.

If you do not comply with my request, you will receive her piece by piece. Instructions to follow.

Sawyer looked up. Keating moved in to read the note.

'He is a fantasist,' said Strickland. 'Clearly obsessed with our diverging fortunes since leaving school. My son suffered at his hands, and now it's my wife's turn. There is no evidence I was involved in any assault on his mother, and we need to move quicker this time to find where he's taken Eva. Because I am not confessing to something I didn't do.' He leaned forward, hands flat on the desk. 'You've had your chance. I'm now going my own way.'

Sawyer glanced at Strickland's hands. Trembling, fingers spread wide. 'When Crawley took Luka, I spoke to a woman named Tracey Manning. She claimed to have been present at the assault.'

'And was this assault reported at the time? Was it investigated? Is there any evidence? Are there living witnesses?' Strickland slammed his hands down on the desk and pushed his face close to Sawyer's, eye to eye. 'This is *hearsay*. Fantasy. Ancient history. This problem is in the here and now. And it's real. I will not waste any more time arguing about the delusions of a mentally deranged man who's stuck in the past. So, unless you have any new ideas, I'll bring all my private resources to bear.' He tilted back slightly. 'I wonder, Sawyer, if your stunt with the ring at the press conference might actually have inspired Crawley, rather than deterred him. Given him the idea.' He wrinkled his nose and hissed the words through an angry sneer. '*A tooth for a tooth.*'

Flashes.

His dog, bludgeoned. Twitching.

His brother, face down in the grass.

His mother's raking screams. Her mortal terror.

Sawyer kept his eyes locked on Strickland's. The nausea churned, taking longer to pass than usual. He focused on small details. Distractions.

The moving hand on Strickland's vulgar watch.

An ingrown hair in his stubble, trapped beneath the skin.

His sallow cheeks. Anaemic lips.

'We'll find Eva by understanding Crawley's world view,' said Sawyer. 'Not by calling in an army of reject bouncers and freelance sycophants.' His eyes flicked to Cameron. 'Crawley does not see the world as we do. His hunger for revenge has corrupted his thinking. He has a different sense of justice, of cause and effect, of time. His only actions so far have been designed to make you suffer, not to correct some kind of imbalance.' Sawyer got to his feet and walked back to Keating, seeking more details to calm his roiling thoughts.

Wooden door frame. Chipped near the lock.

Keating's cap.

His mother's sobbing.

The cap again. Finger smudges on the brim.

A dusting of dandruff on Keating's collar.

He continued. 'Crawley has fetishised the idea of your suffering. His sadism is pure, personal. His goal is to rob you of your happiness, just as he thinks you robbed him of his own. And he seems inspired more by your increased profile than by my actions at the conference. It's written right there.' He pointed to the note.

Strickland said nothing for a while. He stood up and walked over to a diamond-finish turntable on a shelf at the corner of the office and toyed with the tone arm. 'So, what if he gets his way, Sawyer? What if I confess? Will that feed his fetish? Will he return Eva unharmed and then disappear into the ether?'

'Do you know a man named Farouk Abadi, Mr Strickland?' said Sawyer.

Strickland flicked up the tone arm lever. 'Yes, I do. What does that have to do with—'

'He's on the mayor's security detail, isn't he?'

Strickland ran a finger over the stylus. 'Yes. Your point being?'

'I'm wondering if Crawley might have contacted him. As someone you trust. Could he be getting help from Mr Abadi? Information on your dealings, whereabouts?'

No reaction from Strickland.

'I believe Mr Abadi has visited Victoria Kendal's house sometime after Crawley left there. Were you aware of that?'

Strickland didn't look up. 'No. I wasn't. Farouk is a reputable employee. Comprehensive background checks. Where are you getting this information from? What the hell would he be doing at the house of a random landscape gardener in the middle of Derbyshire?'

'That's what I'd like to know.'

Keating stepped forward. 'Mr Strickland, it's Detective Sawyer's job to pursue lateral lines of enquiry, but I acknowledge we need to concentrate on the acute issue of Eva's safety. We have the resource to deal with Crawley's threats. Specialist officers trained in kidnap negotiation. I certainly don't advise you to take matters into your own hands.'

'I assume Crawley got Eva to this house using a car,' said Strickland. 'Have you found it?'

'Not yet,' said Keating. 'My SOCO team has been at the scene overnight. There's a lot of work to do on the body, location trace evidence, tracks. We're working round the clock—'

'Sawyer's right,' said Strickland, walking back to his desk. 'Crawley wants me to suffer. He has no empathy for Eva's pain or Luka's suffering. He wants us to chase him, to prolong the agony. But he'll always be a couple of steps ahead.' He sat down at the desk, sighed. 'So, we go the other way. We bring him to us.' He looked at Sawyer. 'How badly does he want the tooth ring?'

'It's all he has left of his mother,' said Sawyer. 'It's the one thing that connects him physically to her. That's powerful. The ring is literally a piece of Crawley's mother. The chance of getting it back might shake him up. Make him forget his plan of long-term revenge.'

Strickland dragged his palms down his cheeks. 'But we don't even know if he saw the press conference. When he sends his "instructions" on how I'm supposed to make this confession, we should offer a direct exchange. The ring for Eva.'

Keating moved in, leaned on the desk. 'We can't get into horse-trading. It's better to work on the forensics, let my specialist officers do their—'

Strickland waved a hand. 'Of course. And I won't get in the way of that. And, as the man soon to be in charge of operational policing in this region, I give you my full backing. But as the life partner of the kidnapped...' He glanced at Sawyer. 'I will not sit on my hands and wait for the kidnapper's next move.'

40

Keating shifted in the Mini passenger seat, cap in lap, scowling at his phone. 'Shepherd has interviewed Jared White's PO.'

Sawyer glanced over. 'Interviewed?'

'Rule out the most obvious before you cast around for complex solutions. Occam's razor, isn't it?'

'Sort of.'

'Let's discuss at the morning briefing.'

Keating slipped the phone into his uniform breast pocket and lowered his head, peering through the windscreen at the Strickland home across the road; the largest in a quiet estate of semis on the fringes of Bakewell. Cameron came out of the front door and beckoned to a white Mercedes S-Class parked in the drive. A short man in a grey suit got out and followed him inside.

'We could have talked in your car,' said Sawyer, 'which is roomier. But you're parked further up the road and you wanted to take a quick look at Strickland's people, and have a nose at my car, which you've never been in.'

Keating gave a grim smile and looked back at the house. 'Had dinner at a friend's place in Heatherdene yesterday. I've been trout fishing up there. Strickland called me direct about the tooth. Put me right off the Eve's pudding. My wife wanted to stay, but he insisted.' He opened his window, freshening the interior with birdsong. 'It's for your benefit.'

'Planting trees whose shade you know you'll never sit in.'

Keating nodded. 'Like I said, I won't be a part of his restructuring plans. But goodwill now will hopefully make his reign easier for whoever comes next, and anyone under them.'

'But...?' Sawyer reached across him and opened the glovebox. He fished out a lemon boiled sweet and unwrapped it in silence, waiting.

'But you're back too soon, and you know it. I made a mistake. This is too much, Jake. Even for you. There's Maggie. Your own recovery. The history with Strickland. And however much you don't want to show it, there's your past relationship with Eva Gregory.' Sawyer started to protest, but he talked over him. 'On top of that, we have two appalling murders—'

'You've spoken to Shepherd.'

Keating turned and fixed Sawyer with a soft gaze. 'Yes, I have. Shepherd has a bright future. He's sharp, book-smart, meticulous. But I've never seen him so preoccupied by your wellbeing. I'm not a dinosaur, Sawyer. I know what this job can do to your mind. How you have to turn yourself off, hide small things, for the good of the bigger picture. How the things you thought you'd hidden can come back. You should at least consider a sabbatical.'

Sawyer slipped the sweet into his mouth. 'Sir. I told you. I was built for this. I do dark, because I grew up with dark. It's the devil I know best. What's the worst that can happen to me? No worse than what happened.' He clenched a fist. 'It's like a callus. An insulation. But also a strength in its own right. What stands in the way becomes the way.'

Keating held his eye, glanced at the fist. 'This sounds like some Buddhist voodoo.'

Sawyer laid his hands flat on his leg. 'Stoicism. Marcus Aurelius.'

'You're comparing yourself to a Roman emperor?'

'Aurelius was sickly. He knew suffering. But it made him stronger. He was a survivor. He lived to sixty when it was rare to get through your thirties. Look, I had this with Hatfield in London. If you haven't truly suffered, it's impossible to understand how much suffering you can take. You project your own limits.'

Keating looked away, took a breath from the window.

'Sir. I can do this. You can't cut me out of the circuit.'

'I couldn't, anyway.' Keating turned back. 'The Chief Constable has given me a blank cheque for temporary resource. Courtesy of Strickland.'

'So, he's already the boss?'

Keating sighed. 'I have it on good authority that the

current mayor will hand over before the Convention of the North next year. But his health isn't good. He's already Strickland's puppet.' He ran a finger across the brim of his cap. 'And Strickland has specifically requested that you take a leading role.'

Sawyer thought for a moment. 'He wants the win.'

'The win?'

'He actually sees this as a fucking competition. Who can get to Eva first?'

Keating shot him the death stare. 'That's absurd. He wants his wife back safe. Why would he care how it happens?'

'He's clawed his way into power. Now he wants to recast his personal life. It's a win-win. If he and his private resources get to Eva first, he's the undisputed top boy to his wife and his son. If I get there first, he can show them how I couldn't have done it without him.' He reached into his pocket. 'We need to put the *de facto* Mayor of Greater Manchester under surveillance.'

'Why?'

Sawyer took a driving licence card from his wallet and handed it over. 'I got this from the house. Farouk Abadi. I wanted to see Dale's reaction to the idea that someone in his office might be working against him. It's a theory we should be checking.'

Keating shook his head, handed back the card.

'It works. They would have access to Eva's routine, Strickland's habits.'

'It doesn't work, Jake. Crawley doesn't collaborate. This is a personal crusade.'

Sawyer leaned in. 'Dale knew Abadi was at the

Kendal house. It wasn't a surprise. He was more irritated that I knew and tried to style it out to look like surprise. I believe he's been to the area himself, with Abadi. He's ahead of us. He knew about the Kendal connection to Crawley, somehow. We need to keep everything off HOLMES.'

'Because Strickland could access regional police intel?'

Sawyer nodded. 'Or he has someone working for him who can.'

41

DCI Robin Farrell swiped the sweat from his brow with his forearm. He dropped the bike resistance rate a couple of points and resumed his focus on the backside of the young woman on the step machine in front.

Bright yellow Lycra shorts. Matching backless vest exposing her sports bra.

The bike was an uncomfortable Peloton knock-off, installed in a musty alcove, and was rarely occupied. But it offered an uninterrupted view of the step machines and cross trainers.

His phone sat on the console. The music in his headphones dropped out and the top of the screen lit up with an incoming call icon. He cancelled the workout and slowed to a stop, then answered the call, transferring the outgoing audio to the microphone in his headphones.

'Farrell.'

'You were going to call me.'

He caught his breath. 'I was about to, Dale. Just got word.' He took a sip from his water bottle.

'Where are you? That doesn't sound like your kind of music.'

'Fucking racket. I'm in the GMP gym. Wife's orders. She insists I've picked up a paunch during my recent repose. I have to—'

'So, what's the word?'

Farrell dismounted and took out his headphones. He switched audio back to his phone and turned to the corner of the alcove. 'Found the original stolen car. It was dumped in Baslow, near to the Kendal house. ANPR shows it was left the night before last, so he must have dumped it, taken another car, killed and buried the woman, then driven away with Eva.'

'Where to?'

Farrell sighed. 'I'm working on that. Looking into stolen reports in the village. Checking CCTV. They might have left on foot, but that's unlikely.'

'So, has he gone to another one of his menopausal pen pals?'

'Working on that, too. I'd say so. But he might have other places in mind. We should watch his uncle's place. If he's clever, and he is, then he's taken a small vehicle he can hide easily. If we're unlucky, it belongs to someone who won't report it missing for a while. Maybe they're away or—'

'Crawley's been in touch.'

'Okay. What does he want?'

'He wants me to publicly confess to assaulting his mother.'

Farrell turned. Yellow Lycra Girl had been replaced by Quivering Sweatpants Man. 'Publicly confess? How? When?'

'He says he'll send more details soon.'

'Do you have experience in this? Ransom demands, whatever?'

Farrell sat on a wall bench. 'We were trained to never accept the first demand. The kidnapper has control over the price of the commodity, but as you're the only buyer in the market, you treat the first demand as an asking price. A place to start haggling.' He waited, listening to Strickland take a few shaky breaths. 'Dale?'

'*Commodity?*'

'Sorry. I don't mean to... Just... That's the theory. It's a negotiation. You can't let kidnappers think they have total power. Then you make sure the... person is still alive. You ask for proof of life. I know you have the photo—'

'He sent her tooth.'

'Christ almighty. You sure it belongs to her?'

'No. They're doing... tests.'

Farrell got up, paced. 'It's hard to use dental records with one tooth. They can match pulp with DNA, but it can take a while. It doesn't matter, though.'

'What doesn't?'

'I mean, in the negotiation. It doesn't matter if it's Eva's or not. We have to assume it is.'

Dale's voice turned shrill. 'If we're still wondering if Crawley is serious, Robin, I think the ship has fucking sailed.'

'Do you have any safe questions? Things you could demand Crawley put to Eva that only she could know.'

'I have things only we know, yes. But I need him to get in touch again first.'

Farrell closed his eyes, cast his mind back. 'We're told the main thing is to help the relatives stay strong and focused, and not to let emotion rule their decisions. For the sake of the hostage.'

'It sounds a lot like you're telling me to calm down.'

'Can you offer money? Do a dead drop. Mark the cash. Hide a tracker in the bag.'

'He doesn't want money. He wants me to suffer. He wants to humiliate me.'

Farrell headed for the door. 'I'll work on the stolen car angle. We might also get lucky and catch him on CCTV, although he probably stole it at night. Let me know if he gets in touch again.' At the exit gate, Farrell waved to a staff member and pointed at the barrier. The man scowled and let him through.

Farrell hurried down the stairs. 'What about your boys? Did they find anything?'

'Nothing the police don't know about.'

He stopped on the first-floor landing. 'How do they know about the house?'

'Sawyer.'

Farrell sighed. 'Of course, Sawyer. Of fucking course. They must have cross-checked with the crazies who wrote to Crawley. There were so many, though. They were quick.'

'There's more to it. Sawyer knew one of my men was there. Farouk. You met him in the car.'

Farrell stared out of the window, across the car park. 'But what put Sawyer on to Kendal? And how the hell does he know one of your boys was at the house?'

'I don't know. I have an idea. But I really hope I'm wrong.'

42

Robert Holsgrove eased his silver Lexus into a short queue of cars outside the main entrance of the Manchester Centre for Clinical Neurosciences. He welcomed the delay. As ever, Radio 3's *Classical Commute* had been a balm for the soul: Bach, Glazunov. And now, Schubert's masterful *Der Lindenbaum* was moments from ending. It was more of a wintry piece, at odds with the morning sun, but he found the mournful melody transformative at any time of year.

The vehicles in front passed through into a small car park in front of the Clinical Neurophysiology building. Holsgrove turned off towards Staff Parking.

He slowed. A pea-green Subaru Impreza was parked, badly, in his private space. He sighed and took out his phone to take a picture of the licence plate, then diverted to a free space in the non-private section nearby. It was probably a desperate or confused patient or visitor, but he had to report the infringement, and it would strengthen the senior clinicians' case for a private garage.

As he got out of his car, a man called from the Subaru driver-side window. 'Mr Holsgrove.'

He moved off, waving him away. 'I'm sorry, but I—'

The man raised his voice: shrill and nasal. 'Just a quick word.'

Holsgrove turned. A chill surged through his stomach as he spotted the sky-blue baseball cap.

Georgi got out and opened the Subaru back door. 'I know you're busy, my friend. But this can't wait.'

Holsgrove looked around. The nearest security officer was round the corner of the Neurophysiology building. He could make it. The officer would close the barrier. He could have the man detained. Report the threat.

Georgi grinned and beckoned him over with an exaggerated, scooping motion. 'For fuck's sake, don't run. And don't shout. That'll be bad for everyone. Particularly Oscar.'

Holsgrove kept his eyes down and walked over slowly. If he took his time, another staff member might arrive.

Georgi yanked the back door open wide. 'Chop, chop!'

As he ducked to climb into the Subaru, the other man, Sergio, turned from the passenger seat and sneered, with a strange little salute. 'Lovely to see you again, Doctor.'

Holsgrove sat down. 'I'm not a doctor.'

Georgi closed the back door and slipped back into the driver seat. 'You're not a fucking postman, are you?'

'I'm a consultant. A surgeon. More training and

experience than a doctor. Higher status. So, I'm traditionally addressed as *mister*, not *doctor*.'

'The fucking English and their status,' said Sergio.

Holsgrove raised his head. 'What do you want?'

Georgi turned in his seat. 'We asked nicely last time.'

Holsgrove held his eye. 'With a grotesque threat.'

Georgi hissed a laugh and raised a handgun, pointing it at Holsgrove but keeping it low in the car. 'Nah, nah. *This* is a threat.' He leaned closer; Holsgrove caught a whiff of the sickly vape smell again, just about taking the edge of Georgi's foul breath. 'I know you're a busy man, yes? But so am I. And I don't like to chase people. I'm a fan of proactivity. So, I'm expecting a daily call from you. An extensive update on the woman's prospects. And, as before, if anything exciting happens, I want to know about that right away.'

Holsgrove took a few steadying breaths. 'I received a report last night. My night duty doctor noted what he thinks are signs of purposeful response.'

'And what's that mean?' said Georgi.

Holsgrove sighed. 'Coma response is purely reflexive. Purposeful response is the next stage up. It indicates possible awareness.'

Sergio frowned. 'So, she might be waking up?'

'These people aren't asleep.'

'And so, what's next? You check it out...'

'Yes. There's a rigorous protocol. Whatever your concerns about Ms Spark, it's unlikely that she'll respond to verbal cues for some time, even if this does prove to be significant progress.'

Georgi got out of the car and sat beside Holsgrove in the back seat. He pushed the gun into his side.

Holsgrove winced and turned his head away. 'Please. There's really no need—'

'I'm not sure you're on board with the sense of urgency, *Mister* Holsgrove. This report you received last night. When were you planning to let me know about it?'

Holsgrove looked at him, then at Sergio's eyes in the rear-view mirror. 'Once I'd confirmed its veracity.'

'See, that's too late. I need you to let me know about the slightest twitch. Because if Ms Spark responds to verbal cues first to anyone but me, then, again...' He prodded the gun into Holsgrove's ribs. 'Bad for everyone.'

Sergio flicked his long hair to the side. 'Nine. Assembly. Nine-thirty to eleven. Core academics. Snack time at eleven. Then practical subjects. Art, music. Elective subjects after lunch, and therapeutic activities from three to four.' He got out of the passenger door and sat on the other side of Holsgrove. 'Life at the Seashell Royal is well organised. But their security is a joke.' He slipped out a long-handled shaping knife with a curved blade and held it to Holsgrove's neck. 'Daily updates. An immediate call on the tiniest hint of improvement. Before your morning team meeting. Before your protocol.' He leaned in, his mouth close to Holsgrove's ear. 'Or I will drown your reject son in his fucking hydrotherapy pool. Then I will cut out his heart and make you eat it.'

43

Keating sat at the head of the packed MIT conference room, staring up at the central monitor, which showed a close-up photograph of a tooth in a transparent plastic bag. He nodded at Sawyer.

'This was sent to Dale Strickland by Dennis Crawley, with a note that makes it clear where it came from.' Sawyer swiped his screen and an image of Crawley's note replaced the tooth. He waited for a moment while the detectives read it, some using their own screens. 'We're waiting on plasma analysis, but we can assume it belonged to Eva Gregory.' He swiped again, bringing up an image of the Kendal house. 'After Crawley escaped during his ophthalmologist appointment, he probably stole a car and drove to Eva's house, where he abducted her. Then he drove here, just outside Miller's Dale. It belonged to Victoria Kendal, a forty-eight-year-old landscape gardener who wrote to Crawley in prison.' He glanced at Walker. 'DC Walker pulled up the lead, and I investigated.' He swiped in a photograph of the shallow grave with Kendal's body. 'I found Ms Kendal nearby.'

Walker spoke up. 'The correspondence with Crawley made it clear she has plenty of money. He probed her for detail. She withdrew over two thousand pounds from separate ATMs in Baslow in the last week.'

'So, that's in Crawley's pocket now,' said Shepherd.

'Presumably, he forced her to withdraw the money. Maybe threatened to harm Eva if she didn't.'

'I believe he took a photograph of Eva at the house,' said Sawyer, 'then had Victoria post it. A few days later, he extracted Eva's tooth, and had her post that, too. Probably coinciding with the cash withdrawals. Then, he either drove away in the first car, or he dumped it and took a second, to clear the trail. He killed Victoria, buried her in nearby woodland, and left.'

Shepherd looked up at the screen. 'Why kill her? He could have just left.'

'His goal is to terrorise Strickland,' said Sawyer. 'He made the grave obvious, and he probably liked the idea that Dale might have thought it was Eva in there.'

'We're waiting on him to contact Strickland again over this confession business,' said Keating.

Myers twirled his pen. 'Do we have any reaction to the conference? With the tooth ring.'

From his seat in the corner, Stephen Bloom cleared his throat. 'Well, the press loved it. A flurry of requests for Sawyer interviews. I'm not sure if it helped, though.'

'Strickland thinks it might have provoked Crawley into sending the tooth,' said Keating.

'He was planning it, anyway,' said Sawyer. 'When he took Strickland's son, Luka, he also extracted his tooth. He was probably planning to send it to Strickland, but we caught him before he had the chance. This is the same pattern. First, the abduction. Then, proof that he's holding the person. In Luka's case, he sent his glasses. With Eva, we have the photograph. Then came the tooth. Something physical. A violation, but nothing too serious or life-limiting. I think if we play his game, if Strickland does somehow humiliate himself with this confession, then it's just the next stage for Crawley. He won't return Eva. He'll brutalise her more. The only thing that will break the cycle will be his mother's tooth.'

'Sawyer,' said Keating quietly, 'you're sounding obsessed. There are better ways to get to Crawley than a grotty old tooth.'

Sawyer pushed back his chair and sprang to his feet, hands on the table, eyes flashing. 'It's not a grotty old tooth. It's his *mother*. The tooth is an avatar for his mother. Crawley is a proxy. He's taking revenge on his mother's behalf. It's *her* revenge, not his. Until he has the tooth, until he has her, back in his possession, that process won't be complete in his mind.'

Keating stood up and leaned on the table, mirroring Sawyer. 'Detective Sawyer. We are not here to help a psychopath with his healing. We are here to get him back into custody and return this woman safely. You've had your drama. Now, we focus on police work. I want to know how Crawley left the Kendal house. Where did he get the transport? Check stolen car reports within a reasonable radius of the house. Check CCTV from the ATMs. Car movements at unusual times. Out-of-character behaviour.' He lowered himself back into his seat.

'And we should rake through the Crawley correspondence,' said Shepherd. 'Could give us an idea where he might head next.'

'While we're on the subject of police work,' said Sally O'Callaghan, 'might I lower the testosterone levels in here by talking about science?'

Sawyer sat down. 'We have tracks around the Kendal house. As with the other case, they're generic, but I might be able to narrow down to vehicle type. Drummond tells me that Victoria Kendal was strangled. No sexual assault. So, not buried alive.'

'He's going soft,' said Myers.

O'Callaghan glared at him. 'He beat her, though. If that helps. The blood in the bedroom is hers. Facial bruising consistent with blunt force. We have plenty of DNA that matches with Crawley, but I suppose that's no surprise. He didn't even bother to wear gloves. Fingerprint impressions all over her neck, other prints on handles, tables.' She paused. 'I also have a bit of mystery blood, from the floor near the dining table. Recent, too. Not matching on NDNAD.'

Sawyer drummed his fingers on the table. 'We should keep all the Crawley intel off HOLMES. It's already loose because of the sharing with Nottingham, and I'm concerned that Strickland might have access, given his position and his emotional connection to the case.'

Myers sighed and twirled his pen again. 'We've got enough to do without faffing around with notebooks and extra briefings.' He flopped forward onto the table in theatrical exhaustion, addressing Keating. 'Sir. We don't have the bodies for all this.'

'There's a lot going on,' said Keating. 'Strickland has released extra temporary resource, and, boy, do we need it. A prison escapee. A kidnapping. A new murder. And there's also the small matter of two other unrelated murders... And now, we've lost a potential target for a third from under our damned noses.'

'Jared White's PO checks out,' said Shepherd. 'He's way overdue. Phone's gone dark.'

'And how are we doing with our missing suspect?' said Keating. 'Dylan Brennan.'

Walker shook his head. 'No joy.'

Sawyer pointed at Shepherd. 'You said Dylan last left Ireland a few years ago.'

Shepherd thought for a moment. 'Four years, yeah. He was definitely on the return flight.'

'So, if he is our killer, he's slipped out unnoticed.'

'Byrne and the Garda are on it,' said Keating, 'but they couldn't find a turd in a bag of flour.'

'I was thinking,' said Walker. 'Burrows was beaten with something that left puncture marks. We've heard that Brennan's brother might have had IRA connections. I read they used to torture captives by beating them with pickaxe handles embedded with nails.'

Myers scoffed. 'Let's hop over to Belfast and do a bit of house-to-house on the Falls Road.'

'What about Brennan's teacher friend?' said Keating.

Shepherd nodded. 'Kieran Leith. I'm seeing him later.'

'Go with Sawyer.'

Shepherd and Sawyer shared a look.

'Sure,' said Shepherd. 'We're getting nothing from connections with the cellmates of the four Brennan killers. Leith might recognise some names from the school. Connections to Brennan.'

Keating flopped back in his seat. 'Can someone please find Jared White for me, at least? If he's gone AWOL off his own steam, it'd be good to knock him off the to-do list. Either way, I want to revisit the fourth man, Morris. Double down on the protection offer. Not a lot we can do if he still won't take it, but with White's disappearance, we have to offer again. What about vehicles?'

'Nothing solid,' said Myers. 'We're looking into transit vans that match the tracks at both scenes. I know we have good vehicle people on the resource team here, but if Strickland is opening GMP resource, I know a guy who's very good on stolen vehicles up there.'

'Bring him in,' said Keating.

'What about the Brennan church? All Saints in Hassop. And the sisters?'

'I haven't spoken to Laura,' said Sawyer. 'But I will.'

'Look into the church while you're at it. If, as Walker said, the Brennans' money kept it standing, I want to know more about the sisters' involvement. There's a local thread here. Maybe in the Catholic community around the church. With apologies to the big man upstairs, I

271

want the All Saints regulars and benefactors triple-checked for records, motives.'

'Be gentle with the Bible-bashers, Detective Sawyer,' said O'Callaghan. 'And please don't get seduced by the divine vibes and come back born again.'

He didn't smile. 'I think I'm beyond salvation.'

44

Luka Strickland puffed his hair out of his eyes and shuffled closer to the TV. On-screen, his character—a burly knight in a silver cloak—leapt onto a mound of blasted stonework, dodging a sword swipe from a gigantic troll. He clambered to the top, where the troll couldn't follow, and turned, aiming a bow at its head.

Dale Strickland hovered by the door, then walked in and sat down on the sofa. He placed a glass mug of hot chocolate on the coffee table and watched the game.

Luka glanced over his shoulder, saw the mug. 'Thanks.'

'You're welcome. Can he get to you?'

'Not from up here. It's a glitch. Mental. Just got to watch his ranged weapon.'

'How are you doing?'

'Okay. Just found a cool place to farm runes. This game is good, but you have to level up quick.'

Strickland closed his eyes, opened them again. 'I mean in yourself.'

Luka shrugged. 'Okay.' He fired an arrow at the troll, hitting it square in the face. It bellowed and swung its sword against the wall. 'What's happening with Mum?'

'Pause it a second. I need to talk to you.'

'Hang on.'

Luka sank a few more arrows into the troll. It gave an anguished howl and tumbled to the ground, then melted into the air. He saved the game and switched back to the home screen. 'Can't pause.' He turned. 'I'm alright. Still dead tired. Wish I could sleep better.'

'Where did you go yesterday?'

'Just a friend's house.' He picked up his phone.

'Luka, the school has sent work for you. But I don't see you studying.'

He flicked his thumb up, scrolling. 'Gonna do it this afternoon. Bit bored with this, anyway.'

'Which friend?'

'What?'

Strickland reached for the phone; Luka pulled it away. 'Put the phone down, Luka.'

He tossed the handset onto the coffee table and sighed, keeping his eyes on the carpet. 'Just... You don't know him.'

'What's his name?'

'Jude. Stayed at his house for a bit and came back on my bike. Dad. Why are you questioning me?' He stood up, grabbed the phone. 'I'll go do some schoolwork.'

Strickland held out an arm, blocking his path to the door. 'Two minutes, Luka.'

Luka sighed and set the phone back down. He sat on the armchair near the TV.

Strickland leaned forward, elbows on knees. 'Did you go to the house in the woods?'

'What house?'

'The one Jake went to. Did he take you there? Did you follow him?'

Luka scrubbed a hand through his hair. 'No.'

Strickland edged closer. 'Luka, whatever you think about Jake, he can only do so much.'

'What do you mean?'

'He has to follow rules. It takes time. And Mum might not have time. And there are things he might find out that I'm not allowed to know, because I'm related to Mum.'

Luka scowled. 'You don't like Jake.'

'We're not best friends, no. But we're both trying to find Mum. So, for her sake, if you know something that I don't, then please tell me.'

Luka held his gaze for a moment, then reached out and took a slurp of hot chocolate. 'Yeah. Okay. Course I will.'

Strickland waved a hand over himself. 'I'll soon be the Mayor of Greater Manchester. That means I have a lot of power. I've levelled up. If I have the full facts, there are things I can make happen that Jake can't. By the time he's followed all the rules, it might be too late.' He got up off the sofa and crouched by Luka's armchair. 'Luka, when you think about Dennis Crawley, how do you feel?'

Luka took another drink, buying time by keeping his mouth on the rim of the mug. 'He's sick,' he said, his voice echoing into the glass.

Strickland gently took the mug away and laid it back on the coffee table. 'He is sick. And so is Jake.'

Luka gaped at him. 'What? Why would you say that?'

'I mean...' He softened his voice. 'They've both had bad things happen to them. You know what that's like. Things that stay in your head. Remember when Jake went away for a while?'

'Yeah.'

'He was accused of murdering a suspect. A witness said she saw him kill this man with an axe. But then she changed her story.'

Luka stared straight ahead. 'But why would he do something like that?'

'Because he's sick, Luka. Some terrible things happened to him when he was younger. He seems like a good guy, but he's dangerous. People like that... It's the people around them. The ones who get close to them. They're the ones who get hurt. They always seem to be fine.' He moved around, in front of Luka, directly in his eyeline. 'Did you go to the house, Luka? Did Sawyer show you how to get there?'

Luka held his gaze.

'Did you see two men there? Did they grab you? Did you slash one with a knife to make him let go? Like you did with that boy who bullied you when you were playing football?'

Luka dropped his head. He got up, tried to push past, but Strickland blocked his way again.

'We both desperately want Mum back, Luka. But

276

you need to help *me* find her, not Jake. Your future lies with me and Mum. Right?' He held Luka by the shoulders. 'I have the power to get her home safe. Stick with me. Getting close to Jake will only get you hurt.'

45

Kieran Leith led Sawyer and Shepherd into a vast kitchen and dining room with a light grey tiled floor, dark grey walls, and laboratory-clean fittings in wood and brushed steel. No clutter, no knick-knacks, no framed vintage posters. Just one concession to personality: an oversized steel fork and spoon hanging beside an undersized wall clock. A wooden stand sat on the central kitchen surface, holding a propped-open cookbook.

Leith waved at the wall. 'I know. It's all about compromise. My partner isn't so pathological about minimalist interior design.'

'Do you still teach, Mr Leith?' said Shepherd.

'Goodness, yes. It's my way of adding something positive and hopefully lasting to the world. Not a lot of opportunity for that, these days. I work for agencies, though. I've stuck to my subject. Geography. But I also do general teacher training.' He gestured to the dark wood dining table, and Sawyer and Shepherd both pulled back a heavy chair and sat down. 'I fear it's a dying profession, though. In a real-world sense, at least.' He walked round the counter and pulled a few glasses from a high cupboard. 'You know. The internet. Autodidacticism. AI. Would you like a drink, gentlemen? I have a few juices. Oat milk? Tea, coffee?'

'I'm fine,' said Sawyer.

Shepherd smiled and shook his head. 'No, thank you.'

'Well, I'm going to have a kombucha.'

'Mushroom tea,' said Sawyer.

He took a can from the fridge. 'You make it sound so appealing. But it's not made from actual mushrooms, rather a symbiotic culture of yeast and bacteria. Also polyphenols, acetic acid. Probiotics to help the good bugs.'

A dog barked in an adjoining room. High and yappy.

Leith pointed. 'That's Susie. She knows we have visitors, and she's unhappy about being confined to her comfy bed in the sitting room.' He sighed, theatrical.

Leith was tall and in decent shape for his vintage; a little tubby round the middle. He was shiny-bald, with a generous salt-and-pepper moustache, and wore well-fitted jeans, Timberlands and a black T-shirt with a phrase constructed from cut-out newspaper lettering in multiple fonts and styles: *NO MUSIC ON A DEAD PLANET.* He put away two of the glasses and emptied the can into the third.

'This used to be a farmhouse. We rent out two of the outbuildings. Sometimes the main house if we go away.' He brought his drink over, sat at the table. 'And we have chickens round the back. Not many, but Felix takes the eggs.'

'Felix?' said Sawyer.

Leith sipped his drink. 'My partner. He's the head chef at the Gallery. Cavendish Hotel.'

'And you're the vegan,' said Sawyer.

Leith smiled. 'I am. Can you tell?'

Sawyer nodded to the counter top. 'Leon cookbook. *Fast Vegan*.'

'Ah.' He consulted his statement designer wristwatch and slipped on a pair of glasses with pale green frames. 'Now. You wanted to talk about Thomas Brennan. My goodness. I haven't heard that name in a few years. A wonderful man, and a huge influence on me.'

'You taught at his school.'

He nodded. 'St Anselm's. There was a lot of good fortune involved. I met Thomas when I saw him speak at an event not long after I qualified. I paid my dues at a few dicey state schools, and Felix pushed me to apply for a job at St Anselm's. I wasn't confident, but, astonishingly, Thomas recognised me from the event. Must have been five years earlier. I somehow talked my way into the role. He was a highly empathic man, an exceptional teacher and headteacher, and it's unconscionable what happened to him.'

'You looked up to him,' said Shepherd.

'Of course. He was a little older. Hardly a father figure, but certainly a mentor. We shared a few passions. The environment. The outdoors. For a while, we played on the staff rugby team, but then he got a shoulder injury and we took to walking.'

The dog barked again.

'*Susie*. Sorry about this. She thinks she owns the place.'

The skin prickled on the back of Sawyer's hand. He ran his fingers over it.

'Were you part of an organised walking group?' said Shepherd.

Leith rolled his eyes. 'For a while. Then... I remember there was some nonsense. Politics over the schedule. So, Tommy and I just walked together on Saturdays. Sometimes Sundays after church.'

'Did you share the same faith, Mr Leith?' said Sawyer.

He smiled. 'I did not. In many ways, that forged our friendship. Tommy would never evangelise. He didn't see me as misguided or, I don't know, a sinner. He was devoted to his faith, but saw it as a private matter. I think he grew more pragmatic as he got older, and became more enthused by the natural beauty of the area. Derbyshire, Staffordshire. The timelessness. We had many discussions on the nature of beauty.'

Shepherd nodded. 'God's creation.'

'I suppose he saw it that way. But he was also fascinated by the landscape. The geographical elements.'

'So, you were the perfect walking partner,' said Sawyer.

'If you like. Tommy was an obsessive note-taker and documenter. He had lots of little notebooks and he'd write down details of the landscape features, historical facts. I just enjoyed having a companion who seemed interested in my meanderings. It bores Felix to tears. Can I ask… Why the interest in Tommy now?'

The dog barked again. Screechy, angry.

'Two of the boys, now men, convicted of Thomas's murder…' Sawyer hesitated.

Flash of Henry's paws, poking out of the grass.

Twitching.

Shepherd picked up. 'They've been found dead, I'm afraid. We're investigating connections from St Anselm's. Ex-pupils who were close to Mr Brennan. The killings could be unrelated, but we're keen to speak to anyone with a motive for revenge.' He took out a sheet of paper. 'We have a few names. Individuals who came into contact with the four men in prison. Cellmates, people on their wing. There are also a few officers in there.'

Leith took the paper. 'And you think they might have links to the school?'

'That's what I was hoping you could tell us. Obviously, we've cross-referenced with the ex-pupils, but there may be a name you recognise here from a school-related activity, or something extracurricular Mr Brennan may have confided in you.'

Leith looked down the list of names, sipping from his glass, stroking his moustache. 'Can I keep this?'

'Of course.'

'I'll have a deeper peruse later.' His head snapped up, as if struck with a revelation. 'Have you looked into Tommy's church work? Maybe someone there has taken it upon themself—'

'We're investigating that, yes,' said Sawyer. 'Tell me about Thomas's notebooks.'

'Yes. They were little things. About the size of your hand. Different colours. This is before everything was digital, of course. Tommy was always involved in helping me choose locations for my field trips. He had books devoted to specific areas, landmarks, his favourite places.'

Sawyer's stomach churned. Leith's face seemed suddenly wrong. Strangely theatrical, as if he were wearing a mask. The washed-out green of his spectacle frames smudged as he moved his head to catch Sawyer's eye.

Moustache.

Watch.

Sawyer looked away, sensing he might be staring.

The face of Leith's watch flashed in the sunshine through the kitchen window.

He tried to shake away the link.

He looked back at Leith. The green of the glasses danced at the outline of the frames, as if detaching.

Sweat on his forehead now.

He squeezed his eyes shut.

Caldwell's face.

His moustache. Watch.

The dog barked again.

Roiling in his stomach.

Eyes open.

'Jake!'

Leith, leaning in to him, mouthing something.

Shepherd standing up.

A hollow rush in his ears. Distorted barking.

He stumbled out of the chair, retching, clawing towards the kitchen table-top.

Shepherd's hand on his shoulder.

Sawyer shoved him away, got to the sink, took out a glass.

Leith's voice breaking through the rushing sound. 'It's okay. I'll get it—'

Sawyer pulled him back, filled the glass with tap water. He leaned on the sink, gulping it down.

Leith again. 'Jesus Christ!'

Sawyer looked round. Leith was down on the floor, groping to get to his feet, Shepherd helping.

More barking. Louder, angrier.

Eyes closed again.

Caldwell's face. Smiling.

On the chair in his father's basement.

On the verge, silhouetted in the sunshine.

Sawyer opened his eyes, clambered out of the kitchen, past Leith, now standing.

'Jake!'

Past the cookbook. Past the table.

'Don't look back!'

Hand on the wall. Why was there a giant fork and spoon there? Had he shrunk?

Push out into the hall, to the front door.

He gagged. Diffuser on a bookcase. Sickly honeysuckle.

Outside... Fresh air...

His legs, though. Like rubber.

Stumbling to his knees. Get up. Stumble down again.

Barking, barking, *barking*.

Sweat, lashing off him.

Sawyer holding the gun on Caldwell in the basement.

Hands on him, trying to help him up.
From the grass verge.
From Leith's floor.
Keating to his AFOs. 'Stand down!'
Soil on his face. Grass between his fingers.
Toppling forward.
Nose to the floor. Wood. Wax.

46

A voice came through.

'Can you hear me, mate?'

Sawyer opened his eyes. A middle-aged man in a reflective jacket crouched beside him.

He looked around. Sitting room. Ceiling fan. Topographic map of the Peak District on one wall. A painting of Debbie Harry on another; Warhol-style but with a line of black paint running vertically down one eye, like an exaggerated teardrop. Photos: Leith and another man in chef whites standing in a gleaming kitchen; Leith on the Mam Tor summit, arms aloft; the other man with a small dog, running side by side.

'Can you tell me your name?'

He looked at the man. 'Jake.'

'I'm George. Can you tell me what happened, Jake?'

Shepherd stood by the tall bay window, arms folded.

Sawyer took a few slow breaths.

'Take your time.'

'I had a moment,' said Sawyer.

'A moment?'

'Yeah.' He sat up, on the sofa: grey, velvet. He ran his hand against the grain of the fabric. 'Haven't been sleeping well.'

George cast a doubtful look to Shepherd. 'Are you in any pain, Jake?'

Sawyer shook his head. 'I'm fine. Sorry to have wasted your time.'

The man smiled. 'This is my job.'

'Leith called the ambulance,' said Shepherd. 'He's okay. Bit freaked out.'

'Where is he?'

'Garden with the dog.'

George took out a blood pressure cuff. Sawyer rolled up his sleeve.

Mint on the man's breath. Coffee.

'Have you taken anything today, Jake?'

'No.'

'Are you on any prescribed medication? Any medical conditions I should know about?'

'No, and no.'

George inflated the cuff. 'Have you had panic attacks before?'

Sawyer winced at a sharp pain in his wrist. 'Sort of. How long have I been out?'

'Fifteen or twenty minutes,' said Shepherd. 'We had to drag you in here. I'll update Leith.' He walked out into the hall.

George removed the cuff, checked the reading. 'Bit high, but nothing scary.' He took Sawyer's pulse. 'Same there. I can give you something if you feel you need it?'

'Diazepam?' said Sawyer.

'Something similar, yes.'

Sawyer shook his head.

'You're a police officer?'

'Detective, yes.'

George stood up. 'Well, Jake, I'm happy to take you to Cavendish for a deeper assessment. But it's your call. It's probably best to get checked out after something like this.'

Another paramedic moved in and handed Sawyer a glass of water.

He drank half the glass in a few gulps. 'I'll be okay. Thanks for this.' He turned his head from side to side, flexing his neck muscles.

George stood up, packed his bag. 'Well, if you have any more moments, I'd get yourself to A&E. Even coppers are human, you know. So I'm told.' He grinned. 'Take care of yourself, Jake.'

They headed out, the wooden floor creaking under their heavy boots.

Sawyer's phone sat on a side table. It buzzed with a message.

Shepherd stepped back in. 'Leith's not happy, but he's cooling off. Could have been worse. You just swatted the poor bastard out of the way.' He paused. 'I used to get that, you know. A craving for water. Your sweats are worse than mine, though. I'd say you owe Leith a new tea towel.'

Sawyer finished the water. 'Say it.'

'Say what?'

His phone buzzed again.

'Say how this can't go on. How I have to step back. How I shouldn't be working. How I'm not fit for work. Whatever you've been telling Keating.'

Shepherd walked over to a tall white bookcase and browsed the spines. 'For a while, my trigger was blood. Then confrontation. Then confined space. But the root was blood. At least, that's what the therapist focused on. During our sessions, it transpired that when I was young, and still at nursery school, our teacher, Miss Willis, fainted. Hit her head on the desk. There was a lot of blood. The other kids were crying, screaming, as you would imagine. I remember going up to the front and looking at her. It was like a switch flipped in my head. I'd never thought of grown-ups as... breakable. They always seemed so confident and in charge of it all. I was perhaps too young to find out that wasn't true. Someone else ran to get help, and I crouched down by Miss Willis. She had a deep cut on her forehead. I reached out and touched it. I kept asking, "Is she dead? Is she dead?" She wasn't, but... It was the blood. How it leaked out, showing how everything is so fragile. How you can be happy one minute, but then the rug gets pulled out from under you. Why? Who's doing it? Who's controlling that? From then on, it was all just fear. The slightest thing, and my brain would extrapolate instantly, rush to the worst possible conclusion. So for a while, I buried myself in books. I got really into natural history, especially local stuff. Life as this constant struggle. Then I moved on to biographies of historical figures, inspirational memoirs. All these people who had faced much worse than me, but somehow got through it. The books were my friends, and

I hid myself away with them for a while. That was the way I dealt with it, and I thought it was the only way I'd get stronger. Nobody could tell me any different.' Shepherd sat in an armchair. 'And I don't think anyone can tell you different. Jake. This is the way you deal with it. You survive. But you've survived so much, you think you can survive anything. You think you're invincible. That kind of strength... It's more of a weakness. And until you accept that, it will not get better.'

Sawyer stared at him.

'Say it,' said Shepherd.

'Say what?'

'Something deflective. Something funny or flippant or... mordant.'

Sawyer gave a weak smile. 'Good word.' His phone buzzed again. 'Have you had any calls?'

Shepherd checked his pocket. 'Oh, shit.' He looked up. 'I left my phone in your car.'

Sawyer handed over his car key and Shepherd dashed out, retrieved his phone and scrolled through, noting the many missed calls, reading the messages.

Shepherd's feet, thumping back up the hall. He burst in.

Sawyer was up. 'Jared White.'

47

Leon Stokes twisted the cup out of the Nutribullet and filled a glass with greenish-brown gloop. He settled into a lemon-yellow sofa, set before a widescreen TV in the corner of his home gym. Boyd Cannon walked in through the double entrance doors and strode across the wooden walkway set around the room edge. The gym was an overlarge, overstocked indulgence for one man; a place to grunt and preen. Mirrored facing wall, flecked rubber exercise floor, treadmill, rowing machine, elliptical, bike. Weight bench and rack. Punchbag. Pull-down bar. All mostly ornamental. Stokes's regime had dwindled from a strict daily rotation of upper, core and leg work to an occasional circuit of pull-downs and weights, closing with a theatrical work-over of the punchbag. These days, he was more interested in the inside of his body than the outside. Chia seeds, fish oil, fistfuls of multivitamins with plant compounds. Low effort, high benefit; as long as he stuck to the partisan websites.

'You visit your mum?' said Cannon, sitting on a matching side chair.

Stokes took a slurp of his protein shake. 'Yep. You never know what you're gonna get. Last week, she gave me a fucking backhander. Accused me of stealing her money. The week before, I was the best son in the entire world. Today, she was just... there. Still breathing, not much else. I talked to myself for half an hour and fucked off.'

Cannon slipped on his glasses and opened his iPad Pro. 'Business is far from booming, Leon.'

'Strickland will come through once his immediate troubles ease up.'

Wes Peyton and Jakub Malecki pushed through the main doors, jabbering to each other.

'Once your midfield starts ageing,' said Peyton, 'you're fucked. But the trick is to replace it *before* it starts ageing. That takes bollocks.'

'Easy to say when you have the money and goodwill,' said Malecki.

'Fuck me. I can't help it if City has money. Premier League is big business. If you want a fair go for everyone, watch wheelchair tennis or something.'

Stokes took a long drink of his protein shake and wiped his mouth on his tracksuit sleeve. 'House meeting, gents. Just the one item on the agenda.'

'Doctor says she's improved,' said Malecki.

'Improved?'

'*Purposeful response,*' said Peyton, laying out the syllables like a small child parroting something phonetically.

Cannon sighed. 'There are still plenty of doors to unlock before this becomes an issue. This doesn't mean she's ready to point the finger at Malecki. She's not just going to sit up straight and announce what she heard. If she can even remember it.'

Malecki glared at him. 'It's not your name she'll speak.'

'I'm just saying, we need to shift focus onto our earners. All still spooked after the raids. And Doyle is ominously quiet.'

'What's the latest on Mavers?' said Malecki.

Stokes caught Cannon's eye. 'Strickland has sent him away.'

'Away as in *away*?' said Peyton.

Stokes clunked his glass down on the wooden floor. 'As in soon to stop Doyle's nagging. Sometimes it's best to not make a move. Stay in a holding pattern.'

Peyton walked over to Stokes. 'Leon. The Maggie Spark thing is already an issue.' He glanced at Cannon. 'We've got Holsgrove ready to squeak if he sees a drop of drool on her mouth, but by the time he's contacted us, we might have the double nightmare of getting to her when someone knows we're coming. Better to make it a surprise.'

'You been talking to your brother, Wes?' said Stokes.

'Why wouldn't I? He knows the score.'

Cannon scoffed. 'That's why he's where he is.'

Peyton paced over to Cannon and got in his face. 'Yeah. And I don't fucking fancy joining him. Which is why we need to deal with this now instead of waiting for it to get worse.'

293

Stokes got to his feet. 'A stitch in time...'

'Yeah,' said Peyton. 'This is our number one problem right now.'

Stokes shot him a dark look. 'A problem of your own making.'

Peyton walked back to Stokes, stopping too close. 'Whatever caused it, we need to deal with it now. You can sit in here, in your *holding pattern*, drinking your fucking cabbage juice. If the shit comes down, it's Malecki that'll get it in the neck. And me. We were fucking there. You weren't.' He was ranting now, his face inches from Stokes. He nodded to Cannon. 'You two can relax because you know if we get collared, there's no way we're dropping you in it.' He took a couple of steps back and shrugged in challenge, holding his arms out, palms up.

Stokes smiled. 'Did Eddie do this when you were kids, Wes?'

'What?'

'Clean up your shit. Did you go running to him when some kid nicked your Lego?'

Peyton stared at the floor in fury, shoulders rising and falling.

Malecki stepped across and stood between them. 'Listen. We need cool heads, okay? We are in a win-win here. If this bitch doesn't wake up, we win. If she does, I will make sure she doesn't wake up again. The doctor shit his pants. He is sending daily messages now. We will have time. And I can get to her.' He squeezed out a derisory smile. 'Easy.'

A moment of silence.

Music leaking from Stokes's Bluetooth headphones. He turned them off.

Peyton looked up. 'Eddie's inside, yeah. But that's a mistake he's learned from.'

'And what did he suggest, Wes?' said Stokes.

Peyton leaned in. 'Why take the risk?'

He held Stokes's eye for a few seconds, then turned and stormed out, shoving open the double doors with force. Malecki held up a hand, then followed.

Cannon swiped at his iPad. 'He's right about thinking ahead. Planning. We have columns to balance. Can we help Strickland get his wife back?'

'No, we fucking can't. That's just another plate to spin. I'll remind him of his pledge when the time is right.' Stokes picked up the protein shake, swirled it around the glass. 'And remember. If he walks it back or tries to stiff us, we have insurance.'

48

Sawyer and Shepherd flashed their warrant cards to the inner cordon officer and joined a well-maintained path beneath a canopy of birches. Sunlight shimmered through the emerald-green leaves, dappling the parched earth.

Sawyer forged ahead, almost tripping over the tendrils of a tree root, steadying himself with a hand on the trunk.

'Birch tree bark starts white,' said Shepherd. 'But all the years of winter have turned it blue-grey, with black splotches.' He called from behind. 'You okay, sir?'

'I'm fine. Bit groggy. Like I just got up.' Sawyer shielded his eyes from the sun flare.

'A ranger says he saw a dark-coloured minivan around 3am yesterday,' said Shepherd. 'Parked on the verge back near where the unit van is now. Didn't get the reg. Might be nothing, but, y'know. Trace, eliminate.'

'What kind of ranger?'

'National Trust. Stanton Moor is protected. It's

owned by a combination of private landowners, public organisations, conservation charities. Some bits are the property of local farmers and private individuals. The National Park Authority also has a hand in.'

Sawyer turned. 'And Mother Nature has signed all this off?'

'I don't think she has much choice. Sad that we need to work so hard to keep our beautiful places beautiful. It's either that or barbecue fires, tipping, overuse, dodgy development. Hell is other people. Particularly when they're tourists.'

The trees thinned out, and they crunched across a springy patch of heather, vivid in lilac and mauve. A layer of fallen leaves and needles led to a clearing that overlooked nine rickety stones, around the size of gravestones, gathered in a circle. The air bristled with the scent of resin, soil, fresh moss.

A yellow-and-white forensic tent sat on the far edge of the clearing, tended by a group of workers in white Tyvek suits. The cordon extended to the back side of the stone circle, where two groups of forensics conducted an overlapping grid search.

Sawyer stopped, and Shepherd caught him up.

'Have you been here before, sir?'

He edged forward, looking out at the stones. 'No, but my mum has. She came to a mini festival here for the summer solstice back in 1976.'

'Bronze Age, they think. Nine women turned to stone as a penalty for dancing on a Sunday.'

'Different times,' said Sawyer, walking towards the tent.

Sally O'Callaghan approached, in her turquoise Tyvek suit. 'Bad news and good news.'

'Bad, please,' said Sawyer.

'We have Jared White. Or what's left of him. Some kind soul carried him here in a taped-up bin bag. I've had a new girl only just get to a sick bowl in time. Be my guest, but don't expect much sleep tonight.'

Shepherd exchanged a glance with Sawyer. 'And the good news?'

'Victoria Kendal's car has been found dumped in Baslow. My skeleton staff are all over it as we speak. Oh, and the plasma analysis confirms the tooth is Eva Gregory's.'

'That's not good news,' said Sawyer.

O'Callaghan waggled a hand. 'I'll take every ticked box I can get at the moment.'

Sawyer paused, thinking. 'It's why he's waiting. He wants Strickland to be in no doubt. We'll hear from him again soon.'

'And he switched transport. We double down on freshly stolen cars in the area.'

Sawyer and Shepherd pulled on masks and gloves, and ducked inside the tent. Shepherd hung back as Sawyer moved in on Jared White's clothed body, propped against a rotting log, the black bin bag cut open and peeled away.

A thick layer of dried blood plastered his hair across his face, coating his head and neck. His left eye socket had collapsed, revealing a dislodged eyeball, perfectly smooth and intact, resting on the cheekbone. Sawyer moved his head in close, entering the eyeball's unseeing sightline. The socket seemed to have caved in under a heavy impact on the left side of White's forehead. The fabric at the shoulders of both shirt sleeves was stretched taut over jutting spurs of bone. His jaw was smashed, partially detached.

Sawyer lifted the polythene. White's ribcage was concave beneath his shirt, and both forearms had snapped and hung at unnatural angles; one broken at the wrist, the other nearer the elbow. Smears of gore had congealed on White's face, neck and chest.

He leaned in closer. A wound across White's neck: puncture marks. Similar-sized holes down one arm, across his chest.

Sawyer jerked his head to the side, recoiling from the smell; too strong for the mask. Faeces and vomit, with a vague metal tang.

'Dog walker?' said Sawyer.

O'Callaghan's voice from behind. 'No. Peace-seeker. Said he comes to the circle twice a month to meditate. It'll take more than alternate nostril breathing to come down from this.'

Sawyer looked at the face again. The eye socket. The eye.

He expected his mother's face, demolished by Caldwell's hammer.

But nothing.

'He's been beaten by something studded, like Burrows,' said Sawyer, standing up. 'And there's a lot of blunt force trauma.' He looked at O'Callaghan. 'Can you let me know if he's left us anything?'

'Of course. His form so far suggests not. Drummond

will have the body within the hour. I'm sorry to be the stuck record here, but the only trace so far is tracks. Again, generic. Van, pick-up.'

Sawyer nodded to her as he left the tent, trailed by Shepherd. 'Talk to the ranger. Did he see anyone? Anything unusual he remembers about the van?' He walked out to the edge of the clearing and turned to gaze out across the stone circle.

'Beaten?' said Shepherd from behind.

'Looks like it. Burned, beheaded, beaten...'

Shepherd's phone buzzed. 'You might be overthinking the "B" thing. Walker says he's combing through the Crawley admirers. Nothing yet. No further contact from Crawley.'

'I'll go to the church. Maybe we need to get more lateral. Ask about Brennan's church connections. Can you speak to Laura Brennan? I'll follow the money. Let's find out more about the family's involvement. How much they put in, where it came from.'

'This could still be a beef the four of them got involved in since Brennan's murder.'

Sawyer turned, gave him a look. 'It's linked to Brennan somehow. Damon Morris is the only one left now. We need to watch him.'

'He won't accept it.'

'I said watch, not protect.'

'If it is linked to Brennan, maybe he was into something? Could his murder be about more than just teenage boys objecting to his request to be quiet?'

Sawyer turned back to the circle. 'Maybe he told his priest something he didn't tell his family.'

'Good luck getting the priest to break confessional confidentiality.'

O'Callaghan came out to them. 'Keating has expedited PM. Early briefing tomorrow. I should hopefully have my findings by then, too. Don't expect any revelations, though.'

'He wasn't killed here,' said Sawyer, turning again.

Shepherd nodded. 'Bin bag from van to tree. Over his back. White could have just been unconscious. Jesus, could he have beaten him while he was still in the bag?'

Sawyer shook his head. 'No. It's about maximising the suffering. The killer wanted them to see, to know what was coming. Why bag him up first? Like the others, he killed them somewhere he could take his time, with no danger of discovery.' He glanced at O'Callaghan. 'It'd be good to know where.'

She offered a thin smile and walked back to the tent.

'And we need to find Uncle Dylan. Now we have more bodies thanks to Strickland, get some of them on his case.' His phone vibrated in his pocket. A call. 'Everything points to revenge killing, but I'm just not feeling it. There's something oddly dispassionate.'

'Dispassionate?' said Shepherd.

'Too much method to the madness.'

'Brennan's killing was a long time ago. Tempers cool.'

Sawyer took out his phone. 'The fury doesn't fade. Whoever's doing this is efficient, savage. They want the victims to suffer. So, why the presentation as well? All that effort. Getting the bodies out to places like this.'

Caller ID. Mia.

He connected.

'Uncle Jake?'

'Mia. How is—'

'There's...' She stuttered through tears. 'There's progress. It's *good*, Uncle Jake. The doctor says there are signs of... response.'

'Purposeful response?'

'Yeah. Purposeful response. He says she can probably hear us. He says there's a chance she might be back with us soon.'

49

Sawyer snapped a shortbread finger in two and dunked one half in the foam of his latte.

Mia Spark looked up from her phone, laid flat on the corner table at the back of the Costa concession. 'You won't sleep. It's too late for caffeine.' She'd tinted her hair strawberry blonde and let it grow past her shoulders, and she'd discovered make-up: light pink lips, a dash of foundation and eyeliner. She wore a wrist wrap with a silver heart in the centre, which jiggled as she tapped the screen. Her violet crop top featured a black-and-white screen print of a moth-like symbol with wide wings and long tail.

'What's your T-shirt?' said Sawyer.

Mia pulled the front fabric taut across her chest, revealing a phrase in tiny handwriting beneath the image.

Sawyer leaned in to read it.

LOOK FOR THE LIGHT

'Firefly,' said Mia. 'From *The Last of Us*.'

'A symbol of hope?'

Mia made a face and sipped from a fruit smoothie. 'Yeah. And resistance. Against the dark forces.'

Justin met Sawyer's eye across the table.

'How's Freddy?' said Sawyer.

Mia shrugged, fiddled with her AirPods. 'He's okay. Getting out more now. He's at home. Doesn't like to come here. I text him when we drive back.'

Sawyer took another drink, to fill the silence.

Mia reached into her T-shirt and pulled out a heart-shaped pendant. Male and female figures danced around a sun symbol.

'That's your mum's,' he said.

'Yeah. Relationship Optimism Necklace. I bought it for her. I wear it when I come here.'

'You think it's lucky?'

She scoffed. 'I just like it.'

Justin looked at his watch. 'Holsgrove says we can go up in five minutes.'

'I hear you have a boyfriend,' said Sawyer.

Her head snapped up. '*Dad*. Joshua is my friend, and he's a boy. But he's not my boyfriend. We talk. We went through a lot of stuff. We want to do something together. Help other kids who've been traumatised.' She pointed at the T-shirt symbol and looked back down at her phone.

Sawyer gazed at the top of her head. 'That's wonderful, Mia.'

Holsgrove stood off to the side, giving Sawyer, Justin and Mia access to the bedside. The room was cool and airless; it smelt of synthetic pine, hand sanitiser, freshly bathed skin. Dim fluorescent lighting cast the space in a watery blue. Everything was drained, washed out, sepulchral. Grey linoleum floor, ceiling of cheap drop tiles. Plain white walls with no pictures. Why waste the effort when they couldn't be appreciated, anyway? It was a level down from patient care; more like a storage space for something sentient but not quite alive, not quite dead. Halfway to the mortuary, with the final part of the journey— forward or return—still uncertain.

Maggie lay on her back, head sunken into her pillow, her features barely visible behind the oxygen tube wired into her nose, and the tracheostomy fitting installed around her neck and mouth. Her rust-red hair registered black in the light.

Mia moved in and pulled a chair up to the bed. 'Hiya, Mum.' She lifted the pendant from her T-shirt and squeezed it between her thumb and forefinger. She reached out and placed the other hand on Maggie's exposed fingers, then rested her forehead on her mother's shoulder, murmuring to her. Justin stayed by the door with Sawyer, and the three men stood for a moment, still and sombre, listening to the bleep and whirr of the monitors, and Mia's hushed whispers.

'Mr Sawyer.' Holsgrove spoke in a muted tone. 'I'm pleased to see you looking so well.'

Sawyer nodded in acknowledgement.

Holsgrove stepped forward. His normally perfect tie

knot looked rakish and hurried. 'Did you enquire about Ms Spark's condition independently?'

'Mia called me.'

Holsgrove forced a smile. 'Ah. It's just… I don't want to offer any false hope or risk information being filtered. It would be best if everything came through me direct. It's important that family members don't read too much into minor awareness changes.'

'Of course,' said Sawyer. 'Apologies. Is that what we're talking about? Minor changes? I thought you felt Maggie may be on the road to awareness.'

Holsgrove looked flustered. 'I wouldn't go that far. We continue to move in the right direction, but this can be a long, unpredictable journey, and there may be false dawns and setbacks along the way. But loved ones can be helpful, yes. The sound of their voices, encouragement, music. Anything that might normally trigger an emotional reaction in the patient. I can leave you in private for a while, but please let me know if you notice anything that could indicate acknowledgement of your presence. Although I have to say, at this stage, that's extremely unlikely. Ms Spark is clearly a strong soul, though. I always try to err on the side of optimism. But in her case, it may well be justified.' He managed another smile. 'Just come through to my office when you're ready to leave.'

He lowered his head and exited through an adjoining door, closing it behind him quietly.

Sawyer shifted closer to Justin and kept his voice low. 'How are you getting on with Project Glenroy?'

Justin matched his whisper. 'I tried to get a message

to him. But the number he gave me doesn't connect anymore.'

'That's interesting.'

'Interesting good or interesting bad?'

Sawyer thought for a moment. 'Interesting very bad, potentially. I'm surprised you've received no blowback from Mavers's counterattack. But if Mavers had made Glenroy disappear, then his boys would have come back to you by now.'

'How?'

'I assume you set him on Mavers and Wilmot by calling him on your own phone?'

Justin dropped his head.

Sawyer pointed to Maggie's bed. 'Mavers is the key to this. The guy who visited me triggered the station attack. But it was Mavers he wanted.'

'Could he have been one of Glenroy's?'

Sawyer shook his head. 'Eastern European. And he was present at the station attack.'

'*What*?' Too loud.

Mia raised her head, then rested it back on Maggie's shoulder.

'Somebody ordered the attack. The sight of my visitor at the station seals the connection to Mavers. So, I'd really like to know how Glenroy tracked him down, and where to. Because that might help me find Mavers, which should lead me to whoever wanted to find him so bad he sent some psycho to torture it out of me before launching an armed assault on a police station. Which is why we're standing here right now.'

'It's all bullshit.' Mia sat up abruptly.

'What is?' said Justin.

'Joshua's nan was really ill, yeah? And he said at her funeral they were going on about how she "lost her battle" with cancer or whatever.'

'Mum's a strong person, Mia.'

She tilted back her head. 'I know. But she needs our help. Her brain is trying to mend itself. She can't talk, but the doctor said she can hear. So, if she hears the right things, it might help her brain to get better. We can't just leave her like this. To have this *battle* all by herself. We have to do some of the fighting for her.' She walked over and faced up to Sawyer. 'It doesn't matter if you arrest someone for what happened. That won't help Mum now, will it? I'm telling her all the things I remember, from when I was little. Things we've seen and done together. That's not much, but it's more than you are doing.' She jabbed a finger into Sawyer's chest, hard enough to make him stumble back. 'And it's more than *you* are doing.' She did the same to Justin.

Justin reached out for her. 'Keep your voice down.'

'Mia,' said Sawyer.

She glared at him: kohl-streaked tears, eyes raging. 'I'll get her back. She won't have to fight alone. And whoever did this to her, they will pay for it.'

Mia held Sawyer's eye for a second, then spun round and walked out.

Sawyer and Justin stared after her for a moment.

Sawyer held up a hand and spread the fingers. 'Five minutes.'

Justin eyed him, then sighed and followed Mia out of the room.

Sawyer sat on the chair vacated by Mia and took out his phone. He leaned in and rested a hand on Maggie's forehead. 'Mags.'

He took out his phone and opened the Spotify app, navigating to The Aloof's 1996 album, *Sinking*. 'No big speeches.' He pressed play, and the music trickled from the phone speaker: rhythmic pulses of dub bass; shuffling, restless drums; a soft male voice, Jamaican accented.

He sat back, closed his eyes.

———

On the way out, Sawyer tapped three times on the door of Holsgrove's office.

'Yes?'

He stepped inside.

Holsgrove got up from his desk. 'How is she?'

'Sitting up,' said Sawyer. 'Asking for tea.'

Holsgrove twitched for a second, then narrowed his eyes, following Sawyer as he took a seat. 'I assume—'

'Do you have a couple of minutes?'

Holsgrove sat down. 'Of course. But, Mr Sawyer, there's not a lot else I can tell you. I realise that this is a frustrating and upsetting situation for everyone close to Ms Spark. But we're moving in the right direction. People survive this. Her outlook is improving. I gather she's a strong character—'

'She's a loose end.'

'I'm sorry?'

Sawyer tilted his head, studying Holsgrove. 'If I was

the person who tried to kill her, I wouldn't want her waking up and assisting the enquiry into the station attack.'

'I'm not sure I—'

'Of course, I'm a target, too, as I was also there. But I was only present for a short part of the attack. Maggie was there from the beginning. And there's a big difference between targeting a senior detective who's up and about and alert, and a comatose woman in a low-security environment like this.'

Holsgrove frowned. 'I can assure you, we employ extremely high standards of care, and our security staff are trusted professionals. Patient safety is our number one—'

'If I were the person who tried to kill Maggie, and I wasn't keen on her coming round and assisting the enquiry, I'd be very interested in her current situation. Her routines. Her carers. Her clinicians.'

Holsgrove sat back in his chair and swished his mouse around its mat.

'How secure is your communication here?'

'As far as I know, it's very good. I could get you a meeting with our IT Service Manager.'

'I may need to insist on a separate officer.' Sawyer rested his elbows on his knees and rubbed his hands, swirling the palms around each other. 'Earlier, you seemed annoyed at my knowledge of Maggie's improvement.'

'Annoyed?'

Sawyer nodded. 'People in your position can have a tendency towards control freakery. It's understandable.

But this felt like more. I'm sensitive to outliers, Mr Holsgrove. Anything that seems off, out of place, out of character. I like to pick at those threads, see what unravels. You wanted to know *how* I knew. That's specific and, as I see it, irrelevant.' He shifted forward in his seat. 'And it's the irrelevance. That's the outlier. Of course, you want to control the flow of information. But you care too much. *Why*?'

Holsgrove took a moment. 'Mr Sawyer. I must say, I'm unaccustomed to this kind of scrutiny over a perfectly innocent passing enquiry. And I don't take kindly to being intimidated in this way. Please remember you have suffered injury in the same incident. Although your trauma was mild in comparison, I would still advise you to take a longer rest period before returning to work. Have you considered the possibility that your judgement on these matters may be compromised by cognitive impairment?' He consulted his watch. 'Apologies, but I have a clinic round in fifteen minutes.'

Sawyer stood up. 'I'm going to my car. Then I'll come back with a phone for you. We call them burners. Confidential and untraceable. I'll also give you my private number. If you're concerned about anything, please call me immediately.'

50

Sawyer flipped the steak over in the pan, pushed it around. He held his phone in the other hand, browsing the website of All Saints Catholic Church. Schedule for mass, Sacrament of Reconciliation. Details on baptism, weddings, funerals.

He skimmed the *About* section. The priest was Tyrone Reavey. Early sixties. Took the job in the late 1990s. The gallery showed the Neoclassical exterior, with a Greek temple-style Doric portico. It was built in the mid-1800s, but the interior looked recently remodelled: light, clean, contemporary, with a curved ceiling high above the altar. Tall stained-glass windows with bible scenes overlooked the pews on either side, above paintings of saints and scripture.

Sawyer stared into the sizzling meat.

Flash of Jared White's eye.

Back to phone.

He looked through the *Newsletter* section ('News from the Pews').

Bible study every Friday at 11am.

A Saturday talk from one Terry Scully on *A Journey Through The Beatitude* (bring a packed lunch).

Mission statement with standout words capitalised: *Worship, Serve, Grow, Give, Belong.*

A picture of Reavey sat at the top, awkwardly centred. He loitered by the altar in full vestments, with a sheepish smile. Metal-rimmed glasses. Untidy grey hair; neat black-and-grey beard. A rambling article praised his long service ahead of his forthcoming retirement, and a few coy quotes from Reavey himself on the qualities of his replacement candidates.

The only mention of the Brennans came in a short piece about a forthcoming ecumenical gathering, which quoted Laura Brennan citing Dolly Parton's advice that 'if you want the rainbow, you have to put up with the rain'.

Sawyer had little appetite, but chewed his way through the steak with a few overcooked fries and ageing lettuce.

He eyed the wound on his arm as he ate, listening to the craving, feeling it linger, hoping it would pass by. As it intensified, he chased distraction by watching Haneke's 2002 dystopian thriller, *Time of the Wolf*. But the imagery was too incendiary and angular, jangling his already frayed nerves.

He abandoned the meal and walked into the bedroom, where he stripped to the waist and executed a few loose Wing Chun forms before the mirror, then dropped into Jeet Kune Do fighting stance and worked through his lunges, punches, kicks, finger strikes.

Exhausting himself. Trying to deny his brain the space for the flashes, the chatter, the cycling earworms and recurring voices.

He spoke to himself as he worked. Nonsense jabber. Mini scenes. Monologue. Dialogue. Multiple tones and accents. Flitting between characters. Like a child oppressed by the turmoil of his imagination, giving it vent.

He flopped down on the bed and slumped forward, breathing deep and heavy. Now, the backed-up flashes came in bursts.

Eva in the chair, terrified.

Eva up close. The side of her neck. The curve of her back.

Her hair swishing as she tossed her head.

Her tooth.

Jared White's collapsed skull.

The fucking eyeball. Hanging. Shining in the sun like a marble. Like a doll's eye.

Maggie's tube. Nourishing her. Keeping her on the right side of the divide.

Maggie in his student room. Young. In bloom. Self-sustaining.

His mother at the gate.

Movement in the bedroom, on the edge of Sawyer's vision.

His head snapped up and he focused on the chair in the corner, draped in his jacket.

Empty. No Jessica.

He gazed up at the ceiling, let his eyes refocus. A shadow flickered, grew darker as he watched. It seeped to the edge of the wall and trickled down. Not crawling this time. Sliding.

Sawyer blinked, looked away. It remained.

He pushed up from the bed, reached up to the wall. The change of angle re-aligned his perspective, and he caught himself flailing at nothing.

He snatched his wallet from the bedside table and took out the blade, pressing the sharp edge into a clean space at the top of his bicep, above the scab from the first time. The groove deepened, and the skin yielded, spilling blood along the curve of his muscle, dripping to the floor.

Sawyer gasped at the pain: the purity of it. The way it instantly pulled the plug on the thoughts, the images, the voices. He bit down on his tongue and ran the blade back and forth, across the slit, lengthening it, deepening the wound. The pain ramped up, sparking up his arm like a current, crackling across his chest in urgent rebuke.

He drew the blade away and began a new cut, slicing, not pressing this time. As he unzipped his skin, widening the breach with short, jagged swipes, he lifted away from himself, above the agony, beyond his actions. He was an outsider in his own body, watching a hand move across his flesh without agency. And then, panic. Could he even stop it, now he was no longer in control?

Sawyer turned his head, as Bruce hopped up onto the chair, watching him. The cat narrowed his eyes, cool and curious.

He cried out, threw the blade across the room, then reached for a towel, pressing it into the wounds, suddenly appalled by the disfigurement.

He screamed, full-throated, sending Bruce away.

Sawyer wrapped the towel around himself. Soothing, desperate to conceal the cuts, erase them. He howled and sobbed, rocking in place. A rage of mourning for his unsullied skin.

———

After cleaning up in the bathroom, Sawyer basted the wounds in antiseptic salve, and dressed them in plasters and bandages. He swallowed max-strength ibuprofen and paracetamol with water straight from the bathroom tap, and stumbled back into the sitting room.

His arm throbbed, scandalised by the attack.

He poured a glass of Coke and turned to face the sitting room.

Bruce sat on the sofa, gazing over, still curious but more wary now.

'I know, big man.'

Bruce washed himself for a while, then jerked his head towards the vibrating phone on the coffee table.

Sawyer hurried over and took the call.

'Sir,' said Walker. 'Sorry to call late. You okay?'

'Living the dream. What is it, Matt?'

'A woman named Sonya Banks is overdue from Baslow. She owns a café there and was due to meet with the manager yesterday afternoon. But she didn't show. It's out of character, so the guy called it in. Came straight to us because of the Kendal car being dumped there.'

Sawyer sat down, pressing down on the bandage. 'Did she drive? Where's her car?'

'Yes. Grey Toyota Corolla. Hybrid. And it's gone from her house. Banks is a friend of Victoria Kendal's, sir. She owns two more cafés and a florists up in Hope. Lives alone.'

Sawyer watched Bruce as he ate from his bowl. 'Crawley got her address from Kendal before he killed her.'

'Her brother's been to the house. No sign. Her phone's not there, and it's switched off. Rhodes is on it.'

Sawyer lay back on the sofa. 'He wanted a new car because of heat on the old one. But he didn't want the theft to be discovered immediately. It was a safe bet to take Banks with him as he thought she wouldn't be reported missing for a while.'

'But he didn't know about the café manager meeting.'

'No. So we might be ahead of his schedule.'

Walker paused. 'Schedule?'

'Yes. It's all carefully planned. For maximum pain to Strickland. Get on the ANPR. CCTV around Sonya Banks's house. Dashcams. Doorbell cams. Although that's probably all pointless now... Focus on ANPR. The route he took with Sonya Banks's car. Crawley has her and Eva at a new location. He has Sonya Banks's phone...'

'But he'd know we could track that, right?'

Sawyer frowned. 'He'd know. But I don't think he cares.'

51

Sawyer climbed out of the Mini and squinted into the early sun: low and lurking, copper-coloured. He climbed the steps up to the front courtyard of All Saints Church and looked up at the columned facade. Was it appropriated or progressive? Probably both.

He walked round to the side of the building and admired the stained-glass windows, running a palm across the sandstone wall. The church was set back from the roadside, on raised land that opened onto lavish, well-tended grounds. The grass on the verge below was tightly cropped, with a bench in the shade of an abundant beech tree.

He stepped down onto the drive and walked around to the back, onto the dewy grass. Bungalow and outbuildings in matching sandstone, expansive lawn, light woodland beyond.

Sawyer inhaled. Peaty earth, freshly cut grass, a whiff of balsam from the trees. From up here, he could see the land sloped down to a modest river that ran alongside the road and through to the village.

'Lovely morning.'

A grey-haired man in a light-brown blazer with dog collar emerged from a door at the back of the main building. He stopped a few feet from Sawyer and held out a hand. 'Tyrone Reavey. I'm the parish priest.' He carried a slight Irish lilt beneath the flatter local vowels.

Sawyer shook his hand. 'Jake Sawyer. Detective Inspector. I wasn't expecting signs of life so early.'

Reavey grinned. *'He who keeps Israel will neither slumber nor sleep.'*

'I think I need coffee before theology.'

'Oh, I'm the same. Happy to help.' He gestured to the bungalow.

Sawyer walked to a bench on the fringe of the lawn. 'Thanks, but I don't have long.' He sat down.

Reavey joined him at the other end of the bench. 'You must take a quick look at our wonderful church before you go, though.'

'I will. I just wanted to get a sense of the place. But since you're here, could you spare a few minutes?'

'A pleasure, Detective Sawyer.' Reavey turned to face him. He crossed his legs, then decided against it and uncrossed them, clasping his hands and resting them between his closed knees.

'I'm looking into a case we feel might have connections to the murder of a local man, quite a long time ago. Thomas Brennan.'

Reavey screwed up his face in sympathy. 'Ah. A long

time ago, but I remember the funeral as if it were last week. Well attended with considerable press interest.'

'You've been the priest here since the late 1990s.'

Reavey nodded.

'The Brennans were wealthy. They contributed to the church upkeep, yes?'

'Well. We were looking a touch careworn in the mid-2000s. We certainly wouldn't have had the refurbishment without the Brennans. They also did a lot of work in the community. Obviously, Thomas's standing helped with that. I think when the Brennans moved here, they saw the church as an Irish outpost. Thomas denied it, but I'm sure he oversaw the refurbishment to mirror his hometown church.' Reavey was restless. He stood up. 'Come inside, Mr Sawyer. I insist. You should see the church for yourself.'

Sawyer hesitated, but got to his feet and followed as Reavey walked around the side of the main building. 'You're on your way, then.'

Reavey turned. 'Sorry? Oh. You mean retirement. Ah, yes. I'm afraid my sister is approaching the end of her time. And my service here feels... Well...' He put a hand to his lower back. 'I'm feeling the years, Mr Sawyer, y'know? I answered the call, but all missions end.'

He unlocked the main doors and pushed them open. Sawyer followed him across a carpeted hallway and they stood by the back row of pews, looking down to the aisle at the impeccably presented altar. The room was cast in tinted light from the large windows. It was clean and non-stuffy; more like a performance venue than a place of reverence and introspection. It smelt of incense, fresh flowers, beeswax.

Reavey waved a hand up at the curved ceiling. 'The rebuild took the best part of three years. It was exhausting and disruptive, but I'm sure you'll agree, the results are magnificent.'

'It's an impressive space, yes.'

Reavey smiled. 'You're not spiritually inclined, I take it?'

'Does it show?'

'Oh, yes.'

Sawyer shrugged. 'It's all a bit much for me. I'm more interested in individual experiences. How they shape us, dictate our behaviour. The idea of a one-size-fits-all morality seems too neat, too easy.' He looked up at one of the stained-glass windows, constructed from stark shades of red, blue and yellow. The art was elaborate and hyperreal: Mary cradling a cherubic Christ with oddly mature features. 'This is all too comforting. It offers answers rather than poses questions.' He looked at Reavey. 'And, as the history of the Catholic church shows us, an angelic front can cover for some vicious demons.'

Reavey raised his eyebrows. 'Goodness, you're quite the diplomat, aren't you, Mr Sawyer? I take it you're not a fan of a clear line between good and evil?'

Sawyer sat down at the end of a pew. 'It's fine for cartoons. Comics. Bad films. People are more complex than that.'

Reavey sat on the adjacent pew. 'I suppose your profession demands a consequentialist approach.'

'I was reading on the website that you came over

from Ireland in the 1990s. What drew you here, Mr Reavey?'

Reavey laughed. 'How long have you got? I suppose, like many people, it was a matter of fate. Back in Ireland, my father passed when I was fifteen. He was a priest, too. I looked after my mother for a while, then she met someone new and I studied the priesthood to pay tribute to my father. I had various roles at church organisations in Ireland and took the job here at the end of the millennium. I was on the cusp of my forties and thought it was time to get a different angle on the world. A new beginning.'

Sawyer nodded. 'A rebirth. I followed in my father's footsteps, too.' His phone buzzed in his pocket. 'Did Thomas Brennan's daughters follow up his work with the church? I saw Laura's name in the newsletter.'

'Oh, yes. They're regular attendees, and generous with contributions. Their mother, Tanya, was a fine woman.'

'Did you know Thomas's brother, Dylan?'

Reavey lifted his head and thought for a while. 'I knew *of* Dylan. I didn't know him, though. I remember him being terribly distraught at the funeral.' He leaned forward on the pew. 'Can you share the nature of your investigation?'

'Thomas's killers have been recently released. Let's just say that someone doesn't seem too happy about that. Do you recall any connections to the Brennans? People who attended church and seemed linked to them? People who made you nervous? Do you remember anyone expressing murderous intent towards his killers?' He nodded to the confessional.

Reavey followed Sawyer's eyeline, shook his head. 'I'll think it over. Nothing immediately comes to mind. I'm sorry I can't help more.'

They got up and walked to the doors.

'Laura and Catherine,' said Sawyer. 'They wear silver crucifixes around their necks.'

'I assume you're familiar with our creation myth.'

Sawyer smiled. 'I am. I see you have one, too. But you also wear something they don't. Is that a St Christopher?'

Reavey hesitated, then gave an abrupt nod and reached to his collar. He tucked his crucifix away and raised the circular medallion at the end of the other pendant, flashing it briefly for Sawyer before tucking it away. 'Yes. Well, it's a modern take on a St Christopher. My father gave it to me.'

Sawyer took out his Memento Mori coin. 'My father gave me this.' He handed it to Reavey.

Reavey read from the coin, before handing it back. '*You could leave life right now...* I see the value in that thinking. The knowledge of mortality as a blessing. An entreatment to cherish the moment.' He made a face. 'But the imagery is a little lurid for my taste. Was your father a religious man?'

Sawyer smiled. 'He was. But he had his good points.'

52

Sawyer pulled away from the church car park and brought up his phone contacts on the CarPlay screen. He was about to tap Walker's name when a new call came through.

Luka.

He answered. 'Hello?' Silence from the other end. 'Hey, Luka. Are you okay?'

Another moment of silence, and then, quietly… 'Have you found my mum yet?'

'We're trying, Luka. Dennis has—'

'You're not trying!' His voice cracked with emotion. 'You're not doing anything.'

Sawyer joined the road towards Thornhill, listening to Luka's rapid breathing.

'Dad says you're sick. He says you killed someone. *With an axe.*'

'It was self-defence. The man was a murderer. He was going to kill me. Dennis is the sick one, Luka. He's been driven that way. He says your dad hurt his mum when he was younger. I know he denies it, but Dennis won't listen. He wants revenge. And when all you want is revenge, it can blind you to everything else. That's what's happening to Dennis. I know your dad wants to find your mum, but you... You can't be involved. Sit tight and keep yourself out of trouble. Don't do or say anything that might put your mum at risk. I will get her back safely. Let me do what I do.'

A long pause at Luka's end. 'You're not doing *anything*.'

He hung up.

Sawyer drove on in silence, too fast, snaking the Mini along the narrow lane that descended into Thornhill village. He dropped the front two windows and the clean morning air roared through the car.

He glanced out of his passenger window at the painterly fields of the Hope valley below.

Speckles of livestock. Vivid strokes of red and yellow wildflowers. A patchwork of crops, rippling in the breeze.

Rear-view mirror. Nothing.

———

Shepherd squeezed into the car and fixed two plastic coffee cups into the holders. 'We got a new machine.'

Sawyer drove away. 'You're not grinding beans, are you?'

'It's not that hardcore. But there's a steamer pipe thing. For the milk.'

Sawyer glanced over. 'I saw the priest, at the Brennan church. Plenty of their money went into the place. He

325

says he remembers Dylan being angry at the funeral but not much else.'

'How was the priest?'

'Decent enough. Knocking on a bit. He's about to hand over his godly duties to the next generation. Did you see Morris again?'

Shepherd slurped at the spout of his mug. 'You definitely got the better job there. Drop in on the kindly parish priest. Leave the psycho ex-con to me. He's obviously rattled by the murders, but says he's not involved and whatever they were into, it's nothing to do with him.'

'I believe him. The problem is that he's too arrogant to assume someone is reaping what they sowed as boys. He's too removed from the original crime. He thinks he's taken his punishment.'

'He's a nasty bastard, but he's not a moron. Surely he can see the pattern. He's the only one of the four still breathing.'

'He can see the pattern. He just doesn't think it'll continue to him.' Sawyer glanced over. 'Or his lack of fear implies he's involved. He's got someone to silence the other three for reasons we don't know about yet.'

Shepherd offered Sawyer his mug; he declined. 'We've looked into him from all angles. Found nothing. And if he is involved... Why such violence? The effort. The presentation. The locations. It's way too sophisticated and specific for a scrote like Morris.'

'So, he's still refusing protection?'

'Yes. And... You'll love this. He's got engaged. Celebration party tomorrow night at his place.'

Sawyer shook his head. 'Let's push for covert surveillance at the briefing.'

A call came through on CarPlay. Walker.

Sawyer connected it.

'Sir, are you on your way?'

'Fifteen minutes. What's up?'

'Sonya Banks's car. Rhodes has tracked its movement from Baslow via ANPR. Lots of pings on the day and night it was stolen, then nothing. He's drawn up a catchment area based on the last position. I have officers combing the data, cross-reffing locations from the Crawley prison pen pal addresses.'

Sawyer met Shepherd's eye. 'Look for lateral places, too. Farm buildings, bothies. The weather is favourable, and Crawley is a caver, so he won't mind the discomfort, and he's smart enough to know we'll have worked out the pen pal connection, anyway. Anything from the Jared White scene?'

Walker paused. 'Sally's here. And Drummond.'

'How does he look?' said Shepherd.

'Even by his standards, pretty grim.'

53

'This man did not go out on a high,' said Drummond, swiping at his touchscreen.

The conference room central monitor showed a series of garish post-mortem shots. Jared White's face and torso, from multiple angles: bloodied, twisted, broken. Patches of green-and-yellow bruising pooled around his cheeks and forehead, obscuring his features. Similar bruising stained his shoulders and chest. The forehead above the smashed eye socket was distorted by a gaping circular indentation.

'Fist beatings and hand-to-hand combat destroy soft tissue, but when a tool is used, you see deeper damage like fractures.' Drummond swiped to a close-up image: a line of puncture marks at the centre of a bruised indentation. 'So, our killer beat White with the tool he used on Burrows. You can see the indent here. I'd say a bat or pickaxe handle with nails through it. But there are also specific marks. Caved sections, consistent in shape. And these injuries are all on the front side of the body, with defensive wounds on forearms and elbows, indicating he tried to cushion the blows, which wouldn't have been effective as his wrists and ankles were bound.' He swiped to another image: various sections of flesh; some light blue, some darker. 'UV tells us more about what caused the similar-shaped impacts. You see the indentations clearly, based on the pattern of the bruising under UV. I also extracted samples from White's hair. Grass and soil.'

Sally O'Callaghan spoke up. 'The body was definitely moved and placed at the scene. I also picked up deposits from the soil and in the hair. Multiple alloys. Nickel, magnesium, molybdenum, nitrogen. Spectro also shows iron oxides, oxide-hydroxide. You find both in rust. The alloys are typically found in stainless steel.'

'His wrists and ankles were bound,' said Drummond. 'He was beaten with the nailed weapon. Then, based on Sally's findings and the position of the UV indentations and the subsequent bone damage—'

'He was propped up against a wall and stoned to death,' said Sawyer.

Drummond nodded. 'With stones taken from a rusting metal bucket.'

'So far, so vile,' said O'Callaghan. 'But I think he's finally left us something. He probably collected the stones from one location, in his bucket. The grass is too generic, but I might be able to pin down a location based on the soil samples in White's hair. But, like the carpet fibres, I need a match.'

Keating stared up at the screen. 'Damon Morris?'

'The only one of the four Brennan killers alive,' said

Shepherd. 'We've looked into his movements, connections. Nothing. And he's still refusing protection.'

'He's a dead man walking,' said Myers.

'Correction,' said Shepherd. 'He's an engaged dead man walking. He's throwing a party at his place tomorrow night.'

'I want surveillance,' said Keating. 'Treat his place like a crime scene in waiting. Eyes on surrounding area. ID everyone, in and out. Make sure everyone knows what our chief suspect looks like. If this is Dylan, it might be too risky, even for him. But let's be ready.'

Walker swiped through his touchscreen. 'Burning, beheading, stoning. The Brennans were religious. Dylan has rumoured IRA connections, which is consistent with the beatings.'

'I spoke to the priest at the family church,' said Sawyer. 'Thomas Brennan's funeral was held there. He said Dylan was angry at the funeral.'

Myers gave a grim laugh. 'Plenty of anger in this. Unbelievable that someone could keep it so strong for so long.'

Sawyer looked at Walker. 'Do some digging into the priest. Tyrone Reavey. Seemed fine, but he had plenty of connection to the Brennans. Maybe there's a link we're missing. The family money paid for a refurbishment. The sisters are still involved there. Maybe Reavey has a closer connection to the Brennans than he's letting on. Maybe he's protecting someone.'

'Any new vehicle evidence?' said Shepherd.

O'Callaghan shook her head. 'Same as the other. Generic. Looks like a minivan or pick-up.'

'Nothing pinging on rentals or stolen vehicles,' said Myers.

Walker looked up. 'What if he bought it? The van or pick-up or whatever.'

'Too traceable,' said Keating.

Walker nodded. 'Second-hand?'

'I like it,' said Sawyer. 'Get officers digging into that. Local used traders. He might have bought a cheap vehicle for this sole purpose.'

The door opened and Karl Rhodes walked in carrying his laptop. He was short and scrawny, with a narrow moustache that from some angles looked worryingly Hitlerian. 'Newsflash. Got a phone mast ping from Sonya Banks's phone. No nearby addresses that correspond with anyone on Crawley's pen pal list, and the ping isn't exact, but there's a well-established shooting cabin close by in Peak Forest.'

Myers held up a hand. 'Sonya Banks? Shooting cabin?'

'Dennis Crawley has taken the car of Sonya Banks,' said Sawyer. 'She's a café owner up in Hope and a friend of Victoria Kendal's. It looks like he's taken her as well as the car.'

'Shooting cabins are tiny bothies,' said Shepherd. 'A rustic shelter with no amenities. They were originally used as a base for hunting or shooting expeditions.'

Rhodes set down his laptop on the conference room table.

Myers ran a hand through his hair. 'Right. So, we

think Crawley might have taken Eva Gregory to this one? Along with Sonya Banks?'

'Or her phone, at least,' said Shepherd.

Sawyer found Keating's eye. 'Let me look with Shepherd. Before Strickland sends in a fucking attack helicopter. Establish that Crawley is there, then armed response, negotiators...'

'Sorry to break up the action movie,' said Rhodes, 'but there's something else. He's made us a video. He's used the appeal website to send an anonymous link that opens an unlisted YouTube clip. Looks like he recorded it on a phone.' He glanced at Sawyer. 'Hence the mast ping. Sonya Banks's account.'

The team got up from their seats and huddled around the laptop. Rhodes turned off the conference room light, set the screen to full and slapped the spacebar to start the clip.

A colossal, broad-shouldered man with a long, heavy beard stood before a rugged stone wall, glowering into the camera. The scene was dim, even with the laptop brightness at maximum, but the figure was unmistakable. The image blurred and unblurred, struggling to find focus in the low light.

Dennis Crawley pointed to the side, and the image jerked across, to reveal the figure of a bound woman, propped on a basic wooden chair and slumped to the side against the wall.

He cleared his throat. 'To whom it will concern.' He gestured towards the woman and the image zoomed in.

Eva Gregory. Head flopped onto her shoulder. Eyes half-open, fixed on the ground ahead.

'Change of plan,' continued Crawley, off-screen now. 'By the time you see this, Eva will be buried in a box somewhere in the northern Peak District. I won't bury her deep, and the box is big. But she will have only one or two hours of oxygen if she keeps her breathing slow and doesn't panic. Which is unlikely.' Crawley's voice was deep and steady, echoing in the small space.

The framing lurched wildly, then stabilised, as Crawley pushed his face in close.

'Sonya Banks must be filming this,' said Sawyer.

Crawley tipped his head forward and faced the camera with his iridescent blue eyes. He closed them, paused for a few seconds, breathing slow. 'Dale Strickland will film himself confessing to the attack on my mother. He will then post the video on the Greater Manchester Combined Authority website, in the banner window at the top of the home page. It should also be posted on the home page of the *Derbyshire Times*.' He opened his eyes again, but they drifted, off centre, not looking into camera. 'I've included a phone number with this video.' Now his eyes found the lens. 'Detective Inspector Jake Sawyer will send me a voice message when the videos are posted. Sawyer interrupted my justice last time. So it's only fitting that he should help me achieve it now. I'll watch the confession, and if I'm happy, then I'll reveal Eva's location. Please listen carefully. If I see anyone but Detective Sawyer at the location of Eva's burial, the consequences for her will be dire. The same goes for any attempt to contact me before the videos are live.' He managed a slight smile. 'And if the videos aren't posted, then you won't hear from me again, and Eva will not survive.'

The video ended.

'He's included the phone number and the basics of what he wants Dale to cover in the description text,' said Rhodes. 'Pretty batshit. I've ripped the video file in case he takes it down.'

Sawyer pushed back his chair and leapt to his feet. 'Where's the shooting cabin location?'

'I'll send it to you,' said Rhodes, taking out his phone.

Keating sat upright. 'We have options.'

'None of them good,' said Shepherd. 'First, we need to see if he's actually at the cabin. He may have dumped Sonya Banks's phone there just to fuck with us.'

Sawyer checked his phone. 'This is about fifteen minutes away.' He looked at Keating.

'I'll inform Strickland,' said Keating.

'No!' said Sawyer, too loud.

'Detective Sawyer,' said Keating, keeping his voice even. 'I need to inform the incumbent Greater Manchester mayor that the man who has abducted his wife has just threatened to let her suffocate.'

Sawyer paused. '*Sir*. Please. It's close. Let us get there first. Confirm Crawley is actually where we think he is.' He headed for the door. 'That gives us better options.'

54

Sawyer rounded a learner driver dawdling at a crossroads and cut back in at a tight angle, forcing an oncoming car to stop. The driver waved and sounded his horn as he streaked past a roadside sign.

WELCOME TO DOVE HOLES
PLEASE DRIVE CAREFULLY

Shepherd slapped a steadying hand on the dashboard. 'Let's try to get there in one piece, eh?'

Sawyer stared ahead. 'The priest at All Saints...'

'Reavey.'

He nodded. 'He had the same silver cross worn by the Brennan sisters. Also something else. A medallion. He said it was a modern version of a St Christopher.'

'My uncle's family were Catholics. They all had 'em. They're supposed to protect travellers or something, aren't they? Patron saint.'

'Yes. But when he showed me the medallion, he only flashed it. He was quick to put it away again.' He side-eyed Shepherd. 'Why so coy? They're common. Lots of Catholics wear them.'

Shepherd pondered for a moment. 'You think he might be hiding Dylan. Helping him while he takes brutal, biblical revenge on the men who murdered Thomas Brennan. Because of the Irish connection. Something like that.'

Sawyer flashed him a doubtful look. 'Let's see what Walker digs up.'

A call came through on the CarPlay screen. Shepherd glanced at the ID: *Tony Cross*.

'Our friendly neighbourhood rogue sharp shooter,' said Shepherd. 'Please tell me he's not waiting for us at the bothy, ready to take out Crawley.'

Sawyer shook his head. 'I asked him to watch Strickland.' He side-eyed Shepherd. 'Off the books.'

Shepherd dropped back his head and sighed.

'Keating would have never said yes. It's a back channel.'

'A *back channel*?'

Sawyer took the call. 'Tony. One second.' He muted the call. 'Strickland is desperate to get Eva back safe, but if he can look like he's got one over on me while he does it, then it's a double win.'

'But—'

'Even if I'd asked Keating, and he'd agreed to it, he would have still told Strickland. Keating is out of here soon. Strickland has the pull to see him right. And

336

Keating will want to keep him on the end of a phone in case he tires of filling in fishing permits. GMP desk job. Outside the blast zone, but plenty of influence.' He unmuted the call. 'Hey, Tony. Shepherd's here with me. It's fine.'

'Okay.' Cross paused. 'Strickland just left a meeting in Hyde. Same guy driving.'

'Abadi,' said Sawyer. 'What direction?'

'Following now. Traffic has thinned so I'm staying back, but it's not a sightseeing trip. He's motoring. About to head south at Wooley Bridge.'

Sawyer thought for a moment. 'Stay with him. Thanks, Tony.'

He hung up, floored the Mini into a right turn onto the Sparrowpit road towards Peak Forest.

'You actually screeched the tyres,' said Shepherd. 'It sounds like Strickland is heading to Buxton. Keating said he was going to inform him about Crawley's contact, and the video.'

'He's getting intel,' said Sawyer. 'He's heading to the location.'

'The shooting cabin? How would he know? Sir, this is insane. Keating wouldn't play us off against Strickland in a situation like this.'

A speed camera flashed. Sawyer stared ahead, breathing fast, pushing eighty in a forty zone. 'I don't know. Someone on the team. Stephen Bloom.'

Shepherd scoffed. 'He's buttoned up tighter than my old nan's purse.'

Sawyer blasted his horn and a van swerved out of his

way. 'I don't fucking know. Abadi, then. He's... a fucking hacker or something.'

'Maybe he doesn't know about the location.'

Sawyer snapped his head round. 'What?'

'You've got someone following him. Maybe he's got someone following you.'

Sawyer checked the rear-view mirror. He turned off at the Sparrowpit crossroads, but the two cars behind both drove straight on. He braked hard and jerked the Mini onto a verge by a rusting iron farm gate. He killed the engine and lowered his head, grimacing.

Heat rising in his chest. Ripples of nausea.

'Slow yourself down,' said Shepherd. 'Four, seven, eight. In for four seconds. Hold it for seven. Out for eight.'

Sawyer muttered to himself. 'Shepherd... Keating...' He lifted his head, stared at Shepherd with wide eyes and pointed to Shepherd's seat. 'Keating was sitting there for a while, outside Eva's.' He looked around: up at the roof, the back seat.

'You're not seriously suggesting that Keating has planted a tracker on Strickland's behalf? Has anyone else been in the car lately?'

'*Help me,*' Sawyer hissed. He got out of the car and crouched on the verge, shining his phone light underneath. Shepherd did the same on the other side.

Sawyer checked the bumpers, the boot. They stood on either sides of the car for a moment, facing each other.

Shepherd opened the back door and checked under the seats. Sawyer walked round to the passenger seat and slid it back, bumping Shepherd on the head as he backed out.

He shone his light under the seat and reached in, detaching a coin-sized black disc, fixed to the fabric at the front edge with double-sided tape.

Sawyer held it up for Shepherd to see, then threw it over the gate into a field of indifferent sheep.

55

Sawyer turned off the main road through Peak Forest village and joined a tight single-track lane flanked by weathered dry-stone wall, touching distance from the open car windows. After a few minutes' drive with grazing fields either side, the lane steepened, the walls fell away, and they weaved through wild, burgeoning woodland, overhanging branches scuffing the roof. The afternoon sunlight strobed through the trees on Sawyer's side, and he flipped the visor across.

Shepherd checked his phone. 'We're near to the cabin. Ten minutes' walk from here.' He pointed. 'Up through those trees. This is near Eldon Hill. It's the limit of the White Peak, where the limestone merges into the millstone of the Dark Peak.' He glanced over. 'Am I boring you?'

Sawyer shook his head. 'Just because I'm not listening, doesn't mean I'm not interested.'

He backed the Mini into a passing spot at the end of

an overgrown trail that meandered up towards a thinning treeline.

Sawyer looked at his phone. 'Cross says Strickland's car has stopped just outside Sparrowpit.'

They climbed out.

'So how did Strickland get the tracker in your car? It can't have been Keating, surely.'

'Strickland didn't,' said Sawyer. 'His son did.'

'Luka?'

They trudged up through the rough pastureland, towards the trees.

'He was with me at Victoria Kendal's place. He said he'd followed Strickland there, came back later, encountered two of his goons. Luka has obviously decided that helping his dad by tracking me is a better plan than helping me directly.'

'But how did Strickland know Crawley had been to the Kendal house before us?'

'He must have had access to detail on the first car Crawley stole. The one he used to take Eva. No idea how.'

'Farrell?'

'Wouldn't surprise me. Strickland must have helped him wash off the Terry Barker links.'

They ducked into a cluster of silver birches, keeping low.

Beyond, the ground dipped, then gathered to a ridge above Castleton. Shepherd pointed.

The cabin squatted in a strip of lengthening shadows cast by a dense section of trees. It was a tiny single-storey shelter with a narrow gap in the brickwork serving as a door, and a roof built from corrugated iron sheets, savaged by the elements but unbreached.

'There you go,' said Shepherd. 'That's rubble gritstone. Rough as fuck, but solid. Me and the family got caught in a rainstorm last year, up near Kinder. We sheltered in one. Totally dry inside. Don't get me wrong. You wouldn't want to spend too much time in there. Couple of stones to sit on. No Wi-Fi.'

Sawyer led the way as they crept across the edge of the treeline, trying to get a look round the back of the cabin.

He held up a hand; Shepherd froze.

Sawyer pointed to his back, and Shepherd shuffled behind him, looking over his shoulder.

A grey Toyota Corolla was parked tight against the cabin back wall, partially shielded.

Shepherd looked at Sawyer. 'We need to call it in. Assume the worst. Crawley might have Eva Gregory and Sonya Banks in there. We can't risk him seeing us and panicking.'

Sawyer nodded. 'That's not the worst.'

'Sir—'

'The women are his leverage. If he sees us now, he's not going to jeopardise that by hurting them.'

Shepherd got in his face. 'We've been here before. It's repeating a mistake. We need armed response, H&C negotiators.'

'There isn't time. It's Section 17. We assume Crawley has followed up on his threat to Eva. And this isn't about negotiation. Crawley's not interested in getting out alive, going back to prison. He's fixated. It's pathological.

There's only one thing he truly wants now. Watch the front. I'll keep eyes on you.'

Sawyer broke away, scouting along the treeline, staying low, descending a shallow slope around to the cabin. As the ground levelled, he crawled to the edge of the scrubby grass at the raised back side of the building.

He looked back up to the trees. Shepherd raised a thumb.

Sawyer crouch-stepped to the car and ducked down by the front wheel. The back wall of the cabin was pitted with holes where the gritstone had crumbled.

He moved in, taking slow and silent steps, sticking to patches of short grass, soft underfoot. He paused at the back corner of the cabin and listened.

Skylark song, high above.

Bleating and lowing from the grazing fields behind the trees.

A faint rumble of traffic from the Sparrowpit to Castleton road, swept over the ridge on the wind.

Nothing from inside the cabin.

Sawyer leaned forward to peer through a hole in the brickwork. The view inside was murky, but naturally lit by the sun through the gap at the front.

Nothing.

A flash of colour on the ground under the car caught his peripheral vision.

He turned, crept back to the car, and pulled out the phone.

Switched off. Yellow rubber case, scuffed.

Something else behind the tyre: a plastic smart key with a Toyota symbol.

Sawyer stood upright and looked through the car windows. The interior was empty.

He looked up and waved to Shepherd as he walked to the back of the car and pressed the boot release button.

Sawyer leaned forward and looked inside, then stood there with his head bowed, gazing at a flattened patch of pinkish-purple heather.

Shepherd scrambled down the end of the slope.

'Nobody in the cabin,' said Sawyer.

Shepherd reached the car, looked into the boot. 'Oh, Jesus. *Fuck*.'

A middle-aged woman lay folded, foetal, with her head resting against the wheel arch cover.

'Sonya Banks,' said Sawyer. He held up the phone. 'You called it. He's fucking with us.'

Shepherd sighed. 'Message from Keating. Return to base.'

'Why?'

'Strickland. He wants to do the video.'

56

Sawyer stood with his back to the window of Keating's office. He faced Strickland, by the closed door and Keating, seated at his desk. Shepherd stood in the corner. 'Crawley made Sonya Banks film the video on her phone, in the cabin. Then he strangled her, put her in the boot of her car.' He looked out at the football stadium across the road. 'She probably had power left in the phone. He left it under the car, knowing it would ping the mast...'

Strickland slammed both palms down on Keating's desk, sending papers flying. 'I don't *care* what Crawley did or how he did it. Where has he gone with my wife?'

Sawyer lowered his head, thinking.

'We have a forensic team at the cabin now,' said Shepherd. 'There's a trace of Crawley, Eva, Sonya Banks.' He glanced at Keating. 'Splashes of Sonya Banks's blood.'

'He beat her before strangling her,' said Keating.

'He's frustrated.' Sawyer turned and sat at the table by the window.

Strickland frowned. 'Who? Crawley?'

Sawyer nodded, set his phone down on the table. 'He won't hurt Eva. She's his prize asset. So, he's taking it out on the other women.' He raised his eyes to Strickland. 'He's torturing you. Repaying you for what he says you did to his mother. If he hurts Eva, he can't continue.' His phone buzzed.

Strickland threw up his arms. 'So... get... I don't know. An SAS team out on the moorland around the cabin. Send some drones up. Road blocks. Post officers and entry and exit points.' He turned to Keating, red-faced. 'Do *something*.'

'There are other cabins round there,' said Shepherd. 'Bothies. He might wait it out, then check if you've posted the confession video. Then get back in touch.'

'But what about this threat?' Strickland took off his glasses, pushed a hand over his forehead, stretching the skin back and forth. '*Burying* Eva. We have to take him seriously. He's murdered two people since getting out.'

Sawyer checked his phone. 'Dean Logan is here. He's set up the *Derbyshire Times* website to post the video, as demanded by Crawley. Our Digital Media Advisor Karl Rhodes is in touch with the GMCA website manager. You can film the video here in Rhodes's studio and have it live in minutes. I'll leave the message on the number Crawley has given us. He says he'll reveal Eva's location, so I assume he'll contact me.'

Strickland slumped into a chair. 'And how can we guarantee he'll release Eva?'

'We can't,' said Keating. 'But this is all about control. Letting us know he's in charge. We don't know how long he's been on the move with Eva since posting the video, and we don't know if they're on foot or he's taken another vehicle. But I've sent out a ground-based search team, and a police helicopter with thermal imaging is surveying the area now.'

Strickland leapt to his feet. 'Let's do this then. It's a fucking farce.' He threw open the door and turned to Keating. 'But I'm going to record a separate video saying I was coerced into the first out of fear for my wife. I want the videos replaced the *instant* he reveals Eva's location.'

'There's something else, too,' said Sawyer.

Strickland turned. 'What?'

'Dean Logan wants to know if he can have an exclusive interview with Eva once she's safe.'

Strickland glared at Sawyer, raw fury in his eyes. He turned and hurried away, escorted by Keating.

57

Luka slid an ambitious pass between two defenders, into the path of his incoming striker. But the goalkeeper rushed out and fell on the ball, smothering it. He checked the game time at the top of the screen.

Two minutes to go. Two-nil down.

He sighed, switched off the PS4 and trudged through to the kitchen. The sandwich toaster was unwashed from his breakfast toastie, so he scrubbed away the worst of the dried cheese and took out the ingredients for a late afternoon snack: peanut butter, honey, banana.

Luka opened the jar, looked inside, and slammed it down on the table.

'Cameron! We need more peanut butter.'

He scraped out the remains and spread it onto two rounds of white bread, then chopped the banana and layered it on top of one slice.

He squeezed a swirl of honey over the banana, set up the toaster, and placed the slices into the mould.

A crash from his father's office. Something heavy.

He closed the toaster, clipped the latch on the handles and squeezed the slices together. He took out his phone and browsed TikTok. Gaming feeds, football, Marvel, Brent Rivera, Spencer Knight. He indulged each video for two or three seconds, then swished on to the next.

He opened the fridge and took out the carton of Chocomel. Almost empty. He tipped back his head in frustration. 'Cameron!'

Luka tossed the carton across the work surface and stormed out of the kitchen, across the hall, and into his father's office.

Bookcase pushed off the wall, leaning against an alcove. Spilled books gathered around the base.

Printer upended with blank sheets of paper flattened across the floor.

Boots in the far corner. Legs.

Cameron.

Then the smell: loamy and noxious. An outdoor stink brought inside, polluting the diffuser-scented air. As if an animal had fouled the room.

Luka checked on the folding knife, tucked into the fastener at the back of his belt, then pushed the door wider.

Dennis Crawley stood by the window, face bloodied, vast enough to block out most of the light.

58

Sawyer entered his office and closed the door behind him. He drew the blinds and sat at his desk in the dim light, eyes closed, watching the faces swirl around, melding and melting.

He whispered to himself. 'Four, seven, eight...' Breathe in for four seconds. Hold for seven. Out for eight.

Repeat.

And again.

A knock at the door. Walker.

Sawyer waved him in.

'Sorry to disturb. You asked me to look into the priest at All Saints. Tyrone Reavey.'

Sawyer sat back, tuned in. 'Anything?'

'Well... Registry details for the church all check out. Reavey became parish priest in 1998. Drawing a blank on anything personal before that.' Walker checked his phone. 'The church has a connection to something called the Trócaire. It's a Catholic foreign aid charity. Also the

Legion of Mary, which is all about evangelising, spreading the word.'

'1998. The Good Friday Agreement probably smoothed his path to the UK.'

Walker nodded, thinking. 'Sir. There's nothing to suggest this guy is hiding anything or is involved in the Brennan killings. He knew the family well, but there's no obvious history of violence or IRA connections. What are you thinking?'

Sawyer's phone buzzed in his pocket. 'I want to know what he wears around his neck. There's two things. A silver cross and something he said was like a St Christopher. But he wasn't keen on me seeing it for too long. When someone doesn't want me to see something, I get curious. We're in the thick of it with Crawley right now, but try to find out what it is. And I know he knew the family, but dig deeper into his past in Ireland. Church records back from his earlier years. Associations that followed him. Is there anything that connects him to the Brennans before he came to the UK? All Saints Church is common to all the main players.'

He pulled out his phone. Call from an unknown number.

Walker gave a nod and exited, closing the door behind him.

Sawyer took the call. 'Sawyer.'

'How's life, Detective?' Hushed voice. Scouse accent.

Sawyer cleared his throat. 'Pretty busy, Curtis.'

'Good time to talk?'

'As good as any. I was hoping you could drop in and help us with our enquiries.'

Mavers laughed, wheezy. He lapsed into a brief coughing fit, recovered. 'I'll pass. More than happy to take questions over the phone, though.'

'Okay. Here's my first. Why would an Eastern-European torturer be so desperate to find you, he's willing to attack a senior detective, then take part in an armed assault on a major police station?'

Mavers whistled. 'Well... Now, you probably think this call is going to be all cat and mouse. Cryptic and evasive. Lots of dinky little metaphors. An underlying buzz of mutual respect. Like that coffee shop scene in... What's it called?'

'*Heat.*'

'That's the one. Well, it's not. I'm going to be straight with you. I'm in a confessional mood. So I hope you can spare me a couple of minutes. Sounds like you've got a lot on, but I might ease a few of your pains.'

'So, who's the torturer and why is he so keen to find you?'

Mavers paused. 'Your torturer is a fella called Jakub Malecki. Polish. He's a heartless bastard, Sawyer, and I fucked off his boss good and proper. Y'see, there's a toxic triangle at the heart of this. You, me and Mr Strickland. Dale hired me last year, to disrupt the Manchester drug gangs.'

'How?'

'By robbin' 'em. Setting 'em against each other if I could. Making 'em paranoid. He told me it was because he wanted to combat drug dealers, but it was his way of eliminating opposition for his own business. And to curry

352

favour with the mayor. So, I took Levi along, and we dropped in on most of the middle men and a couple of bigger cheeses. You'd just shooed me from the lad Justin's house, with his missus and the kids. You'd taken out Levi, humiliated me... So, when I robbed Leon Stokes, one of the top boys out in Fallowfield, I dropped your name.'

Sawyer pushed back his chair, turned away from the door. 'Why?'

'I know. Sorry about that. It was petulant. I wanted to cause you a bit of grief. I also thought it might give me some extra pull with Strickland, who's not your biggest fan. I used to do a bit of lifting for him. Went down for it. Kept quiet. So, he was straight on me when I got out. I'm sure you know he was running county lines when I was inside. Drugs. But he knew about my sister, and he told me he'd stopped all that. So, once he'd got his seat at the top table, endorsed by the Chief Constable, he starts his clean-up. He sold me out to Stokes and his pet psycho. But I spawned my way out of that, and now I'm his final loose end.'

'So, why Justin? Why Maggie?'

Mavers slurped at something. 'To flush you out. Provoke you. I wasn't into it. I didn't share Levi's appetites. But then Justin set this Yardie lad on me. I handed him his arse, went back to Justin's place... And that's where you came in.'

Sawyer took out a boiled sweet, twirled the edges of the wrapper. 'You helped him with Crawley. The man who's abducted his wife.'

Mavers laughed again. 'Now you're getting it. I was

outside Dale's place when his missus got taken. Saw the car reg.'

Sawyer slipped the sweet in his mouth, rolled it around. 'What now, Curtis?'

'*What now* is Dale Strickland.' His voice deepened, found an edge. 'He lied to me. Fucked me over. Then pulled me out of the fire only to fuck me over again. So, here I am. Fucking *him* over.'

'I'm losing this, Curtis. Didn't you have a guarantee after you'd given him the car reg?'

'Course I did. He's sold it well. Sent a fixer over to set me up with ID, travel, a place near my dad's home town in Jamaica. Dale's a clever lad, Sawyer. But I know something he doesn't know I know. The Yardie lad, Glenroy Valance. I sent his boys back to him in one piece, and I called in the favour. He looked into my new pad in Jamaica.'

'It doesn't exist.'

Mavers scoffed. 'Yeah, it exists. But the fella who runs it has Shower Posse connections, friendly to Glenroy's original crew. Strickland's fixer is a slimy counterfeiter called Crutchley. These boys owe him. I wouldn't last five minutes out there. So, it's a good set-up.' The wheezy laugh again. 'Just not good enough.'

Sawyer turned back to face the window that looked out to the office. 'Tell me more about Dale's operation.'

'Fuck me, Sawyer. You need to catch up quick. He'll be your boss soon. What can I say? He's a fuckin' snake. He's cleaning house because he can see the potential in legitimate power, instead of ducking and diving with high-maintenance business fronts. Listen, Dale's trick was to take a page out of the terrorist playbook. Run his operation with lots of little cells of associates. Not your standard top-down deal. Divide and conquer, I suppose. The cells don't associate or infect each other if something goes wrong in one.' He dropped his voice. 'So, when I was robbing the dealers, we used a graft phone. Private between me and him. There are messages and voicemails on there that will implicate him fair and square with the dealer attacks, along with a couple of side hustles he had me settle for him.'

'Terry Barker.'

Mavers paused. 'If all this got out, it would be the shortest Manchester mayor term in history. Your IT boys would be all over it. And I'm sure they could throw in his tame detective with the dyed hair.'

'Farrell.'

'Now, here's the really good bit. Dale thinks I ditched that phone long before we fell out. But it's somewhere safe. I should have kept your name out of everything. You were only doing your job. So, take this as an apology.'

Commotion outside in the office. Detectives running.

'The phone is at a safe house, isn't it? Somewhere Dale kept you.'

'I'll send you the address. If I can find your private phone number, you can find a phone in three rooms.'

Shepherd at the door, beckoning; Sawyer held up a hand. 'I appreciate this, Curtis. But you'll forgive me if I don't immediately reinstate you on my Christmas card list.'

'There you go,' said Mavers. 'Probably the sweetest

bit of intel you'll ever get. And... Yeah. Sorry for the inconvenience.'

Sawyer got to his feet.

'Before you go, Sawyer. One last thing. You were wrong about me. I *am* a wolf. I'm not a good guy. But I don't think you are, either. The difference is, I wear the badness up front. I'm at peace with it. But, I see you, *Detective Inspector*. You're a wolf in sheep's clothing. A bad guy in a good guy's disguise. You'd be good at the darker arts. You should embrace it. Dale is the same, but he's made it work for him. If you see him, give him a slap for me, would you?'

59

Sawyer burst out of the lift and hurried down the entrance corridor, pursued by Shepherd.

'Rhodes says he was about to post the confession video, when Strickland got a message,' said Shepherd, panting. 'He bombed out with his right-hand man. Keating called ahead to Matlock station and raised their response team.'

They shoved through the entrance doors.

'So, how did Crawley get to Bakewell from Peak Forest?' said Sawyer.

'He flagged down a car on Clement Lane. Minor road between Peak Forest and Bradwell. Coshed the driver. We had checkpoints across the top of the Hope Valley. Castleton, Winnats.'

'He took the hard way. Doubled back. Used the back lanes around Peak Cavern. Probably knows the area well. Was Eva with him when he took the car?'

'Driver didn't see. He was out for a while. Young lad.

Only passed his test a few months ago. Crawley took the car and left him there.'

They bundled into the Mini and Sawyer screeched out of the station car park.

Shepherd continued. 'The driver had to walk nearly into Bradwell to get a signal. Called his dad, who works in Longsight. He called 999. Got routed to GMP. It shot up the chain because of the lad's description of Crawley. And it looks like it got to Dale before us.'

'Farrell,' said Sawyer, climbing out of the town, flooring it along the snaking Bakewell Road.

'The car last pinged an ANPR on Buxton Road, east of Ashford. Nothing after that.'

'Luka will be there.'

Shepherd slapped the dashboard. '*Fuck!*'

'So, Keating has gone ahead to oversee the ARU?'

'Yeah.' Shepherd opened his window an inch.

Sawyer handed his phone over. 'Call him.'

Shepherd turned. 'Who?'

'Crawley. The number he left on his video is on my contact list.'

Shepherd swiped through the phone. 'He said—'

'If Eva's in a box somewhere, we can't hang around for negotiators to work through their playbook.'

Shepherd tapped the number, linking the phone audio to Sawyer's CarPlay.

They sat in silence while the phone rang a few times.

Sawyer pointed to the glovebox. 'What's left in there?'

Shepherd opened it, rummaged. 'Just wrappers. Couple of sweets stuck to the hinge.'

The call connected. Silence at the other end. Then light breathing.

Sawyer glanced at Shepherd. 'This is Sawyer.'

'I know,' said Crawley. 'You're the only one who'd have the bollocks to do this.'

'Or be stupid enough,' said Sawyer.

Crawley gave a grunt of amusement. 'I saw your press conference.'

'Dennis. Is Luka with you?'

Crawley waited a long time before answering. 'How he's grown.'

'And where's Eva?'

Crawley inhaled, then exhaled, slow and noisy. 'I see no video, Sawyer. No confession.'

'He filmed it at Buxton. But then realised you were revising the deal.'

'No revision. Luka is safe.'

'But you've changed your mind again, yes? You're back at Dale's place. Why?'

Silence from Crawley. Slow breathing.

Sawyer looked at Shepherd. 'You want to see it first-hand. You realised that Dale's humiliation wouldn't be enough. You were there when he brutalised your mother. You want him there when you do the same to his wife.'

Caldwell's face. Smiling.

'You've had years to plan, Dennis. But this desire. The hunger for revenge... You told me it was like a stone in a lake, sending out ripples. But it's more like a parasite. It takes you over, controls you. You're just a host now.'

The gun barrel sinking into Caldwell's cheek.

'But it's a pain you're used to. So, there's a fear, isn't

there? A fear in satisfying it. A fear of what comes after, once it's been indulged. It's all you've ever known. So, although the pain and trauma is real, you fear the unknown version of you, out there beyond the revenge. But there's still a chance to heal. Focus on what you can control. Your reactions and decisions. You can wait for the armed response unit to take you out. And they will. Or you can choose to change. You'll go back to prison, but you can learn there. Reinvent yourself. Heal. Kill the infection.'

Sawyer paused, found Shepherd's eye.

They drove on in silence, listening to Crawley's measured breathing.

When Crawley spoke next, his voice sounded fractured, almost frail. 'And Strickland goes on living his life? How have you carried that, with your own mother's killer?'

His father's blood and bone, dripping from the skylight.

Sawyer accelerated out of the curve at Sheldon Moor, swooping towards Bakewell. 'We've both been changed. But we can be more than what's happened to us. We can change again, if we understand and accept how we were changed before. We can override it. This desire for our enemies to suffer forces us to act like them. The best revenge is to be unlike the one who performed the injury. That's what I mean by healing and change.'

Crawley was silent for a moment. Sawyer turned up the volume and the car flooded with the sound of his breathing; frayed and unsteady now. 'You talk about fear, Sawyer. When you've experienced the worst, you don't fear the worst. But fear keeps us alive. Fearing nothing is close to feeling nothing. I coped by zooming out. By setting the events onto a different scale of time. You know. People call it *the grand scheme of things*. How you and I and our dead mothers are just blips in history.' He took a breath. 'You see her, don't you? You talk to her. And I bet she's young and unharmed, as she was before that final day. You've repaired her. You've kept her whole in your heart. But my mother was already broken. Diseased. And then Strickland broke her some more.' Crawley raised his voice, anger rising. 'My mother was taken from me twice. Once when she died, and once when I went into prison, when you arrested me and put me there. Strickland was responsible the first time. You were responsible the second. I will have her back. And then I can end this.'

He hung up.

Shepherd stared at Sawyer. 'I think you just talked him round.'

60

Sawyer parked roadside on the edge of a cordon at the end of a side street opposite Strickland's house. He and Shepherd got out and jogged over to an unmarked black BMW. Further down the main road, a group of officers in Hi-Vis jackets were busy evacuating neighbours and bystanders into a buffer zone.

Keating moved out from behind the van to greet Sawyer. He was shadowed by a stern officer in body armour and helmet, cradling a carbine rifle. Strickland sat on the bonnet of a red-and-black Tesla, next to a grey-suited man with a dense black moustache.

'He's on the ground floor,' said Keating. 'Sitting room. He has Luka.' He gestured to the man with the gun. 'This is Clay Hutchcraft, ARU co-ordinator. DI Jake Sawyer, DI Ed Shepherd.'

'Just the man,' said Hutchcraft, nodding at Sawyer. 'We're in contact. We've heard from Luka. So, as far as we know, he's safe. No evidence of anyone else inside. No direct demands or threats yet. But the subject says he wants to see you, DI Sawyer.'

Strickland sprang off the bonnet and walked across the road to his gate, trailed by the moustachioed man. Two armed officers stepped into their path.

Strickland stopped, turned to Keating, red-faced. 'This is my home. I am not hanging around waiting for a fucking multiple murderer to release my son and tell me where he's keeping my wife.'

Hutchcraft stepped forward. 'Mr Strickland. If you go in there, what are you planning to do? How will it help? The subject has told us he'll only speak to Detective Sawyer. I have to assume that he'll react badly if we ignore that demand. I understand your anxiety. But in my experience, this kind of situation ends better when we act with cool heads. I have a tactical response team at my command, and two highly trained crisis negotiators are inbound. The subject has control here. We have to focus on de-escalation. Active listening, empathy. Build a rapport. Establish an exit strategy. It takes patience.'

Strickland jabbed a finger at Sawyer. 'He is not going into my house. It's too dangerous.'

'He might have to,' said Hutchcraft. 'Sawyer, is there any reason Crawley would ask for you specifically?'

Sawyer glanced at Keating. 'There's history. Where's the car Crawley used to get here? And was anyone with Luka? Is Cameron in there?'

Abadi stood up. 'He was, but we've had no contact. No response.'

'He's dead,' said Sawyer. 'What did Crawley say about me?'

'To come in alone,' said Keating.

Sawyer looked at Strickland. 'And the car?'

'There's a garage round the back. It might be there. But we can't tell from here.'

'Sorry, but what's your role here, sir?' said Hutchcraft to Abadi.

'Farouk Abadi,' said Strickland. 'He's my assistant. Ex-Egyptian military.'

'Sa'ka unit,' said Abadi.

Hutchcraft studied him for a moment. 'Okay, Farouk. As a civilian, I'll need you to stay well behind the cordon with Mr Strickland.'

Abadi smiled. 'I assist Mr Strickland. Not you.'

Hutchcraft cracked a weak smile. 'Okay. Let's focus on you, Detective Sawyer. We have no intel on what weapons the subject might be carrying. Are you familiar with him? How is he going to react when he sees you?'

'You mentioned empathy,' said Sawyer. 'I have that with Crawley. I spoke to him on the way here, using the number he provided in his video.'

Strickland threw up his arms. 'For fuck's sake.'

'Unlike Mr Strickland,' said Sawyer, 'I can be calm. I also have a good relationship with the hostage. Mr Strickland's son, Luka. I can focus on exit strategy while giving Crawley the impression he has control. Give me a two-way radio. I can keep it open so you can hear everything. He won't mind. You'll also learn about specific demands directly.'

Strickland walked over to Sawyer. His eyes were wild and unfocused, and he didn't smell good. 'Find out where Eva is, Sawyer. Offer him whatever you think might help.'

'Lie to him?'

'Yes. We can worry about our consciences when Crawley is in a maximum-security prison. Do your job.'

'And what's that, Dale?'

Strickland leaned in close to Sawyer's face. Morning breath in the afternoon. 'You have a duty of care to protect the safety and well-being of everyone.'

'Including the hostage-taker,' said Sawyer.

'Correct,' said Keating. 'We use force as a last resort. Clay handles his team, but I have gold command.'

Strickland turned to face Keating and pushed his mouth next to Keating's ear. 'If this goes wrong, it'll be the last thing you ever command.'

———

Sawyer walked around the side of the house and tried the door that led into the kitchen.

Unlocked.

He let himself in and closed the door quietly behind him.

He walked down the hall. The door to Strickland's office was wide open, and he stepped in, noting the mess, the tilted bookcase, the body in the corner.

Sawyer crouched beside Cameron's body. He checked for injury signs, took the pulse, listened for breathing. Heavy bruising on the face. Blood on the side of the head and upper body. He spoke in a low voice, towards the walkie-talkie clipped to his belt. 'One adult male. Ground floor office room. Deceased. Mr Strickland referred to this man as Cameron on a previous visit. Severe head injury. Looks like blunt force.'

He rose, and walked into the hall, then stopped. Listening.

'I hope that's you, Sawyer.'

Crawley's voice from the sitting room.

He walked in.

The room was lit by a sliver of external light peeking through the side of the drawn blinds. Crawley stood by the wall, near the sofa. Luka sat on the floor by the TV, behind Crawley, mouth taped, hands bound with what looked like a bathrobe belt.

'Dennis,' said Sawyer.

Crawley's shoulders rose and fell. He was bigger than Sawyer remembered: mallet fists clenched, broad chest raised. He wore a dark T-shirt with a sleeve torn away. The fit was saggy, but the tee was taut against his sturdy frame. As Sawyer's eyes adjusted, he could see the shine of liquid spatter across the cheek near the window.

Sawyer squinted. 'Are you injured?'

'No. The blood isn't mine. Or Luka's.'

Sawyer rested on the arm of a facing chair. 'Where's Eva, Dennis?'

Crawley dipped his head, spotting the radio. 'Who's listening?'

'My bosses. The co-ordinator.'

'Clay. He seems human enough. Is Dale there?'

Sawyer hesitated. 'Of course. His wife and son are under your control.'

Crawley grinned. 'You're good at this, Sawyer. Reminding me I'm in charge.'

'Why did you change your mind, Dennis? About sending body parts.'

Crawley angled his head. His eyes drifted over to Sawyer, but seemed to focus on a point to the side. 'I thought of a better idea. I'm sure you know the old line about no plan surviving contact with the enemy.'

'And is this the new plan?'

'I don't trust Strickland with the confession video. So, he's going to walk right in here, into his own house, and confess to me. *Live.* I want the media here while he does it. Send in someone with a camera to stream it, so I can see it happen.' He took a step towards Sawyer. 'Dale will confess to me, and the world will watch him grovel for my mother's mercy.' He raised his volume. 'I know you can hear me, Dale.'

Sawyer looked over to Luka, trying to catch his eye. But he stared up at the ceiling, breathing through his nose: sharp and shallow. He writhed and jerked against his bond.

Crawley turned to him. 'Keep still.'

Sawyer refocused on Crawley. 'Your *mother's* mercy?'

Crawley held a long silence. 'You did bring her?'

Sawyer took out a silver ring with a molar tooth set into the centre and placed it on the coffee table.

'I need Eva, Dennis. You have Dale's son now. Give me Eva, and I'll give you Dale. Eva has suffered long enough for Dale's crimes.'

Crawley stared down at the ring. 'They had to sedate me the day I went into prison. I wouldn't take it off. I woke up, realised they'd removed it, and they had to sedate me again.'

'I have nothing physical from my mother,' said Sawyer. 'But she left a journal. I found it at our old house.'

Crawley looked up.

'She started writing it when she was so young. Everything is in there. Her work. Her hopes, desires, dreams. Her loves, hates. Her children. I got to read about me. How she felt about me. She said I lay in my cot, kicking my legs as if I was running. That's the last thing she told me on the day she died. To run and not look back. But I've been looking back my whole life, Dennis. So have you. Our mothers' attackers brought us to this moment. We embody the pain they were subjected to. The pain they dealt out. All paid forward. And now, here you are, passing it on to that young boy in the corner. Are you really going to take his mother from him? Force him to waste his life looking back, too?'

Crawley crouched beside the coffee table, gazing at the ring. 'Eva is in a storage building behind the garage. She's alive.'

'Armed police! Stay where you are.'

A team of officers in body armour and protective helmets swept into the room. Hutchcraft took the lead.

Crawley jumped to his feet.

'Show me your hands!' Hutchcraft aimed his rifle at Crawley's head. 'If you make any threatening movements, you *will* be shot.'

The officers fanned out, guns trained on Crawley,

whose position blocked their path to Luka, still tugging and twisting at the belt around his hands.

Crawley kept still, arms down, as Strickland walked through and stood with his back to the wall furthest from Crawley. 'Mum is safe, Luka. I ordered the police to search the outside of the house, while Sawyer was talking to Crawley. We didn't need him to tell us.' He patted his chest. *'I found her.* She's being cared for by a medical team outside.'

Abadi strolled into the room and stood beside Strickland.

Hutchcraft sidestepped around Sawyer, gun still pointing at Crawley. 'Show me your hands *now*.'

Keating from the doorway. 'The room is not secure. Hold your fire.'

Luka had wriggled his hands free. He lurched forward, reaching behind to the knife tucked into his belt fastener. Crawley grabbed his arm, but Luka swung the knife around and stabbed it into Crawley's ankle.

Crawley roared, kicked out his leg, dislodging the knife. It skimmed across the floor and came to rest in the hall behind Keating.

Luka ran to Strickland, burying his head in his father's chest.

Crawley groaned and reached down to his leg.

Hutchcraft moved in. 'You will raise your arms *now*! This is your final warning.'

Crawley drew himself upright and held up his hands, palms out, eyes locked on Strickland.

An officer ushered Luka out into the hall.

Keating stepped in and stood at Sawyer's shoulder. 'Dennis Crawley. You are under arrest on suspicion of—'

'*Wait.*' Strickland held up a hand and took a pace away from the wall.

Hutchcraft turned. 'Mr Strickland. Do not approach the subject.'

Strickland stopped and held Crawley's eye. 'You've terrorised me, my wife, my son. And now, you've forced me out of my home. Because it's forever tainted. No amount of scrubbing will ever get your stink out.'

'He's trying to provoke you,' said Sawyer to Crawley. He turned to Keating. 'Finish the arrest. Don't indulge this.'

Strickland clapped his hands together in slow, sarcastic applause, and took another step forward. 'After all this, you leave here with nothing. You didn't get your ridiculous confession. You just wasted everyone's time.' He nodded to the tooth ring. 'Your mother would be so proud of you. Murdering middle-aged women. Killing animals. Burying teenagers alive. *Pregnant women*. Ruining lives. What a fucking hero you are. All that suffering. All in the name of one woman.'

Crawley kept his eyes on Strickland. He winced with pain, hovering his wounded foot above the floor.

Strickland edged forward. 'I promise you...' His voice dropped to a hissing half-whisper. 'The caves you used to scuttle around, like some diseased rat... They'll seem like luxury compared with your life from now on. I'm about to take control in this area. I get to choose the top cop. I'll make sure your case is first on his list, and I'll be reviewing it regularly, keeping your privileges beyond reach. Blocking correspondence. Denying visits. Insisting on problem cellmates. Hoping one of them does the decent thing and slits your throat when you're asleep. So, fuck you and your crippled mother. She must have been happy to see the back of you, the day she finally died.' Now, a whisper. 'My only regret is that she didn't suffer more.'

Crawley lunged across the room. Strickland anticipated it and leapt back into the hall, pushing Keating aside.

'Hold your fire!' shouted Keating, as he staggered back, holding on to the door frame. 'This man is unarmed.'

Two gunshots in quick succession, muzzle flash lighting the room.

Crawley bellowed and gripped his left shoulder.

Abadi had pushed himself up against the far wall, handgun trained on Crawley.

One side of Crawley's face was scorched and streaked with blood from the second shot, his ear partially shorn away by the path of the bullet. He collapsed onto one knee, holding himself upright with his right hand.

The two AFOs nearest Abadi turned their rifles on him.

'*Drop the weapon*!'

Crawley swept blood from his eyes and rushed Abadi, head down, barrelling into his stomach, crushing him into the wall before he could get off another shot.

Crawley reached up and pushed Abadi's head back into the wall, holding it firm. He jammed his other hand into Abadi's mouth and tugged at his jaw, pulling it down.

Abadi screamed and flailed, but Crawley was too strong.

His jaw gave a loud crack as Crawley wrenched it unnaturally wide.

More gunshots. Deeper, louder. Brighter muzzle flashes.

Hutchcraft unloaded into Crawley, sending him spinning, away from Abadi, who fell to the floor, howling and holding his mouth.

Crawley lay still, sprawled against the wall.

'Secure!' called Hutchcraft.

'Tac-Meds,' shouted Keating. '*Now.*'

A group of medical responders raced into the room. They huddled around Crawley.

'We need help here, too,' said Strickland, crouched beside Abadi.

One responder broke away and rushed out into the hall while the others stayed to work on Crawley.

Sawyer picked up the tooth ring from the coffee table. He squeezed in around the side of the lead medic and reached for Crawley's arm.

The medics leaned back. One looked up at Keating and shook his head.

Sawyer pressed the ring into Crawley's hand and closed his fingers around it.

61

Three taps on Keating's office door.

Sawyer walked in, followed by Shepherd.

Keating finished typing something, then turned to them, releasing a prolonged and exaggerated sigh. He gestured to the door.

Sawyer closed it and they pulled up two chairs.

Keating clasped his hands together on the desk. He studied Sawyer for a second, then Shepherd. 'Good morning, detectives. Dennis Crawley is no more. I've just filed my report to the IOPC. Crawley's Uncle James has been informed. Clay Hutchcraft and two of his AFOs have been removed from operational duties, and their rifles detained for ballistic examination. Routine. You can both expect to be interviewed for the enquiry. I think it's home and dry, but we'll need to follow up with a standard policy and procedure review.'

'How are Eva and Luka?' said Sawyer.

'FLOs are at home with Luka. Strickland is there, too. Eva is in Spire Claremont up in Crosspool. She's okay. Undernourished and dehydrated, but otherwise well. Physically, at least. Crawley numbed her up to extract the tooth. Victoria Kendal's computer activity shows a purchase for procaine from a website called Over The Counter. She used cryptocurrency. Opened a Coinbase account last year. Probably encouraged by Crawley over time in their correspondence. He certainly didn't wing this.' Keating paused and shuffled some papers. 'Strickland's man, Abadi, will live. Crawley dislocated and broke his jaw. He also has facial nerve damage and dental issues. And when he's all better, he'll go straight to the top of my shitlist.'

'How did Abadi get the gun past the response team?'

'Hutchcraft had him frisked, but he'd stashed it in Strickland's car and he grabbed it when Strickland went in after the team had found Eva. It was licensed, but I'll push for illegal discharge or possession with intent to endanger life. Strickland will probably fight it, though. He's due to give a speech next week, alongside Russell Hogan. It's basically a handover. Open secret.'

'Did he really order the team to go in for Eva?'

Keating hesitated. 'Of course not. I had gold command.'

'But Strickland pushed for it. And you didn't resist.'

Keating busied himself with the papers again.

Sawyer shook his head. 'Strickland got Crawley killed. It was murder by proxy.' He stared into space.

Keating slapped both palms on the desk, startling Sawyer. 'Straight back on the horse, gentlemen. We have an ongoing murder case. I have an engagement in an hour, so we'll have to do a mini-briefing and you can—'

'Disseminate?' said Sawyer.

Keating made a face. 'If you insist.'

'DC Walker has new work on this, sir,' said Shepherd.

'Go find him, then. Sawyer, a minute please.'

Shepherd got up and left, closing the door behind him.

'Strickland sends apologies for having you followed,' said Keating. 'He says he was concerned about your mental state and worried about your decisions putting Eva in danger.'

Sawyer nodded. 'What happened between you, Caldwell, and my father?'

Keating sat back slowly. 'When?'

'June 1987. My mother wrote something in the journal. "Ivan was here, with Harold." I'm assuming that was you. She also wrote that you told my dad you couldn't "let the thing with Bill go away". I'm assuming that was William Caldwell. Who was the Buxton Station Chief. Your boss. My dad's boss. My mother's killer.'

A cloud passed over Keating. He pulled on a pained expression. 'That's a long time ago, Jake.'

'And my father said this thing before he died. *There is nothing in darkness that will not be disclosed. Nothing concealed that will not be brought to light.* It's a bible quote. You were there. You heard him say it. Before he—'

'I don't know what you're asking me. Your father, in unimaginable pain. Desperately obsessed. A Christian, trying to comfort you with biblical wisdom before taking his own life. And... Something your poor mother wrote in a diary a lifetime ago, when I was a young detective. I'd

375

help if I could, Jake. Is there a possibility you're reading too much into this?'

Sawyer took a deep breath. 'There's a possibility, yes.' He tilted his head forward, holding Keating's eye. 'But there is something still in the dark.'

Keating managed a slight smile. 'And you do dark.'

Shepherd and Walker entered and stood either side of Sawyer.

'Sir,' said Walker, nodding to Keating, then Sawyer. 'First thing. Dylan Brennan. Garda found his body at Lough Mahon. A lake outside Cork. Weighted, but not enough to keep it down. Looks like a stab wound to the side of the neck. The state of the body indicates TOD at around two to three weeks.'

Keating pulled his chair back and rested his hands on his head, clasped together. 'There goes our chief suspect. What else?'

Walker continued. 'DI Sawyer asked me to look into the priest at All Saints Catholic Church. Tyrone Reavey. To see if there was a deeper connection to the Brennans, other than benefactors of the church.'

'Are we sitting comfortably?' said Shepherd.

'I couldn't find anything on Reavey back in Ireland, so I had a researcher dig through name changes,' said Walker. 'The Ireland General Register Office shows that a Patrick Butler changed his name to Tyrone Reavey in 1998, in Ireland, just before he travelled to the UK. The Good Friday Agreement loosened up ID checks and gave other concessions to movement across the Irish Sea.'

'That's effectively starting a new life,' said Sawyer.

'New name, new job. And a lot of trouble for someone who has nothing to hide.'

Walker laid an enlarged black-and-white photograph on Keating's desk. 'This is Patrick Butler around the time of the move.'

The image showed a man in his late thirties, with an unstyled mop of greying hair with curling edges, thick and wavy locks growing out in multiple directions. Sawyer took out his phone and brought up the All Saints website picture of Reavey. The beard in Walker's photo was scruffy and untrimmed, but the man wore the same metal-rimmed glasses, and the resemblance was clear.

'He was arrested in 1979,' said Shepherd, 'after a raid by RUC Special Branch on an IRA bomb-making house near the Republic border.'

Walker nodded to Keating. 'Your man Aidan Byrne dug out the reports. Also arrested in the raid—'

'Dylan Brennan,' said Sawyer.

'Brennan was wanted for other offences, and they tried to get Butler to talk. But he kept quiet. And they both did three years for stolen goods. The raid was badly timed and they couldn't make anything stronger stick. Butler was only nineteen.'

'Did you investigate Reavey's father? He said he'd been murdered.'

Walker checked something on his phone. 'Colin Butler. Killed in a notorious loyalist attack on a chip shop in Armagh in November 1975. The place was frequented by senior IRA. The bomb went off early and nine people were killed, including Reavey's father and the bomber.'

'So,' said Keating, 'we have a Catholic kid. Fifteen. His father was murdered by the other side. Probably radicalised him. He's caught four years later in a known IRA bomb-making location. Then, he continues his priestly studies... But we don't know if his IRA links continue. Or if he continued to associate with Dylan Brennan.'

'But we know he came to England,' said Sawyer, 'and re-connected with the Brennans at All Saints Church.'

'I also left a message for an IRA expert called Bob Delaney.'

'How did you find him?' said Keating.

'I googled "IRA expert". He's written a few books on the IRA and The Troubles, and he has a website that he still updates. I thought he might have some ideas on Butler and Brennan, and the 1979 arrests.'

They pondered in silence for a moment.

'Interesting to think,' said Shepherd, 'that Thomas Brennan's funeral could have been the first time Butler, or Reavey, had seen Dylan since the 1979 arrest.'

'It's all interesting,' said Keating. 'But not enough to bring him in. What do we have that could link Reavey to the killings? His ancient history won't be enough for the CPC.'

'I sent Myers to the church,' said Walker.

'Really?' said Keating, smiling.

'I asked nicely. DI Sawyer wanted to get an idea of a pendant Reavey was wearing, because he seemed to be twitchy about showing it for too long. Myers said he had a family member who collected religious artefacts, but Reavey wouldn't show him. So, I pulled out as many pics of him as I could find. Media, events, church documents.' He laid another piece of paper on the desk. 'Two images. I zoomed in to a photo of Reavey in a group of wedding pictures on a Facebook page found by Rhodes. He, uh, wrote a script to scrape the site for references to All Saints.'

Side-eyes all round.

'I'm not sure what it means, either. I matched it to a symbol related to the archangel Michael I found online.'

Sawyer picked up the photo and studied the image. The lower left was obscured behind Reavey's collar, but most of the markings on the circular pendant were clear. A scattering of symbols lay in the centre: crosses, interlocking geometric shapes, mathematical signs, the letters 'S' and 'M'. Four words ran around an outer circle: *SADAY, ATHANATOS, SABAOTH, MICHAEL.*

'It's a sigil, apparently. I've contacted a professor of Religion and Society at Oxford University to tell me more. Bloke called Paul Weller. Not that one. Haven't heard yet. I'll chase him up after this.'

'Did Myers go inside the church?' said Sawyer.

Walker frowned. 'Yes. Earlier today. He said he spoke to Reavey first in the entrance hall, then they went into the main room.'

'Get his shoes to Sally. See if there's a match for the fibres she found at the scenes. Look into Reavey's recent travel history. Did he go to meet Dylan in Ireland?'

'Did he kill him?' said Shepherd.

Sawyer nodded. 'And why?' He gazed off into space, to the side of Keating's desk. 'We haven't found his vehicle, but if Reavey did this, then we know that

Burrows and White were killed away from the scenes. It would have been somewhere he felt secure. Somewhere private where he could take his time.'

'*The name of the Lord is a strong tower,*' said Walker. '*The righteous man runs into it and is safe.*'

They all looked at him.

'It's from Proverbs, I think. I tried to misspend my youth but my mum made me go to Sunday School.'

'Surely not the church,' said Keating.

Walker pointed. 'Myers said the place was busy. Closed to the public. Reavey told him they were setting up an event there this evening.'

Sawyer stood up, nodded to Shepherd. 'A good opportunity for a confession.'

62

Shepherd rummaged in the glovebox.

Sawyer glanced over. 'What are you looking for?'

'Something sweet.' He reached further in. 'Coffee breath. There's literally nothing in here but empty packets and wrappers. When's your next consignment of sherbet lemons due?'

'I think I've grown out of them.'

Shepherd laughed. 'It's the End Times. Hell frozen over. Pope not Catholic. Sawyer off his sweets. And another thing... Can you hear that?'

'What?' said Sawyer.

'Exactly. No strange music.'

'My music only sounds strange to simple minds.'

Shepherd turned to the window. 'I like their earlier stuff.'

Sawyer turned off at the Yondermann Café, towards Wardlow. He sped along the connecting road, straight as a train track, bordered by endless sloping farm fields of olive-green wheat and golden corn.

Shepherd opened his window halfway, then closed it to a couple of inches.

'It's always breezy down here,' said Sawyer. 'Even on a summery day.'

Shepherd looked at him. 'This is your home village. You could have turned off back at the campsite.'

'I won't melt down just by driving through my old stomping ground.'

Shepherd shrugged. 'Just not as direct.' He turned back to the window. 'How's the head?'

'Still pretty scrambled. Yesterday didn't help.'

'You did okay. Strickland hijacked it.'

Sawyer slowed as he drove through the village. Dusty red phone box; uniform grey-stone semis and farm buildings. White-gated driveways. Topiary.

'What was it like,' said Shepherd, 'growing up in a postcard like this?'

'Idyllic, to start with. Then I hardly noticed.'

'My counsellor said to be careful of the tendency to shut yourself down as a way to cope with traumatic reliving. Panic attacks and other symptoms. He said the point wasn't to forget, but to reframe the trauma as bad memory. Something that doesn't trigger that sense that you're experiencing it all again.'

Sawyer nodded. 'Wise words. But I've tried it.'

'He said that going the other way... Turning off your feelings. It shuts out most of the pain, but it can also reduce your capacity for pleasure. You get nothing from the things that make life worth living. Sport. Culture. Sex. Music.'

'Sugar,' said Sawyer, flashing him a smile.

Shepherd rested a hand on the dashboard as Sawyer took a hard corner too fast, onto the road towards Hassop. He left it there as the car steadied. 'How is she?'

Sawyer let the question hang for a long time. 'Still alive. But if she survives, she'll be changed.'

'As you've told me before, change is the only constant. Hephaestus, wasn't it?'

'Heraclitus.'

Shepherd kept his eyes on the fields. 'It's trite, you know. Sir. Thinking you could have done more.'

'I've moved on from that. It's a lot clearer in my head now. A simple beautiful truth.'

Shepherd turned. 'In what way?'

'Should have been me.'

———

The car park was full, and Sawyer had to wedge the grubby Mini onto a side-road verge, between a crimson Porsche and a Land Rover Defender, both spotless.

Sawyer reached over, opened the glovebox and took out an empty Starburst packet. He exited and hurried off in the direction of the church. Shepherd squeezed out and caught him up. 'We just parked illegally.'

Sawyer aimed the transponder over his shoulder and locked the car. 'You just told me I need to get more pleasure from life.'

'So, what's the plan? I doubt Reavey is going to break down and lay it all out for us.'

'I'll talk to him.' Sawyer handed Shepherd the empty packet. 'You go for a walk.'

'Where?'

'Down to the river. Do a little digging. Sally's soil sample.'

———

Sawyer stepped off the front path and crossed the freshly mown front lawn. Laura Brennan stood by a line of white trestle tables, arranged in a line along the lawn perimeter. A small group of well-dressed men and women milled around the main doors. A few scurried back and forth, covering the tables with bright cloths and laying out boxes of books, clothes, handicrafts. A few sat on the grass at the side of the church, helping children write signs.

Laura indicated something to a stern-looking man in a church-branded polo shirt and gave Sawyer a little wave as she caught his approach.

The man pointed. 'There is a path, my friend.'

Sawyer looked around. 'But no sign.'

'Sorry?'

'Nothing that says to keep off the grass.' He smiled. 'I prefer the path of least resistance.'

'Whatever,' said the man. He sighed and headed off towards the back of the church grounds.

Laura shook Sawyer's hand. 'Detective Sawyer. I was about to introduce you to Leonard Podmore, our groundskeeper. He's a man of many talents, but he's funny about his lawns.'

'How's the preparation going?'

She brightened. 'Splendid. It's for our annual soirée

tomorrow. Mainly for the children in the morning. Games, cakes, usually overtired tears. Then barbecue and fund-raising with the grown-ups later on.'

He looked around. 'How is Catherine? Is she here?'

'She's good. She's at home today. She had to work.' Laura reached to her neck, twirled the silver crucifix. 'Ralph and the girls are helping with the music stage on the back lawn. We usually set everything up, then go for pizza in town.'

'Catherine will join you for that?'

She tidied a plastic box of prayer cards. 'Yes. I'll head back to her place when I'm done here. Then we'll change and meet up with everyone later. I know it's not your scene, spiritually, but you'd be welcome.'

'I wouldn't want to sully the occasion with heathen vibes.' He nodded to the church. 'Is the man at home?'

She frowned.

'Not *the* man. Tyrone.'

Laura smiled. 'Whoever told you God was male?' She waved a hand. 'Don't worry. This isn't the time for a debate on biblical anthropomorphism.'

'It's certainly the place.'

Laura forced a laugh. She thought for a moment, then turned back to the box. 'Father Reavey isn't here. He had to leave on a family matter. I believe one of your detectives spoke to him earlier. Can I help in any way?'

'We spoke to Kieran Leith.'

'Ah. How is he?'

Flash. Shoving Leith to the floor.

'He's well. He mentioned some notebooks. Small, different colours. Local places your father enjoyed.'

385

She pondered for a few seconds. 'I remember them, yes. Cat has them in a box at her place. I'll ask her to dig them out later.'

'I need to look at them urgently. I'll head over to Catherine's after this.'

Laura jerked her head around. 'Don't worry. I'll get them and bring them to the event later. I know she's really busy.' She laughed. 'Cat can be fierce if she's interrupted when she's working. She's not great with being hungry, either.'

'There's something else. I'm sorry to say, but your Uncle Dylan was found dead yesterday, near his home in Ireland.'

She froze, looked up at him with pained eyes. 'Oh, no! What happened?'

'The investigation is ongoing. I'm sorry, Laura, but I need to ask you something. Catherine told me that Dylan... came on to her. Did she tell you?'

'What? When?'

'The time he stayed with you for a while, when he travelled over for your father's funeral.'

Laura steadied herself with a hand on the table. 'She never mentioned that. Dylan wasn't... He was upset, but he wasn't like that.'

Sawyer moved closer, dropped his voice. 'Dylan is dead. Two of the other men who murdered your father have also died since I last saw you. I think your sister tried to distract me by painting your uncle as a suspect. Could you blame me for joining up the dots?'

She turned away. 'I'm sorry... That's awful news about Dylan, but I didn't know him that well, and I have no idea what you mean by joining up the dots.' She gave her shoulders a brisk shake, visibly pulling herself together. 'Now I really don't want to say any more, Detective Sawyer. Come by later and talk to me when Catherine is here. Excuse me.'

She walked away and fell into a breezy conversation with two small children lying on the grass, colouring a vast *ALL SAINTS SUMMER FETE* sign with crayons.

He looked up. Podmore was working with another man, setting up a barbecue in a concrete recess along the near side of the main building. He saw Sawyer clock him and turned his eyes away.

Sawyer wandered around to the back of the church grounds. A modest stage area sat partially constructed, close to a marquee tent with white garden furniture stacked outside.

He walked on, away from the fete activity, to the sandstone bungalow. He ran a finger along the frame of a wide blue door set into one outbuilding. The paint was weathered and peeling.

'Can I help you, my friend?'

Podmore called from the perimeter path. He walked over, head held high in scrutiny.

Sawyer pointed. 'What's in here?'

Podmore stopped and squinted at Sawyer, amused. 'Unless you're the Holy Father in disguise, I can't tell you. Father Reavey lives in the bungalow. This is all his private land. Note the use of the word "private".'

Sawyer grinned. 'Isn't the Pope supposed to be God's man on Earth?'

'Yes. He's considered the Bishop of Rome and the

Vicar of Christ. The earthly representative of Jesus Christ. He's the successor of Saint Peter.'

Sawyer tried the door handle. Locked. 'And Saint Peter... He decides which way you go, right? Up or down.'

Podmore sighed. 'What exactly do you want, my friend? Are you a copper or something?'

'You're a sharp one, Leonard.' Sawyer showed his warrant card.

Neither the revelation nor the use of his name fazed him. 'Okay, Detective Sawyer. Can I suggest you come back next week and speak to Father Reavey? I'll let him know you were here.'

'As the groundskeeper, you have a key for this, yes?'

'Yes. And I suppose you're going to tell me I can either open it now or you'll have to get a warrant.'

'You're a mind reader, Leonard.' Sawyer held his eye. 'I'd really appreciate it. Five minutes and I'm gone. *We're* gone,' he said as Shepherd walked over from the perimeter path. 'This is my colleague, DI Ed Shepherd.'

Podmore nodded at Shepherd. 'I hope you went to a different charm school.'

'Oh, definitely,' said Shepherd. 'I'm the good cop.'

Podmore rolled his eyes and unlocked the blue door. 'There's a light round the corner. Storage room up top. Cellar down below. It's just junk, though. Building materials. Bits and pieces. Also, deliveries. They come through from the side road. There's a ramp for trolleys.' He held up a finger. 'Five minutes.' He stood there, arms folded. 'Anything else?'

'You should be careful, Leonard,' said Sawyer.

'What about?'

'Assuming people are your friend.'

Podmore glared at them both. 'Whatever.' He headed back round the front.

Shepherd held up the Starburst bag. 'Got your soil.' He stuffed the bag into his pocket. 'Couple by the river having a picnic, watching me like I was some kind of freak.'

Sawyer opened the door and stepped into a musty hallway adjoining a side room with a windowed door.

Shepherd followed and turned on a weak overhead light. 'Walker called. Reavey travelled to Dublin three weeks ago. Looks like he rented a car, but no details on his movements. He was there for two days. Oh, and Sally has the fibres from Myers's shoes and she's fast-tracking.'

Sawyer cupped his hands and looked through the side-room window. Teeming but tidy. Linens, candles, candle holders, books, vestments. A collection of statues and artworks sat on a high shelf, alongside various artefacts, featuring the usual saints and religious scenes. Low shelves held chalices, crucifixes, tabernacles, bells.

Shepherd held back, and Sawyer led the way down a set of stone steps into a large cellar with a ceiling so low, he had to duck to keep the top of his head from scraping on the stone.

His eyes adjusted and he looked around, helped by the light from the top of the steps. Ancient barrels were lined up at the base of the longest wall. Stacked crates and cases, a battered workbench with tools. The air was stale and dank, peppered with chalk dust. Faded leather, mildewed wood, clay, a hint of sulphur.

Sawyer's nose twitched. Something soapy.

He switched on his phone light and walked to the stone wall furthest from the steps, crouched down. A large patch of floor on this side of the room was clear of dust, freshly stained. He ran a finger across it and lifted it to his nose.

'Disinfectant.'

He turned. Shepherd was trying the handle of a heavy-looking door set into the wall by the bench.

'Locked?' said Sawyer, walking over.

Shepherd nodded.

'What could be in there? All the churchy stuff is in the top storeroom.'

Shepherd coughed. 'Spare pews? Ark of the Covenant?'

Sawyer checked the lock. An ancient Yale. 'When someone doesn't want me to see something, I get curious.' He took an oblong black case from his pocket and removed two kirby grip hairpins.

'Ah, okay,' said Shepherd. 'So, we're breaking into church property now?'

Sawyer bent one pin and inserted it into the keyhole, using it as a wrench to turn the lock and feel out the tension, then slotted in the other pin above, using it as a pick. He raised the cylinders into place, one by one, turning the lock further with the wrench each time, until the lock opened.

He pushed at the door and it swung aside.

'We're definitely going to hell now,' said Shepherd.

Sawyer found a light switch and pressed it.

An overhead light flickered then burned steady,

revealing a long, thin chamber, walls lined with shelves.

'*Hello?*'

Laura's voice, from the steps.

Sawyer walked along the shelves. White packets, plastic pots, black bottles. Boxes with wires, batteries, switches.

'*Mr Sawyer?*'

He crouched. The bottom shelf was neatly loaded with a selection of saws, hammers, drills. Boxes of nails, ball bearings. A welding torch with fuel tanks, gloves and goggles. Sawyer looked over to the far wall. A rusted steel bucket sat in the corner.

His eyes carried up to the corner.

Shepherd read the labels from the materials on the shelf. 'Ammonium nitrate. Potassium chlorate. Nitric acid.'

Laura arrived at the door. 'I'm sorry. Leonard told me you were here... This is Father Reavey's property and I must insist—'

Sawyer stood upright and held up a long piece of wood with several nails hammered into the end. 'Pickaxe handle. Modified. Ms Brennan, could you please explain the theological significance of this item?'

She moved into the room. 'That can't belong to Father Reavey.'

Sawyer set down the weapon. 'Laura. I'm afraid you're going to have to disappoint the congregation. The fete is officially cancelled. I'm going to call in some smart people in hazard suits to come down here and take the contents of this room away for forensic examination. Also, I'm keen to speak to the good priest of the parish about his plans for all this, and about the murders of Jermaine Cunliffe, Rory Burrows and Jared White.'

Laura lowered her head and held her face in her hands.

'I also suspect you and Catherine were involved. Maybe giving financial support. And Dylan. I think something went wrong, and Tyrone had to kill Dylan. Maybe to keep him quiet.'

Laura shook her head. 'Oh, no. No, no, no...' She turned away from Sawyer and Shepherd, facing the wall.

'We'll put out a call to find Tyrone, but for now, I'd like you to come with us to pick up Catherine. Is she really at home?'

Laura nodded and her face crumpled.

'Then we can talk at the station. I will have to arrest you, Laura. But I don't want to put you in handcuffs for the walk back to my car.'

Laura was sobbing now. She sniffed, composed herself, and turned to Sawyer. 'Thank you,' she said, in a small voice.

'I don't know how much you know about Father Reavey's past,' said Shepherd.

Laura stared at him. 'I know everything.'

'Do you know where he is now, Laura?' said Sawyer.

She shook her head, then walked between them, to the far wall, and looked up at the tall item propped in the corner: an upright post, in rugged dark wood, welded to a thick crosspiece.

Laura sighed deeply and crossed herself. 'This was for Morris. I wanted to save him until last.' She turned to them. 'I wanted to watch.'

63

Laura sat in the back seat with her head down, weeping softly. She pushed herself low into the corner, almost reclining.

'Does Catherine know we're coming?' said Sawyer.

She sniffed and shook her head, catching his eye in the rear-view mirror.

Sawyer stopped at a red light and navigated to his phone photos. He passed the device to Shepherd. 'What does this all mean, Laura? It's a pendant Tyrone wears. He not keen on others seeing it, though.'

Shepherd held the phone up for her to see. She studied the image. 'It's the sigil of Archangel Michael. It's about protection, courage, strength. According to the holy book, Michael is the commander of the army of angels.'

'Isn't he in *Paradise Lost*?' said Shepherd.

'Yes. Michael commands the angels loyal to God against the fallen angels of Satan. Wielding a sword from God's armoury, he defeats Satan in combat.' She zoomed in on the image and scrolled around. 'The circle represents unity. The infinite divine. Michael's unending protection. The triangle is Michael's power, wisdom, and love. The cross is the symbol of sacrifice, redemption. And the Hebrew letters speak to different elements of Michael's power and personality.'

'What about the words?'

'*Saday* is a Hebrew name for God. *Athanatos* is Greek. It means immortal or deathless. Sabaoth is another Hebrew term that means hosts or armies. Here, it refers to the armies of angels led by Michael.'

Shepherd handed the phone back to Sawyer.

'So, Father Reavey doesn't have a God complex,' said Sawyer. 'He has a protector complex. He sees himself at God's side, ridding the world of evil.'

They moved off. Sawyer diverted from Wardlow past the view of the Monsal Head viaduct and onto a tight tree-lined lane in shadow from overhanging branches.

'Mum held out for so long,' said Laura.

'How do you mean?'

'It was the cancer that changed her mind. Or it certainly concentrated her mind.'

Sawyer's phone rang. Walker.

He took the call on CarPlay. 'Matt. We have Laura Brennan in the car. She's under caution.'

'Sir. I have some detail on Tyrone Reavey.'

He paused. 'Let's hear it.'

'The Irish journalist, Delaney, got back to me. Delaney was a major thorn in the IRA's side back in the day. Survived a couple of assassination attempts. As we know, Tyrone Reavey used to be known as Patrick

Butler. Delaney says that Butler's father, Colin, was heavily involved with the IRA, although he believes his son didn't realise it at the time. After the chip shop attack that killed his father, Patrick volunteered and rose quickly through the ranks. He was notorious for the levels of violence he dealt out to loyalist infiltrators and prisoners, and he became one of the Provos' youngest quartermasters, with a talent for weapons and bomb-making. Delaney says that Butler and Brennan would have been routinely tortured for information when serving their time. When they got out, it looks like Dylan relocated, while Butler was recruited into the Internal Security Unit, AKA the Nutting Squad. It specialised in rooting out informants and double agents.'

'So,' said Shepherd, 'he continued to study for the priesthood while maiming teenage soldiers. That's some serious doublethink. But not a problem if you believe you're God's personal executioner.'

'What's that?' said Walker.

Sawyer checked on Laura. Head still down. 'Never mind. We're taking Laura Brennan to her sister's place. Reavey is missing. We found plenty of evidence in a room at the church. Sally's team are there now. Call a meeting. Say you're acting on my direct authority. Get Myers to check on Morris's place. Take an assault team. Reavey might head there to finish the job. Set up an arrest warrant. Alert the NCA. Border Force. Stations, ports, airports. Garda. In case he tries to head back to Ireland. Check travel bookings. Given Reavey's history, get Keating to alert security services. I think Myers spooked

395

him, so he's taken off. But there was bomb-making equipment at the church, so we can't rule anything out.'

Walker blew out a breath. 'Is that it?'

'Trace evidence. The CPS will need more than unprovable war stories. Get Sally onto those carpet fibres. Shepherd has passed on a soil sample from the area near to the church. Hopefully, it'll match with the deposits in White's hair.'

'Just the soil? How will she tell?'

'If Reavey took the rocks from around the church, the river would narrow down the biome. Google it. But not now.'

Sawyer hung up, and they drove in silence for a while. He looked up to the rear-view mirror. 'You were saying...'

'Hmm?' said Laura.

'Your mum. Tanya. The cancer changing her mind. About what?'

She sat up in the seat, took a few big breaths. 'We had the years of forgiveness. I know Dylan spoke to Mum about taking revenge when the four got out of prison. He even said he wanted to go after their families. Mum wouldn't have any of it. She just kept saying that it wouldn't bring Dad back, so what was the point? Dylan had met Tyrone at Dad's funeral and recognised him. He got back in touch, and tried to use his religious standing to sell it to Mum, but again she said no. Now, I know Dylan wasn't great with money. Mum used to send him some. But he was in trouble with gambling debts and needed more. Dylan wasn't a well man, Mr Sawyer. The Irish aren't exactly known for their temperance, but Mum always said Dylan could drink the island dry.'

She paused, sinking back into the seat, as if the truth was letting the air out of her.

'Dylan came over to the UK a few years ago, right?' said Shepherd.

'He did. That was when she'd found out about the cancer. She was Stage Four on diagnosis, and they put her at twenty-five per cent chance of a five-year survival. We all worked on her. Catherine was busy with her family, so I did most of the talk. Then Morris had his release confirmed, and he heard about the cancer. He sent her these foul messages, saying his life was about to begin and hers was going to end. He sent more after he was released. What *is* that, Mr Sawyer? Why do people have to do that?'

'Some people are like cancers. They exist just to spread poison. They enjoy the pain of others. Usually to get back at a world they feel has poisoned them.'

Rear-view mirror. Laura had hitched herself up, and rested her head against the window, staring out at the sunlit pastures.

She turned to him again, wiping her eyes. 'I think that pushed Mum over the line. She spoke to Tyrone, then Cat and me. She released a lot of money to us, saying it would all just look like a legacy. I think the cancer had got into her brain, because she was ranting. I'd never seen her like that. Saying how they all got off too lightly, and Satan must have been involved. But she wanted Dylan kept out of it.'

'Maybe she had Tyrone offer Dylan money to stay out. But if his life was a mess, he might have demanded more. Threatened to expose Tyrone...'

Laura turned back to the window. 'That makes sense, yes.' She dropped her head again. 'In her last days, Mum said the men had to be denied the rest of their lives, as they'd denied Dad. But she said it wasn't enough. She wanted them to suffer as much as possible. She said to "make it Biblical".'

Shepherd nodded. 'Looks like Tyrone took that literally. I assume the locations in your father's notebooks inspired the body dump scenes?'

'Yes. Tyrone said Mum told him that would be like a tribute. Thomas's killers presented to the Lord, in the places he loved in life.'

'Like sacrifice?' said Sawyer.

She nodded. 'But it got inside me, too. The pain of his death. All those years of sadness and torture. A simple moment of retribution just didn't seem enough. I needed it to be extreme. That's what I took Mum to mean by *biblical*. Transcendent. Catherine wasn't so sold. She wanted it quick and efficient. After Cunliffe's death, we argued. I wobbled and spoke to Tyrone in confession. But he steered me back on track.'

'Onto the path of righteousness.'

'Dylan had been angry, but he couldn't see the moral sense in the method of retribution. He just wanted to right the universe. Keep it *proportionate*.' She sighed. 'I know we'll be judged. Cast out by our faith. Labelled as fanatics. Dismissed by atheists as an example of how religion corrupts. Have you ever done something wrong in the name of a greater right, Mr Sawyer?'

He caught her eye in the mirror again. 'Many times.'

'Well.' She sat forward. 'That's life, isn't it? *Fear*. It's the root of our survival. How we react to the things we're afraid of. How we avoid them, overcome them. Death, disease, harm coming to our loved ones. Fear drives our behaviour. And we learn to justify it in different ways. And when you have a fear of God, you have the ultimate justification.'

Sawyer turned the Mini onto the road that curved up out of the valley, to Catherine Brennan's house. 'My question now is, what does Tyrone Reavey fear?'

'In what sense?'

'He doesn't know you're with me, but he thinks you're going to your sister's house later, before the fete. If you want to keep your sister safe, I might need your help.' He caught her eyes in the rear-view mirror again. 'If I were Reavey, and I was trying to get away, I wouldn't leave the only two people who knew about my involvement in the killings still alive.'

64

Catherine Brennan's generous detached house was perched on a rise, with a gently inclined path leading to a tan-coloured front door. The late afternoon sun shimmered through the trees at the back of the house, casting a greenish-golden hue across the front lawn, flat as baize.

Sawyer parked the car on the corner of a side road and turned to Laura. 'Okay.' He unlocked Laura's cuffs and handed over her confiscated phone.

Laura made a call, putting it on speaker. It rang a few times, then connected.

'Hey there.' Catherine sounded flustered.

'Cat...' Laura glanced at Sawyer, who gave her a nod. 'Bella's had a bit of a mishap. Don't panic. It's just a cut. We've patched her up, but she's upset. Can you come over?'

A pause. 'Isn't Ralph there?'

'Yeah, but she's asking for you. Please, Cat. I've got so much on here.'

A longer pause. 'I'm... I have to work, Laura. If we're going to be on track for later, I need to finish this.'

Another pause. Laura started to speak, but Sawyer shook his head.

'Listen,' said Catherine. 'Can you bring her over? If it's just a minor thing, there's no need for me to do a mercy dash, is there? I'll set her up with some TV and ice cream while I work.'

Laura looked at Sawyer; he nodded. 'Cat. I can't do that. There's no way—'

'This is my girl, Laura. You're telling me you can't just drive her over here? Half an hour round trip. Get someone to cover. You'll be back before you know it. I've got to go.'

She hung up.

Laura sighed. 'Goodness. That's not like Cat. Like I said, Bella is her pride and joy. She'd be over there in a shot. Can't you get... back-up here?'

'The back-up is backed up.'

Sawyer pondered for a moment. He took back Laura's phone and recuffed her. 'There is trouble ahead for you and Catherine, Laura. But there will be sympathy, given the background and the way you've co-operated so far.' Sawyer took out his phone and tapped out a note on an app. He screenshotted the note, then repeated the process with another.

'But... Are you just going to walk in there? Tyrone Reavey isn't as young as you, but he's a dangerous man. He's not someone you take on lightly. You need help.'

'Does the Lord listen to prayers in favour of the faithless?'

'Nothing prevents him from answering a prayer. It's all according to his will.'

He nodded at Shepherd and got out. 'Okay. Put a word in for me, will you?'

Sawyer walked across the road and climbed the path to the front door. He stopped at the door and listened for a moment, then rang the bell.

Catherine answered quickly. Her red hair was gathered over one side, but the ponytail band was low, making it unkempt. 'Detective Sawyer.' She forced a smile.

'Catherine.'

'Mr Sawyer. What can I do for you?'

He held up his phone, showed her the first note.

IS TYRONE HERE?

She looked up, nodded.
He swiped to the second note.

IS HE ARMED?

Her eyes widened and she shrugged.
He swiped to a third note.

DOWNSTAIRS?

Catherine gave him a grave look and shook her head.

'Can I come in for a few minutes? Just a couple of quick questions.'

'Uh, sure.' She stood aside.

Sawyer walked through, past the sitting room. He glanced up the central staircase as he entered the kitchen and stood by the smoked glass dining table.

Grey coasters in place.

Flowers undisturbed in the vase.

'Well, now.'

Tyrone Reavey stepped out of an alcove in the corner of the kitchen. He held a handgun at his hip, levelled at Sawyer.

'Not a sound. Not a movement without my permission. Take a breath out of turn and it'll be your last.' Reavey stopped at the far end of the dining table. 'You got your cuffs with you?'

Sawyer shook his head. 'In the car.'

Reavey pointed down with his other hand. 'Sit. Both of youse. At that end.'

Sawyer and Catherine sat at the table, beside each other. Sawyer tried to catch Catherine's eye, but she just stared ahead, jaw set. Reavey took a seat at the far end. His eyes stayed fixed on Sawyer, and his skin was flushed, sparkling with sweat.

'He went upstairs,' said Catherine to Sawyer. 'Must have come back down.'

Reavey scowled at Sawyer. 'You expected me?'

'Did you kill Dylan, Tyrone?'

Catherine gasped and looked from Sawyer to Reavey.

Reavey sneered. 'Collateral. I assume the Bella thing was to see if Catherine was free to leave. And did you write out some questions for her at the door, in case she couldn't speak?'

Sawyer nodded.

403

Reavey shifted in his seat. 'So, listen. We're not doing the bad guy gives you the whole plan thing. I assume you've worked things out. I should shoot you on principle, just for sending that idiot with the slicked-back hair this morning. I've seen better acting at a school nativity play.' He studied Sawyer for a moment. 'So, what now? Are the cavalry coming?'

'No. I've had enough sieges for one week.'

'I got a call from Leonard, saying you'd been snooping. So, I was ready.'

Sawyer's phone vibrated in his pocket. A call.

He took a breath. 'Where did it go wrong for you, Patrick?'

Reavey flinched at the name.

'For me, I was six.' Sawyer sat back, caught Catherine's eye. 'It was a lovely sunny day, and I saw my mother battered to death with a hammer before my eyes. Her killer tried to kill me, too. It changes you, doesn't it? Having a parent snatched away. You had such good intentions. Serving the Lord. Following your father. You were going to do so much good. But here you are. The bad guy.'

'I thought you didn't believe in absolutes?'

'You just switched from one enemy to another, didn't you? Spiritual to existential.' He waved a hand. 'Primeval demons to young British recruits.'

Reavey's eyes burned. 'I was a soldier. I *am* a soldier.'

Sawyer nodded. 'A soldier of God. An angelic protector. Ridding the world of evil, in whatever form suits you. Back in Northern Ireland, it was someone who went to the wrong church, carried the wrong flag. You justified it as a cause. A struggle. In the name of the greater good. Now, though...' He sat up. 'The cause is yourself. You're happy to slaughter addled old alcoholics for a bit of cash. You're not a soldier. You're a mercenary. And back we are again, at the absolutes. The love of money. You're not an archangel, Patrick. You're more like Judas.'

Reavey flinched, jabbing the gun forward. 'Judas has always been a convenient scapegoat. Many believe he wasn't motivated by money, and he was trying to provoke Christ into leading a revolt against the Romans.'

Sawyer nodded. 'And how did that go? Jesus wouldn't compromise, would he? He stuck to that old-fashioned stuff you've been preaching for years. Love, forgiveness, non-violence.'

'I should shoot you in the mouth,' said Reavey. 'Shut you up. Watch you die slow.'

The phone in his pocket, still vibrating.

'Before you do that, I have one question. What gives you the right? To be righteous? I liked that idea, too. Following in my father's footsteps. He was also a policeman. I saw his agony after my mother's death, and I thought that seeing his son doing good would take it away, and I could channel my pain into hunting the evil that took my mother. But I realised something recently.' Sawyer slowly got to his feet and held up his hands. 'I thought I was seeking vengeance, but what I really need is salvation.'

'Well, as you know, Mr Sawyer. I'm retiring from that business.' Reavey stood up. 'There's a five-pound car bomb under Damon Morris's car. Ammonium nitrate fuel oil. It's fitted with a tilt switch that will trigger as he drives away from his flat. As he normally does around this time.'

'What happened to your showpiece crucifixion?' said Sawyer.

Reavey raised his eyebrows.

'I've seen the cross in your cellar.'

'This one.' Reavey pointed at Catherine; she winced and bowed her head. 'It was too much for her in the end. Her sister was all for it. Catherine didn't like the implications, though. Fair enough. He's a waste of good nails, anyway. Now. A couple of things. First. It's more than "a bit of cash". Don't tell me you're squeamish about putting a price on these things.'

Catherine spoke up. 'Two hundred thousand pounds each, and another two hundred thousand when all four are done. I'd say that's good value for a man like my dad.' She raised her head, aiming a defiant glare at Sawyer. 'Money is only one part of this. It's a war. Surely you understand that? Tyrone is a soldier of the church. You're a soldier of the state. But the system you enforce is set up to favour the rule of law. Fair trial. Due process. Making sure everyone, particularly the lawyers, get their pay day. The victims and victims' rights are a side issue. The rights and needs of offenders are served at the expense of victims. I'm just using my wealth to balance a broken system.'

Catherine glanced at Reavey, then stood up and moved around to stand at his side, both facing Sawyer from the far end of the dining table. She held her silver crucifix between her fingers.

The phone fell silent.

'He's planning to kill you, Catherine,' said Sawyer. 'And Laura. Why else is he here? He knows Laura was planning to come over before the fete. Like he said about Tyrone. *Collateral*. This mighty divine warrior would have been fine to let your husband and children discover your dead body.'

'Laura's in your car, yeah?' said Reavey. 'Hence, no cuffs.'

Sawyer nodded. He lowered his hands slowly and rested them on the edge of the table.

'Okay, then.'

Reavey was swift for his age. Wrapping an arm around Catherine's neck, he yanked her into him, keeping the gun on Sawyer. Catherine yelped in surprise.

'I won't ask for much. Safe passage will do. I've got a car out back, so... Let's be sensible, now.'

Sawyer wrenched the heavy dining table upward, tipping it onto its end, and shoving it towards Reavey. The vase flew into the wall and fell to the floor, spilling its contents.

He dropped low. Reavey fired at head height.

The bullet shattered the table. Sawyer dived towards the open door, shielding himself from a cascade of shards.

Reavey shoved Catherine aside and crunched across the glass, following Sawyer out into the hall.

Sawyer stumbled as he made a dash for the front door, and Reavey had him, hand gripping his ankle, dragging him back across the floor on his front.

Reavey tried to line up another shot, but Sawyer

twisted around and lashed a powerful kick into the side of his legs, buckling him.

Reavey reeled from the blow but rose again. He stared down at Sawyer. 'Are you *running away*?'

Sawyer scrambled to the front door, threw it open, dived out.

Another shot from behind, splintering the frame.

Outside, a group of officers in helmets and body armour waited with rifles trained on the house, beside an unmarked black van parked against the far kerb. Two other unmarked cars sat alongside it, with three squad cars forming an outer cordon, lights flashing.

Sawyer sprinted down the sloping path, almost toppling forward.

Reavey emerged from the front door.

The officers advanced.

'*Armed police! Drop the weapon now and raise your hands.*'

Reavey tossed the handgun to the ground.

The vase hit him square in the back of the head, swung two-handed by Catherine. He howled in pain and fell to his knees, holding his head.

Sawyer kept moving, to the cars by the van. He ducked down behind one, joining Walker, crouched behind with two more armed officers.

Reavey crawled away, fumbling for the gun.

Catherine swung the vase again. It shattered against Reavey's head, and he dropped to the ground and lay still.

The officers moved in, restraining Catherine, guns on Reavey.

'Sir,' said Walker. 'Laura is still with Shepherd. I didn't like your talk of bomb-making materials, so I sent Myers to Morris's place with an EOD team. They evacuated and found Reavey's bomb. Contained and neutralised. I came here, saw your car... Are you okay, sir?'

Sawyer steadied himself against the car, breathing hard.

'Sir?'

He nodded.

Walker passed him a bottle of water. 'Can I get a "good work"?'

65

THREE DAYS LATER

Keating took his seat at the head of the MIT conference table and surveyed the packed room. 'It's been a difficult time. We had to dive into two harrowing cases while mourning one colleague, with another critically injured. One case required us to work with a complex figure who will soon take up a senior political position. That could impact us all.' He took off his cap, laid it down on the table. 'The enquiry into the station attack is ongoing, and the refit won't be complete for another few weeks. For now, thank you all for your hard work and resilience. The outcome in the Eva Gregory abduction case was thankfully good. Although the perpetrator lost his life in a confrontation with armed officers, both Eva and her son Luka are recovering well. Moving on, the murders of Thomas Brennan's killers were contracted by Brennan's two daughters and carried out by a local priest, Tyrone Reavey, who had previous links to Irish Republican terrorism. Although three men were murdered, we prevented the killing of the fourth by making safe a large car bomb planted by Reavey. I give special commendation to DC Walker for his support of DI Sawyer, who discovered Reavey's illicit material in a private building on the grounds of his own church, where we also believe he carried out the three murders. Reavey was badly injured in his capture, but it's my hope that he'll recover and stand trial.'

Keating looked over at Sawyer, who had his eyes down, gazing at the table.

'CPS will prosecute,' said Shepherd. 'Sally and her team worked with Frazer to pull everything together quickly.'

'Strong matches on Reavey's boot prints,' said O'Callaghan. 'Also, fibres from the church carpet at all three scenes, and the soil biome in deposits found in Jared White's hair matches with the river around the back of the church. Trace elements, minerals, microorganisms, pH. Nailed on.'

Pen twirl from Myers. 'He used a Fiat Doblo van. Unregistered. Bought it on Facebook Marketplace from a private owner in Grimsby. Single train ticket purchase from Trainline on his bank record, two weeks before the Cunliffe murder.'

'Tyre track match at all three scenes,' said O'Callaghan, 'and we got a DNA match for Jared White from the back. His cellar of doom was a treasure trove, too. We can place all three victims at the scene, and his little bomb lab overlays sweetly onto the present he left under Morris's car.'

'He also had a pet pickaxe handle,' said Drummond. 'Used the same one on Burrows and White. Not Cunliffe, though.'

'Beating Cunliffe by the tree before the burning wasn't enough for him.' Sawyer spoke for the first time, eyes still on the table. 'Reavey has dished out so much violence in his past, it didn't touch the sides. He underestimated. He had to escalate. Just to feel something.'

Drummond whistled. 'So, what's happening to the terrible twosome?'

Shepherd took his cue from Keating. 'Catherine is claiming Reavey extorted the money by threatening her family. Laura claims they were both complicit. Their uncle, Dylan, was initially involved but, according to what Laura told DI Sawyer, Dylan set it all in motion when he recognised Reavey at Thomas's funeral. The mother tried to keep Dylan out of it in the end, but it was too late, and Reavey probably went over there to silence him. Garda still investigating.'

'Either way,' said Keating, 'they'll both get life. Probably whole life order.'

'More than their father's killers,' said Sawyer, eyes still down.

Drummond scoffed. 'Three of their father's killers are dead, DI Sawyer.'

Sawyer looked up. 'And we saved the worst of the four.' His eyes were cloudy, the sharp green muted. 'Reavey. Catherine and Laura Brennan. Crawley. Four people destroyed by violence inflicted on people they loved. Turned into killers themselves. The same grim fucking cycle. And here we are, slapping each other on the back because we kept alive someone who gets off on taunting the bereaved and terminally ill.' He applauded, slow and sarcastic.

'You've picked that trick up from Strickland,' said Keating.

Sawyer turned on him. 'And there's another fine purveyor of violence, walking tall while his victim is in the ground, having taken three more people with him.'

'That's only alleged—'

'And the rest of the violence,' Sawyer ploughed on. 'Here. Gerry, Phil. Sullivan. Ross Moran. All dead. Me sent to hospital. Maggie. My friend. A world-class human being. Fed through a plastic fucking tube. Her massive heart kept beating by a machine.'

'So, what are you saying?' Drummond hitched his glasses down his nose and stared at Sawyer over the top. 'We should all just give up? Grow turnips? Invest in crypto-bloody-currency? Whatever that is.'

'I'm saying that we're more like janitors than police. Mopping up this mess, after the fact. I'm saying the law can only ever do that. This is a cycle. Violence spawning damaged people. Damaged people spawning violence.' Sawyer held his head in his hands, rooted his fingers through his hair. 'I'm saying it's like some kind of fucked-up game.' He thumped both fists down on the table and glared at Drummond, the others, then Keating, his eyes filling with tears. 'I'm *saying* that I can't play it anymore.'

Silence.

Keating waved a hand. 'Give us the room.'

The others hurried out and closed the door. Keating kept his eyes on Sawyer. 'Take a moment.'

Sawyer swiped at his eyes with the palm of his hand. He composed himself. 'Did you come over a lot?'

'What?'

'When I was little. Did you come over to the house? To see Dad?'

Keating leaned back. 'Yes, I did. Jake. This thing Jessica wrote. Harold and I were young detectives. We were probably just bitching about our boss. Caldwell wasn't easy to work for.'

Sawyer sat up. 'On the night you tracked me to my dad's cellar, where I'd found Caldwell. I had a gun on him. Your AFOs were about to kill me, but you told them to stand down.'

Keating frowned. 'Of course I bloody did. You were in pieces. Highly emotional. Out of control. You'd assaulted an officer to get his weapon. They were about to shoot you. I saved you.'

Sawyer broke out a smile, shook his head. He raised a finger, pointed at Keating. 'Your order left it clear for me to shoot Caldwell. Is that what you wanted?'

They faced each other in silence for a long time. Eyes locked. Keating pressed his mouth closed and breathed through his nose, fast and jittery. Sawyer kept his fists clenched, resting on the table.

Keating got to his feet. 'I'm going back to my desk, where I'll write an email to the HR department at the National Police Chiefs' Council. They will be in touch to arrange a formal medical assessment via Occupational Health. I expect your full co-operation. The result will dictate the nature of your duties while you remain under my command. Detective Sawyer. The problem here isn't with society or the system or the rule of law. It's in your head.'

66

Sawyer worked on the wooden man. Thrusting. Parrying. Pummelling the struts with his elbows, palms, forearms. The flashes grew weaker and less frequent if he worked faster, harder. The chattering seemed peripheral. The faces and scenes behind his eyes took longer to form.

In the shower, he kept the water cold, scouring his skin, shocking his system. He knew the steam from hot water would swirl and writhe, carving impossible creatures in the air.

Again, he jabbered and muttered. Imaginary interactions, elaborate vignettes, half-remembered movie dialogue. Soothing himself. Filling the void, lest the faces swoop in.

He dressed in loose running gear and staggered from the bathroom. A call came through as he checked his phone.

He answered, on speaker. 'Luka? Are you okay?'

A pause. 'Fine, yeah. Going on holiday soon.'

Sawyer set the phone down on the kitchen surface as he poured a glass of Coke. 'Where are you going?'

'South Africa. A game reserve. But it's not, like, games. It's animals. Dad says they've got baboons. Remember that polar bear?'

'How could I forget?'

'That was awesome. I thought it was going to bite that guy's head off.'

'Well, that wouldn't have been very awesome for him.'

Luka sighed. 'I mean, you getting him out.'

Sawyer winced and rubbed at the cut on his arm. 'I'm sort of naturally awesome. I don't think I know any other way.'

Luka just about managed a laugh. He paused again. 'I wasn't scared. When Dennis came to the house.'

'Do me a favour, Luka.'

'What?'

'Stop carrying the knife.'

'It helped me get away in that house.'

Sawyer sipped the Coke. 'You've got a much more powerful weapon.'

'What?'

'Your brain. Make the effort to sharpen that up instead. It'll serve you better. You might be shocked about this, but girls aren't impressed by knives.'

'Maybe I'm not impressed by girls.'

Sawyer picked up the phone and walked to the sofa. 'How is your mum, Luka?'

Another sigh. 'She's okay. I'll help her get better. She

wanted to call you, to thank you for everything you did to find her, but Dad said she couldn't.'

'I thought you said I wasn't doing anything.'

'Right, yeah. Sorry.'

He opened his laptop, navigated to emails. 'It'll take your mum a lot of time to recover. Please tell her I said hello.'

'Yeah, I will.'

'I hope you don't want your tracker back. I threw it away when I found it.'

A long pause. 'Not bothered. Battery ran out, anyway. My dad found the one I put in his car and I told him I'd put one in yours.'

He browsed a few emails, including one from Max Reeves with the address of Leon Stokes.

'Are you going to apologise for the tracker, too?'

'Well, yeah. I suppose.'

'No need. We got your mum back safe in the end. It was reckless. But that's coming from a man who picked a fight with a polar bear.'

Luka laughed, louder this time.

Sawyer copied the Stokes address into his phone. 'Luka, enjoy your holiday and make sure you look after yourself as well as your mum.'

'I'll be okay.'

'No, you won't. You'll struggle. You'll have bad dreams. Bad days. You'll play things over in your head. Some things you see or hear might make it feel like it's all happening again. So, that's what I mean when I say look after yourself. Like your mum, you'll need time.'

'I'm stronger than you think.'

'Yes.' Sawyer lay on the sofa, closed his eyes. 'You're a survivor, Luka. But you can't avoid feeling bad. You just have to get good at it. Don't pretend it's not happening. Don't pretend to be tough. It's okay to be scared.'

67

Sawyer ran along the flat path that followed the route of the old railway line. He kept a steady pace, weaving around tourists and cyclists, glancing up at the strip of crystal blue sky laid along the top of the Wetton ridge. He passed the entrance to the track up to Thor's Cave; a group of elderly hikers crowded around the information sign, with more walkers hovering, waiting their turn.

Not today.

He pushed on, past the mill. The car park was filled with gleaming motorbikes, their middle-aged owners huddled around the wooden picnic tables, communing over tea, bacon sandwiches, overlarge hunks of cake.

He would get back to the car, parked at Hulme End Tea Junction, and order a large mug of tea with a cheese-and-tomato Staffordshire oatcake. Browse a couple of reassuringly tedious local history books. Take home a slice of their lardy but moreish apple pie.

Sawyer sprinted away from the mill, passing a group of dawdling hikers. As their chatter faded behind, he removed his earphones and soaked up the natural sounds of this arcadian haven; a place woven so deep into his DNA.

The wind worrying the trees, jostling the tall grass that lined the path. Faraway sheep cries, shrill and urgent. The trickling river, shrivelled by summer, eager for autumn rain.

Out here, he felt an easing of gravity's pull, as he basked in something infinite and unknowable. Nature rallying itself for the eternal cycle of ruin and rebirth. Untroubled by ego or events long departed.

Nothing extraneous.

Nothing unnecessary.

Just being.

Sawyer slowed through Swainsley Tunnel, closing his eyes as he ran, tuning in to the echoes of his footfalls.

He accelerated out into the light, crossed a miniature bridge spanning the parched river bed, then plunged through the narrow, overgrown path that led back to the Tea Junction car park. To civilisation.

His phone found service and buzzed in his pocket.

He took it out. Four missed calls.

Another came through, from the end of the world.

Holsgrove.

68

Wes Peyton got out of the pea-green Subaru. He screwed on his sky-blue baseball cap and stalked across the visitors' car park.

Jakub Malecki nudged him from behind. 'We stay clean. We do it properly.'

'I don't fucking care how it's done, as long as it gets done. I'm sick to death of stressing about this.'

Malecki tugged at Peyton's shoulder and they stopped. 'Listen. I told you. They have security. Let me deal with that first. Then Holsgrove has access to the ward. He won't jeopardise his son by doing anything stupid. I threaten him. He lets you in. Looks like he's been forced. We go in calm. No running. No shouting. We are visitors. *Invisible.*'

Peyton stared at him, shook his head. 'Do you want to get a fucking latte before we go up there?' He spun away.

Malecki caught him up. 'And we have to get a ticket.'

Peyton stopped again. 'For the car?'

'Yes,' hissed Malecki. 'Your fucking car is already bright enough. We don't want to draw more attention by getting a parking fine. Tickets come from the machine in there. You then use the same machine to pay when you leave.' He leaned in close. 'We have plenty of time. Holsgrove won't dare call the family before he lets us in.'

Peyton sighed. 'Get the ticket. I'll check the access.'

'Remember,' said Malecki. 'Clinical Neurophysiology.' Malecki nodded to Peyton's jacket. 'What've you got?'

'Glock 17. Suppressor.'

'No bombs? Missiles? *Grenades?*'

'Get the fucking ticket. Back here in two. If it looks okay, in and out in ten.' Peyton turned and walked away.

Malecki raised his hood and walked into a multistorey parking garage with an adjoining kiosk signposted *VISITOR CAR PARK PAY & DISPLAY.* Inside the kiosk, a man crouched at a large and complex-looking ticket machine at the far end, staring into the screen.

Malecki stood a few paces back. He rubbed at the strapping around his elbow and gave a loud impatient sigh.

The man stood back from the machine and held up his hands, palms up. He shook his head.

'You having trouble?' said Malecki, stepping closer.

Curtis Mavers turned and caught Malecki with a crunching right hook. Malecki staggered, lost his footing and toppled backwards, clunking his head on the tiled wall. His heels scraped across the ground and he yelped in pain as he pushed himself upright, off his injured elbow.

Mavers pulled out a handgun, but Malecki rushed him, swiping at his gun arm. Mavers jerked it away and smashed the barrel of the gun into Malecki's face.

Malecki spun away, stumbled, went down again. He sat with his back to the wall, head down, blood streaming down his chin and chest.

Mavers walked towards him, gun aimed on his head. 'Off to hell with you, soft lad.'

Malecki sat there for a moment, staring up at Mavers. Then he twitched, and thrust his upper body over to one side. Mavers fired, hitting the wall. Malecki pulled out the shaping knife and launched himself up off the floor, plunging the blade into Mavers's side. Twisting.

Mavers screamed, fired again, taking out a strip light, showering them with splinters of plastic.

Malecki held Mavers close, hanging on like an exhausted boxer, keeping his head down. He yanked out the knife and stabbed, again and again. Quick and shallow. Taking advantage of the knife's short blade.

Above, the light flashed on and off, buzzing and clicking.

Mavers wrestled himself clear, backing off to the door, gaining enough distance to raise the gun again.

Malecki came for him, but Mavers got his shot away. Clean this time. Between the eyes.

Malecki's blood splashed up onto the flickering light. He skittered backwards on the smashed plastic, slamming into the ticket machine, dropping to the ground.

Mavers walked over and held the gun above Malecki's head, pointing it vertically down. He buried two more bullets into Malecki's brain, then dropped to one knee, blood flowing from the knife wounds. He released the gun, and it tumbled away.

A young woman appeared at the door. She froze, as Mavers fell forward, then screamed and turned, bumping into Peyton.

The woman ran, as Peyton absorbed the scene. He edged forward and crouched by Malecki, studying his shattered face, as if confused. He turned to see Mavers crawling towards his gun, then pushed the silenced Glock barrel into the side of Mavers's head and fired, propelling his body into the tiled wall.

More screaming outside. Shouting. A revving engine.

Peyton turned and broke for the door.

He barged past a middle-aged man in a security uniform and sprinted to the Subaru, hammering the door unlock button on his key.

He threw open the door but then fell into it, barged from behind. His head tipped over the top of the door and the sky-blue baseball cap flopped onto the bonnet.

Sawyer pulled him back, spun him round.

The Glock fell onto the ground as Sawyer slammed Peyton into the neighbouring car and held him by the throat.

Sawyer punched and punched, sending Peyton's head whipping to one side, blood splashing onto the roof and wing mirror.

More shouts. Screams.

Running feet. Pleading.

Another security guard dragged Sawyer back. He turned, swung a side kick into the man's legs, dropping him to the ground.

Sawyer swivelled back to Peyton, slumped into the side of the car, sliding down.

He grabbed a fistful of hair and dragged Peyton out into the open, threw him down. He dropped onto his chest, knees first.

Peyton coughed, choking on blood, spraying it onto Sawyer's face. Sawyer stepped up the attack, driving his fist into the centre of his pulverised face, over and over.

More car engines. Shouting.

Two men bundled into Sawyer, trying to haul him off, but he resisted still, and a third had to grapple with his legs before they dragged him away.

More screaming. Shouts. A group of men and women in surgical scrubs charged out of the main building, across the car park. Two ran into the parking machine kiosk. A man and woman fell to their knees on the bloodied ground around Peyton, tending him.

The three men who had pulled Sawyer away stood in a ragged line, blocking his access to Peyton and the doctors.

Approaching sirens.

Sawyer drew himself upright and faced them. His arms hung at his side, blood dripping from his clenched fists. Eyes ablaze.

He ran.

69

Leon Stokes lay back on the lemon-yellow sofa and browsed his streaming channels. He sipped a caramel-coloured drink, straight from the blender carton.

Boyd Cannon sat on the rowing machine, rocking forward and back, browsing his iPad Pro.

Stokes looked over his shoulder. 'We heard from Doyle?'

Cannon shook his head. 'Take your pick. Ominous silence, or no news is good news.'

Stokes cued up a film on Netflix: *Sicario*. He stared at the title screen, sloshing his shake around. 'Too many things up in the air, Boyd. I like to be grounded. Get Peyton and Malecki in here. Updates.'

Cannon swiped and tapped at his screen.

Stokes set down his drink on the floor by the sofa. 'Gotta see the old dear later. The manager wants to make a few adjustments to her care package.' He sighed and bent forward, dropping his head. 'It's so fucking hard to see her like that. Sometimes I think it doesn't matter because I'm not sure she knows what's happening, anyway. But other times I think, what if she is in there somewhere? Aware of it all. Deep down. She wants to communicate, but she can't get through this... padding. That's like a living fucking death.' He took a gulp of his drink. 'Do you think about it much, Boyd?'

'What?'

'Y'know. The big sleep.'

Cannon shrugged. 'If it's coming, it's coming.'

Stokes scoffed. 'There's no *if* about it. My mum was healthier than me, then *whoosh*! She had a stroke. Few months later. Vascular dementia. They tell me she's in moderate cognitive decline now. Couple of years left, if she's lucky.' He stared into the screen. 'That's our problem, isn't it? We know where we're going.' He turned to Cannon. 'I was watching *Blade Runner* the other day. The bit where Rutger Hauer comes in to see Doctor whatsit...'

'Tyrell.'

'Yeah. And Tyrell says, "What seems to be the problem?"'

Cannon nodded. 'And Roy says, "*Death*."'

A crash from the front of the house.

Shouts. Male voices. Another crash.

Stokes sprang to his feet, as the gym double doors burst open.

Sawyer walked through and stopped at the edge of the wooden walkway. The front of his light-coloured hoodie had been turned almost entirely dark by a deep red stain. His hair was knotted and congealed, his face streaked with dried blood.

He fixed Cannon with a bone-chilling stare. 'Leon Stokes?'

Stokes picked up a baseball bat propped against the wall and padded over, barefoot. 'That's me. Who the fuck are you?'

'Jake Sawyer,' said Sawyer. 'Detective Inspector.'

Stokes grinned. 'Well, fuck me twice. I've heard a lot about you. By the looks of things, you're off duty, yeah? Heavy night?'

Cannon got up from the rower and backed away, eyes on Sawyer's bloodstained fists.

Sawyer advanced on Stokes. 'Curtis Mavers is dead. Jakub Malecki is dead. Your boy with the Man City cap...' He held up his fists. 'This is his blood.'

Stokes backed away, but held the bat ready.

'*It was Strickland.*'

Sawyer stopped, turned to Cannon. 'What was?'

'He encouraged it. The attack on your station. He came here. He practically fucking ordered it. He said he'd make it easy for our business once he was mayor.'

Sawyer carried on towards Stokes.

'*Listen!*' Cannon dashed over, keeping a safe distance. 'I recorded it. When Strickland waltzed in here, talking about how he could help. I set my recorder running on my laptop.' He fumbled at his phone, then played an audio file.

Strickland's voice came through.

'*I want Sawyer gone. Off the board. He's become too complicated for me, in too many ways. He was a sparring partner for a while, but he's an obstacle now. And anyway,* he's corrupt. A liability. The brass will be happy to see the back of him.'

Peyton's voice. *'So, we your fucking hitmen now?'*

A pause. Footsteps. Strickland's voice again. More distant, but still clear. *'Your brother blew up some low-ranking lowlife in his stolen car, Wes. Sawyer is a Detective Inspector. He's known. High profile. The newspapers call him hero cop. This would be like you bagging big game compared to your brother taking out a scrawny pigeon. You would be the one getting talked about. No longer in your brother's shadow.'*

Cannon scrubbed the audio forward a few seconds.

Strickland's voice again. *'I can give you Mavers. He's worked with me before. Ask around. He trusts me. He can't get out of the country without my help. Get me Sawyer and I'll get you the time and destination of the private airfield where I'll arrange for Mavers to fly out. Everybody wins, Leon. You balance your personal books, regain respect, get more freedom to operate.'*

Cannon's voice. *'And you?'*

Strickland. *'I get Sawyer. At a safe distance. No blowback.'*

Cannon stopped the audio.

Sawyer kept his eyes locked on Stokes. The fire had left them, replaced by something cold and primal.

He pushed a hand through his blood-soaked hair and walked out.

70

'Yes, Luka. They have pizza there.' Strickland hitched his feet up onto his desk. 'Special South African pizza.'

Luka moved in close to the camera at his end. The image blurred as his eyes filled the Zoom window. 'I can tell if you're lying, you know.'

'Yeah? Well, ask me a question then.'

Luka sat back. 'Anything?' Strickland turned to his open window. 'You have to face the screen, Dad.'

He turned. 'Go on. Anything.'

Luka hesitated. 'Do you think Mum is okay to go?'

'Yes. We have a lot of security detail. She'll feel safe. And you have to go through the lions' territory to get to our game lodge accommodation. I think she'll be okay.'

'Also,' said Luka, 'Dennis died.'

'He did. Like I said, Luka. He was sick. But that's all over now.'

Luka dropped his eyes. 'So, that stuff he said you did... You didn't really do it, did you?' He looked up again.

Strickland paused, fixed the camera with a rigid gaze. 'No.'

Luka moved in close to the screen again.

Strickland startled at a shout from the office outside.

He swung his feet around and wheeled his chair across the room to see what was happening.

The door crashed open.

Reuben Gaines filled the frame, panting, his forehead slick with sweat. 'Mr Strickland. I tried to get up the stairs before him.'

Glass shattered from somewhere behind Gaines.

Strickland's PA, Oliver, shouting. '*Call them now*!'

A crash. Something else smashing.

Gaines turned, then fell to the side, clattering into Oliver's standing desk.

Sawyer moved in on Gaines as he tottered and flailed, trying to correct himself and face his attacker.

More shouts, as Sawyer hit him with a right, then a left. The other staff scattered to the edge of the room as Gaines went down on his knees, and Sawyer aimed a solid right kick into the side of his head, knocking him out cold.

Sawyer turned and stalked into Strickland's office.

'*Dad*?' Luka cried from the screen.

Sawyer drilled a punch into Strickland's stomach, doubling him over. He thrust a knee up towards his face, but Strickland read it, and dodged to the right. He swung around, hitting Sawyer with a clean punch to the jaw, sending him tumbling into the desk.

'*Dad? What's going on*?'

Strickland tried to follow up on Sawyer before he

could compose himself, but Sawyer aimed a quick snap kick at his knee. It connected to the bone and Strickland cried out, winding up another punch.

Sawyer was ready for him now, and he swayed away from the strike and hit Strickland in the face with a left, then right, then left, forcing him back to the wall.

Strickland collided with a chair, knocking it sideways. He grabbed the legs and swung it into Sawyer's side. But Sawyer had already shifted away, dampening the contact.

With Strickland off balance, Sawyer shifted inside and hit him with another body blow, then a brutal uppercut that slammed him into the wall by the window.

Luka, screaming now. '*Dad!*'

Strickland slid down the wall, dazed. Sawyer pushed the window open wide and lifted him up, shoving him out, head first. Strickland flopped forward but held on to the frame, his upper body now out in the open air, facing the Deansgate pavement, six storeys down.

Strickland kicked his legs as Sawyer tried to wrap them around his arms and bundle him forward, head first.

A uniformed security team crowded into the office. They took in the scene and hung back by the door.

Luka, screaming and sobbing. '*Jake! Please!*'

Sawyer froze.

The lead man held up both hands. 'You don't want to do that, mate. Trust me. You don't want to do that.'

Sawyer found his eyes.

'That's it. Jake. Look at me. We will not hurt you. You don't want to hurt him. Keep your eyes on me.'

Luka, sobbing. '*No, no, no, no...*'

Sawyer pulled Strickland back into the room. He rolled over and limped to the security team, bent double, clutching his knee.

Sawyer climbed up into the window.

'No! *Jake*.' The security man stepped forward.

Sawyer perched on the sill, crouched, with his back to the room.

He tipped his head back, face to the sky.

71

THREE WEEKS LATER

Shepherd parked his boxy grey Range Rover on a deep grass verge and killed the engine. He took a few slow breaths, climbed out, and walked down the lane, shielding his eyes from the low morning sun lurking behind the Kinder summit.

He crossed the private driveway bridge and took out a key, then spotted the door was already ajar. He pushed it open and stepped inside.

'*Tea?*'

Sawyer stood in the kitchen, back turned.

'I'm okay, thanks.'

Sawyer set down a dish of cat food. Bruce hopped off the sofa, inspected the dish, then left through the cat flap.

Shepherd took a seat on the sofa while Sawyer rummaged in the fridge.

'How is she?' said Sawyer.

'Eye movement increasing. Breathing pattern more regular. The doctor said she yawned the other day.'

Sawyer took out a bottle of Coke, filled a glass.

'It'll take time,' said Shepherd.

Sawyer walked over and set the glass down on the coffee table. He wore jeans, trainers, fitted orange-and-black sweatshirt. He'd cut his hair—short but scraggy—and had started on a beard.

Shepherd turned to face Sawyer as he sat on the arm of the sofa. 'Is that the regulation look?'

'They don't have a dress code. But you're expected to wear...' He looked up, recalling. '"Comfortable clothing that isn't too revealing or provocative".'

'You'll have to leave the arseless chaps here, then.'

Sawyer sipped his drink, staring. 'Anything from Strickland?'

Shepherd sighed. 'Nothing you'll want to hear.'

'It can't hurt me now.'

'Good news or bad news?' Sawyer gave him a look. 'He made a speech a couple of days ago. Patched up. Crutches. Good news is you're forgiven. He was Mr Magnanimous. After all he's been through, he's realised that compassion is the answer. He wants to make his term as mayor world famous for championing the downtrodden and disadvantaged. Give them the tools to get themselves back on their feet and contributing to society again. Standard self-reliance dog whistle for the right, with a dash of bleeding heart for the left.' Shepherd paused. 'He mentioned you by name, saying how police wanted to press for GBH or even GBH with intent, but he realises that... What was it? "Forgiveness is the only response that can change the narrative."'

'And that's the good news?'

'Well, yeah. Bad news is that he's forcing Keating out early.'

Sawyer shrugged. 'He was retiring anyway.'

'Yeah. But we now have a new DSI overseeing Buxton MIT until the Great Restructuring.' Sawyer closed his eyes. 'You've guessed it. Mr Robin Farrell. Silver lining is that Keating is pushing for a bump for Walker within the year.'

'He's the best of us.'

'Speak for yourself.'

Shepherd smiled; Sawyer just about managed a grimace that might resemble a smile from some angles.

A car pulled up outside. Sawyer walked over to the window. 'My brother's here.'

Shepherd got up. 'So... Are you evaluated? Isn't it normally twenty-eight days?'

'That's the holding order. I was down for ABH, then Sec 136 for the first three days. Then Strickland stepped in, and they waived the detention as long as I agreed to self-admission. Voluntary patient. I didn't like the colour scheme at the Cavendish psych unit.'

'This Trafalgar Lodge place can't be cheap.'

Sawyer opened the front door wide. 'If I'm going to fix myself, I might as well use the money Dad made trying to fix himself.'

Michael Sawyer walked towards them, over the driveway bridge.

'There's no *fix*, Jake. My fella said you have to accept

there's work to do on yourself. Until you commit to that, you can never expect to enjoy fulfilling relationships, or any kind of inner peace. But it's always in progress. You don't go from broken to fixed. And even you can't do it alone.'

Sawyer turned to him.

'I'll visit,' said Shepherd. 'I'll smuggle in some humbugs in a quinoa pie.'

They were silent for a moment. Sawyer averted his eyes, but not before Shepherd spotted the tears.

'Now I'm getting your trick,' said Shepherd.

'What do you mean?'

'I know what you're thinking.'

He drew Sawyer into a crushing hug. 'I've got this, sir. Don't worry about the cat.'

72

They sat in Michael's car, in the drop-off zone, at the side of a steep, curved road that led directly from the main gates.

'Better than Rosemary House,' said Michael, peering out at the one-storey outbuilding a few paces from the car. 'Their reception area was the door. How big is it?'

'A hundred and sixty beds across all the different levels of security. Medium, low and step-down. Twenty-two private inpatient rooms. It's all purpose-built. It'd look space age to the Victorians.'

Michael groaned. 'Well. They were terrified of the likes of us. Lunatics. Madmen.'

'Weak,' said Sawyer.

'So, how secure is a medium-secure?'

Sawyer angled his head. 'You've seen the fence. CCTV. Twenty-four-hour security. Mainly to protect the gym equipment. Stop the multi-sensory room from being vandalised. They have a tailored nutrition programme.'

'So, it's a cross between a low-risk prison and a spa hotel?'

'This one is. The lunatics without money don't eat so well. They still do electric shock therapy in some places.'

They watched as young well-dressed staff strolled in and out of the reception building.

'Please be here when I come to pick you up. Whenever it might be.'

'What do you mean?'

'Don't... escape or whatever. Picking locks. Stealing keys.'

'Have you read *The Myth of Normal*?'

Michael sighed. 'Of course not.'

'Dr Gabor Maté. He's a sort of mental health Yoda. He says that addiction and self-destructive behaviour results from unprocessed trauma from childhood, which continues to play out in our daily lives. So, the question isn't why the addiction or why the behaviour. It's why the pain. The behaviour is all about coping with the trauma. The feelings.'

'You're going to crush the group therapy with this stuff.'

'And I've been trying to anaesthetise the feelings, rather than address the pain behind them.'

Michael squinted at him. 'And you've only just worked this out?'

'It took you thirty-odd years.' He opened the door, then leaned over and hugged his brother. 'I'm off to feel some feelings.'

As they broke apart, Michael lowered his head. 'You

said you wanted me to live a life of my own, Jake. I got there in the end. So, how long for you?'

'I reckon I can do it in a year. Maybe two, if the sauna is decent.'

Sawyer got out, closed the door, and walked up the pavement towards the reception area, a slight tilt to his gait but no swagger.

At the door, he paused and looked back, held Michael's eye.

Then was gone.

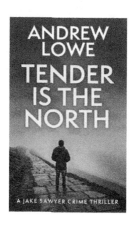

BOOK NINE IN THE **JAKE SAWYER** SERIES

JAKE SAWYER is isolated. A year after checking into a psychiatric unit, he has found peace by cutting contact with his previous world, living offline and refusing visitors.

When Sawyer's ex-colleagues arrest a single father for abusing bodies at a hospital mortuary, the man records a desperate video confession, sealing his fate. But with his young daughter missing, the case soon develops into something more complex and sinister.

Sawyer resists the urge to end his exile and step back into the fray. But when his own mother's ailing killer contacts him with an unrefusable offer, he realises that no matter how hard he works to build a brighter future, his past has a way of hunting him down.

https://books2read.com/tendernorth

JOIN MY MAILING LIST

I occasionally send an email newsletter with details on forthcoming releases and anything else I think my readers might care about.

Sign up and I'll send you **a Jake Sawyer prequel novella**.

THE LONG DARK is set in the summer before the events of CREEPY CRAWLY. It's FREE and totally exclusive to mailing list subscribers.

Go here to get the book:
http://andrewlowewriter.com/longdark

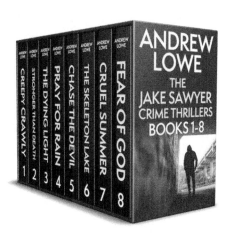

BOOKS 1-8 IN THE **JAKE SAWYER** SERIES

AVAILABLE IN EBOOK and PAPERBACK

READ NOW WITH **KINDLE UNLIMITED**

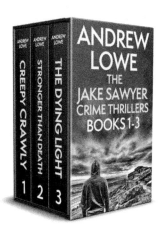

BOOKS 1-3 IN THE **JAKE SAWYER** SERIES

AVAILABLE IN EBOOK and PAPERBACK
READ NOW WITH **KINDLE UNLIMITED**

https://books2read.com/sawyerboxset1

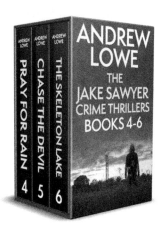

BOOKS 4-6 IN THE **JAKE SAWYER** SERIES

AVAILABLE IN EBOOK and PAPERBACK

READ NOW WITH **KINDLE UNLIMITED**

https://books2read.com/sawyerboxset2

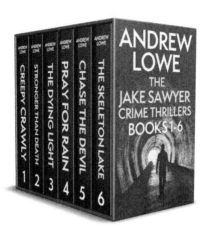

BOOKS 1-6 IN THE **JAKE SAWYER** SERIES

AVAILABLE IN EBOOK and PAPERBACK
READ NOW WITH **KINDLE UNLIMITED**

https://books2read.com/sawyerboxset3

ACKNOWLEDGMENTS

Detective Constable Ralph King, for helping me with my police enquiries.

Forensic scientist and author **AJ Scudiere** for the gory details.

Oisin Feeney and his excellent **The Troubles Podcast** for the background. (To follow me on my trip down the rabbit hole, read *Killing Rage*, *Bandit Country*, *Provos*, and *A Short History of The Troubles*.)

Bryony Sutherland for the focus on consistent syntax and cat welfare.

Book Cover Shop for the cover design.

Special thanks to **Julia**, for listening to me go on about it all.

Andrew Lowe. London, 2023

PLEASE LEAVE A REVIEW

If you enjoyed **FEAR OF GOD**, please take a moment to leave a review or rating on the book's **Amazon** page.

Honest reviews of my books help bring them to the attention of others, and connecting with readers is the number one thing that keeps me writing.

Go here to leave your review:
https://books2read.com/fearofgod

THE JAKE SAWYER SERIES

THE LONG DARK
CREEPY CRAWLY
STRONGER THAN DEATH
THE DYING LIGHT
PRAY FOR RAIN
CHASE THE DEVIL
THE SKELETON LAKE
CRUEL SUMMER
FEAR OF GOD
TENDER IS THE NORTH
BLOOD NEVER SLEEPS (2025)

BOOKS 1-3 BOX SET
BOOKS 4-6 BOX SET
BOOKS 1-6 BOX SET
BOOKS 1-8 BOX SET

GLOSSARY

ACT – Acceptance and Commitment Therapy. A form of psychotherapy that uses acceptance and mindfulness strategies along with commitment to behaviour change.

AFO – Authorised Firearms Officer. A UK police officer who has received training, and is authorised to carry and use firearms.

ALF – Animal Liberation Front. A political and social resistance movement that promotes non-violent direct action in protest against incidents of animal cruelty.

ANPR – Automatic Number Plate Recognition. A camera technology for automatically reading vehicle number plates.

AWOL – Absent without leave. Acronym.

BSE – Bovine Spongiform Encephalopahy. Colloquially known as 'mad cow disease'. A neurodegenerative condition in cattle.

CCRC – Criminal Cases Review Commission.

Independent body which investigates suspected miscarriages of justice in England, Wales and NI.

CI – Confidential Informant. An individual who passes information to the police on guarantee of anonymity.

CBT – Cognitive Behaviour Therapy. A form of psychotherapy based on principles from behavioural and cognitive psychology.

CID – Criminal Investigation Department. The branch of the UK police whose officers operate in plainclothes and specialise in serious crime.

COD – Cause of Death. Police acronym.

CPS – Crown Prosecution Service. The principle public agency for conducting criminal prosecutions in England and Wales.

CROP – Covert Rural Observation Post. A camouflaged surveillance operation, mostly used to detect or monitor criminal activity in rural areas.

CSI – Crime Scene Investigator. A professional responsible for collecting, cataloguing and preserving physical evidence from crime scenes.

CSO – Community Support Officer. Uniformed but non-warranted member of police staff in England & Wales. The role has limited police powers. Also known as PCSO.

D&D – Drunk & Disorderly. Minor public order offence in the UK (revised to 'Drunk and disorderly in a public place' in 2017).

Dibble – Manchester/Northern English slang. Police.

EMDR – Eye Movement Desensitisation and

Reprocessing. An interactive psychotherapy technique used to relieve psychological stress, particularly trauma and post-traumatic stress disorder.

ETD – Estimated Time of Death. Police acronym.

FLO – Family Liaison Officer. A specially trained officer or police employee who provides emotional support to the families of crime victims and gathers evidence and information to assist the police enquiry.

FOA – First Officer Attending. The first officer to arrive at a crime scene.

FSI – Forensic Science Investigator. An employee of the Scientific Services Unit, usually deployed at a crime scene to gather forensic evidence.

GIS – General Intelligence Service (Egypt). Government agency responsible for national security intelligence, both domestically and internationally.

GMCA – Greater Manchester Combined Authority. Local government institution serving the ten metropolitan boroughs of the Greater Manchester area of the UK.

GMP – Greater Manchester Police. Territorial police force responsible for law enforcement within the county of Greater Manchester in North West England.

GPR – Ground Penetrating Radar. A non-intrusive geophysical method of surveying the sub-surface. Often used by police to investigate suspected buried remains.

HOLMES – Home Office Large Major Enquiry System. An IT database system used by UK police forces for the investigation of major incidents.

H&C – Hostage & Crisis Negotiator. Specially trained law enforcement officer or professional skilled in negotiation techniques to resolve high-stress situations such as hostage crises.

IED – Improvised Explosive Device. A bomb constructed and deployed in ways outside of conventional military standards.

IDENT1 – The UK's central national database for holding, searching and comparing biometric information on those who come into contact with the police as detainees after arrest.

IMSI – International Mobile Subscriber Identity. A number sent by a mobile device that uniquely identifies the user of a cellular network.

IOPC – Independent Office for Police Conduct. Oversees the police complaints system in England and Wales.

ISC – Intelligence and Security Committee of Parliament. The committee of the UK Parliament responsible for oversight of the UK Intelligence Community.

MCT – Metacognitive Therapy. A form of psychotherapy focused on modifying beliefs that perpetuate states of worry, rumination and attention fixation.

MIT – Murder/Major Investigation Team. A specialised squad of detectives who investigate cases of murder, manslaughter, and attempted murder.

Misper – missing person. Police slang.

NCA – National Crime Agency. A UK law enforcement organisation. Sometimes dubbed the 'British FBI', the NCA fights organised crime that spans regional and international borders.

NCB – National Central Bureau. An agency within an INTERPOL member country that links its national law enforcement with similar agencies in other countries.

NDNAD – National DNA Database. Administered by the Home Office in the UK.

NHS – National Health Service. Umbrella term for the three publicly funded healthcare systems of the UK (NHS England, NHS Scotland, NHS Wales).

NHSBT – NHS Blood and Transplant. A division of the UK National Health Service, dedicated to blood, organ and tissue donation.

OCG – Organised Crime Group. A structured group of individuals who work together to engage in illegal activities.

OP – Observation Point. The officer/observer locations in a surveillance operation.

Osman Warning – An alert of a death threat or high risk of murder issued by UK police, usually when there is intelligence of the threat but an arrest can't yet be carried out or justified.

PACE – Police and Criminal Evidence Act. An act of the UK Parliament which instituted a legislative framework for the powers of police officers in England and Wales.

PAVA – Pelargonic Acid Vanillylamide. Key component in an incapacitant spray dispensed from a handheld canister. Causes eye closure and severe pain.

PAYG – Pay As You Go. A mobile phone handset with no contract or commitment. Often referred to as a 'burner' due to its disposable nature.

PM – Post Mortem. Police acronym.

PNC – Police National Computer. A database which allows law enforcement organisations across the UK to share intelligence on criminals.

PPE – Personal Protective Equipment designed to protect users against health or safety risks at work.

Presser – Press conference or media event.

RIPA – Regulation of Investigatory Powers Act. UK Act of Parliament which regulates the powers of public bodies to carry out surveillance and investigation. Introduced to take account of technological change such as the grown of the internet and data encryption.

SAP scale. A five-point scale, devised by the Sentencing Advisory Panel in the UK, to rate the severity of indecent images of children.

SIO – Senior Investigating Officer. The detective who heads an enquiry and is ultimately responsible for personnel management and tactical decisions.

SOCO – Scene of Crime Officer. Specialist forensic investigator who works with law enforcement agencies to collect and analyse evidence from crime scenes.

SSU – Scientific Services Unit. A police support team which collects and examines forensic evidence at the scene of a crime.

Tac-Med – Tactical Medic. Specially trained medical professional who provides advanced medical care and support during high-risk law enforcement operations.

TOD – Time of Death. Police acronym.

TRiM – Trauma Risk Management. Trauma-focused peer support system designed to assess and support employees who have experienced a traumatic, or potentially traumatic, event.

Urbex – urban exploration. Enthusiasts share images of man-made structures, usually abandoned buildings or hidden components of the man-made environment.

VPU – Vulnerable Prisoner Unit. The section of a UK prison which houses inmates who would be at risk of attack if kept in the mainstream prison population.

A WOMAN TO DIE FOR

AN EX WHO WOULD KILL TO GET HER BACK

Sam Bartley is living well. He's running his own personal trainer business, making progress in therapy, and he's planning to propose to his girlfriend, Amy.

When he sees a strange message on Amy's phone, Sam copies the number and fires off an anonymous threat. But the sender replies, and Sam is sucked into a dangerous confrontation that will expose his steady, reliable life as a horrifying lie.

https://books2read.com/dontyouwantme

WHAT IF THE HOLIDAY OF YOUR DREAMS TURNED INTO YOUR WORST NIGHTMARE?

Joel Pearce is an average suburban family man looking to shake up his routine. With four close friends, he travels to a remote tropical paradise for a 'desert island survival experience': three weeks of indulgence and self-discovery.

But after their supplies disappear and they lose contact with the mainland, the rookie castaways start to suspect that the island is far from deserted.

https://books2read.com/savages

ABOUT THE AUTHOR

Andrew Lowe was born in the north of England. He has written for *The Guardian* and *Sunday Times*, and contributed to numerous books and magazines on films, music, TV, videogames, sex and shin splints.

He lives in the south of England, where he writes, edits other people's writing, and shepherds his two young sons down the path of righteousness.

His online home is andrewlowewriter.com

Follow him via the social media links below.

Email him at andrew@andrewlowewriter.com

For Andrew's editing and writing coach services, email him at andylowe99@gmail.com

facebook.com/andrewlowewriter

x.com/andylowe99

instagram.com/andylowe99

tiktok.com/@andrewlowewriter

bookbub.com/profile/andrew-lowe

amazon.com/stores/Andrew-Lowe/author/B00UAJGZZU

Printed in Great Britain
by Amazon